DOROTHY KOOMSON

The Flavours of Love

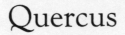
Quercus

First published in Great Britain in year of 2013 by

Quercus
55 Baker Street
7th Floor, South Block
London W1U 8EW

The paperback edition published in 2014

A CIP catalogue record for this book is available
from the British Library

ISBN 978 1 78087 503 3
EBOOK ISBN 978 1 78087 502 6

10 9 8 7 6 5 4 3 2 1

Printed and bound in Great Britain by Clays Ltd, St Ives plc

Typeset by Ellipsis Digital Limited, Glasgow

For M & G & E

I love that we're on this super-plane together.

The Flavours *of* Love

prologue

'Are you going to tell the police?' she asks.

'I think I have to,' I say. My mouth is dry, my mind is racing to so many different places and thoughts and decisions all at once, I can't keep up. I can't hold a single thought in my head for too long because another dashes into its place. Air keeps snagging itself on the way in and out of my lungs so I haven't taken a proper breath since my daughter started to speak, and my heart is running cold with the knowledge of who it was that killed my husband. And why.

I have to tell the police this, of course I do.

'Please don't, Mum.'

'But, Phoebe—'

'Please don't, Mum. Please. Please. Please.' Her twelve-year-old body, nestled on my lap, shakes with fretful sobs. 'Please. Please. Please. I'm scared. I'm really scared.'

'Phoebe, we can't—'

'Please, Mum. I'm really sorry, but please, don't.'

'Shhh, shhhhh,' I say, rocking her, trying to hush her. This isn't fair. None of this is fair. 'Let's not talk about it now. It'll be OK, I'll make it all OK.'

I

I

What's the difference between folding and stirring?

I'm sure I knew that once upon a time, I'm sure someone told me. Apparently, you can tell whether an ingredient has been folded in or stirred in. I've always been a bit dubious about that, have often wondered if it's one of those things that cooks/chefs add to the instructions to make a recipe sound more interesting or more difficult than it actually is.

Fold or stir. Stir or fold.

'Ah-he-hem!' The man sitting across the desk from me, whose body and clothes bear the hallmarks of a person deeply mired in a mid-life crisis, clears his throat in an uncomfortable manner. He's obviously got something big to say. He needs my attention, even though my attention, my gaze, causes him to squirm a little in his seat every time I direct it at him. *Every* time. He doesn't know how to share space with the woman whose husband was murdered. With me.

I know that's how he refers to me in his head, how he talks about me to other people, because that's how everyone refers to me – I've heard the whispers at the two different playgrounds I drop my children off at, in the toilets at work, in the conversations of people in the local shop and supermarket. It's not meant nastily, it's simply an easy, defining shorthand of someone on the edges of their life. Even now, eighteen months later, I am The Woman Whose Husband Was Murdered. Or, to give me my full title: The Woman Whose Husband Was Murdered And His Killer Was Never Caught.

'*Ah-he-hem!*' Another throat clear. Another squirm in his seat when I look at him.

The last time I met this man properly he wasn't having a mid-life crisis and we were discussing how to reintegrate my daughter back into school after what had happened. He'd avoided eye contact, shuffled papers on his desk, clicked his pen on and off, and fumbled over his words, scared and uncertain of what to say. And here we are again today: same room, same nervous unease but with different clothes and a different form teacher standing beside him.

This form tutor, positioned like a silent bodyguard beside his headmaster, is male. I know him by reputation – he's *The* Mr Bromsgrove. 'The' having been installed by playground mothers because he is youngish and good-looking, the subject of some scandalously outrageous sexual comments (despite how married they are and him not necessarily teaching their children).

Across the room, on the same side of the desk as me, sitting in a chair that couldn't technically be further away from me unless it was outside the room, is my daughter. Phoebe Mackleroy. I don't know, yet, what she's done, why I've been called up here on my first day off in nearly a year.

She's a good girl, I want to be able to say. *This is just a blip; she's a good girl really.* But I'm not going to be able to say that, am I? Things don't work out like that for people like me.

'*Ah-he-hem!*' Another throat-clear before the headteacher speaks: 'Mrs Mackleroy. There is no easy way to break this news to you. Phoebe has made a disclosure today to her form tutor, Mr Bromsgrove.' The headmaster's chubby, pale hand goes up to indicate the man he's referring to. I want to correct him, remind him that he is in fact *The* Mr Bromsgrove, but I know that wouldn't be appropriate so instead I allow myself to briefly glance at him and in return, *The* Mr Bromsgrove continues to studiously avoid my eye. The headteacher continues to speak: 'He was unsure what to do, so came to me. We thought it best to contact you as soon as possible. Especially if it looks like we're going to have to involve social services.'

My heart skips three beats at those magic words. I'd braced myself when the school secretary had called, I'd put down the pile of recipes scrawled on different types of paper I was leafing through and readied myself to hear the worst. But when they'd asked me to come in here and not to a hospital, when I arrived and saw Phoebe sitting in a chair, moving, breathing, *living*, I'd allowed myself to unclench a little, to almost fully relax.

Stupid woman that I am. I'd let myself forget that your life can be devastated on the whim of the wind, the change of mind, a friendly push that becomes a deadly shove. Your life can change when you're looking right at it but don't notice the tiniest cut in a major artery.

'There's no easy way to tell you this, Mrs Mackleroy.' The headmaster is still talking, as though mentioning social services doesn't merit allowing me a moment to take that in properly, to steel myself because everything is heading in a direction that has a destination marked: 'Hell'. 'I'm sorry you have to hear this from me instead of Phoebe herself. We felt – all three of us – that this was the best way to tell you.'

It took two police officers to tell me an 'incident' meant I'd never see my husband again, why shouldn't it take three people to tell me whatever it is that my daughter has done?

I shift to study her. The way she sits in the tulip-shaped seat – turned away like she is a sunflower and the sun is situated in the opposite direction to me – means I can't see the top part of her body. Her grey, pleated uniform skirt exposes her knees; her long, grey regulation socks with the turquoise edging hide all the skin below her knees, disappearing into her flat, black shoes. Her hair, which she is presenting to me instead of her face, is split into two equal sections and secured into two perfect afro-puff pigtails by matching black elastic hairbands. She doesn't look like a troublemaker, but then she never does. She looks like a girl who follows the rules, does as she's told and is *mortified* at being sent to headteacher's office.

I know what you've done, I think at her.

'*Ah-he-hem!*' goes the headteacher's throat again, and I swivel back to him. I should know his name but I don't. It's a piece of information that has skipped right out of my head, replaced by the knowledge of what my fourteen-year-old daughter has done. I don't need him to say it because I know what's going on.

He says it anyway, because it needs to be uttered out loud, this needs to be confirmed.

'Mrs Mackleroy, I'm afraid to say, Phoebe is about four weeks pregnant.'

II

16 years before *That Day* (June, 1995)

My fingers were curled tight into the edges of the armrests, my body forced back into the seat as the aeroplane, Flight 4867 to Lisbon, lurched sickeningly to the left, then was immediately flung to the right. This was why I hated flying. This was why I'd thought long and hard about whether I really, actually needed to 'get away from it all'. I hadn't been sure that my need to escape the anxiety and stress of being at home was worth this. Was worth taking the chance of being trapped in a metal box with only the thought of teetering in the air, waiting for the aeroplane to either glide into calmer skies or to suddenly plummet meaning I'd have to scream or cry or pray my way to impending death.

Go to Portugal, I'd told myself. *It's only two hours on a plane*, I'd told myself. *It'll be fine. It'll only be one hundred and twenty minutes. How much turbulence can be crammed into that short amount of time? Some movies are longer than that. You'll be fine, Saffron. Absolutely fine.*

I was not fine. I was clinging to the armrests of an aeroplane seat, securing my mind firmly to the present, refusing to allow my life to replay itself before my eyes because if I could stop that happening, the rest of it, the screaming/

9

praying/crying to impending death wouldn't happen, either.

The man seated next to me, whose girlfriend had his left hand in a vice-like grip, turned to me as the plane rollicked sideways and held out his right hand. 'You can cling onto this hand if you want,' he said. My gaze went from his large hand with its square, neat nails to his girlfriend. Her green eyes were wide and terrified, her straight red hair ruffled, it seemed, by fear itself, but she still managed a nod to me to communicate: '*Go on, you idiot, grab on and squeeze tight. We're all in this together.*'

The plane swooped into a dip and his girlfriend and I both closed our eyes after letting out simultaneous 'Ohhhhhhh's. I immediately clamped my hand over the one proffered and clung on for sheer life as we rocked and rolled our way into Lisbon.

I've fallen through a pothole in time, been to one of the places in my past with Joel, and I have come back to the present with a rising and falling tide of nausea at the pit of my stomach. Usually, the memory pockets that feature Joel and our life before *that day* give me an unexpected little boost, a little something to allow me to carry on in the present, but not this time.

This time, the cauldron of uncertainty and worry that lives where my stomach should be continues to whisk itself into a frenzy because I'm one of those parents. *Those* parents. The ones you read about in the papers or magazines and shake your head at; the ones you think *Where were the parents?*

about when you hear of something terrible involving a child. I know I'm one of those parents because here I sit with my hands folded on my lap, my face set in a neutral expression, replaying the secrets a stranger has seconds ago revealed to me about my own life.

I hate feeling sick.

I hate feeling sick even more than I hate being sick because at least once you've vomited, have excavated your stomach of its contents, apart from the ache in your ribs or your throat, it's done with; gone. Nausea, though, sits at the pit of your being, mixing itself slowly and potently, occasionally rising up, threatening to spill out, before it subsides again, folding and stirring, stirring and folding itself a little more intensely as a sensation that won't be shifting any time soon.

Right now, I feel sick.

My daughter, who still wears a school uniform, who I have to take shopping for shoes, who still has teddy bears on her bed, is pregnant.

'Are you going to say anything, Phoebe?' I ask my daughter, revolving in my seat to her.

Her slender, fourteen-year-old body, already twisted away from me, cringes ever so slightly – a tiny reflexive tensing of muscles – at my voice but she does not move or otherwise acknowledge me.

'Phoebe?' I say her name gently, carefully.

Nothing. Nothing from my daughter.

I return my line of sight to the men in front of me and focus on the youthful one, the handsome one. *The* Mr Bromsgrove. Why did she choose to tell him? Of all the people in the world, in this city, in this school, why did she choose to tell him? He is young, but not especially young, probably about my age, actually. Certainly old enough to be her father. He has a grade-one haircut all over, his features are strong – a man who can look like he takes no nonsense very easily, but also able to look soft and understanding an instant later. He's slender, bordering on skinny, and wearing a form-fitting white shirt, navy suit jacket and tan corduroy trousers. His eyes, from what I can see behind his gold wire-rimmed glasses, are the same dark hazel-brown of his skin and seem kind. This is the first time I've regarded him properly, have *noticed* him, and now I can understand what the others in the playground have been whispering about. Why they have crushes on him. Why I would have had a crush on him if I were a teenager. Does my daughter? Is that why she told him this thing first? Because she thought it might bond them? Or is it more nefarious than that, does he have something to do with her condition?

My gaze goes to the headteacher. *How could you allow this to happen?* I want to say. *When she's not at home, she's here, at school, so this thing must have happened on school time.*

I contemplate *The* Mr Bromsgrove again. Has she mentioned him a little too much? Have I seen anything with his name on in her bedroom when I go in to check her computer? I am plundering my memory, trying to see if there is a moment that featured this man, this potential father of my daughter's child. Nothing. Nothing comes to mind, or pricks my memory. He doesn't even raise a suspicion of anything untoward happening between them.

It could have happened anywhere, I remind myself. *It could have happened with anyone, because I don't know what Phoebe does in the time between leaving school grounds and walking into our house.* At home, she's always studying, with the good marks to show for it, or she's sitting in the corner of the sofa in the living room, phone in hand, texting away or on Facebook and Twitter and all those things I haven't really been paying attention to. She's home so I've always assumed she is safe. All the bad things happen 'out there'. As long as she's where I can see her most of the time, she's safe.

'Phoebe has declined to tell us who the father is,' *The* Mr Bromsgrove says. From the corner of my eye, I see her head turn a little as she looks at him. Is she annoyed and resentful that he's telling me this, or is she incredulous that he's saying that when he is somehow involved? I can't know for certain because her face is hidden from me.

'Mrs Mackleroy, I'm not sure what you want to do right now . . .' The headteacher leaves his sentence open and expects me to fill it.

'Are you going to tell social services?' I say into the gap he has left for me.

The headteacher glances at *The* Mr Bromsgrove, and I wonder if either of them hears Phoebe's almost inaudible gasp. Have they noticed she's now holding her breath? Do they realise that we're already on the social services radar and this sort of revelation would start the whole thing up again?

The Mr Bromsgrove stares at the headteacher, then at Phoebe, then back at the headteacher. He doesn't include me in his assessment of the situation, in fact, he's avoided looking directly at me since I walked in here. I saw him look me over when I entered, but his visual attention to me has been conspicuous in its absence. *It's OK*, I'd love to say, *I know I'm a bad mother, you don't have to avoid looking at me in case your face shows your disgust. I'm disgusted enough with me for the both of us.*

The headteacher finally focuses on me again. 'I think we should play it by ear for now, don't you? We think it would be best if you had a talk with Phoebe, see what you plan to do and then we'll have another meeting to discuss our options.' His face flames a deep crimson. 'I mean, options in the school and education sense, of course. *Ah-he-hem!*' He starts to desperately shuffle papers.

The cauldron of nausea at the centre of my being folds and stirs itself much faster.

16 years before *That Day* (September, 1995)

'What would you like me to make you, pretty lady?' Joel asked me. We'd been dating for two months, not including the time we met on the plane to Lisbon and then not seeing each other again for a month, and this was our first date that didn't involve some kind of physical activity – bowling, hillwalking (disastrous), rollerblading, rock-climbing, dry-slope skiing, clubbing. Tonight, though, he'd insisted on a slower, more relaxed date with dinner and drinks at his shared flat in Hove.

'Nothing. I don't think I could eat a thing.' I rubbed my stomach to emphasise my point. 'I've been eating all day, I'm stuffed.'

'Nonsense.' As always, his rich tones moved deliciously like warmed maple syrup through me. 'You can have anything you like from the rather extensive selection in my fridge.'

Joel opened the door to his tall white fridge, unlocking the gateway to a world of pleasure: fresh vegetables, fresh pasta, apples, blackberries, strawberries, blueberries, butter, cheese, ham, fresh chicken, salmon were all stacked neatly onto the three shelves with raw meat, poultry and fish together, fresh veg and fruit together, deli foods sitting side by side. No open cans with their lids half on, furring up with every passing second; no putrefying foodstuffs that were going to rot away leaving a slimy pool of decay in their wake; no crusty-lidded jars with stained, faded labels.

The rest of the kitchen was pristine, too. Around the room, quite large for a two-bedroom flat, was evidence of cooking, eating, *living*. The wall beside the cooker had two long shelves stacked with many different types of oils, some with suspended chilli peppers, garlic and herbs. The lower shelf had clear jars filled with different types of dried pasta, rice, beans and lentils. Below that stood a rack of dried herbs and spices. On one of the work surfaces there was a wooden knife block with six silver-handled knives – all of different sizes, I'd imagine – protruding from it. Along the sill of the large window that allowed light to pour into the kitchen, small pots of fresh herbs grew – I recognised three of them as lavender, basil and chives.

'So, you and your mate Fynn live here all on your own?' I said to him.

'Yeah, have done since we got proper jobs after uni.'

'And you're both into cooking?'

'No, that's my thing. Fynn's more into cars. And women. But mostly cars.'

'How did two such different people manage to become such good friends?'

'We're not that different. Like I told you, we met at an open day for Cambridge. Kind of gravitated towards each other when we realised within ten minutes or so that we were both there to make our parents happy.'

'Rather be a disappointment, huh?'

'No, rather have a life. I wasn't passionate about going there and it wouldn't have been fair to take a place away from someone whose whole life was about going there. Same with Fynn. We met again at the interviews and exchanged numbers. After A-levels we decided to run away and live by the sea to escape the sound of our parents' hearts breaking. We literally did nothing but work and party for a year before we both started college in Brighton.'

Closing the fridge door, I took his hand and stood staring at him for a few seconds. Just staring at him. He was easily the best-looking man I'd been 'involved' with. Easily. He was six foot or so, solidly built, with long, lean muscles that I kept eyeing up whenever he wore short-sleeved shirts. I hadn't seen the rest of him in the flesh, as it were, but I was hoping to change that. I was always trying to get lost in his eyes because they were like twin whirlpools of melted mahogany fringed with pitch-black lashes. His face could have been carved from a piece of walnut wood it was so smooth and dark, and begging to have my fingers stroke it. And his mouth – it was always smiling at me. Whenever I caught him looking at me, he was always either grinning or seemed to be on the verge of doing so.

'Didn't see anything in the fridge you fancied, no?' he asked and reached for the silver handle again.

'Not exactly,' I said. To distract and get him to focus on me, I led him out of the kitchen and into their spacious living room, where I encouraged him to sit so I could drop onto the sofa beside him. 'I'd much rather hear more about what you got up to in that year of work and partying.'

'Really that interested?' he asked and his smile lit up his twenty-six-year-old face again. I was instantly jelly-like inside. He reached out and slipped his arm around my waist as I'd been longing for him to do, before he leant back onto the sofa and pulled me towards his body.

'Oh, yes, I'm very, very interested.'

We're at the bus stop near the school. I'd been too shaky after the call to come to St Allison to even contemplate driving and spent all the spare cash I had on a taxi to get here. I had enough to get home on the bus and Phoebe had her pass.

We are propped two widths of a normal-size person apart on the moulded plastic bench under the shelter. It's April and I, like everyone else, am still waiting for the faintest hint of spring to join us but the weather is not cooperating. The air around us is cool but not hostile. I wish it was warmer, though, waiting for a bus would be far more pleasant if the cool air wasn't seeping in under my jacket and playing across my skin.

'You're going to have to talk to me at some point,' I say to Phoebe. The first thing I've said to her since, 'We're going to have to get a bus' as she stood waiting to see which direction I'd go to get to the car.

In response to this, she turns her head even further away from me, not in the direction the bus will be coming from, but towards home and back towards the school.

I stop watching her, she's not going to look at me. I focus myself instead towards where the bus will come from and I wonder: *Is she wishing herself at home, is she wishing herself back in the safety of school, or is she wishing she was anywhere but near me right now?*

III

There's an area of faded purple on the white tiled floor of our kitchen. It's an irregular-shaped patch that I've tried to remove over the last fifteen months but it's still there. No one else can see it, apparently, or maybe no one else is bothered by it – I'm the only one I've noticed who stares at it. I've tried white vinegar, bleach, cream cleansers, everything I know to get a stain out, but nothing has worked. It's still there, splashed across six tiles, reminding me of the time I dropped a bowl of blackberries and didn't have the presence of mind to clear it up before the black, viscous juice leached into the surface of the white tiles and left a permanent dark bruise in our home.

Every time I walk into the kitchen I look at it first. I glance at it and fleetingly remember the numbness that overtook my body with frightening speed; the phut, phut, phut of black-berries exploding on the tiles; the sound of the bowl, already chipped and scratched with age, smashing as it hit the floor; the sensation of all the air leaving my body in one go.

I watch the grey-sock-covered heels of my daughter walk across the patch as if it's not there. She plonks herself at the table, in the seat nearest the sink, where she always sits, and immediately takes her phone out of her jacket pocket.

She shouldn't be wearing her jacket in the house, but in the grand scheme of things, I don't think it matters.

'Zane's staying at Imogen's house tonight. He and Ernest have got a new game to try out,' I explain to her. I talk to her as normal even though she hasn't even acknowledged my existence since the headteacher's office. Or was it before that? Did I stop existing for Phoebe all that time ago, when I did what she wanted and agreed not to go to the police? Did getting her own way make her lose all respect for me?

Zane, Phoebe's ten-year-old brother, is with Ernest, his best friend since reception. Ernest's mother, Imogen, has been sweet, and kind, especially in the last eighteen months, but I haven't told her what has happened today. I can't even begin to find the words to explain it to myself, let alone someone who has brought up three children – two of whom have made it past teenage-hood without this kind of scandal.

14 years before *That Day* (June, 1997)

I ran through our Hove flat, my heart sounding like stampeding buffalo in my ears after I threw aside the cloth I was using to clean the kitchen surfaces, and answered Joel's urgent cries from the other side of our flat. We were renting a beautiful art deco place right on the Hove seafront and I was bordering on obsessive with keeping it clean.

'What, what, what's the matter?' I asked him. He stood in the bathroom, naked apart from his white underpants that were so tight, so moulded to his body, I was surprised they didn't cut off circulation between his torso and his legs.

'Ffrony, I think it's time. I need you to shave my back for me.'

'That's what you were calling me like that for? I thought it was an emergency. Or at least important.'

Like a blanket of short, black wool, his chest hair lined the sink in front of him, and his chest was smooth and hairless. Each of the well-defined areas of his six-pack was emphasised now it wasn't covered in hair.

'It *is* important,' Joel replied. He frowned at me in the mirror, his beautiful face knitting together in mock horror that I didn't realise this. 'It's extremely important. I need you to shave my back.'

'Erm, I think we can pretty much say that's a no,' I replied. Even though I wasn't going to shave anything, I perched on the roll-top edge of the white bath with its brass claw and ball feet, and took the opportunity to watch my boyfriend. I loved to examine, whenever I could, the way his body contracted and expanded, how many tiny, seemingly inconsequential expressions flitted across his face without being manifested as words or actions. I adored watching him.

'Excuse me, Babes, I think you'll find it's part of the whole "for better and worse" deal,' he cajoled. 'Come on, it won't take long – a few strokes and we're done.'

'How many times have you said that?' I laughed.

With a grin on his face, he spun towards me, tugged me to my feet, then pressed the electric shaver into my hand.

'Why do you need to shave your back, anyway? I wouldn't mind you being hairy.'

'Yes, but it's unbelievably uncomfortable having a hairy back, especially when it's hot.'

21

I examined the shaver in front of me; the prongs seemed vicious and dangerous, like they'd slice off chunks of flesh instead of efficiently and effectively snipping off hair. 'Hang on, we've been together two years, lived together three months, how come this is the first time you've asked?' The answer, of course, was immediately obvious. 'Fynn does it, doesn't he? Still? *Still?* Do you do his as well?'

'That's between me and him, Ffrony, there are some things you can't know.'

'I swear, you two . . . I don't know whether to be jealous or impressed sometimes. You're way too close.'

'No such thing. Come on now, Babes, sort me out here.'

I pushed the large rubbery on button and the buzzer jumped to life, vibrating violently in my hand.

'This is a very important moment in our life together, Ffrony. Not just anyone gets to do my back, you're the first woman I've ever asked to do this. You are about to be initiated into the Great Hall of Joel.'

'The Great Hall of Joel. Riiigggghhhttt.' I sounded confident, but I was trembling, shaking with anxiety. I didn't want to hurt him, not ever. My hand quivered as I pushed it against the hairy area over his right shoulder blade.

'Don't worry about hurting me,' he said seriously. His whirlpool eyes held my gaze steadily in the mirror. 'I know you'd never do that.'

I steadied my hand, willed myself to stop quaking. He was right, I wouldn't hurt him and I *could* do this. 'OK.'

'You can't anyway, it's got a safety guard,' he added before laughing so much it was a full five minutes before he was still enough for me to try again.

'I was going to make chicken pesto with mash and veg for dinner,' I say to my first-born child. Joel and I tried for her for what seemed like for ever. Every month my period started I would feel such extreme disappointment, and the second the two lines turned blue on the test the dread and panic that bolted through me was like nothing I'd ever experienced. 'I've made the pesto already, so how about we have it with gnocchi instead, it'll be quicker?' Her head is lowered and her right thumb is flying over her phone's keyboard as she types away. For Phoebe, it seems, everything is normal, nothing has changed.

She lifts her head, looks briefly at me and then shrugs a 'Suppose' before returning to her phone, to her important, real life. My tongue hurts from how hard I clamp down with my teeth, reining in the scream that has flared up in my chest. With the scream still bubbling at the back of my throat, I quickly rotate to the chrome kettle and take it to the sink. All the while: *I will not scream, I will not scream, I will not scream* pirouettes like a clockwork ballerina through my mind.

13 years before *That Day* (August, 1998)

'What do you want the baby to be?' Joel asked, resting his hand on the ever-so-slight swell of my three-month-pregnant stomach. 'I know we'll be happy whatever we get, but what, ideally, would you like the baby to be?'

'Human?' I replied. I placed both my hands over his, pressing him closer to our child and holding onto him at the same time.

'*Human?* As opposed to . . . ?' he questioned.

'Klingon?'

He used his free hand to tug me closer as we reclined on our sofa together, then he snuggled his face into the curve of my neck, where he was always pressing his cold lips, which made me giggle and shudder at the same time. 'Now, what have you got against Klingons?' he asked, mid-nuzzle.

'Nothing. I'm going to marry you, aren't I, Mr Ridge Face?'

He immediately touched his forehead, as if he needed to check, as if I wasn't always calling him that. 'I do *not* have a big forehead.'

'No, course you don't,' I giggled.

'Don't listen to her, baby,' he laughed. 'Your dad doesn't have a big forehead.'

'He doesn't,' I conceded, 'it's *huge!*'

'I know what you're doing, Ffrony,' he said, suddenly setting aside his laugh, 'and it's not going to work. Stop avoiding the question.'

'Sorry.' I closed my eyes and thought of the future; thought of him and me and a bundle of a baby. Immediately the white-hot fear of uncertainty started to close in around the edges of my thoughts and set off the tumble of worry, about what would come next, what could go wrong, how I could fail, that was always precariously balanced like a stack of fragile tea-cups inside me. I couldn't pin down the thoughts, the needs, the wish list of what I wanted for our future, because that might jinx it, that might make it a real thing that could be taken away from me. 'I don't know what I want, Joel, I really don't.'

'Don't be scared,' he said. He knew what I was thinking, how I was worrying and wrapped both his arms around me instead of just around the baby. 'It's all going to be fine.'

'You can't know that.'

'I can, and I do.'

'What do you want, then?' I didn't want my anxieties to spoil this for him. This was his time, too. Even if I couldn't completely relax, the least I could do was give him that opportunity.

'A girl, I think. I'll be as happy with a boy, don't get me wrong, but I'd love a girl.'

'Why?'

'Don't know, really. I . . .' He stopped talking and then glided into one of his now familiar and comforting silences as he considered my question from all angles. 'I don't know, I guess it's one of those things you think you want and you have no real reason for wanting it.'

'I see,' I replied, even though I had no clue what he was talking about.

I'm standing at the sink, looking out of the window, watching the last of the light outside recede into early evening darkness through the gaps in our curtain of butterflies. When she was ten, Phoebe spent weeks stringing together multicoloured crystal butterflies. Night after night she'd take up her seat on a cushion in the corner of the living room, using a large needle to string butterflies onto jewellers' wire, before twisting a knot on either side with jewellers' pliers then adding another butterfly. When she'd finished, her dad tied them to a curtain pole and hung it up over the part of the window by the sink.

The curtain dots our kitchen with splashes of different-coloured light during the day, intensified, of course, when the sun is out. Some mornings I come in here before the sun comes up and sit at the table with a cup of coffee, staring at the blackberry stain while the room gradually becomes a multicoloured glow.

'Who's the father?' I ask Phoebe, clattering our plates onto the butterfly-covered place mats I have laid on the table in the two minutes it took to cook the gnocchi.

Phoebe picks up the fork I placed in front of her earlier, and spears a rocket and basil pesto-covered potato dumpling. When I ask my question, she doesn't raise the food from the plate to her mouth, instead she leaves it there, jammed onto the fork, sitting against the plate. Eventually, she gives a small, discreet shrug of her bony shoulders as her reply.

Panic billows up inside. 'You don't know who the father is, or you're not going to tell me?' I ask.

Phoebe treats me to another shrug, this time with one shoulder.

I inhale slowly and deeply, then exhale at length. I know what Joel would say right now. He'd remind me that she's fourteen, she's terrified and that there are worse things you could do than get pregnant. He would tell me not to scream.

He would tell me to remember how it felt to be in a similar position to her. He'd tell me all these things and he would be right.

Picking up my fork, I remind myself of the sheer terror of sitting in front of a parent you are already scared of upsetting after they've been to the headteacher's office about you, after they've learnt things about you that you thought would go away. I remember the words that came quietly spilling out of my mother's mouth when I was in a similar position to Phoebe, how each syllable was a stinging blow that I can recall without trying too hard. I remember the way I didn't speak at all until she stopped, and how I stayed silent as she ignored me for a whole week because I'd brought such shame onto our family.

This is different, though: ignoring this will not make it go away; pretending it's not happening is not going to cure anything. I lower my fork and rest its prongs on the edge of my plate. 'The thing is, Phoebe, you can't shrug this away.' My voice is calm and reasonable, not at all how I feel inside. 'It might be the way you want to deal with this, but you can't handle an adult problem by behaving like a child.'

'That's how you see me, isn't it?' she says on the edge of a screech, her face screwed up like a wounded, cornered wild animal about to attack. 'As a problem! That's all I am to you, isn't it? A problem!'

I have no idea what I'm doing here, of course. Joel would probably know. He'd work out how to deal with this, the right thing to say, the correct way to act. Me?

I keep thinking: SHE IS PREGNANT.

I keep thinking: SHE HAS BEEN HAVING SEX.

I keep thinking: SHE DIDN'T TELL ME.

Twelve months ago my daughter was still asking me to buy her cuddly toys. Six months ago she was still racing her brother to the top of the slide in the park and screaming in joy as they slid to the bottom. Three months ago she was thirteen and still a little girl. My little girl. But she's been having sex like an adult for God knows how long. And getting pregnant like an adult. Then reacting like a child. How am I supposed to know how to deal with it?

'Are you going to deal with this *situation* like an adult or a child, is what I meant to say. You can't shrug what is happening away. I need to know what's going on. Who the father is. If you've told him. What he thinks if you have told him, if we're going to tell him if you haven't already.'

Despite her outburst, Phoebe has been eating, but now she stops shovelling down food and instead moves gnocchi around her plate with the tip of her fork, smearing the creamy green-flecked pesto in its wake. Joel used to do that with the sauce on his food. He would move it around and around as if trying to paint a picture on the plate. Phoebe probably learnt it from him – or maybe it's a genetic thing, something they were both predisposed to.

'Have you told the father?' I ask.

She shakes her head, staring at that piece of gnocchi as it continues its round-plate journey. I stare at it, too, a plump, creamy oval of potato and wheat flour and milk solids and all the other things the manufacturers add. Joel made gnocchi once. He'd used egg, though, and cream, I think. Or was it

28

parmesan? Or was it both? He never made it again, because the effort-to-gain ratio was all wrong for him. Every week, whenever Joel made pesto, Phoebe and Zane would try to convince him that he wanted to make gnocchi, too. That nothing would be better. He held firm, though, unmoved by their appeals to his better nature.

'Is he your boyfriend?' I ask Phoebe, snapping myself back to the present. I keep falling through those potholes in time, finding myself back there, with him, with them, with us, how we used to be. This isn't the moment for that, though. I need to stay focused, I need to stay *now*.

Phoebe pauses, then nods once. Stops. Shakes her head four times. Nods five times. Then 'shrug'. The ubiquitous shrug. I could scream the house down because of those shrugs.

'Are you in love with him?' I ask. I need to know what this pregnancy means to her. I need to know if she is thinking of this as something that will become her love child, something she possibly did on purpose so she could bind herself to this boy without a name or if it was a huge mistake that she is horrified as well as terrified by.

Phoebe doesn't reply, or even look at me, because we both know that is a stupid question. Fourteen-year-olds are always in love. They are made up of the fizzy, popping, spinning feeling of falling in love. Love is something that happens for them with every in and out breath.

I want to tell her that this isn't 'love'. That 'love' doesn't stay the same, it changes like we do, it is shaped by our experiences, by what we do, who we meet, what we learn. I'd like to explain that falling in love now is not how it'll be for ever, and even if you stay with the same boy for the rest of your life, this incarnation of love won't stay the same, it never does.

Apparently, in relation to the teenager in front of me, it's a stupid question for different reasons: 'Everyone hooks up, Mum,' she says. 'It doesn't mean anything. It doesn't mean love or anything like that.'

'What do you mean "hooks up"?' I reply. I'm not thick, I simply need to clarify that I've understood her properly.

'You know, *hooks up*.'

I really don't. Or, rather, I don't want to. 'So you're pregnant as a result of "hooking up"?'

She says nothing because her food is suddenly very interesting, and it's absolutely necessary to put two pieces of gnocchi into her mouth at once and chew very slowly, rendering her incapable of speech.

I lower my head to my food, too, and we eat in silence. After five minutes I look up at her. Her childish afro-puff pigtails, her grey, turquoise-trimmed school uniform, her friendship bracelet on her left wrist that is studded with pink, clear plastic butterflies. *Hooking up? This girl in front of me has been hooking up?*

'You're fourteen,' I remind her. 'Who "hooks up" at fourteen?'

I can't see her abdomen, the place where the answer to my question is growing, because of the wood of our table. *Who hooks up?* Everyone 'hooks up' apparently.

5 months before *That Day* (May, 2011)

'For the love of . . . Why are you doing this to me, Joel? What

30

Earthly reason could you have for trying to scrape away the inside of my head like this?'

'I'm only making porridge,' he laughed. His laughs always filled the room like the divine scent of freshly baked bread, slipped through me like syrup to remind me of all the good things in my world.

'No, you are making porridge in a metal saucepan with a metal spoon. You know what it does to me. And why, anyway? Why?' I indicated the metal container beside the stove, crammed with upturned utensils – a potato masher, a handheld grater, a spatula, and most importantly, loads and loads of wooden spoons of various sizes. 'You've got a million wooden spoons there, we can't move sometimes for wooden spoons, and you insist every time on using a metal spoon with the metal pan.'

'I'm trying to save on washing up. If I use this I can eat with it, too.'

'Like you do the washing up!' I scoffed at him. 'And, by the way, in case you haven't noticed despite me telling you this all the time – that is not porridge, it is cement.'

'It's the only way to eat porridge,' he said. As he spooned the 'porridge' into the white bowl with the ring of red flowers around its rim, he made theatrical cracking sounds as though the cement-like substance was breaking the bowl.

'I'll go get the kids up,' I said, while he switched on the television. His fingers reached for the remote to click on BBC breakfast news, and he took his seat at the table. As I passed him on the way upstairs, I ran my hand over his hair, pausing to twist a tiny section between my fingertips, twirling the black strands back into its piece of a budding dreadlock.

Joel caught my wrist before I moved on, pulled me back and kissed the palm of my hand. 'I'm proud of you and how you're doing,' he said quietly, before going back to his beige cement and catching up with the world news, his few minutes of peace before the world became full of our family.

Like his smile, like his laughs, those words diffused warmth through every cell in my body.

The sickness is still turning, but now it's burrowing itself deeper and deeper into my stomach. I probably need to eat more to make it stop, I feel this more acutely when I'm hungry, but I can't eat any more. My mouth will not allow me to chew any more, or swallow any more. The sense of failure I'm feeling right now, the horror that is accepting I am a bad mother, has dragged me closer and closer to actual vomiting. Once I've done that, have stopped this pervading sense of wanting to chuck up, maybe I'll feel better, maybe the nausea will subside enough for me to think clearly.

'Do you have any idea what you want to do?' I ask her.

She shakes her head.

'Do you want me to stop talking about it?'

A nod.

'Me, too,' I admit. 'Look, I know it's early, but let's go to bed, sleep on it. Talk about it again in the morning.'

Shrug. 'If you want.'

I squeeze my fingers onto my temples, close my eyes and fight the bile that has gushed unexpectedly up my throat.

I will not scream. I will not throw up and I will not scream.

'You know what, Phoebe, it's not a case of what *I* want, actually. I'm trying to be ... This is something I seriously never thought I'd be dealing with. You don't go out to parties or even ask to go to your friends' houses – as far as I know you go to school and come home. This is not something I thought I had to worry about right now.

'And because this is all such a shock, I've not thought through how I was going to react. So, I don't know what to say or do right now at all, let alone what to say or do that won't set you off. Also, I'm trying not to take it personally that you decided to tell some teacher at your school before you told me, like I'm some ogre who's going to shout at you. I thought you knew you could trust me. After last time, after— What I'm saying is, I didn't shout at you last time, did I? I understood, I did what was best for you. But still, you go off and tell some stranger this news first.'

'He's not a stranger,' she states simply.

'Well he's a stranger to me!' I snap, astounded that amongst all the other things wrong in this situation she's defending her teacher. I inhale to push air right to the bottom of my lungs, to gather all my strength together. I exhale to release the anger and tension. 'Look,' I sound normal again, 'let's go to bed and talk again tomorrow. Hopefully we'll both have clearer heads and maybe you'll be able to tell me more. OK?'

Shrug. Then: nod.

I stand first. Both of us have left little mounds of food on our plates, me more than her but I think for a moment to tell her to finish it, to remind her she's going to need her strength in the coming weeks and months whatever she decides. I can't do that, though. It's wrong on every level, and it'll become something else for us to fall out over.

Before she can escape, I move around the table to her and swamp her in a hug. I may want to scream at her right now, but I love her and I want her to know that. She's my world. She and Zane are my world, especially after what happened to Joel, especially after the secret I was forced to keep and the choice I had to make. I want Phoebe to know that I did what I had to do, it wasn't easy, but I did it for her because I love her so much.

In my hold, she freezes. She's unable or unwilling to accept anything like that from me. I hug her and Zane all the time, and while he hugs me back or rolls his eyes until it's over, this is almost always Phoebe's reaction nowadays: a rigid body in my arms as another reminder that no matter how hard I try to pretend, our family is shattered and my attempts to put us back together aren't working.

'I love you, baby,' I whisper, as I used to do every day when she was a newborn, a toddler, a child. '*I love you, baby*', I used to whisper because she had saved me. In ways I didn't even admit to Joel, she'd helped me to put my life back on track and overcome some of my greatest fears. And then she turned twelve and a half and those days ended; cut short by the guillotine of losing Joel.

I'm treated to another shrug from Phoebe, this time to get me away from her. She doesn't need me, she's telling me. And she certainly doesn't need my declarations of love.

I hold out my hand as she is about to turn for the door. 'I need your mobile.'

'What?' she asks, incredulous.

'You need to sleep, you can't do that if you're texting or on the net all night. Phone.'

'No!'

'*Phone,*' I insist.

She bunches the two plump lines of her lips together over her gritted teeth, her eyes narrow to slits of naked disgust. I stare back at her, silently reminding her of the rules: after what she did last time, she can only have a phone if she gives it to me whenever I ask, and as long as I know the password so I can check it whenever I want.

Her breath comes in shallow, outraged bursts as she reaches into her rucksack that she's decorated with blue, purple and red jewelled butterflies like the ones she used to sew the curtain, and throws the retrieved shiny silver and black gadget onto the table. Before I can pick it up, she snatches it up again, fiddles with the back until it is open, then slips out the rectangular battery and pockets it. She doesn't want me to know the secrets that live in her phone.

That isn't part of the deal, but I'm not sure I have the energy to fight about it right now. I certainly don't think the sickness is going to be held back much longer. I am breathing through my nose, trying to stem the flow but even that's ceasing to be effective.

Without bothering to reassemble her little box of secrets, she throws it onto the table and storms out of the room.

'Just so you know,' I call, causing her to pause on the fifth step to listen to what I am saying, 'I'm taking the router up to bed with me, too.'

After she realises that I am cutting her off for the night, that she won't be able to email or get onto social media on her iPod or the computer in her room, every stamp upstairs is increased to earthquake level. The slam of her bedroom door is so hard I swear the very foundations of the house shake.

I don't make it to the upstairs loo. I dash to the small tiled room with a little wall-hung sink, that's just off the kitchen. I drop to my knees, lift the lid of the toilet and finally let go of the anxiety and worry and horror that have been mixing inside me since the phone rang and my life took another turn for the worse.

That Day

My fingers are numb, my body is numb, my entire being is suddenly without air. There are a dozen little splattering thuds of blackberries falling onto the ground, there's a crash of a white ceramic bowl hitting a white ceramic tile.

I snap myself out of there, drag myself from the pothole to the past and into the present where I need to be. And where I need to be is outside my daughter's bedroom.

She's quiet, careful, but I can still hear her small sobs, only partially muffled by her pillow. She needs to sleep, and she needs to cry. She needs to be alone with herself so she can feel this. Hiding from the pain will not help her, it'll become a habit that's virtually impossible to break. That's why I took

36

away her interactive distractions, made her come up here to be alone, so she can start to feel this. I don't want to punish her, just help her to start to accept what's going on. Unlike losing her dad, there's a clock ticking over this situation; avoiding it, pretending it's not happening, will only work for a very short amount of time. With losing her dad, with losing Joel, we can try to defer that grief for the rest of our lives.

I walk past her room to the main bedroom – it always smarts like a flick at my heart how quickly it became *my* bedroom after being ours for nearly ten years – but I don't enter. Instead, I open the door, place the router inside, then shut the door as I usually do, so Phoebe thinks I've gone to bed. Next, I navigate the uneven, noisy corridor floorboards and creep back to my place beside her room. I sit on the floor and briefly touch my fingers to the mottled dark wood door. '*I love you, baby,*' I mouth and I hope she feels it. That it seeps through the wood, that it floats through the air to her and she can breathe it in.

This was all I could do eighteen months ago. Neither Zane nor Phoebe wanted to sleep in the big bed with me, and I couldn't split myself in two to be with them, so I'd sit here, in the space between their rooms, whisper 'I love you' to each of them, then listen powerlessly as they cried themselves to sleep.

It's all I can do for Phoebe now, because at the moment she really does need to be on her own, and to feel whatever it is she's going to feel next.

*

'Saff? What's up? What's happened?' The familiarity of Fynn's voice immediately trickles ease through my tense, troubled body and frantic, fretting mind.

'I'm sorry, I know it's late and I didn't want to wake you, but I didn't know who else to call.'

'I'm on my way,' he says, followed by the rustle of bed-clothes being thrown back, of someone sitting up, preparing to slide out of bed.

'No, no, you don't need to. I just need to tell someone this before my head explodes.'

'Right,' he says cautiously, bracing himself for the worst. But what is the worst? He's heard it, is he preparing himself for that? Is he bracing himself to hear that another person he dearly loves is lost to him?

'*You need to come,*' I'd said. '*Something's happened. To Joel. Something's happened to Joel. I need you to come here. I have to go to the hospital.*' He didn't respond straight away that time. He'd been silent for many, many seconds that felt like hours, and then he snapped out of it and said he was on his way. I called him before I called Joel's parents, before I called my parents or my sister, because I didn't know if I'd be able to speak again after I'd said it once. I needed him to come and I needed him to tell other people, because I had other things to do. I had to go and identify him, I had to go and get the children then tell them. I had to pretend I believed any of it was happening. I could only cope with that if Fynn was there, too.

In the present, he exhales quietly but at length and I imagine his navy blue eyes slipping shut, his broad shoulders moving downwards as they're forced to relax, his torso contracting as he holds himself ready. *You can do this, Fynn,* he's telling himself, *you can cope with whatever it is.*

'Phoebe's pregnant,' I say. I was going to gently lead him into it, explain about being called to the school, the headmaster, that *The* Mr Bromsgrove fella, how I realised what was going on right before I was told – but doing it like that would have been cruel. Revelations this huge should be delivered straight away – you can comfort and cosset the blow afterwards, the preamble takes the listener to all sorts of places they don't need to visit before fully receiving the news.

Fynn's inaudible reply is obviously shock. Incomprehension at what I've said. 'Phoebe who?' he eventually says. Not shock: confusion; he's been trying to work out who I could be talking about because it's *that* ludicrous an idea it could be the only Phoebe he knows.

'Your goddaughter, Zane's sister, my and Joel's daughter.'

Silence returns to his side of the phone. Eventually he speaks again: 'But she's fourteen,' he states. 'You need to . . . You know what you need to do to get pregnant and she's only fourteen.'

'I know,' I reply.

'Are you sure about this, Saff?' He thinks I've lost it, that I am out of my mind.

'Yes. She told a teacher at school and they called me in. She's about four weeks pregnant. Or whatever it is in real terms of last period etc.'

Silence. This time it is shock. 'Bloody hell,' Fynn breathes. '*Bloody hell.*' He understands, he knows why I am panicking:

there is no easy way out of this; whatever happens next, Phoebe, my baby, will be changed for ever.

'She won't tell me who the father is,' I explain before he asks. 'She pretty much won't talk to me at all. If I ask a question I get a shrug or a handful of words, but nothing that makes me understand why and how this happened. I mean, I don't know if she was forced or pressurised or manipulated. If she wanted to. If it was all planned or a hideous mistake. I don't know, so I don't know how to help her. Or what I'm supposed to be doing. I wish she would talk to me. I wish I could think properly. I wish I could stop wanting to scream at her.'

'Do you want me to talk to her?'

'I'd love it if you could, and if it meant she'd open up, but not yet. I think she would completely lose the plot if she knew I'd told someone. But I had to because my brain was about to explode. There are so many things going on in my head and I had to get a little bit of it out. It was either you or go dig a hole in the garden and shout into it and I don't think our garden is big enough for the hole I'd need.'

'This isn't your fault,' he says, reading my mind as Joel used to.

'Oh, really? How did you figure that one out?'

'This isn't your fault,' he repeats, his voice taking a firmer tone.

'Fynn, I know I've said this to you before, but when you have children and something bad – or even something not very good – happens to them you try as hard as you can to work out what you could have done differently to get a different result.' To not have a terrified fourteen-year-old crying herself to sleep because adulthood, which was meant to come to her as drips of experience over the coming years, has submerged her with a flood of the real world in one go. Again.

'What could you have done differently?' Behind his reasonable question, his attempt to soothe my guilt, is a man who is quietly but definitely freaking out. I can hear it in the timbre of his voice, in the spacing of his words. 'Bloody hell' is probably on loop in his mind and he's anxiously rubbing the area above his right eyebrow.

'I don't know,' I admit.

'Exactly, there is nothing you could have done differently, none of this is your fault. Do you want me to come over?'

'No, it's fine. I'm so grateful, though, that you don't blame me.'

'Of course I don't. Joel wouldn't have, either. Please listen, Saff, this isn't your fault, and you know yourself that there's nothing you could have done to change it.'

'Yeah, you're right. Night, Fynn.'

'Night.'

I must have sounded convincing to him because he didn't keep me on the phone, insisting we talk, he didn't insist on coming over to reassure me in person. It was almost believable that I don't know how I could have stopped this happening.

It's obvious, though. No matter which way I try to spin it, look at it, take an alternative view – this wouldn't be happening if Joel was around. Phoebe's slow decline into this wouldn't have occurred if I hadn't got her father killed.

IV

Slugs have been nibbling at my plants.

It goes through phases when it's fine and there's no sign of them, and then I'll go out to water my 'crop' of vegetables first thing in the morning before work and the silvery, slimy evidence of something unwelcome will glisten up at me. This morning, it seems the slugs have had an orgy on the vegetable plot, despite the carefully laid border of broken eggshells. Maybe I wasn't diligent enough, maybe there was one that had been a Trojan horse, hiding under the spinach leaves, which then made plans to admit the others once my back was turned, because they have decimated the area. Where the spinach grows is obviously where they partied the most – I'm sure if I look hard enough I'll find tiny discarded beer bottles, Rizla papers and condom wrappers.

It's after nine, Phoebe hasn't surfaced and I didn't bother to wake her. I had to organise things for the day, take another day off work – even though my compassionate leave from all that time ago somehow segued into being part of my annual leave over two business years and it's still frowned upon if I take *any* time off. Kevin, my boss, who is Director of Operations, paused a long time earlier when I told him I had a medical emergency and had to take today off as well. With icicles hanging off his every syllable, he asked if I'd *definitely* be in tomorrow. In reply, I'd wanted to sing a couple of lines about no one knowing what tomorrow would bring from 'Love Lifts Us Up Where We Belong', and a better man would have appreciated it, would have laughed. Instead, I'd crossed my fingers behind my back, even though he couldn't actually see me, and said, 'Yes, of course.'

Then I'd made an appointment for Phoebe with the doctor. Despite me calling at one minute past eight (when the appointment lines opened at eight), I'd ended up with six people ahead of me in the queue, and the doctor she normally saw was booked up.

I couldn't take any more judgement from semi-strangers, at least I knew Phoebe's doctor well enough to withstand her scorn, so I'd made her an appointment for the next day, and then I'd called Zane before he left for school. We live one street away from the school, literally around the corner, so I'd been tempted to go and wait for him outside school so I could hug him, hold him, remind myself that he was all right. I'd failed with the older one, but the younger one was all right. I couldn't, though, because that would mortify him, me acting the crazy mother in front of his friends. Instead, I'd settled for speaking to him on the phone, checking he was behaving, checking he'd done his homework, checking he knew how much I loved him. Irritation ran like a throbbing vein through every 'Yes, Mum' he'd uttered. I smiled after each one, that irritation told me he was indeed all right.

And now I am here, kneeling in front of the vegetables in the shady part of the garden, against the back, whitewashed wall, surveying, like a parent who has returned from holiday without two teenage children, the damage done by the slugs to my vegetables.

That's a big one. Perfectly spherical, its clear skin glistening and swirling as it spins away. I dunk the long, purple bubble wand again and take it out, wave it through the air to release different size bubbles into the bright sunlight of this clear April morning. Today's weather is perfect for making bubbles. Joel and I would, much to the mortification of our children, stand in the garden, one of us with the wand, the other giggling and laughing as we chased around after what looked like large, fragile crystal balls. Then we'd swap and carry on for as long as we had enough mixture. 'You're behaving like you're three,' Zane would say after fifteen minutes of watching us. 'What he said,' Phoebe would add. And we'd laugh even louder because we were their parents and embarrassing them was our job.

I still buy bubble mixture refill, but this is the first time since *that day* I've glugged the yellow liquid into an empty bubble wand container, stood in the centre of the lawned section of our garden and done this. It's another of those things I haven't been able to do because it doesn't work without my partner in crime. Except today, I need to feel close to him, I need to do something that reminds me of him and how we used to be, how I used to be, how I was once able to feel something other than numb. I am constantly numb, as though I am surrounded by swathes of cotton wool and gauze, as though life is filtered through those thick layers and I'm not actually allowed to fully experience anything. Maybe it's too much for me, maybe, like the glimpse I got with yesterday's news, engaging fully with the world, actually touching it by living in it properly would completely overwhelm me. If I do this, though, maybe I'll connect with Joel. Maybe I'll get some feeling back and I'll know what I need to do next.

I could do that with cooking something, but right now I need to be outside, I need to have the air on my skin, the sun in my eyes. I need to watch the bubbles rise effortlessly into the air, catch the light, and settle themselves on the wind to be carried away. I need to do all this and see if it can bring a smile to my face and feelings into my body.

'What are you doing?' Phoebe asks. She steps out of the kitchen door, which I left propped open, still in her silky blue pyjamas, her fluffy pink dressing gown tied firmly over the top.

I dunk my wand, then slice it through the air to free the flawless spheres. 'I'm making bubbles.'

'Why?'

'Because it's Tuesday. Because I'm not at work. And because a bunch of slugs have trashed my vegetable patch.' I've got my green and white striped gardener's apron on, and my gardening gloves, so I probably look either strange or eccentric depending on how you viewed these things. 'It's surprisingly calming,' I add. I hold out the bottle to her. 'Want a go?'

She rolls her eyes and curls her lip in disgust. If I'd ever looked at my parents like that, I think they'd have slapped my face clean off my head.

'Can I have my phone back?' she asks and shoves her hands into the neat square pockets of her dressing gown.

I lower the bubble wand. 'Not until we've talked a bit,' I say. The eye roll and lip curl turn into a full-body sigh.

'Come and have a look at what the slugs have done,' I say to her. 'It's really quite impressive, if you're not the person whose plants they've destroyed.'

She has her trainers on, so drags herself across the patio, across the lawn, across the other part of the patio to the vegetable patch in the corner. It's shaded a little by the overhang from the large oak tree that grows in next door's garden. We stand side by side, looking at the leaves of my spinach plants, which look like badly crocheted doilies; the slimy trail that is all over the rocket leaves, which have huge chunks taken out of them but not as artistically as the spinach; and the glistening trail that links the near-black earth between the rocket, spinach, watercress and cabbages.

'Wow,' Phoebe breathes. 'They did this all in one night?'

'One day and one night,' I say.

'*Wow.*' She's impressed, probably imagining what it'd be like to go to the human equivalent of such a party. 'Wow.'

'Do you have any idea what you want to do?' I ask her now that I've impressed her and we're on a neutral subject.

The shutters around her immediately come down, whatever positive emotion she had towards me is whisked away in an instant. 'Whatever you say,' she mumbles.

'This isn't my decision,' I reply.

Phoebe starts to prod at the edge of the earth around the plundered tomato plant with the toe of her trainer, openly unsettled by what I've said. I watch her as she avoids touching the areas of dirt that glisten with slug goo. 'I knew you wouldn't care,' she eventually says. 'That's why I didn't bother telling you first.'

I'm not going to bite at that. I'm not going to let her goad me into shouting at her. 'Do you know what I wish?' I say. I extend my foot and prod at the earth, too. It's pointless, but enjoyable. 'I wish you'd come to talk to me before you did anything like that. I really thought we could talk about anything, Pheebs. Admittedly, I probably would have gone off at the deep end *at first* because I would have thought you were too young to have sex. Not your body, I'm sure you think your body is ready, and I'm sure you thought your mind was ready, but really, I would have liked to have discussed it with you. I didn't even think this sort of thing was on your radar.'

She bunches her lips up and continues to poke at the soil in front of her, but doesn't interrupt what I'm saying so maybe she's listening.

'I would have loved to have found out what you felt about it. Who he was. If he was nice to you.' I stop what I'm doing and focus on my daughter. She is so young. In my head she'll always be that big-cheeked bundle of screams that was handed to me minutes after she was born. In my mind, she'll always be the little girl who managed to lose her black shoe with the red bow on the way home from school and still to this day doesn't remember how. She'll always be the little girl sitting on the bed beside me crying because it's finally hit her that her dad isn't coming back. Phoebe will probably always be young to me, I don't think she'll ever be old enough to have sex in the nostalgia of my mind. 'Was he? Was he nice to you?'

She also stops jabbing at the dirt. She doesn't move as she considers my question. With her lips twisted thoughtfully to the left she starts to chew on her inner cheek. Then: shrug. 'I suppose.'

'Did he pressure you into it? Or did you want to?' *Or was it 'hooking up'?*

'I wanted to feel close to him, Mum,' she says.

'And you didn't feel close to him before?'

'Kind of, I suppose. I just wanted him . . .'

'To like you.'

'Yeah. I like him. I like him so much, and he makes me feel really funny in my stomach, and it feels really awful when I'm not with him and sometimes even the texts aren't enough. I just wanted him to feel the same way. Is that bad?'

Bad? It's *horrific*. She's having sex to make someone like her. Not because her body's telling her it's ready, not because she wants pleasure from it, not even because she's curious what the fuss is all about, but because it's currency. It's to get something. 'No,' I reassure her. 'It's not bad. I completely understand, although it's probably not the best reason to do it? I mean, it might have been better to do it because you felt he was as close to you as you feel to him, and with the both of you feeling so close, that was the natural next step.' *Is this the right time for this?* I wonder as I speak. It seems a bit like locking the stable door after the horse has not only bolted but has made it to the other end of the country in a clear, unhindered run. 'I can't tell you what to do in any way that will stop you having sex, but I think it'd be great for you if you could promise yourself that you're only ever going to do it because you want to enjoy it. Not because everyone else is doing it, not because you want someone to like you, not because you think you have to after someone's nice to you, but because you want to feel the pleasure from it. OK?'

'But . . .' she begins.

'But?' I ask.

'Nothing,' she says, shaking her head. She buries her hands deeper in her pockets, hunches her shoulders over as she resumes digging at the slug earth with the toe of her shoe. 'Can I have my phone back?'

You didn't say, please, I want to point out to her. *I spent years teaching you to always say please and thank you.* 'What contraception were you both using?' I ask to stall her. I suspect the second I hand over the little silver and black box of circuits and buttons I have in my apron pocket, I will not get anything else out of her.

She shrugs briefly and dismissively with both shoulders.

In Phoebe-shrug speak, this reply causes my stomach to turn over right before my heart does the same. I rotate on the spot and look at her. When she continues to stare downwards, I take her shoulders and force her to look at me. 'You did use contraception, didn't you?' I ask.

'You don't need to the first time because if you're a virgin then you can't get pregnant.' She shrugs me off.

Nervously, I unscrew the bubble wand from its bottle. Then screw it on again. Then unscrew it. I promised myself I wouldn't let this happen. That I wouldn't let my daughter become like me: too scared to talk to my mother; too terrified to tell my mother my periods had started (and only did in the end because I needed money from her to buy towels); too ashamed of my body and what was happening to it to ask for help when I needed it most. I promised myself that I would always be there for my daughter, and I've let this happen. I've managed to blink, to close my eyes over the period of losing Joel, and open them again to find I have missed the most important time of my daughter's life. And I've missed the chance to not turn into my mother.

'Did he tell you that?' I ask her, still anxiously unscrewing and screwing on the lid of my bubbles bottle.

She nods. Her eyes, mouth, forehead, chin are set with pure defiance as she challenges me, *dares* me to tell her he was wrong. Even though her body has proved that all by itself, she would still believe anything he said.

'Well, it's not true.' There should be some comfort, I suppose, that it was her first time. That the 'hooking up' talk was all for show.

'But he said—'

'Sweetheart, come on now, you're a clever girl, you know where babies come from and how they're made. You know that every time you have sex you take the chance of getting pregnant except if a person has had a tubal ligation, or a vasectomy.'

'But—'

'Pheebs, you're pregnant. Your own body has told you it's not true.'

She scrunches up her face in rage, like a six-year-old told

50

there'll be no Christmas this year because Father Christmas isn't real.

Something occurs to me as I face her silent wrath: 'If you really believed what he told you, why did you use the test so early? Surely you would have waited until two periods had passed.'

She sighs. 'Cos I thought I'd better be doubly sure so I got the morning-after pill.'

'And when you were late you knew it might not have worked?'

She nods. 'But that doesn't mean it's not true,' she adds, quickly.

'Erm, obviously it does.'

'I need my phone back.'

I need my Joel back. He'd know what to say, what to do, how best to navigate this unknown rocky road our lives have veered onto.

'Are you going to tell him you're pregnant?' I ask.

'I need my phone,' she insists.

The slug-damaged plants all need to go in the bin. The earth needs to be turned over, aerated, then left to rest before I replant things. I could make her do it. I could make her dig up all this stuff and dig over my land before I hand back her phone. Or, I could accept that right now, when I'm still blind-sided by the situation, I need to pick my battles.

I place my gloved hand into my front pocket and take out the phone. 'You've got a doctor's appointment tomorrow,' I say before I return her secrets, her line to the boy who helped to get her into this situation. 'Nine o'clock.'

'What for?'

'You're pregnant. You need to see a doctor about that.'

'Fine. Whatever. You obviously know everything about everything.'

My lip hurts when I clamp down on it, like my tongue did yesterday. Giving in, picking my battles, is not something I'm good at. I like to win. I like to do things the proper way. Talking to her much longer could involve me attempting to win this battle by any means necessary. I hold out her phone. She snatches it out of my hand, scowls at me before storming towards the house.

'You didn't say thank you,' I call at her retreating back.

I drop to my knees and start to dismantle the last days of Sodom and Gomorrah as played out in my vegetable patch.

12 years before *That Day* (February, 1999)

'She's a girl,' Joel said. His face was a mess of tears, his eyes a bright red after he scrubbed at them with the heels of his hands. 'We got a girl one.'

'Is she OK?' I sobbed. I couldn't hear her crying, I hadn't seen her in the seconds after she was born and I was scared after nine months of taking care of her that I hadn't done it right at the last minute. That once again I'd let everyone down and there was something wrong.

'She's perfect,' Joel said.

'Are you sure she's OK?' I sobbed. 'Why isn't she crying?'

'Not all babies cry,' the midwife said. 'Some are really chilled.' The midwife laid the squirming bundle on my bare chest for skin-to-skin contact.

I was sobbing so much I could barely move my arms to hold her. I hurt so much I didn't know what part of me was sinew, blood and bone and what was pain. My heart felt as if it had expanded to fill my entire chest cavity, which was why I could only inhale and exhale in gasping, sobbing breaths.

My gaze focused on her, and I could see I'd done it. She was here. She was a wrinkled milk chocolate brown smeared with white; her right arm was extended towards my face, her mouth was wide open, showing us the two parallel ridges of her gums.

I stared at my chilled daughter. 'We did it, Joel. We did it.'

'You did it, Babes,' he said, scrubbing at his eyes again. 'You did it and you were amazing.'

'"Phoebe" is right for her,' I said. This was the name he'd chosen. He'd had a reason for it, but I couldn't remember right then what it was. But it was right for her, it was who she looked like. Phoebe.

'You sure?' he asked.

'Yes, absolutely. She absolutely looks like Phoebe.'

'She does. And she is absolutely amazing.'

My mobile vibrates in my jeans pocket. I tug the thick gardening glove off my right hand before I retrieve the phone. I vaguely recognise the number flashing up but it's not stored so I almost don't answer it. After my recent history, though, I know that would be folly. That would be like convincing yourself that you believe you can't get pregnant the first time you have sex.

'Hello?' I say into the phone, half-expecting a pause then a recorded message claiming I need some sort of financial advice.

'Mrs Mackleroy?' the person on the other end asks, politely.

'Yes?' I reply cautiously because although I recognise the voice, I can't quite place it.

'This is Felicia Laureau from the retirement village where your aunt, Betty Mackleroy, is living?'

'Oh, hello,' I say, pleased that I don't have to play the 'pretend I know who you are' game. Then it strikes me: this is Felicia Laureau from where Joel's Aunty Betty is staying. I close my eyes and ground myself, like I would if I was about to be battered by a hurricane.

'We were wondering if you could come in and see us tomorrow? Nothing to worry about, we'd simply like to discuss a few things with you.'

'It has to be tomorrow, does it?' I ask, trying to gauge how bad it is this time.

'Yes, it has to be tomorrow.' It's really bad.

'Right, fine. I'll see you about midday.'

'Perfect.'

I sit back on the grass, not bothered that the damp from the lawn seeps into my jeans and slowly soaks through to my knickers.

I'm not bothered because I know without question that tomorrow is going to be a repeat of yesterday.

II

V

15 years before *That Day* (February, 1996)

'Saffron, meet Aunty Betty,' Joel said proudly.

Aunty Betty reclined on the red velvet chaise longue in the living room of her Ealing mansion flat, her gold and silver cigarillo holder installed between the fore and middle fingers of her right hand. Her shiny black hair was piled up on top of her head in an elegant bun, at its front an ornate silver bun clasp. Her large eyes, heavily made up with gold and plum eyeshadow and what I suspected were false eyelashes, inspected me carefully. She lingered over my chin-length straightened black hair, she noted my lack of jewellery, she debated with herself over my knee-length blue silk skirt, and cream jumper secured at the middle with a blue patent belt. She openly disapproved of my blue and white shoes. Once she was done checking me over like a farmer might do a new pig at an animal auction, she took a long, theatrical drag on her holder. (You could tell it was all for show as little smoke came out when she exhaled.) Slowly, her rouged lips parted and she grinned. She was watching me like a predator watched the walking takeaway meal that was an injured, bleeding deer – it wouldn't take much to devour her prey, but there'd still be enough fight in the creature to give her some fun.

'Saff-aron.' Her beam grew wider. 'I like that name, you know.' She had a Jamaican lilt so slight I wondered if I imagined it. 'She'll do. In fact, I think she's perfect.'

Aunty Betty turned her slender, slightly wrinkled neck towards Joel, her smile growing by the second. 'Ashtray.' She indicated the blue and white porcelain ashtray on the teak sideboard with a wave of her hand. 'Your parents are going to hate her,' she informed him. 'That makes me like her even more.'

'Aunty Betty!' Joel laughed as he handed her the ashtray then returned to my side, casually taking my hand. 'Ignore her. She loves to cause controversy.'

'Don't I just?' she said, the grin now taking up most of her face.

'It was Aunty Betty who bought me my first cookbook and apron when I was seven,' Joel said. 'She unleashed my love of cooking.'

'Yes, and his parents think that's the reason why he didn't go to Cambridge,' she said, laughing. 'They still hate me for it.'

'Aunty Betty!'

'It's true. I don't care, though. And that's why it doesn't matter that Ma and Pa Mackleroy are going to hate you, darling Saff-aron – I like you. And in the Mackleroy family, what I say is the law.'

'Ignore her,' Joel said. He was smiling indulgently at his aunt but not denying what she was saying: in his family, Aunty Betty was the law. And his parents were going to hate me.

*

Another office, another person who is uncomfortable, tense, shuffling papers and repeatedly clearing their throat in front of me.

What's going to happen now? Is this woman going to tell me that Joel's sixty-six-year-old Aunty Betty is pregnant, too?

Felicia Laureau finally sits back in her big black leather armchair, and faces me properly with a strained smile. Her bobbed hair is like a silver-white curtain across and around her face, she is small, round and distinctly curvy, but dressed well in a form-flattering pale grey suit.

Like the headteacher, she's nervous about talking to me, not only because of what she's got to tell me, but because she doesn't know how to talk to someone like me, the woman whose husband was murdered. I'd imagine this nursing home is filled with widows, women whose husbands died and left them alone, but how many of them were bereaved in the same way as I was? Were any of them forever saddled with the image of a large kitchen knife entering their husband's stomach, and him bleeding to death an hour or so later on the side of a road they'd never been down before? If any of them were like me, then this woman would be awful to be around. She'd be uncomfortable, unnerving and most of all, fake.

'Mrs Mackleroy, it's good to see you,' she says brightly.

I sigh. 'It probably isn't, is it?' I sigh again, a deep exasperated sigh. I've spent the morning stopping Zane from winding up Phoebe, sitting in the doctor's office while Phoebe told her GP nothing and then intervening when Phoebe began freaking out at the idea of taking folic acid and going for an early scan. This was followed by driving around the M25, something I avoid wherever possible, to get here. 'Sorry, but I can't think of a single, realistic reason why you'd call me to come in at such short notice if it was going to involve good news.'

Mrs Laureau's features twitch, fluttering as if out of control, especially around the mouth area. With horror, I realise she's trying to arrange her face into a sympathetic, gentle smile – something that clearly doesn't come easily to her. 'You're right, of course,' she replies. 'This isn't going to be an easy meeting.'

'Where is she, anyway?' I ask. I had genuinely expected to find Aunty Betty sitting in a chair in the same position as Phoebe had adopted in the headteacher's office, waiting to have someone tell me what she'd done. 'I thought she'd be here.'

'We thought it best we talk first without her,' Mrs Laureau says.

'Why, what did she do?'

'We've tried to make allowances,' she says gently, 'since, since the events of . . . Since your husband . . . Since . . .'

I am meant to leap into this sea of discomfort she's in to rescue her, stop her floundering by supplying *Since my husband died*, but I'm not going to. I'm going to stay where I am, nice and dry, and wait for her to wreak havoc on me as she's about to do. People like Mrs Laureau never need to see you unless they want more money, or they're about to screw you over, or sometimes, even, both.

7 years before *That Day* (March, 2004)

Aunty Betty's face slowly became an intricate picture of disdain and horror when she had fully digested what Joel had said to her.

'Live with you?' she spat in disgust. '*Live* with *you*? You don't smoke, you barely drink, I'm still not certain if you actually ever do the do, even though you have two children. Always wondered if that was turkey-baster-assisted. If I live with you, I might as well get down to the nearest cemetery and start digging my own hole.' She frowned sternly at Joel, then cast her expression at me. 'You don't want me living in your house. I'm selfish, rude and messier than that pink squiggle thing in those children's books. I wouldn't wish me on my worst enemy.'

Joel seemed deflated, the worry of the situation rested heavily on his shoulders. He'd thought the best thing would be for Aunty Betty to live with us after her accident. A few days ago she'd slipped in the shower, fallen and knocked herself out. She'd woken up with a hairline fracture to her left hip and, because she'd always lived on her own, had screamed her way through the blinding pain she was in to drag herself out of the bathroom, along the carpeted corridor to the bedroom to get to her phone. She couldn't live on her own any more. We all knew and accepted that. Joel's solution was to ask her to live with us.

'Admit it, you don't want me living with you, do you, Saffaron?' Aunty Betty was appealing to me because she knew I'd be able to convince Joel it was a bad idea.

'Of course we want you to live with us,' I replied, because we did. We loved her and wanted her to be safe. Joel and I had both been shaken and tearful at the thought of her being alone and in pain.

She laughed bitterly. Shook her head. 'You two are out of your tiny minds, you know. I want to get into one of those nursing homes with my own flat, see if I can meet some nice widowers who'll spend their weekly allowance showing me a good time.'

'You really want to go to a nursing home?' I asked.

She grinned and nodded mischievously. I wasn't sure if Joel could see that despite the smile, despite her rejection of our offer, she was terrified. Of the encroaching years, of having to drag herself naked to get help because of the choices she'd made in her life. The flames of pride burned in her eyes, though. She made no apologies about the way she'd lived her life, you only had to spend a few minutes in her company to realise she'd enjoyed every single second of it, and she wanted that independence for as long as possible. Living with us would be a slow, lingering death by boredom. I could understand that. When you've travelled all over the world, when you've been one of the first black women to have a starring role in a West End play, when you remind anyone who'll listen that you're better-looking than Eartha Kitt ever was, when you've told the world every day for sixty-odd years that you'll do things your way, thank you very much, the last thing you want to do is live in a four-bedroom house in Brighton with Mr and Mrs Boring and their two children. Independent living when there was someone around to help if she needed it let us all pretend that she could still be whoever she wanted to be no matter how old she was.

Over five weekends, Joel and I took it in turns to pack up her flat. We put most of it into storage, and she moved into Rose Bay Manor three months later.

'As I said, Mrs Mackleroy, we've tried to be understanding, but we feel it's time for your aunt to move on,' Felicia Laureau says. Sandy Fields is the third home she's been in. The others didn't 'work out'.

'What did she do?' I ask again as I wonder how much it would cost to make the 'moving on' go away. In the last home, she'd got into a fist-fight with another resident because she didn't like the way the woman had looked at her. Aunty Betty neglected to mention that she'd flouted every single piece of dating etiquette when she moved in. The poor woman who'd punched Aunty Betty had been quietly and carefully working long-term on a widower with cups of tea, afternoon walks, listening to Radio 4 together. Within days of Aunty Betty moving in, she'd asked him whether he was going to buy her a drink, and had basically been dating him ever since. That had cost us quite a lot of money to make it go away and to suppress potential assault charges even though Aunty Betty was technically only defending herself.

'Maybe it'd be easier to list what she didn't do,' Mrs Laureau says without a shred of humour.

'I see.'

'The incident that inspired this call, however, was her

being caught having . . . *intimate relations* with another resident in one of the out-of-bounds areas of the main complex.'

'Oh, God,' I sigh.

'The member of staff who caught them was most upset.'

'Old people have sex you know,' I said, channelling, it seems, my inner Aunty Betty, ignoring the fact it would permanently traumatise me if I walked into a room and found two rutting people – whatever their age.

'Yes, but in private, you would think,' she replies, as sour as an unripe Granny Smith apple.

'What's going to happen next?'

'We feel . . . We have no choice but to ask your aunt to leave.'

'Leave?' I reply tiredly. 'Only her, I take it?'

'Pardon me?'

'The man she was caught with, is he being chucked out for not doing it in private or is it just my aunt?'

Mrs Laureau's eyebrows twiddle themselves into position, as she prepares to put me in my place. She probably tried this with Aunty Betty and got a mouthful. We've been here, together, for ten minutes, enough time for a people-watcher like Mrs Laureau to realise that I'm most unlikely to 'do an Aunty Betty' no matter what she says to me.

'If it was merely this "incident" we might be able to overlook it. But in the last three months alone, your aunt has managed to set fire to the rug in her apartment three times, she has roped in half a dozen residents to try hitchhiking to the next village so they can go to the cinema, and has been spotted walking around with only her bikini top and a miniskirt when she knows we have a dress code. In short, it's really quite a miracle that we've lasted this long.'

My cheeks are puffed up like over-inflated balloons and I blow out slowly as I exhale my biggest sigh yet. 'When do you need her out?' I say. A month should give me enough time to find her a new place; a fortnight would work at a push.

'She's just saying her goodbyes and then you can take her home with you.'

'*Excuse me?*'

'Her belongings are packed and ready. Anything we can't fit into your car, we'll send on to you, at our expense. And we've already agreed we'll refund this and last month's fee as a gesture of goodwill.'

'*What?*'

'I know this must come as a surprise to you, and believe me, we wanted to tell you sooner, but she insisted this was the best way. She said it would be easier on you after all you've been through recently.'

'And you believed her?'

'Why wouldn't I?' she replies with a victorious look.

That reply and that expression on her face are payback for not helping her out earlier on. I take another gander around her office: the desk has been polished to an unusually high sheen; all the usual accoutrements of a desk – stapler, mouse mat, pen pot, sellotape holder, contacts box – appear to be new. As if they've been very recently replaced, as if someone was attempting to remove all traces of something hideous, like a sixty-six-year-old woman who is the bane of your life having sex on your desk. Aunty Betty did it in here, I'm sure of it.

I really hope it was you who caught them in flagrante delicto, I think at Mrs Laureau. *It would serve you right.*

'Your aunt has signed all the necessary paperwork so you don't have to concern yourself with that.'

'Right, well, I'd better get on with it, hadn't I?' I say to her.

That's the worst thing about all of this, you know, Joel? I say to him in the darkness of our room, staring at where he should be. *No matter how hard it is, because I've got children, because I've got people who rely on me, I just have to get on with it.*

Aunty Betty plugs her seatbelt clip into its holder, having got into the back seat of my car. They have folded down the seats beside her to jam her belongings in. Her stuff has filled the boot, taken up most of the space in the back, and is piled up on the front passenger seat and footwell, too.

'You can look as defiant as you like,' I say to her as she sits, regal and silent, truculent and unrepentant, in the back.

In an expression that is pure Phoebe, she curls her pink, glossed upper lip at me, cuts her black-lined eyes and turns to the window to treat those outside to a full smile. The turnout on this April afternoon is incredible, I've never seen so many people show up to say goodbye to anyone who isn't a celebrity, but here, about sixty people, all of various ages and stages of grey, stand, sit in wheelchairs and lean on walking sticks on the gravel driveway, waving Aunty Betty goodbye.

'Just so we're clear,' I add above the crunch of the tyres on the gravel, 'you're going to have to talk to me at some point.'

VI

Imogen and her son, Ernest, are leaving as I pull up outside the house.

They've obviously dropped Zane back from school because he will have told them that Phoebe wasn't in school today. Imogen is always polished, unhurried and calm. She's a full-time homemaker (her title) and so is always suggesting Zane comes over to hers, that she collects him from school and that he stays over. She started her family young so has a twenty-one-year-old son and an eighteen-year-old son as well as ten-year-old Ernest. The last eighteen months or so, she's been invaluable with Zane. And with me.

I climb out of my car, as they come off the last step and walk down the short, concrete path. We meet outside the black metal gate, pause on the pavement to talk. Without even glancing in his direction I can feel Ernest's large green-hazel eyes on me. He always stares at me, mute and suspicious. When he and Zane are together in the living room or upstairs in Zane's bedroom, or even when they're in the kitchen and I'm busying myself with something, he'll talk ten to the dozen. As soon as I engage with them, or I come near them, he clams up and becomes a mute, wide-eyed mannequin.

'*He's just scared of you,*' Zane explained blithely when I asked him about it.

'*Why?*' I'd asked.

'*I don't know, he just is,*' Zane replied as if that was an answer.

'Oh, hello,' Imogen says.

'Hi.'

Aunty Betty is still ensconced in the car, waiting for me to open the door for her. She's a princess, after all, and she expects people to run around after her. I often indulge her, but not today. Today she's crossed the line and her recalcitrant silence on the journey home has done nothing to endear her to me. 'Thanks for picking up Zane,' I say to Imogen. Ernest's stare doesn't waver, doesn't change. 'I really appreciate it.'

'It was an absolute pleasure, as always.' Imogen comes closer to me and lowers her voice, for whose benefit I'm not sure since we are alone on the street. 'Was everything OK at the school the other day? I've just asked Phoebe and she was less than forthcoming.'

I love Imogen. I can trust her, rely upon her, but I can't tell her this. I don't need any more judgement. I suspect she will judge me, like everyone who knows has judged me so far. Even Fynn, who did his best to reassure me the other night, probably judged me. They were right to – every conversation I have with Phoebe reminds me where I've gone wrong, where I've missed an opportunity to guide her, point her the right way. Even if she wouldn't listen, those conversations – as difficult as they would have been – should have been waiting there like a secondary generator at the back of her mind, ready to kick in and help her when she needed guidance on what to do next.

I've failed her – in pretty spectacular fashion – and I don't need any more external decrees of incompetence about that right now.

'Yes, it was fine. Well, it will be – we have a few things to iron out first.'

'Oh, good.' Her concerned face softens. 'I was so worried. You've been through so much, and you've managed to be so brave, I couldn't bear for anything else to happen to you.'

Neither could I, I think.

'Is there someone in your car?' she asks. I turn to look at my blue four-door parked a little way down from my house. Aunty Betty hasn't moved from the car but she has unwound the window, so she can hear what we're talking about, while doing a very good impression of being asleep. She's not, but she's probably thinking that if she appears asleep we will talk freely and give her access to some of our secrets.

'Yes. That's Joel's Aunty Betty. You met her at the ... at the ... at the funeral. She was the one who sang "Amazing Grace" instead of a reading.'

Wearing a black dress and black hat, Aunty Betty stood at the pulpit with the order of service booklet in front of her. She cleared her throat as if to read and slowly raised her gaze until it was resting on me, on Phoebe, on Zane who were on either side of me, snuggled as close as possible.

She smiled at us and then she began to sing. Her voice carried across the skin of grief on the people in the church, soothing every person it touched, pricking tears into everyone's eyes. I didn't know she could sing like that, or she could make a song sound so enchanting, and every time I think of it, the skin on my body pricks with goosebumps. She'd done it to give Joel something special, something to remind us all of the special place he had in her heart.

'Oh, yes,' Imogen says. 'I thought she lived somewhere near Middlesex? Here on a visit, is she?'

No, she's been thrown out of her home for shagging on the managing director's desk so she's pitching up here until I find her somewhere else. 'Erm, yes, something like that.'

'Looks like she's fallen asleep, would you like a hand?'

'No, you're all right, you've already done so much for me. Thank you. I'll see you later.'

Reluctantly, Imogen curls her arm around her son and they start to leave. I wait until they have got into their car and driven away before I put my hand on the gate to go in. As I do so, a miracle happens: Aunty Betty opens the car door and steps out. She is regal and grand about it, of course, but it's odd seeing her do something this ordinary. Naturally, she has a reason for opening her own car door and stepping out unaided.

'I don't like that woman,' she says. Her line of sight – disapproving and contemptuous – is focused on the direction Imogen has driven off in.

'I'm sure she'll be devastated,' I reply, sourly.

'Child, she's a grief vampire. She feeds off other people's grief.' When I don't comment she adds, 'I'm old, remember? I have been around this for many, many years. I have lost so many people, too many people, and I have seen people like that one several times. They need other people to be broken so they can feel useful. They hook into the bereaved and live off them.'

'You didn't even speak to her just now, and must have spoken to her for about five minutes at the . . . at the funeral, how can you make such bold pronouncements?'

'At my age, you don't need much time to see people for who they are.'

'Obviously not.'

'I don't like that woman,' Aunty Betty repeats.

'So you said. And I find it incredible that you're standing there bold as brass spouting all this stuff about one of my friends when you haven't spoken in over three hours. Call me strange, but I was thinking maybe an apology, or even a simple explanation might have been forthcoming.'

Her silence is my reward.

'I'm back!' I call to my children. The woman behind me '*Ah-he-hem*'s me. '*We're* back!' I correct.

I wasn't exactly expecting a thunderous stampede, but to have no acknowledgement *at all* is humiliating. In the living room Phoebe is on the sofa, on her phone; Zane has his Xbox controller in his hand, a *Star Wars* game on the screen.

'We're back!' I repeat, louder this time.

'Hi, Mum,' Zane calls. He doesn't even bother to turn his head to toss that over his shoulder – he remains focused on the screen.

'Not even a little bit curious who I mean by "we"?' I ask.

'Uncle Fynn?' Zane replies, still uninterested; while silence continues to emanate from Phoebe.

71

'I think you'll agree that I am far more interesting than that giraffe who claims to be your uncle,' Aunty Betty says. She opens her arms and steps out to give them easier access to her.

'Aunty Betty?' Zane shouts. He throws down his controller and jumps to his feet. He hurtles at her, virtually shoving me aside to hug her. From residing in the world on her phone, Phoebe is now here, in the real world, her face lit up like it is Christmas morning at who is here in her living room. She drops her phone and is on her feet, ready to wait in line to steal a hug from her aunt. Guilt oozes into my heart: we haven't been to see her since Phoebe's birthday in February, more than three months ago. Joel used to see her at least once a month because she had no one else, and he'd often take the children. They've obviously missed her, and it's been my responsibility to keep up with those visits and I haven't. These past two days have made me wonder what I've been doing with my life. I know I'm always busy, always on the go, but I seem to have been sleepwalking my way through it all, missing out big, important chunks of time.

Aunty Betty studies Phoebe like she did me the first time she met me – seeking a weakness that will give her something to tease her beloved great niece about. 'Well now, haven't you been the busy little bee?' she says with a cunning but playful grin.

Phoebe, who has obviously forgotten what a wind-up merchant her great aunt is, seems to grow ten feet taller and wider, her face a vicious snarl as she swings to me. 'You told her I'm *pregnant*?' she screams at me. 'I can't believe you!'

Aghast, Aunty Betty draws back, and blinks in fright. Zane stops hugging his great aunt and rotates on the spot to stare at his sister with his mouth open.

How can someone of the 'hooking up' generation make such a rookie mistake? I wonder.

'Your mother told me nothing,' Aunty Betty stutters. I've never seen her panic like this before, she never usually shows remorse for the things she does and says, so to hear her speak so respectfully is as alien as her opening her own car door. 'I say that sort of thing to everyone to get them to confess something to me. You know that.' She keeps looking at me, pleading with her beautifully made-up eyes for help. I ignore her. Even if I did know how to speak to Phoebe without enraging her, which I don't, I wouldn't help Aunty Betty in this instance – apologising will be good for her.

'I'm sorry, Phoebe, I really had no idea what the situation was.'

Zane has closed his mouth, but his ten-year-old face is honed on his sister's stomach. Any moment now he's going to reach out and prod her abdomen. He is fascinated with pregnant women. He knows the biology of how babies are made, but he's currently curious about why they have to stay in your stomach for so long, how they feel when they're in there, and if they'll know if you poke them. I'm always aware when we pass pregnant women that I may need to stop him from making contact with their bumps. I will also need to ask him not to talk about this. It's a burden to put on a child, but until Phoebe decides what she wants to do, it's better no one knows.

Aunty Betty has stopped speaking. She isn't used to apologising, it must taste very strange and unpleasant in her mouth, something I'm sure she won't want to sample again for a long time.

All eyes are on Phoebe in the silence after Aunty Betty's apology – we are all waiting to take our cues from her, wondering what she'll do now she knows she's exposed herself. What she'll do, apparently, is burst into loud, uncontrollable tears.

VII

After the madness, when my family have been herded off to bed, I gather up the post from the day and I sit at the kitchen table. I have the light from the cooker on instead of the main light, and sit still for a moment, pause, catch my breath.

Zane and Phoebe are both asleep, Aunty Betty is unpacking some of her belongings; most of them, though, are piled up in the corridor or in the corner of the living room. Zane and I managed to bring them all in from the car, at which point I admitted defeat – I couldn't take it all up three flights of stairs to her room in the loft, too. And Zane was so exhausted afterwards he could barely bring himself to complain about having fish for dinner.

Phoebe, who I suspect was more distressed by crying in front of us than outing herself, escaped upstairs until dinner time, at which point she made it clear by the look on her face that she wanted no one to bring it up again.

Aunty Betty was contrite and quiet for most of the evening, and even offered to wash up after dinner to show how sorry she was (for upsetting Phoebe, not for tricking me into letting her move in).

Everyone headed off upstairs at the same time and I'd sat on the edge of Zane's bed and asked him if he could bear to keep Phoebe's pregnancy a secret for now. 'Too right!' he'd replied. 'Do you know how babies get inside? I'm not telling anyone she's done that!' Then added: 'She has done that, hasn't she?'

'Yes,' I confirmed.

Now, I can sit at my dining table and be alone for a while. I spend a lot of time in here because it was Joel's favourite room. Everywhere else in the house we shared the input into decorating, but here, Joel took over. He knew exactly what he wanted – the range cooker over there, the stainless steel fridge behind me. The double sink, the roll-top edging on the white marble worktops, the shelves on the walls for the dried food, herbs and oils. The white floor tiles. It all came from his vision, his idea of the perfect kitchen for creating his culinary delights (and his many, many disasters, but we never talked about them).

I pretend to myself I can feel him in here, sometimes. That I can see him standing at the cooker, wooden spoon in hand, turning constantly to talk to me or to catch the latest footie scores on the television on the wall behind. That I can recall him standing at the worktop, fork in hand as he mixed a batter for gluten-free blueberry muffins. I can sense him opening the fridge and staring into it, wondering what it was exactly he wanted when he went there. And I can hear him, dressed in his black Run DMC apron, singing, '*J-J-J-J-J's House!*' right before he started cooking.

The kitchen is about more than just his cookbooks being lined up neatly next to the knife block, and a line of herbs on the window sill, or the selection of pans and utensils he'd assembled. It is about him being there, at the table, at the sink, at the stove, at the window, at the back door about to go out. I remember how he was everywhere in this house, but mostly in here. In this space that was his.

I idly leaf through the mail. A lot of them are white or brown window envelopes containing demands for money and I can ignore them for now. These days, bills don't cause my stomach to clench with the sheer terror of not being able to afford them, but I still don't open them straight away. After Joel died and I spent all those months trying to sort out his 'affairs', I promised myself I wouldn't let things become so disjointed and disorganised ever again. I'd keep on top of things so whoever had to sort out my 'affairs' had an easier time of it. I've let that slip. *Again*. I must get back on top of it, I must sort things out.

Among the bills and leaflets and circulars one letter stands out. It is in a cream envelope without a postmark or stamp but addressed to **Saffron Mackleroy** with my full address. I turn it over in my hands, considering it. The formal nature of fully addressing it suggests the person was going to post it to me but changed their mind and came all this way to deliver it from wherever they were. I assume they live a way away because otherwise, why write to me in the first place?

The writing in blue ink is uniform but not neat, con- sidered but a little wild. It is written in straight lines, perfectly centred on the envelope. I don't recognise it, and very few people I know would write to me. My mother is one, but that's rare these days and she wouldn't travel from London to post it by hand. I slide my finger under the flap of the envelope and rip it open.

That Day (26 October, 2011)

'I'm really sorry to have to tell you this,' the she one says. She stops speaking and looks to the man beside her for help.

'Your husband has been involved in an incident,' the he one continues.

Incident. *'Incident' not 'accident'. What happened was on purpose.*

'Is he all right? Where is he? Can I see him?'

'I'm sorry,' the she one says. 'I'm so sorry.'

My fingers are numb, my body is numb, my entire being is suddenly without air. There are a dozen little splattering thuds of blackberries falling onto the ground, there's a crash of a white ceramic bowl hitting a white ceramic tile.

I knock over the chair as I push myself away from the table, away from the letter I've opened and started to read.

I stand in the centre of the room, trembling as I stare at two sheets of cream A4 writing paper, folded carefully into thirds that are splayed open like an upturned hand on the table.

Suddenly, I'm not here any more. I'm back there.

It's light in the kitchen. It's just after two o'clock. I have answered the door with a bowl of blackberries in my hand, but I have to hurry the callers in because I have left the tap running on full. They follow me into the kitchen and as I reach to switch off the tap, it clicks in my mind who they are, why I didn't think twice about asking them in.

I shut off the chrome faucet and turn slowly, warily to them.

I see myself as clearly as anything. And I watch myself hear the news, I spy on Saffron Mackleroy as she finds out that her husband has been stolen right from under her ever-vigilant gaze.

I watch the words sink in, I see myself drop the bowl, I understand what makes me stagger back against the counter.

I know that I am thinking: *I shouldn't have chosen blackberries.* And in a second, I'm going to look up at the he and the she police officers who stand still and silent in front of me, and I'm going to say:

'Where are my children?'

I'm back there, that letter has ripped me from the present, catapulted me back through time to eighteen months ago. To *that day.* These are not like the potholes that set off memories of my life that can comfort or confuse me, this has dragged me back there. I am there. I am trapped, living it all over again.

That's why I try not to think about *that day.* That's why I try to not think about that time at all. That's why I keep myself numb and safe; if I think about it, I'll have to relive it all over again.

III

VIII

That Day (26 October, 2011)

'I'm really sorry to have to tell you this,' the she one says. She stops speaking and looks to the man beside her for help.

'Your husband has been involved in an incident,' the he one continues.

Incident. 'Incident' not 'accident'. What happened was on purpose.

'Is he all right? Where is he? Can I see him?'

'I'm sorry,' the she one says. 'I'm so sorry.'

My fingers are numb, my body is numb, my entire being is suddenly without air. There are a dozen little splattering thuds of blackberries falling onto the ground, there's a crash of a white ceramic bowl hitting a white ceramic tile.

That Day

'Where are my children?' I ask them. My eyes, wide and wild, stare at them in turn. A him and a her. Two strangers who are standing in my house when I don't even know where my children are.

They look at each other, puzzled, confused, and then return their gazes to me.

'Where are my children?' I ask again, this time my voice on the crest of panic.

The she one says, 'I think they're probably at school.'

'No.' I shake my head. 'That's not right, they can't be. I wouldn't let them go to school at a time like this. I'd keep them here with me. I wouldn't. I just wouldn't.'

'I'll radio the station and have someone contact their schools and check,' the he one says. 'What schools do they go to?'

'St Caroline's round the corner, and St Allison, Hove.'

'I'll be right back.'

'No, I'll go to St Caroline's, it's only around the corner. It'll be quicker if I check.'

The she one, in full uniform, stands in my way, physically blocking me from leaving the room, the house. From tearing into the street and into Zane's school, screaming his name to make sure he's all right. 'No, no, Mrs Mack-el-roy, it's best if you leave that to us. You'll scare him if you turn up like that.' She says this as the he one leaves the room, walks out the front door before he starts to use his radio.

'You think something's happened to them as well, don't you?' I say, hysterically, straining to hear what the he one is saying.

'No, of course not,' the she one says, unconvincing and therefore terrifying.

That Day

He's so still. Quiet.

I need to wake him up, to remind him this is no time to

be sleeping, and no place to be doing it, either. And why is he wearing clothes under a sheet? He always sleeps naked, he hates the thought of being restricted by clothes when he's asleep.

What does he think he's doing, sleeping at a time like this, anyway? He's got a wife to press his cold lips against, he's got children waiting for his rough-and-tumble messing. He's got a best friend who'll be trying to coax him out for a pint or six. He's got parents who haven't openly disapproved of his wife and his life choices in . . . oh, about a week. He's got an aunt he needs to buy a bottle of expensive port for. He's got a life, he should be living it. This is no time for sleeping, for resting, for stillness.

'Is this your husband?' the he one asks from his place beside me.

I should say no because this isn't who he is – he is bouncy, and boisterous, annoyingly always on the go – he is not this. I don't say no. Instead, I nod. I whisper, 'Yes.'

My fingers automatically reach out to stroke across his brow, to retwist a mini-dreadlock that is starting to unravel itself, to cup his face with my hand. All the things I do to touch him, to connect to him a dozen times a day.

'I'm sorry,' the he one says, his hand a vice-like grip around my forearm that prevents me from making contact. 'You can't do that.'

My face distorts in incomprehension. I look at him, then my gaze darts to the petite mortuary assistant, who immediately averts her eyes while sorrowfully curling her lips into her mouth. I stare again at the he one.

85

'I'm sorry,' he repeats, with much more compassion and sympathy. 'It's . . . He's a crime scene now. If you touch him, you might destroy evidence and contaminate part of the crime scene.'

He's not a crime scene, he's not evidence, my closed-over throat replies. *He's my husband. He's the father of my children. He's my Joel.*

5 days after *That Day* (October, 2011)

'Is there anything you can tell us about your husband that might make it easier to find out who did this to him?' the he one asks. He's the one who came to break the news, he's the one who took me to the hospital mortuary. I think he's been assigned to me as my FLO – family liaison officer – from the police because when he told me that Phoebe and Zane were safe in school, I forgot myself and threw my arms around him, sobbing a grateful thank you. I think they think we have a rapport, a connection. So he's always around. When the other officers come, he comes to sit with me, to try to be a comfort. Sometimes, like now, he asks me questions on their behalf.

'Is there anything you can tell us about your husband that might make it easier to find out who did this to him?' The question is inscribed in the air between us. I consider it over and over.

I can tell them a lot about my husband, but not right now. I can't remember a single thing about him. Am I meant to? I have all these sensations about him, these things in my head that make me smile, how can I describe them, though? His warmth? How do you describe someone's ability to draw people to them because they were as warming as the sun? How do you describe the wattage of his smile? How do I tell that he made me feel perfect? How can I do that? If I can't describe that, if there aren't enough words in the universe to describe that, then what's the point of talking about him? Anything else isn't important; everything else is stupid and meaningless.

'I don't know who did this,' I say. I've told them this before. In the last five days I've told them this. They aren't listening.

'Is there anything he might have said, might have told you? Was there anyone who might have had a grudge against him? Was he worried about anything? It could be the smallest thing, something you don't think is important but it could be the clue we need.'

I'm using the wrong words. I'm not saying it right. 'I don't know anyone who could do this,' I say. That's what I mean. 'I don't know anyone who could do what they did. I don't know what to tell you.'

The other he one, the one who isn't the FLO, looks sympathetic. As if he has finally heard what I am saying he nods, before saying: 'Tell me about his friends? His work colleagues? Anyone you've had a funny feeling about, maybe?'

He doesn't understand. No one understands. 'I don't know anyone who is capable of this. Please stop asking me. I don't know. I want to know, I want to help. But I don't know. I don't know. I don't know.'

The first he one, the one who is always here, drinking my tea, always standing near me whenever I turn around, suddenly understands. 'It's the shock,' he says carefully. 'It'll become easier as it starts to wear off. Unfortunately, this is the most critical time in helping us to find the monster who did this.'

'It wasn't a monster,' I say to him. 'Monsters aren't real. If a monster did this, Joel wouldn't be . . . Monsters aren't real.' That's the shock talking, of course. Monsters are real. They are very, very real.

2 weeks after *That Day* (November, 2011)

'We'd like you to take part in a television appeal to see if we can urge anyone to come forward with any information relating to your husband's death,' the he one who is my FLO says. He is concerned, quiet, slightly protective in the way he sits so close on the sofa, while the other officer stands beside the fireplace.

'No,' I reply with a shake of my head.

'No, Mrs Mack-el-roy?' he says.

'I've told you before, it's Mack-*le*-roy,' I say tiredly. 'And no, I'm not doing it. I'm not sitting in front of TV cameras appealing to the better nature of a killer.'

'You wouldn't be, you would be trying to jog the memory of anyone who might have seen something and didn't realise what they were seeing. Also, we want to drive home to anyone who might know something the continued suffering behind not knowing who did this. We want anyone who has any information to realise that they can't not come forward.'

He's probably right, people out there do need reminding that Joel isn't simply some man whose picture they see on the news, who was most likely in the wrong place at the wrong time. He was real, he was human, he was mine. 'Ask his parents to do it,' I offer as a compromise.

'We really think it'd be better if you – the grieving widow – did it,' the other one says.

People need to know, but I'm not sharing him with anyone out there any more. I've lost him physically, and I only have snatches of time – in between the form filling, taking care of the children, going to work, organising my life – to think about him. About *him*, not his death, not the investigation, but him as the person who went through life with me. I'm not sharing one precious moment of that with anyone else, not people I know, not the television cameras. No one.

'Ask his parents,' I repeat. 'They knew him for longer than me. And they'll be more sympathetic than me.'

They might not mind giving away the memories encapsulated in the droplets of time they have to think about him.

17 days after *That Day* (November, 2011)

'You look awful,' Fynn says to me as he follows me from the front door to the kitchen then takes a seat opposite me at the kitchen table.

'Thank you very much, it's always great to get updates from the talking mirror.' I do look awful. I do look strange. I've taken to wearing my jeans and T-shirt, then slipping on one of Joel's jumpers or hooded tops as well. I'm always cold, the chill lives in my bones, so I need to wear something of his to warm me, to comfort me. My hair is in a ponytail and it'll probably stay that way until a time when washing my hair seems important again.

'Sorry, didn't mean anything by it,' Fynn says. 'I worry that you're not taking care of yourself.'

'I know, I know. Just don't, all right?' I rub at my tired eyes with my forefinger and thumb. 'I can't cope with comments like that on top of everything else.'

'When was the last time you slept?' I don't need to look at him to know his navy blue eyes are overloaded with concern. I could ask him the same question and would probably get a reply to match mine.

'Who needs sleep when you're facing financial ruin?'

'Is it that bad?' he asks.

'It's worse. I can't do anything until I get a death certificate. I can't access any of the money in his account, I can't claim on his life insurance, I can't ask to defer payments because I haven't got a death certificate. And I can't get a death certificate because I haven't got his . . .' My voice snags in my distress-lined throat, my eyes are suddenly awash with tears I have to blink away. I don't have time to cry. 'I can't get a death certificate because he's still "evidence". I can't even organise a funeral because I haven't got him back and I don't know when I will get him back.'

'They haven't said when it might be?'

'About three months, maybe longer.'

'*Three months?*' Fynn's outrage – acute but raw, like sharp nails clawed across a tangle of exposed nerves – is enough for both of us. Like most things, I can't feel that indignation because it burns up energy, sucks away the reserves of spirit I need to make it from one end of the day to the other. Being numb is the only way I'm surviving right now. 'What? Why?'

'People keep telling me that's just the way it is with a death that's a crime.' *With a murder*. I can't say the word most of the time. It's too much, too unreal, too 'stuff that I see on TV'. My life doesn't include 'murder'.

I can't feel my face as I run my hands over it, I know my nose is still there at the centre, I know my cheeks flank my nose, that my eyes are above it, that above them is my forehead, my lips are below my nose and below my lips is my chin, but these are things I sense from memory, I can't believe I am actually touching any of them right now. I am numb, shut off from the sensory world.

'How much money do you need?' Fynn says.

'No, thank you, but no.' I remove my hands from my face and stare into the face of the man who knew Joel first. 'You don't have the kind of money we need right now. And I couldn't take it from you even if you did have it. I've gone through everything, all the figures, what savings I can access, and to keep going for three months I have to . . .' I sigh. 'I have to sell the beach hut.'

'What? No, surely not.'

'Yes. I've done that crunching numbers thing that you hear people talking about, which is just adding up everything you've got and then taking away everything you owe or are going to owe and seeing what you've got left. Or in my case, what you haven't got left. I have to sell stuff. The only things I can sell that will give me a big hit of cash to tide us over are the children, my car or the beach hut. Even if I was allowed to sell the children before all the probate was settled seeing as Joel did contribute towards making them, I think I'd miss them too much.'

This curls the edges of Fynn's lips in the vague conjuring of a smile. Seeing his face relax like that reminds me that one day it might be possible to joke again, to feel unburdened again.

'All that's left is the beach hut,' I say.

'Please let me lend you some money. That beach hut ... you had Zane's first birthday party there, the blessing of your tenth wedding anniversary there. Every year you couldn't go on holiday you—'

'You're not helping, Fynn,' I cut in. That moment, that little sliver of hope for a future that could be full of laughter again is gone, whisked away on Fynn reminding me of what else is about to be lost. 'I don't need a trip down Memory Lane.'

'Sorry,' he mumbles.

'It's a lot to ask of you, but I need you to sell it for me. I can't do that. If you'll talk to the estate agent and then deal with everything, and when it's done if you could empty it, put the stuff somewhere for me. I know it's a lot to ask, but I can't—'

His hands cover mine, sheltering and protective, anchoring us together. 'It's the least I can do. You're in real dire straits, aren't you?'

'You have no idea. Let this be a lesson to you. If you get married again, make sure you each have a separate account in your name in case something like this happens. And make sure you know each other's passwords. And don't let them out of your sight for even a second so they can't go and do this to you.'

'It'll be OK,' he reassures.

'Do people actually believe that when they say it? Do you actually believe it?'

'I have to, otherwise, what else is there?'

What else is there? 'Yesterday, I saw this parking inspector walking down the middle of our road and he stopped at this one car that maybe the ticket had run out on. He looked so self-important getting his little keypad thing and camera out and I had to stop myself dashing out to remind him that it was the end of the world, so he should have something better to do. But, of course, he didn't have anything better to do because it's not the end of the world for him. Just for me. Just for the kids. Just for Joel's parents. Just for Aunty Betty.'

'Just for me.'

Fynn is so incredibly pale, the lines of his face greyed and thinned by what has happened. His dark brown hair, usually neatly cut, is messy, growing in untamed curls; his eyes are dull. He looks how I feel. 'Yes, just for you.'

'It does get better,' he promises. 'The pain doesn't go away, but it does get easier to live with. It doesn't feel like it's going to consume you for every moment of every day; it's muted a little.'

'How do you know?'

He gives a one-shouldered shrug. 'I know lots of things.'

'I don't believe you.' I don't believe I'll ever not feel like this. That the world after *that day* could ever be less painful, less agonising than it is now.

'I wouldn't believe me either.'

'Right,' I say decisively as I stand. 'I'd better get back to trying to magic up money from nowhere.' After rooting through the drawer beside the fridge, I manage to pull out the three little padlock keys, looped onto a flimsy metal ring Joel and I kept meaning to change. Every time it came out of its resting place to be used, we'd say to ourselves or to each other, *Must get a proper keyring for this.* I hand them to Fynn. He looks at the keys, then at me, and in that moment, he lets his guard down, and I can experience his pain: I can see the enormity of losing Joel, how it's eating him up, how he has to steel himself constantly to get through the day.

'Please get as much as you can for it.' I avert my gaze because looking into his face of torment, seeing what grief looks like, how I must appear to the outside world is more than I can handle right now. 'I've, erm, I've searched online and most of them are on sale for twelve grand so if you can get ten for ours, it'll probably sell quicker and we could breathe a bit easier for a while.'

'I'll do my best.'

'Thanks, Fynn.' I want to hug him, but I can't. I can't make this any harder than it already is. For the first two weeks Fynn slept almost permanently on our sofa. He would get up in the darkest hours of the night when I'd be walking around and around the kitchen looking for something I had lost, and he would lead me back to bed. During those nights I would grip desperately to him. He was like an anchor that I tied myself to, a fixed point that kept me grounded. I mustn't start that again now, I'll never let him go.

Without warning, he takes me in his arms and pulls me towards his body. He buries his face in the curve of my neck, his lashes flutter against my skin as he closes his eyes and his hold around me intensifies. It's his turn to grab onto the anchor and cling on.

3 weeks after *That Day* (November, 2011)

A loud, mournful squeal in the middle of the night stops my heart and yanks me fully awake from that half-conscious state that is as close to sleep as I can get. Phoebe? Or Zane? I throw back the covers, out of bed like a shot ready to dash down the corridor to them.

The sound happens again, this time louder and accompanied by a couple of clicks, and it's obvious now that I'm upright that it is coming from outside the house. I move towards the window. The clicks – five short, ear-splitting animalistic clicks of large front teeth hitting together – are followed by an equal number of mournful, deep-throated squeals. It happens again, the clicks, the squeals, and again, and again, and each time they increase in intensity and volume, louder and louder until the sound swells enough to fill my room.

I know what the sound is without looking, but still I pull apart the slats of the blinds at the left-hand window in the bay of my bedroom, and peer out. The outside world is bathed in darkness, and despite the street lamp a little to the right of our house, I can't locate her. I know who she is and I know that she's just found him.

The squirrel was the first thing I saw this morning when

I glanced out of the open blinds in my bedroom. He was motionless on the ground, his grey-brown fur smooth and unruffled, his body stretched out, as it would if he was leaping from one branch to another. He looked as if he'd been struck down in the midst of doing something he did a million times a day.

My eyes are too heavy and vein-threaded to make out any shapes amongst the parked cars and bases of trees, but I keep searching for her as she continues her piercing, feral keening.

A cluster of emotions – shock, fear, sadness – had imploded in my chest as I stared at the squirrel this morning. Dead. He was dead. He was dead and an unwelcome reminder of what death looked like in the physical world. I'd stared at him for several minutes before running out to move my car to hide it from view from the pavement – I didn't want the children to see it, to notice it and be reminded what 'dead' meant. When being dead was talked about you could use the words 'gone' and 'lost' and 'left', but seeing a physical body would negate all that, would make it horrifically real. Remind them that their dad's body was like that, somewhere 'out there' because we hadn't got him back yet. I'd gone to work and called the council about having him removed and had been grateful when I hadn't seen him when I came back from work. But now, with the clicks and squeals rising up from outside my window, I realise his body is still there somewhere and she, his mate, has just found him.

She's probably been searching all day for him – and she can't quite believe that she's finally found him here, like this.

I'd dropped blackberries, I'd wanted to know where my children were, I hadn't been allowed to touch him, I'd woken up every morning and gone to bed every night, but three weeks later, I still can't believe it. I still feel like that inside, I still feel like I am back at *that day*, hearing the news of what happened to Joel all over again. I still feel like screaming the world down.

I give up looking for her, she who shares my grief, and instead stand at the window, my hands over my eyes, my ears full of the clicks and squeals of the lamenting squirrel, knowing exactly how she feels.

25 days after *That Day* (November, 2011)

'The estate agent can do a direct transfer to your account as soon as you sign the paperwork.'

'Can't you do it?' I whine over the constant flow of traffic outside my office building. It's located just behind Queen's Road, the street from the train station that leads down to the sea, so cars, taxis, vans are always cutting down this way to lead them down into shops in the North Laine area.

A white van rumbles by as Fynn replies, 'No, sorry, I'm not the legal owner. I can run you down there now, if you want. I know it's a pain, but ten thousand pounds is a good price and if we go down there now, it should be in your account today. Tomorrow at the latest.'

'I won't be able to go now, I've already had so much time off—'

'For compassionate leave.'

'Yeah, compassion starts to wear pretty thin when they

think you're not pulling your weight,' I whisper. I might be outside, but I know the ears have walls or is that the walls have ears? Nowadays, I often forget how phrases work, how jokes are told, sometimes how the days of the week are arranged. In this minute, all I remember is that I don't want anyone to hear what I'm saying.

'It'll have to be in your lunch hour then.'

'Lunch hour? Which century do you work in?'

'Do you really want to wait until Saturday?'

'No, no I don't. What time do they close?'

'Seven.'

'OK, do you mind watching the kids and giving them dinner while I go down there?'

'Sure, no problem.' He pauses, wondering if he should say something to me, then says it anyway: 'Do you want to know who bought it?'

I hesitate because I am curious. I want to know who'll be sitting on my box seat, who'll hang up different deckchairs on the brass hooks we installed, what colour parasol they'll have. But do I *really* want to know? When they'll be using the place Joel, Phoebe, Zane and I loved to make new, radically different impressions in time? I'd been saving to go travelling again when I saw the sign stuck on the front and, in an impulsive moment, bought it. I'd been dating Joel for a year and in that moment I decided not to go travelling because I had a man that I had a future with, and instead I'd bought the beach hut. And we'd used it as our holiday home ever since. It was always ours, never just mine. Did I really want to create in my mind the image of these people who would be replacing us by hearing their names? 'No. I want to sign on the dotted line and move on.'

'Fair enough. I'll see you later.'

I stand on the street outside my office, my phone resting uselessly in the palm of my hand, as the recollections of our little beach hut with the bright yellow doors fall like a heavy rain on me: Joel tripping over his feet and dropping Zane's birthday cake and watching in fascinated horror as the circling seagulls dive-bombed to swallow chunks of it, almost like a scene from *The Birds*. Phoebe doing a handstand outside the beach hut and Zane holding onto her leg while giving a thumbs up to the camera as though she was a huge fish he'd landed all by himself. Me falling asleep on our double deckchair while reading a book and them leaving me there to go for ice cream and a paddle in the sea, then coming back to gleefully tell me what I missed. Joel making a dent in the roof with the cork from the bottle of champagne he opened after our tenth anniversary blessing. The photo I took of our family last summer, each of them pulling a stupid face at the camera right before I hit the button.

I had to sell it, I remind myself. *There was no choice, for the greater good I had to do it.*

6 weeks after *That Day* (December, 2011)

'Police today confirmed they have arrested a thirty-two-year-old man in connection with the brutal murder of Brighton man, Joel Mack-el-roy. Forty-year-old father of two Mack-el-roy was found on Montefiore Road in Hove, bleeding from a stab wound, and died on the way to hospital without regaining consciousness.'

I pause in the middle of the kitchen, staring at the stain on the floor, listening to the radio tell me things I do not know about my life. I didn't know they thought they knew who did it. I didn't know they'd arrested anyone. I didn't know anything.

'Police are still appealing for information in relation to the murder. In other news—' I don't hear the news item that comes next because I am bracing myself. The house was silent until I put the radio on ten minutes ago, and now I'm waiting for the howling, the noise of the outside world wanting to know everything they think I should know, to come for me.

My mobile wins the race, lighting up on the table; the house phone is next, trilling from its place beside the kettle. I push my hands over my ears – drowning out the radio, blocking out Mum on my mobile, silencing Joel's mother on the house phone.

It's all too noisy.

8 weeks after *That Day* (December, 2011)

'Why do you think it's taking so long for them to find out who did this terrible thing?' Mum asks.

'I don't know,' I reply listlessly. 'The police are doing the best they can.' She is sitting on my sofa while my dad is in the attic sleeping off Christmas dinner and the children are hiding upstairs.

This wasn't how Christmas was meant to be. We had planned to spend it alone so we could start to sort out how it would work, how the three of us would cope on important occasions.

Despite me explaining that, my parents – my mum – insisted they come. At the moment we have to break up time with other people who knew him, section them into little chunks or it all becomes overwhelming. We've found that you're almost expected to take on their grief, too, acknowledge what they have lost too, when really, all we want to do is focus on ourselves, examine how we feel and not worry about the others. With the grandparents it is harder still, because they are family and family always comes first, even if that means putting their grief above yours. Joel's parents have gone to Jamaica for Christmas and have taken Aunty Betty with them, they couldn't stand to be here this year, knowing they wouldn't see Joel.

'I still don't understand why they let that man go,' Mum says. 'If they thought he did it, why did they let him go so easily?'

'Because he can prove where he was at the time it happened. For the whole day it happened, in fact. He didn't tell them straight away because he was somewhere he shouldn't have been.'

'But—'

'He was innocent, Mum! OK? He didn't do it.'

Mum's entire body bristles and she sits back in her seat, lifts her chin slightly and fractionally purses her lips into a pout. I've upset her. She has been virtually no help preparing Christmas dinner, instead sitting around expecting us to serve her. She's told me that I should still be wearing black but not near my face as it drains me. She's explained at length – and in their hearing – that I shouldn't let the children stay up so late, even if it is the school holidays and they are often scared to go to bed because it's the time they cry and sometimes they simply don't want to cry. She has told me that I should think about moving my wedding ring to my right hand because I'm not married any more. But this, my raising my voice a little because once again she isn't listening to me, has offended and upset her. Joel made this possible. He made seeing my parents bearable.

'Sorry,' I mumble. I can say that because it'll make the next two days of their visit easier on all of us. I can say that because she's not coming back to stay again. Without Joel, there's no way I'm going to allow this to happen again. 'It's been a long few days. I'm a bit tired.'

'You look tired. And you've lost so much weight. It doesn't suit you at all.'

My mouth bends into a smile. 'You always used to say I . . . Never mind.' *You always used to say I needed to lose weight*, I complete in my head. *I was always too large for you, I was always eating too much even though I always had to clear my plate or I was a bad girl who didn't care about all the starving people in the world. I'd have thought at least this would make you happy.*

My mother doesn't notice that I stopped mid-sentence, she continues to speak: 'How you look now isn't good at all. You need to eat. You need to put on weight.'

'Yeah,' I say. 'You're probably right.'

I focus on the tinsel-surrounded photo of Joel and the children that stands on the mantelpiece. It's of our first Christmas as a foursome. Phoebe is four, Zane is nine months and the four of us had the best time together. That photo, that snapshot of who we were, has sat there since our first new year together. I focus on the picture, on what we did that day, and tune out everything else around me.

9 weeks after *That Day* (December, 2011)

'Mum?' Phoebe's voice is so quiet, so fragile-sounding, it is almost drowned out by the noise that is raging inside me.

'Yes?' I say. I'd had my head resting on the table, staring at the purple bruise on the kitchen floor but now I sit up as though I wasn't doing that at all. Phoebe doesn't turn on the light as she moves into the room.

I blink a few times, clearing my vision so I can look at her properly, clearing my head to allow myself to speak. I'd sat outside her bedroom until she'd stopped sobbing by slipping into sleep, the same with Zane. I'd been in and checked they were both asleep, both still where they were meant to be. Fynn had been and gone, and I'd come down here because I couldn't face another night up in the attic, going through papers and filling in forms.

Phoebe's walk is slow, cautious, like a girl approaching the gallows, like a twelve-year-old with a heavy burden on her shoulders. I open my arms to her and she comes to me, allows me to pull her onto my lap and wrap myself around her. She smells of sleep, and of Phoebe – that unique mixture of aloe vera conditioner, shea butter hair cream, mint toothpaste, and fresh air.

'I have to tell you something,' she says, gravely. The last

time she said that in that tone, she'd been seven and had gone on to inform me that one day she was going to have to leave home and live somewhere else, but I mustn't be sad because she would still love me.

'What is it?' I ask. I could do with a laugh, something that would lift the heaviness from my heart.

'Please,' she says inside a sob. 'Please don't be cross with me. Please.'

'I won't,' I say without thinking. I clasp her closer to me to reassure her that whatever it is, I will understand. And I say it because my ravaged heart can't bear to have her cry about something else when we all have so much to sob about already.

'I know something about what happened to Dad,' she says.

I am silent, terrified suddenly. What she is about to say will change how I feel about her, I know it will. It will damage us all over again and I don't want that. I almost ask her not to tell me. I don't want anything else to batter our family.

'I didn't tell the police about it because I was too scared.'

'Tell me,' I say to her.

She shakes her head, breathless sobs falling from her lips. 'Please don't be cross with me. Please don't shout at me. Please don't hate me.'

'I won't,' I reply. 'Whatever it is, just tell me, Phoebe.'

And she does.

'Are you going to tell the police?' she asks afterwards.

'I think I have to,' I say. My mouth is dry, my mind is racing to so many different places and thoughts and decisions all at once, I can't keep up. I can't hold a single thought in my head for too long because another dashes into its place. Air keeps snagging itself on the way in and out of my lungs so I haven't taken a proper breath since my daughter started to speak, and my heart is running cold with the knowledge of who it was that killed my husband. And why.

I have to tell the police this, of course I do.

'Please don't, Mum.'

'But, Phoebe—'

'Please don't, Mum. Please. Please. Please.' Her twelve-year-old body, nestled on my lap, shakes with fretful sobs. 'Please. Please. Please. I'm scared. I'm really scared.'

'Phoebe, we can't—'

'Please, Mum. I'm really sorry, but please, don't.'

'Shhh, shhhhh,' I say, rocking her, trying to hush her. This isn't fair. None of this is fair. 'Let's not talk about it now. It'll be OK, I'll make it all OK.'

10 weeks after *That Day* (January, 2012)

'Do you know if your husband ever used prostitutes?'

I stare at the he one who is my FLO for long, uncertain seconds, then rise from my seat and go to shut the living room door. The children don't need to hear this. No one needs to hear this, but certainly not Phoebe and Zane.

'No, he didn't,' I reply. I stand behind the door, needing the solidity of the wood to keep me upright. My body is simultaneously hot and cold, I'm trembling. What is he about to tell me? Is he going to take Joel away from me all over again?

The FLO sits back in his seat, looks uncomfortable. He lowers his voice, makes it soothing and caring. 'It's just there were long blonde hairs found on his clothing from the time of his death, but no way of knowing who they belong to because they didn't have the bulb at the end with the DNA.' His tone doesn't fit with what he is saying – he sounds concerned while he is being accusatory.

'Why immediately assume prostitutes? Why not an affair or a female friend or colleague, why straight to a prostitute? Why would you try and hurt me like that?'

'I'm sorry if this has upset you, but we do have to follow all lines of enquiry.'

'He'd had sex just before he'd died, then?' I ask. The cold-hot-cold feeling siphons itself from my heart to my feet, from my feet to my head and back to my heart.

'No.'

'You found out that he'd likely kissed someone?'

'No.'

'Someone had gone down on him?' I am desperate to understand why this man would say this to me if there was nothing more than blonde hairs on his clothing.

'No.'

'He'd had a shower right before he died, meaning he was maybe trying to hide something?'

'No.'

I am suddenly aware of every muscle in my body, I am aware of them tensing, contracting, adrenalin pumping through like drivers on a Formula One circuit.

I say nothing, so he does: 'You just mentioned an affair, do you think your husband might have been seeing someone else?'

'No. I was just . . . You know what I meant. And, anyway, wouldn't his phone records tell you if he was calling one number more than any other?'

'Men who have affairs or have some other kind of secret life involving drugs, prostitutes, gangs and the like often have more than one phone.'

'Do they? I wouldn't know.'

'It wouldn't be entirely surprising if you had no idea what your husband was up to. We thought we'd ask in case . . .'

'You're not searching my house for another phone,' I state.

'Mrs Mack-el-roy—'

'Like I said, wouldn't you have found something else – known prostitutes who recognised him, secret bank accounts, maybe drug dealers who . . . you've talked to all those types of people and no one has even vaguely recognised him, have they?'

The FLO says nothing because he doesn't want to say no again, because for some reason I'm the one now conducting the interrogation. We stare at each other across the room – me the sudden investigator, he the potential criminal.

In the seconds that slide by in silence, I know with a clear certainty I haven't had since this all began that I can't tell them what Phoebe told me. She's right to panic about them not understanding. They *will* twist it, they *will* sully Joel's name. Not even intentionally, they'll simply want to 'cover all angles', not realising what that is doing to the people who loved him in the process. Phoebe won't be able to cope, either. Not if they're like this with her. Not if they start asking questions that imply Joel was someone other

107

than who he was. I can't protect her if they'll say things like this to her.

'Please don't come back here again,' I say, even-tempered despite the adrenalin that is fluttering rapidly and fiercely in my chest. 'I can't answer your questions because you're not taking this seriously.'

'We are taking this very seriously,' he protests.

'All right, let me put it this way: my husband didn't take drugs – he tried them once in his late teens and hated it. He didn't go with prostitutes or go to lap-dancing clubs no matter what his mates did because he had a brain of his own and he hated those places. He drank too much occasionally but no more than anyone else. He didn't gamble. He didn't sleep around. He wasn't part of a gang. He got one parking ticket in his whole life. He paid his bills, he paid his tax, he visited his parents at least once a month, he visited his elderly aunt the same amount. He occasionally gave other people the wrong impression because he was so friendly he didn't realise they thought he was flirting. Those are all the things I can tell you.'

'Don't come back here. If you do come back here, I will not let you in nor speak to you.' I stand aside and open the living room door. 'Please leave now.'

'Mrs Mack-el-roy, I'm you're FLO, I'm here for you. I'm sorry this is so upsetting, but all we want to do is get to the truth.'

'It's Mack-le-roy. And go now, please, just go away and leave us alone.'

IX

The letter sits on my kitchen table, placid and deadly.

I inhale as much as I can and my body moves. I am no longer frozen as I relive the past, I am in the present and I can move.

I take a step back. I take another step back. And another step. And another. Until I step back and I am on the other side of the room. I have the solidity of a wall behind me. I have the ability to press my body against it, the coolness of the painted plaster, a welcoming, shocking reminder that I am back in the present. I let myself go, slide to the ground and stare at the letter.

If I touch that letter again, if I read any more of those words, I'll end up back there, I'll end up re-experiencing the moments of what it was like to be *her* again.

Right now, I am the woman whose husband was murdered, the woman who the world thinks is successfully 'moving on' and 'coping'. If I read the letter, even touch it again, I will be her all over again. I will be the woman stuck in the loop of dropping a bowl of blackberries and being told her life is over again and again and again.

Dear Saffron.

I'm not sure how to start this letter because I think you probably know who I am even though we have never met. I feel like I know you, too. I knew your husband, Joel. He was my friend. That's why this next thing I'm going to say may shock you, and I hope you're sitting down as you read this.

I need you to know I didn't murder him.

It really wasn't like that.

Murder means you plan something, but I didn't plan it. It happened. It was fast and it was immediate and it was deeply shocking for both of us. He was my friend so I felt the pain too, when he was hurt.

I'm telling you this now, eighteen months later, because it has stayed with me. What happened is in my thoughts every day and I want to share it with the one person I thought might understand? Also, I think it is only fair for you to know how it really was, not how they described it on the news and not in the way the police probably told you. It wasn't a callous, malicious act. It was nothing like that. I did not want him to suffer and no one can feel as traumatised as I was when I had to leave him on the side of the road. I did not simply dump him there, like they said on the news and in the papers, I had no choice but to leave him. Even he understood that. I don't think he'd hate me for it if he had lived.

It's a sad truth that you've probably had letters like this before, that people claiming to have killed him will have contacted you and said all these terrible things. How are you supposed to know if this is another letter like that or if this is genuine? I can assure that I am 100 per cent the real deal.

No one ever mentioned this in the papers or on the news, not even in the coroner's court but he died with his phone near him. Not beside him, it was out of reach. And it had an unsent text message to you that read: Love you xxxxx

I think he was trying to get it to you but didn't manage to send it before he died. I hope you realise this is a genuine communication from someone who was there.

I'm writing this letter because I hope it will be of some comfort to you. I hope now you know it wasn't how it sounded – it wasn't a viciously planned murder, it was a sad misunderstanding between two friends.

We were very close friends, we cared for each other, deeply. I am only sorry it ended so tragically.

Please take care of your beautiful children. Life is short and precious, and we should cherish every moment we have with the people we love whenever we can.

Kind regards

IV

X

The Mr Bromsgrove is sitting today.

He stands when we enter and shakes my hand, firmly, formally, almost as though he hasn't met me before. As I take my hand away, I admit to myself that this is another of those situations where I don't know how to be, how to act.

'*Be yourself*,' Joel would say to me if I was stressed about something.

That's easy, if you know who you are, I'd silently reply.

'*And who you are is amazing*,' he'd add because sometimes, just sometimes, Joel could read my mind. He could look at me and know what he had to say to make me believe in myself.

Be yourself.

Who am I in this moment? Oh yes, a widow with a knocked-up teenager; one of those don't-have-a-clue mothers that are only fit for condemnation.

After our hellos, we all sit in our designated seats. Phoebe is nearer to me this time, not through choice, obviously. She hasn't spoken this morning. She grunted at me when I asked if she was going to eat anything for breakfast; she gurned at her brother when he asked her if she was going back to school for the rest of the week; she shrugged at Aunty Betty when she asked if Phoebe's school hairstyle was always afro-puff pigtails. Any meaningful communication had been conducted between her and her mobile. She knew she wasn't meant to use it at the table and I'd been tempted to take it off her, but decided not to. I needed her onside. If we're going to work out a way through this, I needed to not alienate her.

Especially since that letter arrived. Mostly unread, but what I have read has told me I need to not alienate Phoebe right now. She, like me, could be in danger.

'Mrs Mackleroy, it's good to see you,' the headteacher says and brings me away from the cream A4 sheets of paper back to the present and his modern, bright office. I glance at the black lettering on the bronze nameplate on his desk, something I didn't notice the other day. Or maybe I did because his name – Mr Newton – isn't a surprise to me. I simply didn't take it in – too busy being shocked, I think.

Mr Newton is lying if he is trying to convince himself, me or anyone else it's nothing short of a disaster that he's having this conversation with a parent. I'm sure he's had this conversation before, but that doesn't make it any easier. I've had the conversation many, many times before about my husband dying, about who might have done it, about why the police investigation never found the killer, but it's never got any easier. In fact, I search the lined face of the middle-aged-crisis-ridden man in front of me and wonder if, like me, he finds these conversations harder the more he has them.

'How are you, Phoebe?' He is tender and compassionate when talking to her, highlighting how clipped and hard-edged his manner is towards me. Why wouldn't he treat me like that, though, when I am the woman whose daughter was too scared to tell her she was pregnant, who allowed her daughter to get into that condition in the first place? They blame me. Of course they do. And they've probably been imagining the horrors I've subjected Phoebe to in the intervening hours since leaving here.

My instinct is to tell him that I wouldn't hurt her. To explain that while I don't know why she couldn't tell me herself about this, it's not because I would hurt her. Even when she's done something awful in the past I haven't hurt her.

'I'm OK,' Phoebe says, proving that she's capable of speaking nicely to people.

'Good, good,' Mr Newton replies, and manages a not-very-subtle look to *The* Mr Bromsgrove. *Good, good, she didn't beat her,* he's obviously thinking at his colleague. *Or least, nowhere the bruises can be seen.* 'Well, are you able to tell me what decisions you've made about Phoebe's . . . condition?' he asks, focused on me again and back to snipping the edges off his words.

I turn my head to Phoebe. 'Have you made any decisions, Phoebe?' I ask.

All eyes on her and in response she silently lowers her head and stares at her feet.

'Understandably, Phoebe hasn't wanted to discuss much of anything with me since I found out,' I confess. 'I think she's still in a bit of shock, so she's considering her options. We had a doctor's appointment on Wednesday, and we'll probably be having another next week, when hopefully we'll be in a better position to decide how we proceed.'

The Mr Bromsgrove and Mr Newton both look at me as if I have grown another head or two. I've done something wrong, clearly. Possibly I have not taken proper control of the situation and laid down the law about what was going to happen next, maybe I've been too hard on her by making a doctor's appointment, or maybe, just maybe, whatever I do is not going to be right for these two. Maybe, being me, being in this situation is always going to mean I am in the wrong. I used to hear that phrase: 'A mother's place is in the wrong' and smile to myself, understanding the vague sentiment behind it. I never realised that I would be living it at some point, that other people would be rephrasing it to: 'Saffron Mackleroy's place is in the wrong'.

A knock on the door accompanies an '*Ah-he-hem!*' from Mr Newton clearing his throat and we all wonder for a moment if he's created that sound. Then it comes again: *Rat-a-tat-tat!*

Mr Newton knits his whole face into a frown as he looks up at the door, bemused at the interruption. 'Yes?' he calls.

His secretary, Ms Taylor, opens the door and appears in the doorway, purposely filling the gap with her slender frame. She has the manner of a woman who is trying to hide something outside from those of us in the office.

'Erm, Mr Bromsgrove, may I have a quick word with you outside?' she says, nervously. She keeps moving her body, blocking something from being seen, or, rather, stopping someone from seeing into the room.

Perplexed, *The* Mr Bromsgrove replies, 'Not really, Ms Taylor, we're in the middle of a meet—'

'Dad!' A boy's voice calls out from behind the school secretary when he hears *The* Mr Bromsgrove speak. 'Dad, I need to talk to you.'

The Mr Bromsgrove stands, embarrassment pouring off him like sweat off a man who has just run a four-hour marathon on a summer's day. 'Curtis?' he says.

Mr Newton throws himself backwards in his chair, irritation and contempt plain on his once flabby face. *I'm surrounded by amateurs*, he's thinking with an unsubtle look of disapproval in my direction.

Resigned, but not a little disgruntled, Ms Taylor steps aside and allows the boy into the inner sanctum. In walks a tall young man, impeccably turned out in his school uniform, a short, neat haircut, his skin a gorgeous hazelnut brown and large, inquisitive eyes. Apart from the lighter shade of his skin and the absence of the gold-rimmed glasses, he is almost a miniature replica of *The* Mr Bromsgrove, right down to the way he walks and sets his face as his eyes scan the room to see what is going on.

The boy, Curtis, now that he has gained entry, ignores everyone and goes to what he came for: Phoebe. Their eyes lock and horror immediately overtakes her features, settling in her eyes, in the way she holds her body. She shakes her head really fast at him.

'I'm doing it,' he says. 'I don't care.'

'No,' Phoebe replies. 'No, don't.'

Anyone would think they were conducting this intimate, short-handed conversation alone.

'*Yes*,' he declares. His voice has broken, but it does not have the slants and nuances of maturity that are added by experiences of the world. He is tall but does not have the height of a fully grown man. He is good-looking, but in a youthful way that will develop with time.

I study him and my daughter, watch them talk verbally and non-verbally. The language of their bodies shows a certain closeness, a familiarity of non-physical touching.

'*No!* Just *don't!*' Phoebe insists.

He is on his knees now, crouching at her side, staring into her eyes, trying to communicate with her.

'Excuse me, Mr Bromsgrove, perhaps you would care to explain what you think you're doing in here?'

'Yes, Curtis, what do you think you're doing?' *The* Mr Bromsgrove says.

My gaze shifts back to the two older men. 'Do you two really not understand?' I ask, because no one can be that clueless. The two older male faces that were full of judgement and disdain merely a few minutes ago swivel towards me with confusion.

'OK,' I say, stupefied by them. 'This young man, Curtis, is the one responsible for Phoebe's "condition" as you called it, Mr Newton.'

If I didn't know how awful it felt to be in that situation, how shocking and sickening and frightening, a trickle of Schadenfreude, pleasure at the misfortune of others, would have run through my veins at the look dawning on *The* Mr Bromsgrove's face. But I take no pleasure from this moment. No one needs to find out that no matter how hard they've tried, they've let their children down.

'Is that true?' *The* Mr Bromsgrove asks. I'm not sure if he is questioning Phoebe or his son but my daughter lowers her head as tears spring into her eyes. Young Bromsgrove stands to face his father, his stance one of a prize-fighter about to go toe to toe with his greatest opponent.

'Yeah, Dad, it's true,' he says.

And for a moment I think I'm going to stand up and punch his stupid lights out.

XI

Outside the school, I lean against my car and centre myself.

By 'centre' I mean I take a moment to stop the shaking, to stop my mind going to those words on that letter which will cast me back to reliving the events of eighteen months ago all over again.

Phoebe is in class, having insisted that she wanted to stay at school. Curtis, in the year above, is in class, too. The office after the revelation had exploded with quiet pandemonium: Mr Newton had virtually kicked Mr Bromsgrove to my side of the desk with stern looks to go and stand with his son. (He was obviously stripped of his *The* and downgraded from heart-throb, 'good guy who teens confide in' status to common or garden bad parent.) Phoebe sobbed for a bit, not loudly, but enough to have Curtis drop to his knees again and awkwardly encircle her with his arm, putting his head against hers and whispering that it would all be OK. Mr Bromsgrove, diminished without his *The*, stood near the pair of them, impotent and confused. I'd watched them all like I watched myself relive the early weeks and months of losing Joel last night – there but with no real role in it. Sometimes it feels like no one would notice if I fell off the face of the planet.

Except, Kevin. He'll notice I'm not there. He will be sitting in his little glass-walled office, looking at the clock he's had installed on the wall to the right of my desk, noticing with every tick of the red second hand that I am not there.

I'd wanted to take Phoebe home, to cuddle up with her and talk to her about this guy Curtis, ask her again how she felt about him. Ask her again if she had any idea what she wanted to do. Not what she wanted, though. She wanted to get back to normal, stay at school, be away from me.

'Mrs Mackleroy,' Mr Bromsgrove shouts to me from the school gates. I pause in opening my car door and stand waiting for him to approach.

'I hoped I hadn't missed you,' he says. He is a little breathless because he's probably run from wherever he was in the maze that was the school. Understandably, neither he nor Mr Newton offered to show me out. They allowed me to walk Phoebe in the general direction of her class and then probably hoped I'd drop off the face of the Earth. 'If I were you, I don't think I'd be able to simply drive away, either.' He smiles a smile that would make a couple of dozen other playground mothers swoon. He is undeniably good-looking.

I say nothing to him because his pleasantness and smile have been so absent since all this began.

Disconcerted by my lack of response to his small talk, Mr Bromsgrove tries again: 'Would you like to go out and have a drink so we can talk about this situation?'

'Not especially, no.'

He blinks at me in surprise, obviously not the reply he was expecting from a mother as bad as me. I am supposed to be grateful, I think, that he wants to talk to me at all, and desperate to share this with him. Mr Bromsgrove shuffles his surprise away behind a serious expression. 'OK, how about if I put it this way – I would like to talk to you about the fact our children have not only had sex, but they've potentially created our grandchild and what that will mean for our families. I would like to do that in a non-school environment. Would you be so kind as to meet me at eight-thirty tomorrow at The Cuthbert, which is near where you live, I believe?'

'Fine,' I say. Phoebe talks to him, she talks to his son, it could help me to talk to him, find out what she's thinking. 'Seeing as you asked so nicely.'

'Eight-thirty, then.'

I nod and don't bother with goodbyes before I get into my car and leave. Mr Bromsgrove is openly puzzled as I drive away. Probably because his good looks let him get away with treating most people however it suits his mood. And if his mood changes, if he decides the person is now in favour or has fallen out of favour, they usually accept it, allow him to dictate the terms of their interactions because, well, he's the good-looking, confident one. I am not most people.

As I navigate the roads from Hove to Brighton, two things keep nibbling at my mind, like a caterpillar chewing on two different leaves that can't decide which one to settle for and finish completely: the opening words of the letter; and the awkward way Curtis put his arm around Phoebe – it was almost as if he'd barely touched her before.

XII

I'm hoping Kevin is in a meeting when I get out of the lift at work.

I swipe myself into the office, and as I head for my desk, I risk a look at his glass-walled office at the other end of this floor. He isn't there. I'm grateful for that small mercy. His responses to my calls about not coming in or coming in late have been decidedly frosty. I used to be his second in command, Assistant Director of Operations, in our business strategy firm, the person who he trusted to do his job when he wasn't there. And now he thinks of me as someone to whom he can say . . .

'Oh, it's a nice surprise to see you, Saffron. I wasn't sure if you'd be dropping by today or not.'

I continue with the action of putting my laptop and bag on my desk while I close my eyes and count to ten, wish myself somewhere else again.

4 months after *That Day* (February, 2012)
'Saffron, we wanted to sit down today to touch base and find out how you feel you're getting on at the moment,' said Gideon, CEO and President of Houlsdon Business Solutions.

I might have been working through the fog of losing Joel,

but I could see clearly what was happening: at the end of the day, when I'm about to turn off my computer and dash out to collect Zane and Phoebe from Imogen's house, I'm 'invited' into the Managing Director's office via email – so all officially noted – for a 'chat'. The other people in there apart from Gideon were Kevin (my direct boss) and the HR Manager, Mrs Piller. Once in the oak-wood-panelled office, I was asked to sit down in the smallest chair in the room. The HR woman was positioned beside the door in her roomy chair, so not 'officially' there; Kevin, who would normally sit beside me, was on the other side of the desk and had his seat placed to the right of Gideon's. A quick glance at each of them wearing identical concerned expressions was enough to tell me I was about to be sacked. Not only that, they were going to do it in a way that would make me agree that it was the *only* way forward, meaning I would get minimal money and I would be too humiliated to even think about suing them for constructive dismissal.

'Isn't it more important how you think I'm getting on?' I replied. I wasn't playing. If they were going to sack me, then they'd have to do it the old-fashioned way – I wouldn't be manipulated into 'resigning'.

Helpfully, I looked down at my hands to allow them to visually decide who was going to do what was necessary. I'd obviously scuppered their plans: they thought I was so stricken with grief that I would willingly fall on my sword out of embarrassment because I was no longer over-achieving for them.

'We appreciate that the last few months have been *difficult* for you,' Gideon said, his words painstakingly chosen and quietly delivered. 'It's obviously taken some bravery for you to continue to come to work every day when things have been so . . . *difficult* . . . We simply think, after assessing your work of late, that . . .'

His flow of considered words halted when I directly faced him. It's easy to sack someone when they won't look at you, it's easy to impart news of someone's failings to their bowed head, but only a complete bastard wouldn't hesitate when a widow looks you in the eye as you're about to cast her and her children into the fires of financial ruin. Gideon wasn't a complete bastard, simply a businessman who wanted the results he'd been getting from me for the past seven years, who wanted me to work double my stated hours for the same pay so he could make his profits and keep his shareholders happy.

'This isn't easy for me to say, Saffron, you've always been a good worker but . . .' *'But we're not a charity. But we're not going to make a profit if you can't put in your horrendously long hours any more. But we're no longer going to underwrite your inability to "get over it".'*

'I'll take a demotion,' I said in the gap between his words. I wasn't going to help them sack me, but I needed a job. I'd never find another one when most of the time I could barely think to the end of the sentence that was coming out of my mouth. And what would I say when any potential new employer asked me why I left my last job? *'My husband was murdered and because I couldn't put in ridiculously long hours any more, I was sacked.'* Any other job I got would want those hours, they wouldn't want to 'carry me', either. What would I say, too, when they asked me who killed Joel and why? *'The thing is, I do know who did it, and I think I know why, but I can't tell the police. All I can tell you is that he bled to death alone on the side of a road in Hove and I dropped a bowl of blackberries when I found out.'*

'I'll take a demotion,' I repeated to the vacuum of sound in the room. 'I'm sure you've already got someone lined up for my job.' Right on cue, Kevin flushed a deep crimson, confirming that he'd been working tirelessly to stitch me up. 'I could help do a comprehensive handover and I'd be on hand if they needed guidance on how we work here. Also, I doubt you'd find someone as experienced as me who wouldn't mind doing a job a step or two down the ladder for less money.' No one said anything. 'Without possibility of promotion,' I added to let them know that I wasn't going to be hanging around, expecting to get my job back – because heaven forbid I asked for a bit of time to get myself back to full strength. Heaven forbid that after seven years working for the company, after bringing in and retaining more than twenty per cent of their new, big-money accounts, I expected them to cut me a little slack.

'Are you sure about this?' Gideon asked.

'I have to feed my children,' I replied.

He stared at me across the desk. He understood. He had children, he had a wife, he understood that I'd do anything to keep my job when I was all they had to rely on. He understood so much he avoided eye contact with me for the rest of the meeting while we 'thrashed out' the terms of my degradation. Sorry, demotion.

*

'Kevin.' Everyone on my bank of desks either keeps their head down, picks up their phone or focuses intently on their computer screen. We aren't friends any more. I used to be their boss, albeit the one they came to with pretty much everything because there was no way on Earth they'd approach Kevin, now I am one of them. I am also that weird woman whose husband was murdered as well as the employee who Kevin spends a lot of time picking at. They are grateful for that, because if it wasn't me, it'd be them. In a way, like I was when I was his second in command, I'm still their buffer from Kevin.

I manage to create something approximating a contrite, apologetic smile by the time I fully face my direct manager. My life is imploding, but I've actually done all my work I'd needed to do this week, I've fitted the reports on three ongoing projects as well as the two initial pitches to encourage companies to use us to plan their business communications and sales strategies, around everything that is going wrong. However, because I haven't been sitting at my desk while doing these things, Kevin feels he has the right to be like this.

'I'm sorry about the past few days, Kevin,' I say. 'I've had quite a few family things crop up this week but we're back on track. And I'm back at my desk.' I pull out my chair. 'Raring to go.'

'I hope this isn't going to become a habit,' he says. 'We've all got families, Saffron, but most of us don't let them interfere with our work.'

Of course we don't, if we've got a stay-at-home partner who does everything while you swan in and out of the office being a cock. It

129

wasn't until Joel died and Kevin shafted me because I wasn't over-performing that I regarded him again, properly, fairly. And I saw him for what he was: an over-entitled weasel who could work whatever hours he wanted because he had someone at home to do the stuff he wouldn't lower himself to do.

Joel and I always shared the home stuff, carefully plotting our lives so one of us was there to make dinner, supervise homework, do bedtime, look after a sick child, listen to anything that troubled them. With just me, I was running really fast to stand still: I'd had to take a demotion, I barely had time to speak to my son, and my daughter was pregnant.

3 years before *That Day* (April, 2008)

'Would Madame care to join me for some champagne on the beach?'

My husband had draped himself over my desk with a couple of champagne flutes and a very expensive bottle of Veuve Clicquot Vintage beside him. I'd found him there when I returned from the toilet.

'How did you get past security?' I queried.

'I'm Joel Mackleroy, do you really need to ask me that?'

'Ah, yes, the cheek of a baboon and the charm of a swan.'

'So, how about it?'

'Where are the children?'

'With Fynn, so we can go celebrate our anniversary down at the beach.'

I frowned as panic spiralled up through me. I'd been so taken up with work lately, had I forgotten an important day? 'Which anniversary?' I asked.

'Which anniversary?' he scoffed. 'Can't believe you've forgotten. The anniversary of our first—'

'Joel Mackleroy as I live and breathe,' Kevin interrupted. He came towards us with his hand outstretched. Joel took himself off my desk and towered over Kevin as he shook his hand. 'What are you doing here?'

'I'm taking my wife away from all this.'

Kevin kept hold of Joel's hand, because he did that with men taller and better-looking than him. It was his way of trying to make those qualities rub off on him. 'I don't blame you coming all the way here to tear her away. I'm always telling her she shouldn't be working so much.'

'No you're not, Kevin,' I said with a laugh.

'Well, maybe not, but I mean to.' He turned to Joel again. And with a nod to the champagne and flutes: 'Special occasion?'

'Anniversary.'

'Oh, I thought your wedding anniversary was in September?'

'It's not that anniversary,' Joel said and hitched his eyebrow at my boss. In response Kevin's weaselly face became a ball of puce embarrassment.

'Oh, erm, right. Well I'll leave you to it then.'

'You are so mean,' I whispered to Joel once we were alone.

'Sometimes that's the only way to deal with people like him.'

*

In the present I face Kevin. 'Yes, I know others don't let their families interfere with their work,' I say in the sort of tone Joel would use. I don't want this to get out of hand, for me to start having crazy thoughts about telling Kevin where to go when I need a job. 'I'm really sorry about Tuesday and yesterday. Did you get the stuff I sent you?'

'Yes,' he says sourly.

'Is there something wrong with it?' I ask.

'No. It simply would have been easier to have you here to go through it.'

I don't reply to Kevin. Instead, I sit down and turn on my computer, decide to clear my head by concentrating on work. I force my lips together while I wait for the computer to flash through its waking up process. I have so much I want to say to Kevin.

Since Monday, when I was brutally ripped from the shell of numbness I'd spent the last eighteen months living in, since I was shown that how I have been existing in the world has not worked, I am starting to re-experience the world. Rapidly, painfully, the numbness is thawing. Who I am, is coming back. And who I am is someone who would normally call out people like Kevin. I want to tell Kevin that after the way he used to fawn over Joel, for him to not acknowledge (even with a mealy mouthed 'I'm sorry') what happened makes him despicable. For him to not take into account how hard I'd worked but to instead screw me over when I was still shocked and bewildered, makes him a lowlife. For him to continue making comments even now, eighteen months later, makes him a slimeball. All of these statements sit like a bitter herb on the tip of my tongue, begging to be spat out at him.

'I expect the Ibbitson and Howell files to be on my desk before you leave tonight,' he says.

I nod with my back to him, unable to speak. If I do, all the sourness I feel towards him will come gushing out in a torrent. Eventually, he walks away and my shoulders want to relax, to unclench so I can slouch a little in my seat, chill out slightly. But I can't. Not when Kevin has unintentionally set off a line of the letter crawling like news tickertape through my head: *I need you to know I didn't murder him.*

XIII

5 years before *That Day* (May, 2006)

'Do you think you'd cope if something terrible happened to me?'

'I'd have to, everyone has to cope, but I'd be incredibly sad.'

'I'd be sad, too.'

'But I couldn't mope around all the time.'

'*What?* Have you already got in mind who you'll be moving on with, then?'

'Eh? I said I wouldn't be moping around for ever, not that I'd be moving on.'

'Well, why wouldn't you move on with all the not moping around you'd be doing? I knew it'd take you no time at all to find someone else. You can't just replace me like that, you know. I'm irreplaceable.'

'I'm not going to replace you. Who could replace you? You're nuts in a very special way. I mean, you're irreplaceable as you said.'

'You must *never* replace me. I want you to miss me for ever. Even if you do meet someone else, it has to be years and years and years later. And even then, you can't love them more than you loved me. All right?'

'Erm . . .'

'*All right?*'

'All right.'

'I'm not being unfair, you can fall in love again, just remember to—'

'Not love them more than I loved you.'

'Absolutely. And, you know, I'll do my best not to do it, either.'

'Why *you* . . . Come here! You deserve a good tickling for that. Come here, come here.'

Dear Saffron.

I hope you don't mind me writing to you again. Like I said, I feel like I know you. It was oddly cathartic writing all that down before, knowing that you, like my mother confessor, would read it and understand.

I haven't been able to talk about it to anyone since it happened. I tell people that I've been so down because I have lost someone dear to me and their reactions vary wildly, but I'm not sure which reactions I prefer, really.

Is it harder or easier, since it was so public for you? All I could do at the time it happened was say that I knew him and say it was shocking. I could never have confessed how well I knew him because I'd be forced to admit that despite how close we were I was living out of the country so hadn't gone to the funeral.

You seem to be doing well, which is something at least. I thought your life would come to a standstill and you wouldn't be able to function. But, I see you're doing well.

What I meant to ask you before when I mentioned people's reactions was how was it for you? Whose reactions did you find the worst? The people who pretend it hasn't happened, the people who won't let you forget and expect you to stay frozen, or the ones who expect you to get over it already cos you've been grieving for long enough? It's a minefield, isn't it, dealing with other people's responses to your grief.

But, as I say, you seem to be doing well. I'm glad, in a way, because I don't have to feel so guilty for how things turned out.

As an aside, I hope you aren't going to do anything silly such as show this and the other letter to the police. It will only cause trouble and upset. However, I don't think you would do that. If you were like that, Phoebe would have told the police what happened, wouldn't she? I do hope I'm not speaking out of turn here. I'm sure your daughter confides everything in you and will have told you the truth already.

If she hasn't, do please go easy on her. She's only a child.

Thank you again for the reading eye/listening ear.

Kind regards

XIV

I've never been to this gastropub before. It's a short walk around the corner and down towards the sea from our house. As soon as I enter to meet Mr Bromsgrove, slightly harassed because I have rushed, the smells of the food unexpectedly assault me. It feels like an assault of my nasal and taste senses because I haven't had time to eat. After making dinner for the children and Aunty Betty, and cleaning up, and making sure Zane was OK going to bed, I only just made it here in time.

'What are you going to talk about?' Phoebe had asked when I told her where I was going. She probably wasn't aware of it, but she was wringing her hands and moving anxiously from one foot to the other.

'I don't know. Mr Bromsgrove wants to talk about this situation from the parents' perspective, I suppose.'

'Right.'

'But we're not going to make any decisions, that's all up to you and Curtis, if you want him involved.'

'Right,' she said, and left the room without further question.

Mr Bromsgrove arrives seconds after me and when I see him cross the threshold, I double-take: he looks like a different person. His clothes have been upgraded from cords and suit jacket to navy blue designer jeans, white collarless shirt and smart black leather suit jacket, he's also without his wire-framed glasses.

'Don't tell me, you have plain glass in your glasses,' I say in lieu of a hello when we meet at the bar.

'No, I'm wearing contacts.'

'Why?'

'Because glasses at school give me more gravitas, it seems. Kids expect a teacher to dress a certain way and they seem to respond better to the glasses.'

'I see,' I reply.

'Would you like something to eat?' he asks. 'I picked this place because the food's meant to be good.'

A swirl of the scents of curry, chips and risotto rice, which shouldn't work together, is driving me insane – my mouth is watering like there is a tap at the base of my throat, my stomach is quietly grumbling, complaining like a teenager with all its access to the outside world stripped away. 'No, thanks. I ate with the children earlier.'

'Ah, right. Do you mind if I eat?'

'If you want.'

He orders a steak (medium rare) and chips, with a beer and I order a glass of white wine from the tall, auburn-haired barmaid. Without thinking, I open my purse and pay for it all, while he still has his card mid-air.

'Oh,' he says. 'I, erm, didn't mean for you to pay.'

'It's no bother,' I say.

The woman busies herself with the till and we stand at the

bar waiting in a strange silence. It's the uneasy silence of two people who've gone on a date a week after a one-night stand that began within half an hour of them meeting – they know 'stuff' about each other because they've had sex, but finding something to talk about is the awkward part for them. Our children have got the sex part out of the way for Mr Bromsgrove and me, now we have to talk about it.

'Is that your husband?' Mr Bromsgrove asks.

I have my purse open as I wait for my change, so it is not as if he is prying, but my response is to immediately shut the leather pieces together, to hide away from scrutiny the picture of my once-upon-a-time family. I forget the picture of Joel, Phoebe, Zane and me is there. I don't look at it and I certainly don't show it to people. When it first happened, not long after he . . . died, there were pictures of Joel everywhere – in the papers, on the TV, A4 sheets in shop windows – and I stopped looking. I didn't want to look, to be reminded. Over time, the pictures went away, they stopped being published in the papers, they didn't appear regularly to hijack me when I turned on the television, the posters in windows curled up at the edges, the Blu-Tack dried out and they were taken down. And it was back to normal, back to only snatching glimpses of him where he should be – in our photo frames, in my photo albums, on my phone, in my purse.

My fingers curl around the top of the wine glass that has been placed in front of me even though Joel taught me to only pick up a wine glass by the stem because your fingers around the bulb of the glass warmed up the wine. I take a sip and avoid looking at the man next to me.

'I was about to ask you how you were feeling about what happened,' he says, 'then I realised you probably wouldn't want to talk about it and I probably wouldn't understand.'

'You're right, you probably wouldn't,' I say after I've swished the wine around my mouth. It's Gavi, slightly tart with a hint of lemon. I only know that because two friends – Angela and Lisa – from my first job educated me on the taste of Gavi when they were on a mission to make me more sophisticated.

The pub is small, intimate, with splashes of bright colour breaking up the cream walls. Hung on the wall above the archway to the back of the pub is a black, metal-framed bike; suspended from the ceiling is a small wooden aeroplane. The bar is ringed with high-legged, multicoloured bar chairs. It's not very busy for a Friday night, and there are seats free in the snug area at the back as well as near the area laid out with table, chairs and eating place-settings. 'Seat?' he asks and nods towards the restaurant-type area.

'Yes, sure, why not?' I reply and move in the opposite direction, to a small table and two leather armchairs. I'm too hungry to sit surrounded by lots of people eating, but I can't eat because that would be committing to spending a longer time than necessary with my daughter's form tutor.

'I'm sorry, I shouldn't have asked about your husband.' He has a smooth tone, it matches his smooth good looks.

'So, how about our babies making babies?' I say in a fake bright voice to change the subject. I don't want to talk about Joel, not with this man.

'Yes, an easier subject,' he says with a smile. 'I knew they were friends, but I didn't realise they were that close.'

'I didn't even know they were friends. This whole thing has served to remind me that I don't know my daughter at all.' *I thought I did, I thought she trusted me, could tell me anything, but apparently not.*

'I thought I knew my son and it turns out, I don't. I didn't know he was . . . I've had "the talk" with him several times. Not only the biology, the stuff about respect, mutual affection and consideration. I've sat him down regularly, even though it's been excruciatingly embarrassing for both of us, and I thought I'd drummed it home to him to always use a condom. For health protection and to prevent pregnancy.' He sighs heavily, wearily. 'I suppose no contraceptive is one hundred per cent effective.'

I toy with whether or not to tell him, to shatter his illusions about his son and how his chats have gone across. I remember that time, two years ago, when I thought the talk I had with Phoebe about personal responsibility had gone in. It'd ended with her begging me not to tell the police what we knew about Joel's murder six months later.

Do I want to visit the same sort of knowledge upon this man? To let him know that you can talk all you want, but if they won't listen they won't listen. Want to? No. Have to? Yes. 'According to your son, you can't get pregnant the first time you do it,' I say. I sound snippy, fuelled a little by the way he and Mr Newton treated me four days ago and yesterday.

Mr Bromsgrove's handsome, chiselled features go through many shades of disbelief and shock, settling in his black-brown eyes. 'He wouldn't say that. He doesn't believe that. Is that why . . . ? No, I don't believe he'd say that.'

'You don't have to believe something to say it if it'll get you what you want. Do I really have to spell that out to a man of your age?'

'I don't believe my son would do that.'

'Oooooo-Kaaayyyy,' I say, stringing those two syllables out after they've been doused heavily in sarcasm.

'I'll wring his scrawny little neck.'

'You mean you haven't already?'

'Awww, I can't . . . Do you have any idea what Phoebe plans to do?'

'I was going to ask you that question, since she seems to talk to you and pretty much anyone else on Earth apart from me.'

My entire body jumps when he rests his hand on my hand. His hand swamps mine and I stare at it, surprised. The whorls of his knuckles are dark, the skin on the back of his hands a gorgeous, delicate hazelnut-brown colour. My hand below his is very different – permanently marked, scarred and blemished, something I tend to keep hidden. I wonder if he can feel the ridges in the skin against his palm, if he's curious how I came by them. Most people don't notice but then, few people touch me.

'What does your wife say about all this?' I say, removing my hand from under his.

'My wife,' he says quietly, almost forlornly. His eyes become unfocused and reflective as he says those two words. As suddenly as he slipped into that reverie, he brings himself out of it again: 'Phoebe and Curtis get on so well because they both know what it's like to lose a parent.'

'Oh. I'm sorry,' I say, my apology meant to encompass my earlier sarcasm. Immediately I am uncomfortable because I've forgotten what it's like to have people suddenly excuse your bad behaviour because you're bereaved. How patronising it is to be on the receiving end of undeserved understanding. 'I didn't realise.'

'It was four years ago. Not sudden, but hard on Curtis. When Phoebe came back to school after losing her father, I asked Curtis to keep an eye on her, talk to her because he knew what it was like and was further along the process. They've been good friends ever since, even though he's in the year above. I see them hang out together at school, and I think they saw each other as kindred spirits. Especially when people were gossiping about her at school, he stepped up and protected her.'

I knew about the gossiping, the school kept me informed and I talked to Phoebe about it. According to her, it was fine. It was always fine. It didn't stop me talking to her, trying to help her but, according to her, it never stopped being fine.

'Do they still gossip about her?' I ask, scared of the answer.

'Not about that any more. But it'd be naive to think they won't when they find out about this. People always find out.'

'This is what I hate about all of this. Like last time, we can't hide away, we can't pretend it didn't happen because everyone knows. I don't know if emotionally she can stand it.' I *know* emotionally I can't stand it. 'And there's Zane. It's another thing in his life he has to deal with that he shouldn't.

Sometimes I wonder who exactly "out there" has it in for me.'

'It does feel like that sometimes.'

'Wasn't your wife's death hard on you?'

'I don't understand what you mean.'

'You were very careful to point out how hard it was on Curtis, and it sounded like you weren't bothered either way.'

He blinks at me and without his glasses the up and down fluttering of his eyelashes is quite pronounced. 'Of course I was bothered.'

'But?'

Our gazes meet, stay locked together. He is gauging how much he can tell me. I am wondering why I've asked him that when I wouldn't even entertain anyone asking me the same thing. Had the roles been reversed, I would have walked out by now.

'So, what about our babies making babies?' he says in the same fake bright tone I used earlier. His gaze goes to the bar, mine to the snug area through the archway at the back of the pub.

A pair of eyes are avidly watching me. I'm too far away to see the colour of them, but I know what colour they are. I've looked into them enough times over the years, I've stood beside the man whose eyes they are so many times over the years I could easily describe his face without looking.

Fynn. He is staring at me. Of course he's seen me in a bar with a good-looking man. Of course he's seen said good-looking man cover my hand with his. Of course he thinks I am on a date.

I want to smile at him, to maybe wave him over, but I do

neither of these, I simply stare until he redirects his gaze to the person opposite him and I know from the way he holds himself, the way his face is rigidly directed towards his companion, that he will not look at me again for as long as I am sitting there.

'I'm sorry, I can't be here,' I say to Mr Bromsgrove and gather into my arms my bag from beside us on the table and my jacket from over the back of the chair. 'I can't be here.'

Alarmed, his eyes wide in confusion, he says, 'But we haven't—'

'I'm sorry, I'm sorry, I just can't be here.'

My body can't move fast enough. I can't escape fast enough. I can feel the lingering trace of Fynn's gaze burning into me – accusing me of cheating on Joel; denouncing me as a false widow; condemning me for being out in a pub instead of at home grieving.

The worst part of that, of course, as I run-walk my way towards home, is that I know it's not true. Fynn wouldn't think that. He was probably surprised to see me out with someone when I hadn't asked him to babysit; probably confused why I didn't smile and call him over.

The sickness that is twisting up my stomach as it churns itself round and round is from *me* thinking that. Because, above the sickness, blossoming in my chest like a maturing flower, is the sure and certain knowledge that I'm attracted to Mr Bromsgrove.

XV

11 years before *That Day* (March, 2000)

'Do you promise you won't laugh at me?' he said.

'Of course I won't. When, apart from about your Klingon DNA showing in your forehead, have I ever laughed at you?'

As usual, he laughed and pressed his fingers against his forehead. 'I do not have a big forehead,' he proclaimed when he had confirmed his forehead was normal sized.

'I know you don't. I'm sorry, go on, what was it you wanted to tell me?'

'For years and years I've wanted to write a cookbook.'

'I can so see you doing that. You should absolutely do it.'

'For honestly, real?'

'Yes. What sort of cookbook?'

'Well, this is the bit you might laugh at because it may sound a bit stupid and airy-fairy, but I want to make it about the foods that I love. Each recipe will have at least one ingredient that I absolutely love or means something to me. What do you think?'

'I think that's brilliant. I'd love to make stuff from a book that is all about food someone loves and means something to them. All the flavours they love.'

'And it wouldn't upset you?'

'No, why would it?'

My husband took my hand and tugged me onto his lap from my place beside him on the sofa. I was the mother of a four-year-old and just pregnant again, which meant I had a lot of emotional reordering and thinking to do in coming to terms with how my body would change, how my life would change again. If I thought about it full on, though, panic billowed up inside and my heart became a speeding train, while my lungs would not expand fully. Joel understood this, sometimes better than I did. 'You know why.'

'No, it won't upset me. It's something you love so it won't upset me. I like to cook. And I'm fine most of the time. It's just sometimes things are difficult. But mostly I'm fine.' I slung my arms around him, pulled back a little to examine his face properly. 'And this idea of yours is brilliant.' I kissed him. 'Because you're brilliant.' Kiss. 'And everything you do is brilliant.' Kiss. Kiss. Kiss.

'I ain't paying you to help me,' he said.

I took my arms away. 'Fine, well you're on your own then, ain't ya?' I said and put on a toddler-like grump that caused his syrupy laugh to erupt and fill the room. I closed my eyes and the sound of happiness, of my life working out, soothed some of the panic inside.

XVI

Ding-dong! echoes through our otherwise empty house. As usual, I toy for a second with leaving it unanswered, with not inviting whatever is on the other side of the door inside. I often wonder what would have happened *that day* if I hadn't answered the door – if they hadn't been able to tell me their news. Would it still have been true? Would I still have him? Or would they have hunted me down all over Brighton – the world – to tell me, to change my life?

The man at the door could not be more unwelcome if he tried. After last night, as punishment for what I admitted to myself, I read the rest of the letter. It spiralled me back to that time like the other night, but I was prepared for it and I braced myself as much as I could. When it wasn't as sudden, brutal and unexpected as the other night, it didn't precipitate as much mental, emotional and physical trauma as before. It still upended me in many ways. And the letter that was sitting on the mat when I came back last night is unread. It is tucked away with the first one because even I don't need that much punishment.

The words of the original letter, although not as potent as when I first read them, are wrapped around my memories of that time like a red bow, the showy outer binding of something I'd rather keep shoved away in an unexplored corner of my mind and never brought out into the light. That is why I do not want this man here, he has made me confront something I do not want to acknowledge.

'Hello,' he says.

'Hello,' I reply. I want to be cold and glacial, but it seems out of reach, like something on a high shelf I've shoved that little bit too far back so I can't get at it any more, not even on tiptoes.

'My name is Lewis Bromsgrove and I am your daughter's form tutor at St Allison. I am also the parent of the boy who got your daughter pregnant. I would like to talk to you, if that's possible?'

'Yes, it is possible.' Lewis. His first name is Lewis. I don't think I knew that. Or maybe I did, maybe I overheard it in the playground and didn't register it in any meaningful way at the time because he was nothing to me. Or maybe he told me it during the last year or so and I've missed it like I've missed so much else.

'I'm not quite sure what happened in the pub,' Lewis says gently when we enter the kitchen. 'But I thought it best that I came over so we could have a sensible conversation about the situation.' I notice he has gone to the furthest part of the kitchen away from me, while I stand near the door, beside the cupboard where I keep my notebook of recipes, fussing. I pick up my notebook, I put it down. I force it open flat against the white marble, flick through the pages without seeing a single word that is written down. I pick up the notebook, hold it closer to my face, maybe I can read if I hold it nearer.

Eventually I toss the hardcover book, covered in pictures of crystal butterflies, bought for me by Phoebe and Zane for last year's Mother's Day, onto the side and stare into space for a moment. *I think I'll make stuffed cherry bomb peppers for dinner*, I decide. *I have feta, I have cherry bomb peppers, I have basil, I have chilli flakes. I will make them for dinner. Maybe with grilled sardines. No, Zane will hate that. Maybe with home-made pizza and salad. Yes, that'll work. Stuffed cherry bomb peppers, pizza, salad.*

'Are you listening to me, Saffron?' Lewis asks, barging his way into my thoughts. 'If I may call you Saffron.'

My heart is fluttery, unsettled and agitated. It doesn't feel like it is beating properly in my chest. And my breathing is far too shallow, probably because of the odd, staccato, stop-start of my heart.

'You may,' I say. I'm trying to concentrate on something else but he's still getting through. If I focus on something other than him, I may not throw him out and the sickness may not come spilling out of me.

'Did you hear what else I said?'

'Yes,' I say.

He fills the gap between us with a deep inhalation of breath. Frustration. 'Have I done something wrong?' he eventually asks.

Yes. Of course you have. How can you not know that? 'No.'

'If you're sure . . . Anyway, I talked to Curtis, he said first of all that he didn't say that to her. When I asked if he was calling Phoebe a liar on top of everything else, he admitted it. I can't believe he's been that stupid.'

'Stupid,' I echo.

151

'If it's OK with you,' Lewis says, 'I'd like Curtis to come to Phoebe's next doctor's appointment.'

'Why?'

'He needs to go through it as much as he can. He can't carry the baby or give birth, but I want him to know what it's like to have to arrange his life around appointments and scans and so on, like her.'

My fussing stops and I focus on the man in front of me properly for the first time. It happens again: the sudden, almost wholly unwelcome, awareness that he is male. Maybe it's the set of his lip, possibly it's the way he stands tall in his frame, or the way his dark, almost black eyes, highlighted now he is without his glasses, are concentrated on me. He is male, he is here, he is causing all sorts of pleasurably unsettling feelings to spiral outwards through me from the centre of my chest.

'What if she doesn't want to go through with the pregnancy?'

'I'm guessing she'll have at least one appointment for that, too, so I'd like him to go to that. And go with her on the day. As much as is possible, I don't want him to be protected from any of what Phoebe's got to go through. He needs to know what it's like, especially if he's not going to go off and do the same thing all over again.'

'You're serious, aren't you?'

'Yes. I've seen this many times before and I've always thought that boys get off too lightly in these sorts of situations. It becomes the girl's "problem" and the boys are often protected from the reality of it. That's why I tried to drum it into him to always take precautions . . . Clearly my lectures fell on deaf ears. Maybe going through this process won't.'

'Yeah, maybe.'

'Where is Phoebe? And your other child, Zane?'

'They've taken their great aunt out to the shops. That was a while ago, and if you met her, you'd understand why I'm very nervous at the moment. No doubt there'll be somebody on my doorstep complaining about her – *them* – at some point soon.'

I've told him we're alone in the house. My body floods with heat, embarrassment and unexpected, irrational desire. In desperation for something else to do, to look at, I glance down at my hands, something that will sober me up from the intoxicating feelings caused by being around Lewis. Looking at my hands always grounds me: my nails are neat and short, barely crescents above the tops of my fingers; the skin is smooth over a network of pronounced veins because I regularly rub moisturiser into them; but my knuckles are rough and scarred from past times when I haven't taken care of them properly, when I didn't give a second thought to my hands and how they would show up my regular lack of care and attention for myself.

'How is Phoebe holding up?' Lewis asks in another attempt to end the silence, break through my barrier. 'Is she any further along with the decision-making process?'

I flex my hands, promise myself to take care of them before I turn away from Lewis and refocus on the butterfly-covered notebook that holds the secrets to my cooking life. The secrets to my current life, really. Before Monday, before my trip to the school that changed everything, my life had become about cooking: making, baking, creating. I return to Lewis. 'When I said last night that she doesn't talk to me, did you think I was exaggerating or lying?'

The sideways glance and clearing of his throat is all the answer I need.

'I wasn't lying. She doesn't talk to me. My daughter has been through a horrible ordeal in her recent past and that means I have to be careful with her in everything I do and say because I do not want to further traumatise her. So, she doesn't talk to me and I don't push her.'

'What about you? How are you bearing up after the trauma?'

'I don't know,' I admit. 'But in relation to this, at least I know who the father is.' As it has done several times a day since Thursday, how Curtis touched Phoebe plays across my mind: he was cautious, almost reverential in the way he put his arm around her; like he wasn't used to it, like he'd dreamed of it, but hadn't done it very often. Something doesn't ring true, here. It's been niggling and nibbling at my mind since I saw them together. The words fit, but the way they were with each other makes me wonder if he's really the one. Also, someone who convinces a girl she can't get pregnant first time wouldn't have the almost worshipful respect Curtis has for Phoebe, nor would he come forward and confess so easily – boys who lie and manipulate are the types of cowards who hide every which way they can. On so many levels I don't believe Curtis is the father, but why would they both lie?

'If you ever want to talk . . .' Lewis says.

'Thank you. But in case you hadn't worked it out yet, Phoebe's non-talking nature was inherited from someone and her dad was the most open man on Earth.'

Mr Bromsgrove's gaze flits over to the picture of Joel, Phoebe and Zane, reclining on the box seat in our beach hut, that is stuck under a seagull magnet on the front of our silver fridge. Another picture I haven't seen in an age, even though I look directly at it every day, several times a day on my way to and from the fridge.

The Joel I know lives in the spaces of my heart, I carry him in my head; he is all around me and completely inside me. I don't need to see the pictures to know what he looks like, I don't need to close my eyes to conjure him up. He's there. The impression of him, the imprints he made on my life are always there.

'I've made you sad,' Mr Bromsgrove says. 'I didn't mean to.'

'I'm always sad,' I reply. 'I'm simply better at hiding it sometimes.'

'I understand that.'

The air around us is instantly thick and syrupy with something, the thing we shared before I fled last night: *potential*. Something could happen. Something might happen.

Slice the tops off the cherry bomb peppers. Scoop out the middle, making sure to remove all the seeds. In a bowl, mix feta, basil, chilli flakes and olive oil. Ah, olive oil. 'I don't have any olive oil,' I say aloud.

'Is that code for something?'

'I was going to make feta-stuffed cherry bomb peppers for dinner but I don't have olive oil. I forgot to buy some the other day. I used the last of it for pesto and was going to buy

155

some and then I was called to the school and, so, I don't have olive oil.'

'You cook a lot, then?'

'No. I mean, yes. But this is all new stuff. The gourmet stuff was Joel's area of expertise. I guess I'm following in his footsteps. Before he . . . He started writing a cookbook. Just for fun, he wasn't going to get it published or anything. I want to finish it. I'd planned to have it printed up professionally for him as a present once he'd finished it but he never . . . I want to finish it for him. For me and for him. So I've been experimenting with flavours and ideas, trying stuff out really. This feta recipe is a new favourite . . . What was I saying about not being one for talking?'

'I think it's great,' he grins. His smile, which changes the shape of his face, makes me suck in air and avert my eyes. 'The idea of finishing the cookbook and the talking. I especially like the talking.'

'Charmer.'

'Do you have a name for the book?'

'We came up with a title together. The Flavours of . . .' The word hitches itself in my throat, hooked into place by embarrassment. Lewis Bromsgrove waits patiently for me to complete my sentence. The word love shouldn't be uttered in front of one such as him. It's indecent, wrong.

'The Flavours of . . . ?' he encourages.

'Ah, nothing. Don't know why I even brought it up. And it's not as if I've got much time on my hands at the moment, what with my aunt, well, Joel's aunt, moving in and Zane and Phoebe and work. Nah, it's not going to happen.'

I haven't talked about Joel so much in an age. I am using my husband, right now. I am building a barricade around myself; a barrier between me and this man who kept invading my thoughts last night in between the replays in my head of the letter.

Ding-dong of the doorbell brings a new relief. I almost run to the door, throwing it open, hoping for someone trying to sell me something so I will not be alone with this man.

Fynn.

It couldn't be someone from the Church of the Latter Day Saints, it couldn't be someone offering to wash my car, it couldn't be the postman with a delivery – all of whom I would have dragged in for a chat – it has to be Joel's best friend. Who saw me out last night with the man in my kitchen.

'Hi.' He grins at me as he usually does.

'Hi,' I reply. My heart's staccato beat is erratic now, it's also deafening in my ears.

'Am I coming in?' he asks.

'Oh yes, of course, of course. I was just in the kitchen.' Although he's texted almost every day asking how Phoebe is and how I am coping, I haven't updated him on finding out who the father is.

Well trained in entering what is practically his second home, he kicks off his black leather Converse shoes, hangs up his grey hooded jacket.

'So, I'm at a bit of a loose end for dinner tonight and wondered what you were up to?' he says with a sideways grin.

'Would you like to stay for dinner, Fynn?' I ask.

'*Really?*' he says in an exaggerated manner. 'That's so kind of you. I hope I won't be imposing too much.'

'You've the cheek of a baboon,' I say. This joviality is going to last until the end of my corridor, until we step over the threshold of the kitchen.

'Aww, but all the charm of a . . . Actually, what is the most charming animal?' he asks as he crosses from the honey-gold wood of the corridor into the white-tiled kitchen. He doesn't get very far into the room, doesn't even make it as far as the stain before he stops when he sees who is standing there.

'Snake?' Lewis Bromsgrove offers, as though he's been a part of our conversation. 'Or are they the animals that need charming?'

'Snakes are reptiles,' Fynn states, staring Lewis down with the sort of disdainful correction Zane would make.

'True enough.'

'Fynn, this is Lewis Bromsgrove – the father of the boy responsible for, well, what's going on with Phoebe. Lewis, this is Fynn McStone, he was my husband's best friend since they were eighteen and obviously became mine as well.'

Their handshake is firm, short, unfriendly, as if they'd rather punch each other instead. Fynn has always been protective of me, but in the last eighteen months he's been shielding me as much as he can from what can and does go wrong. Without him and Imogen, I would have completely broken down, unable to function because I was frozen with shock; stupefied into inertia. When I needed him to, Fynn stepped in and did what needed doing.

Lewis's problem is that he fancies me. It's arrogant to think

158

that, but it's not a simple case of fancying me because he thinks I'm beautiful or amazing, nor has he fallen in love at first sight; he believes I'm fragile. He fancies me as a delicate little flower, partially crushed by the loss of her husband who needs help and nurturing to reanimate her petals. He fancies himself as the reanimator, the person who will help me get over this. Fynn's appearance, his familiarity and ease with me has Lewis on the back foot – I am not alone, I am not isolated, I have adult support . . . in the shape of a rather good-looking man, too.

'I'll get off,' Lewis says, pushing himself upright so he is no longer leaning back against the worktop. They're the same height and that seems to perturb the pair of them – one of them was hoping they'd be physically superior to the other. 'I'll call you about the appointments,' Lewis says to me.

'Yes, yes, do that,' I say, eager for this to end.

'Fynn, good to meet you.'

'Yeah, right.' At the front door, Lewis lingers, reluctant to actually do the leaving part. 'Take care of yourself.'

'You, too,' I reply.

He openly examines my face, his brown-black eyes almost hypnotic as he does so. 'When I first met you, I assumed you didn't have a clue about anything, despite knowing what had happened with your husband,' he says. 'I secretly thought I was so much more enlightened than you but the same thing's happened to me. Guess I got a reality check, didn't I?'

I nod. I'm supposed to make him feel better, to tell him that I had been a lesser parent, and he had done the best by his son and it was unfortunate, that's all, that we'd both ended up in the same place. I'm supposed to add that we'd work together to make this right. Unfortunately for Lewis's sensibilities, that isn't going to happen.

'Bye then,' he says, disappointed I haven't slipped my fingers into the hand he has been holding out, I haven't committed myself to him because of the circumstances we find ourselves in.

'Bye.' I grin at him and shut the door, pushing him away and out.

'What was that?' Fynn asks the moment I re-enter the kitchen.

'What was what?' I say.

'You and *him*.' He spits out the word that refers to Lewis Bromsgrove like it is dark, yellowy-green infected phlegm. 'He was holding your hand last night and today . . . What's going on, Saff?'

'Phoebe is pregnant. She will not speak to me. For some reason, she speaks to him and she speaks to his son, the boy who got her pregnant. I am trying to find out what I can in any way that I can. That is what is going on.' *Did I decide what I'd make for dinner? Carrots? Maybe I'll make something with carrots. I have two bags of them in the fridge. Maybe I'll add butternut squash, ginger and apple, and make a soup. Joel liked soup. He loved that soup.* 'And he wasn't holding my hand last night, he touched me for some reason and I'm sure you saw that I took my hand away.' *Do I have ginger?* I move towards the fridge and, without seeing the photos I'm staring right at, I open the door, pull out the clear plastic drawer to the salad crisper. I went shopping on Monday, when I didn't realise until I was making pesto how low I was on olive oil, so the vegetable drawer is quite full with various coloured items, some in plastic wrappers, others in brown paper bags, others au naturel, and it takes a couple of goes to open it fully.

'There is obviously tension between the two of you, beyond all this Phoebe stuff,' Fynn persists.

'If you say so, Fynn. But I can't help but wonder if you'd be like this about any man I talk to because he's not Joel.'

'You were not just talking to him.'

Celery . . . tomatoes . . . carrots . . . cucumber . . . rocket . . . carrots again . . . three-pack of peppers . . . lemons . . . ginger. I have ginger. But no butternut squash. *When did I use butternut squash?* I'm ignoring Fynn. It's the only way sometimes. When he gets a bee in his bonnet about something, I ignore him, allow him to ramble on until he runs out of steam.

I remove chicken pieces from the meat drawer, then remove a full head of garlic from the bottom shelf. *No, I don't know what to make with that.* I return them to their places in the fridge. *I'll think of something.* I take them out again. I do this several times and when I shut the fridge, without the chicken or garlic, Fynn is standing right behind it, close enough to make me start.

He's let his hair grow in the past year or so, and it falls in dark, haphazard curls all over his head and around his face. It's his face I focus on now. He has a straight nose, defined cheekbones, gentle eyes, and a beautiful mouth. I know what that mouth is going to say and I wish more than anything it wouldn't. I wish he wouldn't. I wish he would let it go.

'Are we ever going to talk about what happened between us?' is what he says.

I knew this day would come, it had to, of course. But, sometimes I manage to convince myself that it didn't happen so there'll never be a need to have this conversation. Sometimes it seems like the most ludicrous idea that I – *we* – could ever have done such a thing. Sometimes I remember it all and I think I'm going to die of shame.

'I never ever want to talk about that,' is what I say to him.

His navy blue eyes stay linked to mine. 'We're going to have to, though, aren't we?'

Yes, I think at him as I slowly nod my head, *we are*.

Sometimes, I wish I could go back and unmake all the mistakes I've made since *that day* – this would be the first one I erase.

XVII

6 months after *That Day* (April, 2012)

'I don't know what to do with myself any more,' I said to Fynn. 'I've been so focused on getting through the last months with the admin, budgeting for every penny, the funeral, the inquest, and making sure Phoebe and Zane are as OK as they can be, that I haven't had a chance to stop and think.

'Now I've stopped, there's this emptiness inside, and I keep expecting it to be filled up again. For me to roll over in bed and to see him there and realise that it was some terrible mistake. I wouldn't even mind going through all that stuff if it meant I'd be told it was a mistake at the end of it. Do you understand what I mean?'

In the darkness of my bedroom, Fynn looked over at me from his place kneeling up on the brown leather love seat in the bay window and nodded. 'I know I said it gets easier, and it does. Not sure when, but ... Oh I don't know what to say,' he admitted. 'I talk, I hear words coming out of my mouth, at the funeral, for example, I knew I was talking to people and they weren't turning their backs on me or trying to punch me, so what I said couldn't have been terrible, but now, I don't remember what I said. It was all words to fill the space. Like what I was saying just then, they were words to fill a space where a person used to be. None of them can, though. And none of it is meaningful enough to ease your suffering.'

'You're suffering, too.'

'Please don't do that,' he begged. 'Please don't diminish what you're feeling to think about me or anyone else. Unfortunately, there's enough grief to go around. Don't try to comfort someone else at your expense.'

'You're not just "someone else".'

We peered through the wooden slats of the blinds at the outside world. Joel always liked to keep the blinds open, I always liked to shut them. Whenever he wasn't around or if I went to bed first, I would shut them. Since *that day*, I'd left them open. Just like I'd continued to sleep on my side of the bed, not properly close the lid of the toothpaste (even though it used to drive me disproportionately wild when he did it) and place the TV remotes on the floor by his side of the bed. It's not been a concerted effort to do it like he did, it's more a need to keep as many things as possible how they used to be. My life wasn't bad before so there's no need to change it.

The dark orange-brick houses opposite were in darkness, but the orange-yellow glow from the street lamp still illuminated them. Light pollution blotted out some of the stars above the houses, washing out the bright pinpricks and casting the night sky as a shimmering navy grey instead of a deep, endless black.

Joel and I used to kneel like this sometimes, staring out into the night, talking. We'd talk in bed, too, but sometimes, even after sex, kneeling in the dark, spying on the outside world felt like we were in a time machine and we'd been sent back to a shared childhood where we snuck out of bed and stared into the night.

When nothing moved or stirred outside, I returned my gaze to Fynn. He looked how I felt: exhausted; like the drip, drip, drip of grief was slowly wearing him away. The last few months had scored deep, grey trenches under his eyes, had ploughed furrows into his forehead and had shed so much of his weight he looked fragile.

'You look so tired,' I stated.

'It's always nice to get updates from the talking mirror,' he replied, a grin not far from his lips.

'Ouch, I deserved that.'

'Yes, you did. But you're right, I'm tired, you're tired, I'll do the decent thing and go. Or I can stay downstairs on the sofa if you want.' He used to do that, in the early days. When I was still wandering around the kitchen in circles, unsure what to do, what to think, what to feel. I would wake up every half an hour and come down to the kitchen, searching for something, looking for something, never finding it. I think it was Joel I was looking for and I knew I wouldn't find him, but that nagging feeling wouldn't go away. Fynn would let me walk for a few minutes, then would come in from the living room, would take me by the hand and would lead me back to my makeshift bed on the love seat in the bedroom. I'd slept there because I was terrified of losing his smell on the sheets, on his pillow, on the duvet. If I didn't sleep in the bed all the time, I would be able to climb in whenever I wanted and would be greeted with the smell of Joel, I'd be transported to where he was. At that time, I wasn't ready to accept he was gone, but I was even less ready to do anything to destroy something precious he had left behind.

'No, no, those days are over. But it is a good idea if we both get some sleep.'

'Night,' he whispered at the bedroom door, about to open it and not wanting to wake Phoebe and Zane.

I went to reply to him, to murmur my own goodnight, but my voice stopped working. Closed over, plugged up with a sudden thick and heavy sadness. I couldn't get another word out. I could just about breathe, but I could not speak. Fynn turned back to me, concerned. His fingers slipped away from the handle . . . and I desperately wanted him to stay. 'Are you OK?' he asked, still whispering.

Unable to speak, I found another way to communicate what I was thinking. It wasn't a coherent thought, something I'd formulated and considered, it was an urge. I stood on tip-toes and pressed my mouth against his for a long moment. He immediately jerked his head away.

Like modelling clay in the hands of an expert, the thought was quickly taking shape, becoming more certain and clear in my mind, but I couldn't voice it; the words wouldn't find their way out of my throat, through my mouth, into the world. But I could speak without words. I could tell him I wanted – needed – him to stay without saying a thing.

I did it again: I pushed my mouth onto his, wanting a reaction. Again he pulled back, but didn't jerk away his head this time, simply moved it. The lines of his face, partially hidden by the darkness of the room, struggled with something. Probably confusion. I was confused, too. Confused, uncertain, scared.

Terrified.

Terrified of his reaction beyond confusion. Would he scream at me that I had lost my mind? I wanted him to, because I had. Would he push me away and leave as fast as he could, making it clear he'd never come back here again? I longed for him to react like that, too. Or, would he do what I needed him to? Would he lock the door, would he then extend his trembling arm and uncertainly slide his fingers into the dark curls at the nape of my neck and pull me towards him as he lowered his head and returned the kiss?

I'd cried.

I'd cried and cried, when I was alone, when I had nothing else to fill my time, fill my mind, I cried and cried to try to set myself free. Yet, I remained where I had been. I was still chained to this precipice of pain, high up above the world I used to live in, no way to climb down, no chance of releasing myself. I was chained here, like Prometheus in Greek legend, who every day was cursed to experience the same horror of watching his liver pecked out – I was fated to experience the same horror of having my heart plucked out when I remembered every morning Joel was gone. I had cried and cried to liberate myself and I was still trapped. Maybe there was another way.

I trembled too as I reached out to open his trousers. My fingers felt large, clumsy, as I tried to release the buttons of his jeans from their holes. Still kissing me, his fingers came down and moved mine aside to open his flies. He reached for the bottom of my T-shirt and we broke apart for him to pull it up over my head. I tugged his T-shirt up as far as I could before he took over and removed it himself. The T-shirt ruffled the dark brown strands of his messy hair. We came together again and I audibly gasped. Skin against skin. My body, which had felt cold and barely alive, suddenly felt reanimated, wanted, *loved* at the touch of skin against mine.

We half-fell, half-climbed onto the bed; my clumsy, paddle-like fingers urgently trying to pull his jeans over his hips. I wanted more skin-to-skin contact, I wanted all of me to be reminded of what it was like to feel alive again. I'd been living all this time but this made me *feel* alive, my body actually experiencing something.

Fynn used both hands to pull my lower half garments to my thighs and then he was off the bed, standing back to finish taking off his trousers and underpants, while I wriggled and dragged my way out of my grey joggers and black knickers.

The heat of his body, his skin, which pulsed with reminders of what it meant to be alive, was back on mine, and I held him close as his kisses grew firmer. I dug my fingers into his back, into his bum, urging him on, encouraging him to push inside me, to show me in another way what it felt like to be alive.

We moved together, each thrust a delicious blend of pain and indescribable pleasure, each arch of my back an incredible mixture of profound agony and ecstasy. I dug my fingers into his back, whimpering against his lips, encouraging him to move faster, harder, bringing us closer to orgasm; to the sweet emptying feeling of freedom and release.

I wanted emptiness, to purge my body of all the locked-in feelings of grief I'd been force-fed. I wanted to feel my body again, to be in control of it, of something in this world of anarchy I'd been thrown into. My body, what happened to it, was the only thing I had any authority over, and doing this meant I was in total control, I was in charge of what happened. Fynn began to move even faster, harder until I froze as I reached the peak of the build-up, then my body shuddered as waves of pure, undiluted bliss rippled through me. Fynn continued to move fast and hard until he broke away from our kiss, buried his head in my neck and, groaning, he orgasmed with several short thrusts.

Neither of us moved for several seconds and the room felt unnaturally stilted after what we'd done.

Eventually, he placed his hands on either side of me on the bed and lifted himself up until we were apart. His dark blue eyes stared down at me and I stared back up at him. Like an image appearing on developer-submerged photo paper, regret began to take over Fynn's face: faint at first, merely a shimmer, then a slow, stain-like progression that became more defined and solid until it was clear and real. His breathing matched mine: deep but fast; the physical expression of our confusion.

He waited for me to speak. I waited for him to speak. One of us had to say something. After more silence he lifted himself completely off me, and collapsed back onto the bed, unintentionally wedging himself between my body and the foot of the ornate wooden bedstead. Like mine, his breathing slowed as we both stared up at the ceiling. The silence rolled on, neither of us willing to name what we had done by speaking of it. I turned to him but did not try to catch his eye. It was safe here, it was my side of the bed, the side by the door, and it was at the very foot of the bed, which was usually piled up with clothes I hadn't hung up, or hadn't chucked into the laundry basket, so we weren't anywhere near where Joel and I had been this intimate, or even had slept beside each other – there was no danger of blotting out Joel by what I'd just done here.

I curled into Fynn's body, relishing the feel of his skin against mine again. That had been the best part, the warm reminder of what being alive was about. I moved my arm across his body, resting my head on his shoulder, and I closed my eyes. I let go. I wasn't pretending he was Joel. Not now, and not back when we did what we did. I was being in the moment.

And I was doing something that I'd begun to crave: I was having sex. I was ashamed to admit it, but in the midst of it all, I missed sex. It'd been very few weeks, not many days, hardly a blip in the number of hours I was going to have to spend without Joel, but I still missed this. Joel had always been willing, and I'd unintentionally taken that for granted. Having a good sex life with the man I loved had become as usual to me as having a glass of wine – there whenever I wanted it.

Now a lot of the other stuff had been dealt with and what I was staring into was the abyss of a new existence without him, I realised this physicality of life was something I missed. I wanted sex. And I couldn't tell anyone that because they wouldn't understand. They'd think it awful of me to even be considering such a thing after losing the love of my life. I thought it awful of me to be craving such a thing after losing the love of my life, but my body had wanted this, it'd needed this. It'd been yearning for skin-to-skin contact, it'd been longing for the ability to move against another person, it'd been dying to be released.

Fynn's arms cautiously encircled me, as if worried about holding me, then more confidently they came together, tightening until he enveloped me in a secure embrace. With Fynn's arms around me, with the constant beat of his heart against my body, I let go of this reality and drifted away into sleep.

Hours later, I woke up to find Fynn standing on the other side of the room, rolling his grey T-shirt down his once-taut torso. Now he was thinner, his body diminished by the loss of his best friend. He glanced up, saw I was awake and managed an awkward, self-conscious half-smile that was doused in remorse and shame, as he finished buttoning up his jeans. He headed towards the door in bare feet, the sinews of his toes sinking into the deep pile of the carpet. I thought I might speak then: might utter a 'bye', or 'I'm sorry', or even, 'thank you'. Anything. But nothing would come out, there was nothing to say that would mean anything.

As he pulled the door shut after him, he raised his hand briefly in a half-hearted wave. *Don't come back*, I said in my head at him as he negotiated the creaky floorboards and stairs to the front door. *We can never do that again.*

*

In the present, I've decided on carrot, ginger and apple soup. I'll oven-bake some herb-crusted strips of chicken and I'll nip out while it cooks to get some crusty bread. And olive oil. I'll have to fry the onion and spices in butter, though.

I've peeled the carrots in silence even though Fynn is standing right beside me. Now I am cutting up the carrots in the same noiseless atmosphere, with him so close I can feel the heat from his body.

Joel spent many hours teaching me how to slice carrots properly. I was meant to plant the tip of my blade into the chopping board, then to move the carrot along while bringing the knife up and down. 'Almost like you're feeding James Bond through a guillotine,' he'd said. 'Up and down, chop, chop, chop.'

6 months after *That Day* (April, 2012)

The next night, at one o'clock, Fynn sent me

•

in an otherwise blank text. I opened the door to him and we were hushed but quick as we moved upstairs. The kids knew Fynn came over at all hours, they knew we sat in my bedroom talking at all hours, they were used to finding him sleeping on the sofa downstairs, but this was different, for this it felt necessary to sneak around.

The bed was off limits, this time the floor. No words, no speaking. The door secured, clothes cast aside, mouths locked onto each other, movements fluid and natural, the powerful, freeing release at the end. And then calmness that allowed me to sleep. Curled up in his arms, drained for a little while of all the horror and sadness and pain. He left without speaking at five. As he left, I knew it couldn't happen again.

On the fifteenth night, when we'd done it every preceding night since that first one, everything changed. Fynn ignored me urging him to get on with it, instead, after a few long, deep kisses, he held himself above me for a few seconds, capturing my gaze with his. I understood immediately what he was going to do and the fear of that bolted through me.

He broke eye contact and lowered his head to tenderly place a kiss at the base of my throat. Slowly, adoringly, he kissed a soft path from my throat to my navel, setting me alight with every gentle touch of his lips against my skin. As he reached my belly button, he retraced his trail of kisses up my body again until he reached my chest. His gaze flicked briefly up to my face before he took my left nipple in his mouth, sucking and licking it until my nipple was pleasurably, painfully erect.

Instead of stopping him, as I knew I should, I writhed beneath him, encouraged him, as he moved to the right nipple, and worked on that until it was as hard and sensitive as the left. As I gasped silently, relishing the sensations I thought I'd never feel again, he kissed another gentle path down my body, moving lower and lower until his mouth was between my legs. Another inaudible sharp intake of breath from me as he gripped my hips. He held me in place and his tongue immediately began to explore me. Each touch flooded me with what felt like a mini-orgasm, each movement against him drenched me with an exquisite agony until I could feel the approaching rush of bliss that would come with the final release. As it rose through me, he pulled back, took the orgasm away, and instead brought his face level to mine and pushed into me. At the same time he cupped my face with his hand and his thumb stroked across my cheek in time with every slow, precise thrust into me while his gaze held mine.

He was creating intimacy. We'd been intimate, but this was intimacy; closeness and desire – an emotional manifestation of what we were doing. I didn't want that. I didn't want intimacy, nor for him to fall in love with me, which was where doing it like this could lead. I wasn't capable of falling in love with him. I was already in love. The man I loved had left me, yes, but that didn't stop me from loving him; from knowing in the deepest recesses of my heart that it was all a big mistake and he'd somehow find his way back to me. My body and mind craved release and relief, but not love. With my memories of Joel, I had no shortage of that kind of love.

Fynn and I continued to move as one, our bodies in perfect time, our eyes visually locked until we came together; our orgasms shuddering smooth, gentle ripples of euphoria through us and into each other.

Afterwards, he was even more gentle: kissed the top of my head, briefly nuzzled his face against mine, and fell asleep stroking my shoulder. Once his breathing regulated, told me he was drifting in DreamLand, I opened my eyes. Listening to him sleep, I stared into the dark. I had to say something. Before he went home, I had to tell him we couldn't do it again. Not if it was going to be filled with intimacy.

He affectionately stroked my cheek before he left and

I didn't find the courage to say anything before he walked out.

Come back, I silently called at him. *I want to do it again.*

Fynn leans against the worktop, right beside me, his arms folded across his broad chest. He's watching my every move as he waits for me to start this conversation that I never want to have. Even if I did want to have it, where would I start? Frustrated with him, angry at myself, I slam the carrot I have picked up from the colander down on the wooden chopping board. The *thwack* it makes reverberates around the room. Fynn doesn't react, doesn't even flinch. He's going to wait for as long as it takes.

7 months after *That Day* (May, 2012)

'It's Uncle Fynn,' Phoebe said as she returned to the table after answering the door. After three days of ignoring his middle-of-the-night '.' texts, Fynn hadn't contacted me at all in two weeks. I missed him. I ached for him to be back in my life. Everything felt off-kilter without him, but I knew if I didn't take a step back, we'd end up somewhere even more painful.

I'd also had my period in that time, which had been a timely reminder of how reckless I'd been, the risk we'd been taking, another problem I could have added to my list because we hadn't used anything. Joel had a vasectomy six months after Zane was born so I hadn't had to think about contraception in years. In those two weeks with Fynn, during the day, I hadn't allowed my mind to go anywhere near what I did at night, it was a room shut off from my everyday world, and at night when he was with me, all I thought about was the miracle of having the ability to feel again, the release of orgasming and the relief of being able to sleep afterwards. It'd been so irresponsible. The bright red streak on the toilet paper had reminded me of that. '*Dodged that bullet, huh?*' as Joel would have said.

'It didn't even occur to me that it'd be dinner time,' Fynn said. I hadn't heard his voice in a month, I realised. It was such a lovely sound, even and deep and so very kind.

'It's not, usually, is it?' Phoebe said and returned to her seat at the table. 'Usually we've eaten by now and we're doing homework.' She was making a point that I hadn't got myself together quickly enough for her that evening.

'Dinner's a bit late today,' I explained, while not looking at him. 'Don't know why, really, it just is. It's my version of jollof rice with chicken, we've enough if you want some?'

'You sure?' Fynn asked, still by the door.

'Of course.'

'So, Unc,' Zane said. He pulled out the chair next to him, a place for his uncle to sit. 'What you been up to? Ain't seen you for a while.'

Fynn sat in the proffered chair and I dished up the tomato-red grains of rice, studded with pieces of chicken, peas, green beans, carrots and sweetcorn onto the plate I'd got out for myself and placed it in front of him. Instead of sitting down to eat, I began to clean up the kitchen because I had, for some reason, lost my appetite.

Later, Fynn called, 'Thanks for dinner, Saff, I'll see ya' to me on his way out. He'd gone up with Zane to take him through his bedtime routine and had obviously stayed until Zane fell asleep. He'd returned to the kitchen to ruffle Phoebe's hair as she sat watching television – and she'd moved her head in their usual affectionate 'gerroff' shorthand – but he waited until he was at the door to say goodbye to me.

I threw down the tea towel I was using to dry up and dashed to the door. I caught up with him before he stepped out.

'It's been nice to see you,' I offered as an olive branch to check that after my moment of madness which had cast us out into a dangerous flood, we were all right again, we were back on dry land. Our friendship could go back to being safe and grounded.

His face softened, his mouth turning upwards, the creases around his eyes deepening as he nodded and grinned. I'd almost forgotten the warmth that radiated from a genuine, easy Fynn smile. 'Yeah, you too. I'll see ya.'

'I'll see ya.'

The craziness was definitely over with because I'd found a better way of coping, another way to ease the pain and anguish that wouldn't drag in one of the people I loved most in this world, damaging and hurting him in the process.

'I don't want to talk about this,' I admit to Fynn. 'Can't we leave it? I have far too many things happening right now to deal with this.'

'Really? Well, it looked like you were more than able to deal with getting all cosy with your new friend, there.'

'It's not like that, I told you.'

'I don't believe you.'

'Are you calling me a liar?'

'I'm calling you deeply in denial.'

I drop the knife and the carrot, and face him properly. 'Look,' I say. 'Look, what happened . . .'

'I get it,' he says, 'I know what happened was just—'

'Sex,' I say at the same time as he says, 'Grief.'

Fynn draws back, his face bathed in shock. '*Sex?*' he repeats.

I nod.

I can't tell him everything, that it wasn't only 'just sex', because I can't have this conversation right now. There are lots of things I don't want to talk about and most of them do me the courtesy of staying locked away in the box I have tucked them into. If they do escape, try to become seen by the light, I go through the ritual, the stuffing away so that I can function. Fynn isn't allowing that to happen.

'You mean it could have been with anyone?' he asks, bewildered.

'I didn't say that.'

'But that's what you meant.'

'No, no, that's not what I meant at all. I don't know how to talk about this with you. I was impulsive, stupid – not you, you're not stupid, it was. I was. I think I wanted, I mean, I know I wanted se— I trusted you. I trust you. It was safe to—' Everything I say sounds wrong. I can't explain it to him without telling him the rest of it, *all* of it.

Fynn takes several steps away from me until he is in front of the kitchen table. 'I thought it was shared grief. We'd both lost someone we loved so much and I thought what we were doing was sharing that. But it was only sex to you?' He rubs anxiously at the area of his forehead above his right eyebrow. 'Be honest with me, Saff, do you feel anything except friendship for me?'

'You sound like you're dismissing friendship as unimportant. You know it takes a lot more to be a proper friend than a lover.'

'Answer the question, please.'

'This isn't the time to talk about this, Fynn. There's so much going on, we can't talk about this and anything good come from it.'

'I'll take that as a no then.'

'I didn't say that. Don't put words or feelings into my mouth.'

He stares at some point over my shoulder. 'I don't even know what I was thinking. It's not as if we were ever . . . I'm a fuckwit, aren't I?'

'Don't talk about yourself like that. And it's not true.'

'I'd better go.'

'Go? What about dinner? The kids?'

As if my talking about them has summoned them, the front door yawns open and the corridor is alive with the sounds of Zane, Phoebe and Aunty Betty chattering about what havoc they have wreaked in Brighton.

'Who do we know that wears shoes like these?' Zane calls.

'I don't know,' Phoebe says as loudly as her brother.

'Probably someone who wanted to be a racing driver,' Zane laughs.

Fynn stares at me as he desperately tries to pull himself together, tries to mask his pain and shock so he can be normal with them.

'Oh yes,' Phoebe adds, 'that's right, he had to give it all up because he couldn't hack it.'

'Oi!' Fynn says. He sticks his head out the kitchen door and I know he has pasted on a grin. 'I could hack it, thank you, they couldn't hack me showing them up.' A pause. Then: 'Oh my word! Is that Aunty Betty? I knew I felt a sudden influx of beauty into the general Brighton area, I should have guessed why.'

'My darling Fynn,' Aunty Betty drawls. 'It's been far too long.'

'What, since two weeks ago?' he replies with a laugh.

Two weeks?

'Aunty Betty's living with us now,' Zane explains, happily.

'Oh is she now?'

'Yeah, she got thrown out for doing something *bad*,' Phoebe says. 'She won't tell us what, even though we've offered her all our pocket money.'

'Wow, that must have been bad,' Fynn agrees. 'Usually you're all for confessing your wrongdoings. And anyway, Elizabeth Mackleroy, it's a good thing I came here today, isn't it? You weren't going to tell me you'd moved, were you? You would have let me go all the way up there to see you to find you were gone.'

If I thought I couldn't feel any worse before, I was wrong: the shame and the guilt return, this time as a huge, towering wall of emotion that collapses over me, almost completely burying me in the process. Fynn has been quietly, conscientiously, visiting Aunty Betty in Joel's place.

Fynn lurks by the kitchen door because from here they can't see how much of an effort he's making to sound normal, to be normal.

I hate myself for this. I hate myself for starting the madness.

'OK,' I shout. 'You all need to be washing your hands and coming out of the corridor.'

The three of them grumble as they kick off shoes, hang up jackets and generally reintegrate themselves into the house. While they do this, I tug Fynn back into the kitchen.

'Please stay for dinner,' I beg quietly. 'We can talk afterwards, when everyone's in bed. Properly.'

He won't look at me; his gaze flits around various points of the kitchen but avoids me directly. 'No,' he says firmly. 'I need to go. I've got a lot to think about.'

'Please, Fynn? Let's not leave it like this, you're my best friend.'

Now he looks, turns his agony-laden eyes on me. 'And you're mine. Which is why I know you'll understand that I need to go right now. I can't stay here. Will you cover for me with the others?'

I nod. 'Course. We'll talk again soon, though, yeah?'

He gives a short nod but doesn't speak. I don't like it when Fynn doesn't speak. It means nothing good.

'Why didn't Uncle Fynn stay for dinner?' Zane asks as I sit on the end of his bed, chatting to him before sleep.

'He had something to do he'd forgotten about,' I reply.

'Do you think he misses Dad as much as we do?' Zane asks.

I'm hijacked by the question. Zane rarely talked about his dad in terms of people missing him. It was always to ask what I thought his dad would say about something, what he might think, if he'd laugh about something. Even those questions were few and far between, as though asking them would admit to himself as well as me that he was starting to forget. That every day moved us further away from his dad and nearer to a time when he couldn't predict or even accurately guess what his dad would do in any given situation.

I try to help keep Joel alive and present by behaving how Joel would, by reacting as much as possible in the calm, considered way that their dad would, but I get it wrong sometimes. I get it wrong a lot of the time. This question is new, though. Unexpected.

'Yes, he does. Uncle Fynn knew your dad for a long time, even before me, so yeah, I think he misses him.'

'Do you think Dad misses us? And Uncle Fynn? And Aunty Betty? And Granny and Grandpa, and Grandma and Granddad?'

Joel. Joel found it easy, necessary even, to surround himself with others. He had such a capacity to be with people, to spend time with them, enjoy them for who they were, no matter how different they were to the people he knew or to who he was. That's why I hope he's not alone, where he is. I hope he's surrounded by people, even if they aren't the ones he loves.

'Yes, I think he does.'

'I think so, too,' Zane says. 'And that's what Uncle Fynn said when I asked him. He said Dad loved to be surrounded by people but even if he had lots of friends in Heaven or wherever he was, Dad would still miss us.'

That's the sort of answer Joel would have given, of course. I don't know what Lewis would say in that situation, but I do know what Joel would say. What Fynn did say.

I think of Fynn while I wait for my son to fall asleep and my heart aches with the echoes of all the things I want to say to him.

V

Saffron.

This is a genuine question: how is it that you can still function? I mentioned it before but I am truly interested in how you can carry on. I know I can't.

When I lost him my life ended, nothing was ever the same.

It seems nothing has changed for you, really? You still go to work every day, you still hug and kiss your children, you sleep with the blinds open as if you have nothing to hide. Is that blue World Cup 2006 T-shirt you sleep in his? I see it every time you go past your bedroom window with your hair all piled up on top of your head brushing your teeth. See? It's things like that – you can fix your hair for bed and you can brush your teeth. I found it almost impossible to do those things for so long and struggle with them now.

It's just, it seems like you're playing a role? Do you understand what I mean? I'm not trying to upset you, because you do look the part of a grieving widow, with your hair like that, the lack of make-up, and wearing your late husband's clothes. But it's all look and no substance.

I'm genuine when I say I'm not trying to upset you, but I thought you might like to know how you come across to the outside world. And how it comes across to the world is that it's a front and you're not really grieving.

I mean, you even went out to a pub on Friday night. You had two gentleman callers at your house today when you were all alone. That's not how widows behave.

I'm not behaving like that, I'm not really sure you should be, either. If you truly loved him with all your heart, like I did, you wouldn't be behaving like that.

I didn't mean to give so much away or to start to let you know what our friendship was truly about, so I'd better end here.

Just think about it, will you? Think about how you're coming across to the outside world. And if you find you don't care that much, maybe you should think about how much you really loved him. Because, me? I would have done anything to be with him. Anything.

A

XVIII

13 months before *That Day* (September, 2010)

'And you really, really don't mind standing there in your frilly apron making tiny little macaroons?' I asked him.

'No, course not, why would I?' Joel looked down at his dark grey T-shirt which showed off the sleek build of his arms, and navy blue Levi's even though he was standing in front of the floor-length bathroom mirror. 'What're you saying, Ffrony? Is there something wrong with men making macaroons?'

I had my head stuck around the bathroom door to talk to him while he got ready for his first lesson at Sea Your Plate, the cookery course I'd bought him for Christmas. It was a year-long set of lessons that would help him learn about many different types of cooking and their techniques. He was so excited he'd come home early from work to get ready.

He turned away from the mirror, treating me to a full view of him. He was dressed and ready, but had been in the bathroom working on his hair, in other words, gently oiling and twisting the ends of the black mini-dreads all over his head. My husband was a lovely man, but when it came to his hair, he had a streak of vanity a mile wide.

'Oh no, no, no,' I replied, 'there is nothing wrong at all with *men* making macaroons. Just you,' I said with a giggle.

'You with your big hands making all those teeny tiny delicate—'

'Come here,' he said, snatching out to grab me. I was too quick, twisted my body away and ran for our bedroom at the end of the hall.

Phoebe, who was downstairs in the living room, was probably rolling her eyes and tutting loudly, while Zane wouldn't even raise his eyes from the book he was poring over.

'I said come here,' Joel laughed coming up behind me as I shrieked and giggled in the entrance to our bedroom. His arms linked around me and he pulled me close to him while kicking the door shut behind him. 'Now, you were saying . . . ?'

'I was saying . . . something about macaroons.'

'Yes, macaroons,' he said with a huge grin. His kiss was gentle at first, a brief touching of lips before deepening and lengthening, our tongues meeting in the middle.

'Macaroons,' I said, breaking away. 'I like that word.'

'Me too.'

'I think it'll be a good code word.'

'We need code words now?' he asked. He pressed his divine lips together to suppress a laugh.

I ran my hands up over his chest, linked them behind his head. 'No. Yes. Maybe. Imagine it, the next time we're sitting in your parents' house I can say, "These are lovely macaroons, Mrs Mackleroy, did you make them yourself?" You won't be able to contain yourself.'

'My mum's never made macaroons in her life. I don't think she's even given them to us, come to think of it.'

'My goodness, details, details.'

'And I don't want to think about sex when I'm around my parents.'

'Well, there is that.'

'Babes, you are all right with me doing this, aren't you?' He was serious, quiet and concerned.

'Of course,' I replied, blithely. 'I wouldn't have got you the lessons if I wasn't sure.'

'It doesn't feel weird or nothing like that, though?' he said, pushing his point, trying to uncover what was truly inside. Of course it was weird, everything was weird sometimes. But I knew he had to do this, he'd love doing it and it would take him one step closer to actually writing his cookbook. The drawers in our kitchen, the mantelpiece in our bedroom, the various surfaces around the house were filled with his sheets of paper, scrawled on with his ideas for recipes. Some of them were simply sketches of how he wanted the final dish to look. He had many, many ideas but maybe these classes would help him to focus.

'Does it feel weird that my big, burly husband with the deep voice and the *fine* hair, and high-powered job is going to be spending the evening in a frilly apron learning to make macaroons? Nah, course not.'

'I'm not making macaroons. They're really hard to make, just so you know. They take years to perfect.'

'What are you making?'

'Don't change the subject, Ffrony.'

'Sorry,' I said, chastised. 'I'm more than fine with you doing this. It'll be fun. I got you the lessons because I know how much you love to cook. And what makes you happy makes me happy, if I can say that without sounding too pathetic. You know I'm a lot better with all of that. It's fine. It's all fine.'

'I hope so. Because if there's any doubt at all in your mind about me doing it, I won't,' he said.

'You better, mate, those lessons cost a fortune!'

'All right.'

'Although you're not allowed to fall in love with any of those domestic-goddess types on the course, OK? No matter how gorgeous or thin or clever they are, remind yourself that you've got a wife at home who loves you. And that she's the very same wife who'll go proper mental if you take up with another woman.'

His fingers slipped into the curls at my nape as he leant forwards and kissed me. 'So, do you think we've got any time to make some macaroons before I have to head off?' he said, mischievously.

'You can macaroon off,' I said. 'Especially with your children sitting downstairs.'

His laugh resonated throughout the room. I closed my eyes for a second, and indulged myself in the happy moment I found myself in. I didn't realise, of course, that this was where it all started to go wrong. I was too happy, had relaxed too much. And losing Joel was my punishment for that.

XIX

The number '1' flashes on the LCD screen of my telephone answering system.

I hate messages on the house phone. It's never anything good and I won't be able to steel myself for the voice I hear, nor the news it'll deliver. At least on my mobile I can screen, I know who is going to be leaving me messages. After Joel died, the big faceless 'press' somehow found out our home number even though we'd always been ex-directory, and kept ringing. Our house was silent apart from the ringing of the phone. We would sit around not being able to speak, and then the phone would ring and I wouldn't know whether to answer it in case it was someone who knew Joel who'd just heard the news, someone who hadn't heard the news and needed to be told, or if it was someone wanting me to tell them about the real Joel Mack-el-roy.

In the end I unplugged it, and only plugged it in again six months later when I'd changed our number.

It still spikes a little anxiety, though, when I see a message on the answering system because I don't know who it is. I push the triangle button and give myself up to the whim of whoever decided they needed to speak to me.

'Hello, Saffron, Phoebe and Zane.' My stomach flips, seconds before my heart is drenched in ice-cold water. This always happens when I hear her voice. 'I hope you are all well,' she says. 'We'd like to speak to you and possibly arrange a visit in the not too distant future. It feels like we haven't seen you all for a long time. Do please return this call at your earliest convenience. Goodbye.'

My finger heads straight for the delete button and I take a little satisfaction in knowing that I can easily erase her voice – and therefore her unwelcome presence from my house. I can't hate her because she's Joel's mother, but I can maintain my very healthy dislike for her.

15 years before *That Day* (August, 1996)

'It's such a pleasure to meet you,' I said to Mr and Mrs Mackleroy as we sat at a circular table in an upmarket Central London restaurant.

Joel had been very specific about *not* going to their house for this first-time meeting. He said it was because they were extremely house-proud and rarely invited people over, especially ones they didn't know very well, but the truth was obvious: in a restaurant there was a finite time we could be together. Joel was telling me by how he arranged the meeting that his Aunty Betty – who I'd met seven months earlier after being with him for five months – was right: his parents were going to hate me.

I concentrated on not fiddling with the white cotton napkin on my lap, with not reaching out to straighten my cutlery, nor making sure my plate was positioned equidistant to the knives and the forks on either side of my place-setting. I'd already seen the almost imperceptible synchronised hitch of their eyebrows when they arrived ten minutes early at Brown's, a large restaurant in Covent Garden in London that I'd been to before on client dinners, and saw that we were already there. It was like they were hoping we'd be late or even on time so there'd be something to dislike me for straight away.

Restaurants and eating out with people I didn't know already made me nervous. Eating with people who I wanted to impress brought added, deeper angst that I couldn't explain to Joel without unnecessarily complicating things. He wouldn't understand that there was a catalogue of things that could go wrong constantly running through my mind: dropping food on myself, knocking a wine glass over (not that I was going to drink and give them the impression of being an alkie), pronouncing something wrong when I'd been pronouncing it perfectly for years, tripping up a waiter, eating too much so they thought I was a glutton, eating too little so they thought I was anorexic.

I was already working at a disadvantage – I'd dieted for the last fortnight to fit into the perfect navy blue shift dress with a daisy belt I'd bought for the occasion. I hadn't managed it – it still wouldn't zip up smoothly, it was snug across my chest and tight enough around the hips for it to ride up the second I sat down. Instead, I'd had to settle for my pink skirt and red cardigan with my brown belt that gave me the impression of a waist. Joel had said I looked incredible, but I wasn't sure it was going to be good enough for the potential in-laws, especially when I was starting at a loss *and* we were going to be spending time in my idea of Hell.

'Joel talks incessantly about you,' said the beautifully turned out Mrs Mackleroy. Her hair was straightened and set on big rollers to create large curls that framed her apple-shaped face. She had amazingly clear, coffee-brown skin and cat-like eyes. She wore no make-up except plum-coloured lipstick, and her navy blue suit, which I suspected was Chanel, fitted her curvy frame like it had been made for her. She was perfect-looking, and brilliant at avoiding any pleasantries about it being nice to meet me, too, while firmly fixing into the air above our table that most of what her son said about me was inane and unimportant – and that I was likely to live up to that reputation.

'That's cos she's perfect,' Joel said. He immediately slipped his hand around mine, a reminder that I was important. 'She's my favourite subject.'

'Speaking of subjects, did you know that Joel could have read at Cambridge?' Mr Mackleroy said. He came with a serious air sitting on his shoulders, his black hair was threaded with wiry curls of silver-grey, his mahogany-brown skin was lined but not overly so for a man of his age. He had dark, brooding eyes that I had noticed seemed to be relentlessly on the lookout for something to visually dissect to reveal its imperfections. He too wore a suit, a labelled one, but I wasn't sure which one.

'Yes, I did know that,' I said with a bright smile and my hand tightened around Joel's, unsure for the moment which one of us needed the comfort. It was still a sore point for them that with his opportunities, Joel opted to have a year out partying by the sea then go on to study product design at Brighton University. His parents had seen academia for their son, he hadn't. 'Isn't it brilliant?'

'Where did you attend university?' Mr Mackleroy asked.

'Dad,' Joel interrupted, 'there's no need to go into that – we haven't even looked at the menu properly.'

'Am I to infer from the way my son has sprung to your defence that you didn't attend university?'

I desperately wanted to be good enough for them, I wanted them to like me because I loved their son so much it was hard to breathe sometimes. We'd talked about getting married, we'd discussed trying for a baby – I needed them to like me so they wouldn't stand in our way. I didn't want them to keep looking for ways to disapprove of me. If I got this out of the way, then maybe we'd have a fighting chance, Joel and I. I looked at Joel and he grinned at me, willing me on, telling me that my answer didn't matter because he'd always love me no matter what. It did matter, though, it really did. I didn't go to Oxford, I didn't go to Cambridge, I was never going to be up to their standards or good enough for their son. Accepting that wasn't easy, but it was something I had to do.

I faced them, my judges; the people who stood between me and the man I loved. 'Erm, no, no, I didn't,' I replied, unable to meet their eye.

Dismay dawned through Joel, I could see it on his face from the corner of my eye, I could feel it in the way his hand slackened slightly around mine.

My reply had the desired result, though: both of my

potential in-laws relaxed because every single negative, stereotypical thought they'd had about me washed away their tension. I was their worst nightmare, but at least with this knowledge about me they knew how to talk to me, they accepted if I ever got ideas above my station they'd be able to bat me down with some comment about how I wouldn't be able to understand because I hadn't gone to university.

'Please don't do that again,' Joel said sadly to me later. 'I don't care what other people think, not even them.'

In stark contrast to his parents who were chatty and engaging, Joel had been quiet for the rest of the dinner, as had I. He'd been quiet, too, the whole train journey home, even though he held my hand. He hadn't spoken of it until now, until we were cocooned together in his bedroom, our bodies entwined on his double bed.

'But, Joel,' I protested, 'you saw how happy it made them to think that about me. It was easier to pretend—'

'You weren't pretending,' he cut in sternly. 'You lied to them. I don't like lies, Ffrony.'

'Neither do I, but Joel, if I'd told them the truth, that I'd gone to one of the top five universities in the country, they would have spent the rest of our time together trying to find ways to take me down a peg or two. Dinner would have been awful. It was easier that way.'

'I don't care,' he replied. 'Don't do that.'

His parents had been happy and relaxed, jovial and almost welcoming after my lie. In time, I was sure Joel would realise it was the only way, too. Sometimes, a lie is the only way to make things right.

'I won't do it again,' I said. 'Promise.'

If you truly loved him with all your heart, like I did, you wouldn't be behaving like that. The implication of those words from the third letter mix like a poisonous dye in the stagnant water of what Mrs Mackleroy used to say about me, sometimes when I was standing right in front of her.

I stare at the answering system. I wish there was a way I could get the recording back so I can erase it all over again.

Saffron.

Why have you closed the bedroom blinds? You should leave them open. Don't take any notice of what I say.

I'm sorry. I get so het up, it upsets me every day that he's not here and some days are worse than others, which is when I go on the attack. I'm sorry that I've lashed out at you.

You were allowed to see him at the hospital, weren't you? Afterwards? You were allowed to hold and touch him one last time, which must have been so comforting. You organised his funeral. You chose where he was finally laid to rest, you picked out his headstone, and you wrote those words on it. I loved him so much, at least as much as you, and I never got to do any of that.

Do you understand why I say the things I do, sometimes? I feel I've missed out on so much.

Please, you carry on living your life however you want to, you are fine.

XX

'I suppose we can call this our first family meeting of the year.'

'It's our first family meeting, ever,' Phoebe helpfully points out. She's scaled back the outward resentment of me over the past couple of days and I'm not sure if it's because I haven't mentioned the pregnancy since I went out with Mr Bromsgrove or if she doesn't like to talk to me like that in front of Aunty Betty, but I accept it gratefully.

'All right, as I've been so kindly corrected by Phoebe, this is our first family meeting. I would like us to be aware that our new living arrangements mean that we all have to show each other some more consideration and stick to some basic rules.'

'And you're the one making the rules, yes?' Aunty Betty 'helpfully' interjects. She is wearing her shocking pink, bobbed wig today and because of that, everything else about how she's dressed and what colours she's used to make up her face disappears into insignificance.

'I'd say that was a distinct possibility.'

'Is that a yes or no?' Zane asks.

Zane is fresh-faced, his plump cheeks are smooth and dewy, his liquid-mahogany eyes he inherited from his father are clear and bright. He loves having Aunty Betty here, and it's the first time in a while that he isn't constantly showing signs of struggling with his grief.

'It's a yes. Although why I feel guilty saying that I don't know. It's not as if there are any other adults in the house.'

'What about Aunty Betty?' Phoebe asks. I'm surprised she hasn't tried to assert herself into that role.

I regard Aunty Betty, who reclines on the sofa, an e-cigarette holder in her hand with Zane on the floor in front of her, resting his back against the brown leather sofa, and Phoebe on the floor beside her feet. 'Your mother's right, Sweetness, I'm not an adult,' Aunty Betty states.

'As I was saying. I'd like to set some ground rules that we can all stick with.' Over my shoulder, behind me on the mantelpiece is a picture of Joel. I wish I could step into the picture to ask him what I should say and how I should say it. I wish I could fall into a pleasant time pothole and remember the conversation where we agreed how we'd do this. 'I would like us all to clean up after ourselves. I know we usually do, but it's started to slip again and I don't have time to pick up after everyone any more.'

They all seem to agree and nod thoughtfully.

'Next, I am instigating a rule of no mobiles or electronic devices at the kitchen table.'

Uproar. I wait for the protests from my son and daughter to fade away before I continue: 'That used to be the rule and then for some reason it's been lost by the wayside. I want us to enjoy our food, concentrate on what we're eating and take time to enjoy each other's company at mealtimes. Those are the only times of the day we're all together so I don't want you off in CyberLand, Phoebe, and you off in NintendoLand, Zane.'

'Nobody calls it CyberLand,' Phoebe mumbles.

'Wherever it is you go, I want you both to enjoy being with each other and Aunty Betty and me at mealtimes, OK?'

Reluctantly, they nod.

'And one final rule: no smoking in the house.'

Aunty Betty, who has been smugly nodding along to my rules while dragging on her e-cigarette, freezes mid-nod. Zane immediately curls his lips into his mouth to hide the laugh that has built up behind his face, and Phoebe murmurs, 'Ohhhhh, buuurrrnnnneddd' before a loud smirk.

'I don't smoke in the house,' Aunty Betty eventually says. She waves her chrome and ebony holder in my general direction. 'This isn't smoking, it's what we call vaping. No smoke, just vapours. I could get different flavours of vapes if you want.'

'No thank you,' I say. 'Because there's no smoking of any kind in this house. And that includes vapouring or whatever it is you want to call it.'

'But why?' Aunty Betty wails.

'I do not want cigarettes in the house. Or cigars or cigarillos or pipes, before you try to get around it that way. I do not want my children to think that smoking is something I condone because it isn't, OK? If you want to smoke or vapr? Vape? Vaporise? Whatever you call it, then you can inconvenience yourself by taking a trip to the garden.'

'That is so unfair, you know,' Aunty Betty grumbles.

'Yes, it is.'

'What rules will impact upon you, Mum?' Phoebe asks.

'Yes, Mummery,' Zane says, using a nickname for me he hasn't used in at least two years, 'what aren't you allowed to do any more?'

I inhale to the bottom of my lungs, exhale for so long that I'm sure my breath touches the wall on the other side of the room. This is the only way to keep them safe. They won't like what I'm about to tell them, but it's necessary. The woman who killed Joel is seriously stalking me and I have no idea what she is going to do next. I felt intimately violated when I pulled the cords to shut the bedroom blinds when keeping them open was another way I connected to Joel, but she is watching. It's not enough for her to write letters, she has to watch, too. She has to get near enough to notice that I still wear Joel's clothes to sleep in.

I can't have Phoebe or Zane out on the streets until I know what Phoebe is going to do about the pregnancy. Once that is settled, I can talk to her, explain to her that we have to go to the police about what we know and take the wrath of not telling them sooner. Until then, I can't have them exposed, easy pickings for *her* to harm in any way. This is the real reason for the meeting. The other stuff I could have told them about whenever they cropped up, for this I need their undivided attention, I have to underline the seriousness of needing to stick together and doing as I say.

'Lots of things will impact upon me,' I say. 'Like, not coming straight home from work because I have to collect Phoebe from afterschool library homework club and then

Zane from whichever afterschool club he's got on or from Imogen's house.'

'I don't need to go to library homework club,' she protests. 'I'm old enough to come home on my own.'

'I know you are, but you're still going to start homework club. I've already signed you up.'

'But—' Phoebe begins.

'Yes, Phoebe?' I reply. She has no leg to stand on, of course. Not when there is a giant elephant currently sitting in the middle of the room with 'PREGNANT' tattooed in giant letters onto its side, that none of us have forgotten about.

'Nothing!' she snarls and picks up her mobile from the armrest of the sofa and starts to press buttons.

'Ohhhhh, buuurrrrnnnneddd,' Aunty Betty murmurs. She moves to take a drag from the e-cigarette in her hand when she spots my questioning, arched left eyebrow, and stops.

'Child, you really are the fun police, aren't you?' she says.

'And proud,' I say, through the sudden pain that has pleated itself across my chest.

In our house if an adult was going to say no at some point, it would be me. Joel would actually call me the fun police when my foot would hit the ground in relation to him as well as the kids (usually about him buying some unnecessary gadget for the kitchen – who seriously *needs* a bean cutter?).

Without a word or look to each other, even though they've both been catapulted back to a time before *that day*, Phoebe and Zane stare at the photo over my shoulder. It's obvious that the memories of how we used to be are swirling around their hearts, too.

Saffron.

Are you OK?

You seemed so sad on your way to work this morning. Or are you feeling a bit jumpy? I saw you looking around before you got into your car with the children. Were you possibly trying to see if you could spot me? There's no point trying because you can't.

Please don't worry about me being around. Think of me as your guardian angel or something – I'm always there, but you can't see me.

Don't worry, OK? It'll all be fine. Really it will.

A

XXI

My phone beeps with a text and

•

is the message that comes up under Fynn's name.

It's one o'clock Tuesday morning. I'm not even close to going to sleep, but do I want this? It's been a year, things have moved on, and after the conversation in the kitchen on Saturday and his ignoring my 'how are you?' texts, I thought he didn't want to see me at all, let alone be up for this.

I stare at my phone. I want to see him, talk to him, to make things right. But if he thinks . . . Surely he can't believe we'd do it again after all this time?

In one move, I throw back the covers and climb out of bed. I struggle into Joel's large, V-neck Arran jumper, take the purple silk sleep scarf off my head. My heart is back to fluttering out its wild staccato beat, compressing my lungs as it does so. I inhale and exhale in regular bursts, trying to placate myself as I quietly descend the stairs and head to the front door, mobile phone in hand.

He grins at me when I open the door to him, relieved that I've answered, I think, but makes no move to come in. 'Hi,' he says simply.

'Hi,' I reply, confused and wary.

'I know it's late, but I was hoping you'd come for a walk with me. We don't have to go far, I know the kids are asleep, but I'd really like to talk to you away from the house, if that's all right?'

My answer is a hesitant silence. *Well, at least he doesn't want sex*, is my first thought. Swiftly followed by: *Maybe that'd be easier because when we had sex we didn't talk, and when we talked it ruined things.*

I'm not sure I should leave the house in case that woman is out there. But she wouldn't be. Not at this time. When would she have the chance to sleep?

'If anything happens I'm sure Aunty Betty will cope until we come back,' Fynn reasons. 'I promise, we won't go far.'

I reach into my coat pocket hanging on the row of hooks by the door and retrieve my bunch of house keys, before sliding my feet into my trainers. I have to wriggle my feet about before they'll go in and the backs pop up over my heels.

The air is cool, there are no clouds in the dark sky, and the light pollution isn't as potent tonight so I can see the halo of stars that circle the Earth. I probably should have put on my coat, I'm not that warm, but I don't want to go back for it and prolong this any longer.

On the pavement side of the gate, he holds out his hand, and cautiously, I slip mine into his. Again, he grins in relief as we start to walk down the road. Our hands feel comfortable together, they fit, like our bodies had fitted. He runs his thumb gently and affectionately over the back of my hand. Our bodies had fitted like that, too: gently, affectionately.

The road I live on is narrow, hard to navigate when there

are cars parked on both sides, and it seems smaller, more compact being out here at night. A fox darts out from a house across the road and disappears down the narrow walkway along the side of the house next to ours. I'll have to tell Zane about that, he'll be very excited: we thought that all the foxes had gone from this road because in all the nights we'd sat up waiting to see them, we'd been disappointed. We'd guessed they'd moved on, had got on with their lives as we're all supposed to, but they haven't. Or maybe they did, maybe they tried to move on and found that where they landed wasn't right for them and they had to run as fast as they could back to where they had come from.

'I had a sister,' Fynn says when we are six houses down from mine.

'Do you mean "had" like I *had* a husband?'

'Yes, I mean, "had" like that.'

'Oh, I'm sorry. I never knew that. Joel never mentioned her.'

'Joel didn't mention her because he didn't know. She died before I met him. We don't really talk about her in my family. It's too painful.'

'God, I'm sorry.'

'Thanks, it was a long time ago now.' That was Fynn's sadness, what he used to carry around with him like a heavy burden. That was why he knew the pain didn't go away, it simply got easier to live with, to slot in beside the rest of your life, allowing you to continue around it. 'I don't talk about her at all,' he says, 'but I think about her every day. When Joel . . . A lot of those feelings came flooding back.'

'How . . . I mean, was she killed, too?'

'I sometimes think so. She was nineteen and she died of heart failure. That's what the death certificate said and that's what we say if we ever talk about it. But, you know, we *never* talk about it in our family. It's the subject that dare not say its name because Nell actually died of anorexia.'

'I don't understand.'

'She was anorexic from about thirteen, I think . . . I can't be sure because I was a bit younger than her – but the constant not eating and over-exercising, as well as everything else she was doing because she was in the grip of it was too much for her heart.'

My fingers come closer to his, holding him secure like he used to hold me a year ago when we fell asleep tangled up with each other. 'That's awful.'

'Yeah, it is. It was and it still is. I blame myself because I could see what was going on, but I didn't say anything. I literally let her waste away.'

'What could you have done? You were, what—?'

'Fifteen.'

'Fifteen. How could you have helped?'

'I could have told her that I was there. That I understood, even though I didn't. That would have been better than following my parents' lead and ignoring it. I sometimes wonder if what she was doing was a way of screaming at us for attention, for us to notice her.'

'Sometimes it's hard to confront the things that are right in front of you. Like Phoebe and me and what I suspect was her desperate need to be loved which has resulted in her being pregnant at fourteen.' The fear of that rushes up through my body, making me light-headed as the memory hits my brain. My daughter is fourteen and she is pregnant.

'It's OK, it's OK.' He tugs me nearer by taking our linked hands and pressing them to his chest. He changes his mind and takes me in his arms, holds me near enough for me to feel the rhythm of his heart against my chest. 'I'm awake half the night thinking about what to do for the best, so I'm guessing you don't sleep at all with the worry.'

'Not really, no.' If only he knew what else I had to worry about.

'It's going to be OK, Saff. You're going to sort it all out. I know you will.' We haven't hugged, or even touched like this, since before that time. We'd got back on track, had been able to pretend none of it had happened, except in how we were with each other, physically. Physically, there was an unspoken but acknowledged barrier between us that neither of us would breach. Now that it has been, my body relaxes, almost falls completely into the familiarity of being held by him.

He lets me go, hanging onto my shoulders for a second longer than necessary before he takes my hand again and we start to walk. Once we fall into our pace again, our foot-steps like a double-beating heart in the quiet of the night, he barely waits a second before he says, 'Saff, I've fallen in love with you.'

I snatch in a sharp breath, and my step falters but he keeps walking and because our hands are linked, I have to keep moving with him.

'I don't want you to say anything,' he adds quickly. 'I know it's one-sided and I'm going to have to deal with it. I just can't deal with it and be around you. Especially not if I have to see you and that Lewis character together.'

'I'm not—'

'Yes, you are. OK? Whether you want to admit it or not, you are. There's something between the two of you and I don't want to watch it. Not when I'm so . . . I didn't even realise that's how I felt until I saw you with him and it was like all these feelings were suddenly unlocked. And I had no idea until now, really, that I've been hoping that maybe we'd, I don't know, get together properly, settle down, maybe even have a baby – even though we're both getting on. I don't know . . . I've really shocked myself.'

'Fynn—'

'No, don't speak. All that's irrelevant at this moment. Look, the main reason I wanted to talk tonight was to apologise because I've not been a very good friend to you.'

My feet stop, I stop, refusing to move, forcing him to halt, too. 'What are you talking about? You've been the best friend anyone could ask for.'

'No, I haven't and I'm really sorry that I can't make up for that by sticking around.'

'Fynn, you're my best friend. I couldn't have made it through the last eighteen months without you.'

'No, a good friend – a true friend – would have confronted you by now about your eating disorder.'

I try to rip my hand away from his, but he won't let me. He clings onto me and faces me full on for the first time since I opened the door.

212

'What are you talking about?' I ask when it's clear he won't let me unlink from him.

'I don't think it's purely anorexia, I suspect it's more bulimia. Or even a combination of the two, but it doesn't matter. I haven't been upfront with you about it. I've suspected for a long time. It wasn't until you said that what happened with us was just sex that I realised what it was really about. You were trying to deal with the pain in that way, weren't you? You used to do it with food and then you started to do it with sex. That's why you stopped it when I was getting emotional rather than keeping it purely physical.'

I manage to tear my hand away from him, finally. Freeing myself from being joined to such nonsense. I stand back a little distance, glaring.

'Tell me I'm wrong,' he goads.

'You're wrong. You're absolutely wrong. Look at me.' I hold out my arms – my body is large and lumpy, misshapen and decidedly flabby even without the jumper. 'If I had an eating disorder wouldn't I be thin?'

'You are thin.'

'I am not thin. You've seen me naked, you know I'm not thin.'

'*You are thin.* And you don't eat.'

'I do eat. I eat all the time.'

'No, you don't, Saff. You cook, but you never taste any of it. The times I've been there for dinner you give me your portion, or you say you'll eat later. If and when you eat, it's alone away from people. And I doubt very much you keep it down.'

'Well excuse me if I've lost my appetite a little since my husband died.'

'Look at your hands, Saff. They're beautiful apart from the scars on the backs of your knuckles from—'

My hands. The one part of me that always lets me down. That's why he held my hand, why he stroked across my knuckles – not out of affection but to check up on me, to see if there were remnants from what he thought I did. I tuck my hands out of sight, under the crooks of my elbows when I fold my arms across my chest. 'Please stop this. It's nonsense, you know it is.'

Fynn pauses, regards me for several, uneasy seconds. 'I'm doing this all wrong. I shouldn't have blurted it out like that. I'm sorry. I should have said I'm your friend. I love you. I don't understand what you're going through, but I want to help, I want to understand and be there for you. I should have said that it's all going to be OK. That you will be all right if you get help and it'll all work out if you're honest with yourself, honest with someone else, if you find someone you can talk to freely. I should have said there are lots of places that you can—'

'I'm sorry about your sister,' I interrupt, 'and I know what that sort of thing can do to someone and that you start to see the same thing everywhere, in everyone that you meet, but I do not have an eating disorder.'

'There are lots of places that you can go to for help,' he continues as if I haven't spoken. 'I should have said, please get help. Go to your doctor, look online, call a helpline. Reach out to someone, Saff. No one can take that first step for you but they can help you with every other step after that. I should have said, please, *please* get some help before . . . Your children don't need to lose another parent, all right?'

I can't believe he has done this. I can't believe he has scuttled away from the conversation the other day and come up with this. This *nonsense*.

Fynn stares at me, challenges me to tell him he's wrong again.

When I have pushed down my disbelief and shock enough to talk, I say, 'OK, because I don't have feelings for you, because I didn't have to be in love to have sex with you, and doing it with you obviously wasn't a life-changing experience for me, this is how you get me back, is it?' As I speak, he slowly folds his arms across his body, tilts his head slightly to one side but says nothing. 'Because I put a stop to it, and I'm obviously not rushing to do it again, and because it's never even occurred to me to think about having another child, let alone with you, *this* is how you hurt me? This is how you put me in my place? By implying I'm a bad mother, by hinting that I've got some deep problem that will lead to me killing myself and abandoning my already bereaved and traumatised children?

'I really can't believe this. I never thought you'd stoop so low. It was just sex, Fynn. You have one-night stands and flings all the time. Why did it have to be different with me? Why did you have to make it into something it isn't and so end up with us like this?'

Fynn has pasted a neutral look on his face, aloof, unbothered, nonchalant. But I know he is hurt, that what I've said has slashed at a deep part of him. Well good. Because he's hurt me too. By saying all that to me, by accusing me of . . . he hurt me too and he hurt me first.

We have the words we've spoken to damage each other hanging like a thorn-covered veil between us and for long minutes it seems that neither of us is brave enough to breach the gap, to try to sweep it aside.

'It's a good thing we're not going to see each other any more, don't you think?' he eventually says with a sigh and unfolds his arms. 'Before I go, I have to do this.' From the pocket of his grey fleece hoodie, he produces a set of three small padlock keys on a flimsy wire ring that someone would probably spend years promising themselves to replace with a proper keyring. He tries to disguise how severely he is shaking when he reaches out, takes my hand then drops the small, shard-like pieces of metal into my upturned palm. 'These are yours.'

'What are they?' I ask, even though it is obvious what they are.

'The keys to your beach hut. I bought it. I couldn't let you sell it – not when it meant so much to you and Joel and the kids. I kept waiting for the right time to give it back to you, but then it was Christmas, it was the funeral, it was his birthday, it was a year since he died. There was never the right time because it would have added to the pain, brought it all back when you all seemed to be getting yourselves to a better place. But, since I'm not going to be around any more, it's time. Here's your beach hut back. You'll have to register it with the Seafront Office and with the council, but I've already told them you're the new owner so it's yours again.'

'Fynn—'

'Don't say anything, Saff. There really is nothing left to say. I'm going to go. I'm . . . I'm simply going to go.'

'Please don't go like this. Please.' I breathe deeply, to stop the tears, to control the erratic cadence of my heart. 'Please.' The air will not fill my lungs, it will not soothe the mercurial stampede in my chest. 'I'm sorry . . . I'm . . . sorry . . .' I'm hyperventilating. I need to calm down but I can't. If I stop long enough to compose myself, he'll walk away. 'We . . . we can't leave it like this—'

'Take care of yourself,' he says, talking over me.

In desperation, I touch him, on his shoulder, to hold him here, keep him in sight until we can talk. He shrugs me off as if my touch has burned him.

'Take care,' he gasps with tears in his voice.

He puts his head down and starts off up the road. This is why he wanted to take a stroll in the middle of the night, so he could leave, walk away, without doors or walls to hinder him.

'Fynn, please,' I call after him in the fragments between ragged breaths. 'I'm sorry . . . Please. I'm sorry . . . Please. Please. Please. *Please.*'

I silently begged all the way to the hospital *that day*. I begged as I stood in the cold mortuary with a sheet covering the face of a body in front of me. I begged as I went home and with my fingers around the hands of both my children I said to them the words I never even imagined I'd have to find. I begged as the words sank into their minds and they both began to disintegrate even though I was trying to gather them up, draw them to me and keep them safe.

I've begged every day for eighteen months.

This is what I always beg: *Please, please, please don't let this be happening. Please, please, please don't let this be real.*

VI

XXII

6 months before *That Day* **(April, 2011)**

'Ffrony, I'm going to have to quit Sea Your Plate.'

'What, why?' I asked him. I sat up on my knees in bed, watched my husband walk frantically around our bedroom, his body tense, his eyes wild with worry. He sat on the bed, leapt up too agitated to rest, marched over to the brown leather love seat in the bay window, perched on the edge, then jumped up again. He came to the bed, and started the process all over again.

Usually, after a cooking lesson, he fizzed with excitement, would bounce on the bed and take me through the class minute by (sometimes tedious) minute, as he explained the techniques he'd learnt, the flavour combinations he'd experimented with, the people he talked to. Aside from that, he was rarely like this – he was usually rational and clear-minded in how he dealt with problems. I could count in single figures the amount of times he'd been this unnerved.

'It's really humiliating,' he eventually said. He stopped moving and faced me seconds before his embarrassment visibly shuddered through him. 'There's this woman. Audra, remember I mentioned her? The one who asked me if I'd work on a cookbook with her?'

I nodded. He'd mentioned her, and it'd sounded from the way he mentioned her that she fancied him. He couldn't see it, of course. He was way too nice. Blinkered. There was no way I'd ask someone I barely knew, who was potentially a rival, to work on a cookbook idea I'd had if I wasn't after him. It was a book of quick and easy meals that hadn't sounded amazing or unique, but Joel had been enthusiastic for her and I'd said nothing about her clearly being after him.

'Yes.' I sat back in bed and waited to hear the inevitable.

He experienced another moment of mortification quivering through his body, then stalked back and forth across the room again. 'Tonight, we finished class a little early so she suggested we go for a drink to talk about her cookbook, discuss where she's got up to and what I think of what she's done so far. And . . .' He stopped, tensed himself as humiliation trilled through him again. 'She tried to kiss me.'

'Oh.' Inside, of course, I was shouting *I knew she fancied you!* while simultaneously wondering how I could find out her address to go tell her to keep her lips to herself.

'I told her, straight out, that I wasn't interested. That even if I wasn't married I'd not be interested. I've texted the cooking teacher and told him that I can't work with her any more. But on the way home I thought it all through and realised it'd be easier if I quit altogether. She's going to be so embarrassed. There'll be an atmosphere and that's not good when there's only ten of us.'

'*She's* going to be embarrassed? What about you? I can't believe the cheek of her. Didn't she see your wedding ring?'

'Yeah. And it's not like I haven't talked about you and the kids and showed her pictures.'

He climbed onto the bed, grabbed hold of my hands. 'I swear to you, Ffrony,' he said, 'I didn't kiss her back or anything. I just got the hell out of there . . . after I made a total show of her and me.'

'Why, what did you say to her?'

'It's a bit of a blur because I was so panicked. But I said that I wasn't like that. I was married. I had a family. I didn't think of her like that. I liked her but I'd never think of her *like that* whether I was married or not.'

'Doesn't sound too bad. It was honest at least.'

'That wasn't the problematic part. We were sitting in a booth and I shot out of there to put some distance between us. I stood about six foot from her in a crowded bar barking all these things. Everyone heard and they were all staring. She ran out and eventually so did I.'

'Oh.'

'It's such a mess. I panicked. I didn't have a chance to think about what to do properly. I've never been in that situation before.'

'Yes you have.'

'Not like that. People might say something, and you can flirt a little, but there's always the boundary. I always shut it down before it gets that far. In this case, there was nothing to shut down because I didn't think she was interested. And even if you are interested, who tries to kiss a married man?'

'More people than you'd imagine.'

'Well not me!' He was genuinely disgusted by the idea. 'This doesn't happen to me.'

'It does all the time, you simply don't see it.'

'I haven't done anything like that since Lisbon. I swear, Ffrony.'

'I know. And I know you. I know, for example, that you're going to feel awful for hurting her feelings, so I think the best thing would be for you to ring her right now. Apologise for saying all those things in the middle of the pub, and then repeat them but for her ears only.'

'You think I should call her? *Are you mad?* She'll think I'm interested in her or something.'

'Oh, yeah, maybe. Look, tell her your wife's told you to call and apologise. That it was a misunderstanding and you don't want it to spoil going to the classes.'

'You really think so?'

'Yes. You can't give up on your classes, you love them. They cost me a fortune and I get three hours of peace every Wednesday night. I'm not giving that up without a fight.'

'Yeah, you're probably right. But I'll look around for other classes, too. See if anything else is as good for all-round stuff. Then I can migrate over to them.'

'Good plan, Batman. Go on then, get dialling. Better out than in.'

XXIII

'Mum, Mum,' Phoebe says frantically. She is shaking me, her fingers gripped around the brow of my shoulder like she is hanging onto the edge of a cliff with a huge drop below.

'I'm awake, I'm awake,' I say. I force my eyes open and myself upright at the same time. 'I'm awake.' I don't usually sleep that deeply, so it's disorientating to have to be shaken awake, rather than to simply wake up. In the light cast from the corridor by the open door, I see her kneeling beside the bed, and I notice immediately that fear is flurrying across her face.

'What's the matter?' To force myself further awake, deeper into consciousness, I blink hard and fast.

'Someone's trying to break into our house,' she whispers.

My body and mind freeze. 'What?'

'I heard them below my room, they're trying to break in through the back door.'

Automatically, I glance at Joel's side of the bed. *What would he do?*

When we first moved here we lived in fear of this happening: we'd never had so much space, so many doors and windows and points of entry that we were solely responsible for. We'd go around every night and check everything was locked up, and sleep with one ear cocked in case someone tried to get in. *Joel* would go around every night and check everything was locked up. We knew we'd probably be able to handle the idea of things being stolen, but not beloved items being damaged, nor someone walking around our home, infecting it with their unwelcome presence.

Over time, we eased off the worry, found other things to think about. We'd never made a formal plan for something like this happening and I have no idea what to do.

Should we alert whoever it is that we are awake by switching on some lights, making a lot of noise and hopefully scare them off? Or do we hide and call the police? Or, do I check that my daughter is right before I set in motion another drama? 'Show me,' I say.

With Phoebe behind me, we move quickly and quietly down the blue-carpeted corridor, past the bathroom, past Zane's room, past the stairs up to the loft, until we arrive at her bedroom at the back of the house, over the kitchen.

I stand by the window and almost immediately hear it: the scritch-scratching of someone at the back door who pauses regularly to try the handle. The distance from the back door to Phoebe's room doesn't smother the way the person below is industriously trying to enter our home. They're obviously not a professional as they would have got in by now, I'd imagine. They're not reckless amateurs, either, otherwise they would have tried to smash the door in by now. The noise – I cock my head towards it, hoping it will make it clearer – is like the sound of someone trying keys in the deadlock. One after the other, keys are pushed into the lock, then that pause after each go – even though the lock hasn't been thrown – to turn the handle. They are expecting to get in. It's only a matter of time.

I can't look out, see if I can spot them, *identify* them because the back door is hidden from where I am by the brow of the kitchen extension at the back of the house.

Beside Phoebe's bed is her mobile phone, a long black wire trailing from its side as it is charged. I gently unplug it, then as quietly as possible, I back out of the room, almost tripping over Phoebe who is waiting on the threshold, her face still a mask of terror.

'OK, Phoebe, I want you to come with me to wake your brother,' I whisper. 'And then, the pair of you are to go upstairs to Aunty Betty's room and lock yourselves in.' I hand her the mobile. 'After you're all safe together, dial 999. OK?'

Her eyes double in size, leaving her with huge whites of her eyes and tiny melted-mahogany pupils, and she refuses to close her fingers around the phone. She's scared of talking to the police in case she spontaneously confesses what she knows about Joel's death that she begged me to keep quiet. 'I know you're scared of the police,' I whisper. 'But they're the only ones who can help us in this situation, OK?' I push the phone into her hand.

Slowly, she accepts it and gives a reluctant nod.

'When you call them, make sure you say there's someone coming into your house and there are two children and an old lady. That might make them respond quicker.'

Zane has always been a heavy sleeper – I've been known to vacuum in his room while he's having a nap on his bed and not even cause the slightest stir. It takes an age to wake him and, to stop him shouting at us, I have to push my hand over his mouth while tapping my finger to my lips with my other hand. 'Go upstairs with Phoebe to Aunty Betty's room,' I whisper to him. 'Try to be very quiet, she'll explain to you what's going on up there.'

'Wait, where are you going, Mum?' Phoebe asks quietly.

'I'm going to sneak downstairs and turn the light on, see if that'll scare them away.'

'You can't—' they both protest.

'I'll be fine. Especially once you've called the police.'

Both of them are reluctant to leave me, so I stand at the bottom of the carpet-covered stairs to the attic and watch them go up. With Phoebe's phone as a light, they round the corner and go onto the landing up there. I see the bluey glow from her mobile as it illuminates the landing, and I hear them open the door to Aunty Betty's room. When it shuts behind them, and then the lock is turned, I go back to my bedroom. Before I grab my phone, I struggle into Joel's jumper.

The floorboards that creak on the landing and stairs are easy to avoid – I've been doing it for at least nine years, unconsciously mapping them out as I've avoided waking up my children and husband if I need to go downstairs in the middle of the night. At the bottom of the stairs, an unexpected rage overcomes me. I was scared before, now I am angry. That this is another 'difficult' thing coming into our lives: Joel's death, my stupid work situation, Phoebe's pregnancy, the letters. Why us? *Why us?*

I have an urge to pick up the large umbrella that stands at the foot of the stairs in our umbrella stand and charge into the kitchen, screaming my head off and going straight for the back door. I want to scare the life out of whoever it is that is trying to break in. I want them to know, even for a sliver of a second, the fear they've put into us.

'*Your children don't need to lose another parent*,' Fynn said to me. Those words are stopping me going in there right now. I would love to, but I can't. I don't know who they are or what they want, or if they've got a weapon. I don't know what I will be walking into and if it will leave my children orphans.

What I do know is that this burglar thinks they have a key to our house and they have deliberately come here. Our house backs onto other gardens, the only access from the street is from the small walkway on the other side of the house next to us. And that walkway is only to their back garden. Their house is always in darkness, they often come and go so this person, if they were merely on the rob, would have a much easier time of it in that house. Not ours. Ours, the house they think they have a key to.

The way my heart pounds is erratic and volatile: different to the beat from the other night when I was rowing with Fynn, nothing like when I was with Lewis in the kitchen. This beat is violent, forceful, intense, like nothing I have ever felt before.

Deep breath, I tell myself as I wait in my corridor, a few feet away from the living room, staring at my shut kitchen door. *Deep breath*. Joel always used to complain about me never shutting doors on the way to bed. 'It could save our lives in a fire,' he used to say, 'by helping to contain the flames in a single room.' I've had to remember to do that ever since *that day*.

Deep breath. I step back towards the umbrella stand, my fingers close around the cold fake wood handle of the large umbrella Joel was given when he worked on the designs of a series of products for a large Brighton company. As quietly as possible, I slide the umbrella out of the brass stand and I move closer to wait by the white, six-panelled kitchen door. *Deep breath, deep breath*.

In the distance, I hear it. What I've been waiting for, the high, insistent, persistent whine of the approaching police sirens. As they draw closer, the sound definitely coming towards us, I throw open the kitchen door and flick on the light, momentarily dazzling myself with the brightness bouncing off the white surfaces and white floor. The figure at the back door is small, slender, disguised a little by the mottled glass. The person freezes for a second before they snap to their senses, drop what's in their hands, and then run off into the darkness of our garden.

I'm petrified, frozen where I stand. I know who it is that has targeted us in this way.

The night around our house is now a circus of sirens and blue flashing lights and car doors being opened and slammed shut. There's a loud, momentarily terrifying knock on the door, above the crackle of radios giving directions.

I can't move. I stand on the stain in my kitchen, staring at the place where Audra, the woman who murdered Joel, was attempting to break into our home.

XXIV

'I'm sorry we've had to meet again under these circumstances, Mrs Mackleroy,' the he one from all that time ago says.

'It's almost worth it to hear you say my name right first time,' I reply.

The others, still in pyjamas, wrapped in layers of terror, are all in the living room together, huddled up on the sofa with Aunty Betty as the centrepiece the children cling to. It should be me, I want to be doing that right now, but I need to be here, giving a statement. I have to do this away from the children because I do not want to add to this horror, give any type of shape to their nightmares.

The he one manages a weak smile while he keeps an eye on his colleagues who march in and out of the kitchen, dragging mud through from where they have been on the lawn, in the flowerbeds, in the vegetable patch, apparently searching for clues. The world outside is brightening; day approaches without thought for what people like us have been through in the darker hours. None of us is going anywhere this morning – I'll have to take another day off work.

'Are you able to tell us anything?' the he one asks. He's a detective now, and an altered man. Maybe as part of his new role he has been on sensitivity training courses, or maybe he's been told off by a few more victims of crime, or maybe he's simply grown up. Whichever it is, his manner is different, genuinely gentle instead of aggressive and bullying in a quiet voice.

I tell him what I know and he confirms what I thought – that the person was trying keys – by holding up in a plastic evidence bag well over fifty keys (not only deadbolt ones, but Yale ones, too) all slotted onto a keyring the size of a saucer.

'Do you think whoever it was regularly takes a bunch of keys to randomly try to break into someone's house?' I ask.

'To be honest, I haven't ever heard of that,' he admits. 'What I have heard of, though, is someone who has the keys to a house but can't remember which key it is, taking the lot with them with the intention of trying them all until one fits.'

He's only being honest, but that reply releases a shower of ice that starts at my neck and pools at the base of my spine. I didn't change the locks after Joel died. I eventually had his keys returned to me along with his wallet and mobile and clothes he wore *that day*, but I didn't change the locks. It didn't occur to me to do so, nor did it occur to me to even check that all his keys were there. I had a bunch of keys and they were simply keys, nothing unusual or worthy of note beyond being his.

'Do you have any idea who it might be? Did you change the locks when you moved in, for example?'

'Yes, it was one of the first things we did.' I pause. 'I didn't change them after Joel ...'

'Oh, right. I don't suppose you would. I'm sure I wouldn't

think it necessary myself if I thought I'd got the keys back. I wouldn't notice, really, if they were all there.'

'I'm going to have to change all the locks,' I say tiredly.

'Get some window locks fitted as well, on both floors.'

'You think that's necessary?' *Are you saying we're in real danger even though you don't know about the letters and Phoebe's secret about* that day?

'It's the minimum people should have, I think,' he says, gently.

'It never ends, does it?' I say to myself but out loud, so he thinks I'm talking to him.

'Mrs Mackleroy, I'm sorry we didn't catch the person who killed your husband. I often think about the case, and get the file out to see if there's anything we might have missed. That's why I came here tonight when I heard it was your name and address.'

He is a different person. I can probably trust him now. I can probably get the letters out, tell him about Phoebe, explain why I couldn't come forward before. He would probably understand. Then I think of Phoebe.

My tall, willowy daughter who loves to wear her hair in bunches and spends her time consumed by her phone or whizzing through her homework. She is in a state of constant, unrelenting fear at the moment. I know because when I first got pregnant I felt the same, and I'd been trying for a baby with the man I wanted to marry. She is too unstable to go through police questioning right now. No matter how gentle or patient, she will clam up and will retreat into herself like she did in the time after *that day.* If she was further along the decision-making process, if she didn't act as if she constantly hated me, if I knew I had Fynn around as back-up, I could tell the he one everything, I could give them the information that might lead to them catching her and making her explain what happened, why she did it, if he asked for his children before he died.

Those are the scales I'm constantly trying to balance. On the one side of the scale, I would have the answers to those questions, I would see Joel's murderer put in prison. On the other side of the scale, I have my daughter's well-being.

'If you remember anything, Mrs Mackleroy, or think of something, you can always call me at the station.'

'Thanks,' I say.

'We've got a bit more to do here, then we'll get out of your hair.'

'Right. Thanks.' I stand and go to the living room to join my family.

XXV

'Let me guess, the Abominable Snowman pitched up in your fridge this morning and you need to wait in to get the freezer door fixed?' Kevin says nastily.

'No, Kevin, someone tried to break into our house last night and the police only left an hour ago and none of us have had any sleep.'

He sighs. The depth of his concern reaches a sigh. 'I've got into work and worked a full day every day this week, Saffron, do you know why?' he asks.

Because you have a wife who does everything for you including your ironing and, I suspect, wiping your bottom so you have nothing else to worry about? 'No, Kevin, I don't.'

'I am committed to my work, Saffron, that's why. Your attendance record over the last fortnight has made me question your commitment.'

'Has it?' I reply.

'We've got the Mallory and Chilton end-of-year debriefing today. You're meant to be briefing me and Edgar on the meeting, now you're telling me you can't because of *another* drama in your life. Why wouldn't I question your commitment?'

'Technically, Kevin, I should have nothing to do with this

meeting,' I say, pleasantly, placidly, like Joel would. 'I'm not top-level staff and I'm not even supposed to have seen half of the files I have. You could get into a lot of trouble for even showing me that stuff let alone having me do all the actual reports when, with my title, I wasn't allowed to sign the mandatory confidentiality agreement before we took this job.

'It's not my fault Edgar still can't do his job. And it's not my fault that someone terrified the life out of my family last night by trying to break in.'

He contemplates what I have subtly told him – that if he pushes me, I will squeal about him violating company policy by having a junior look after top client accounts – and eventually says, 'Where are the files?'

'On your desk, like I told you last night before I left. The presentations are all printed out, the slides are all on the stick on your desk, the room is booked with refreshments as well. It's all sorted. So, good luck. I hope it goes well.'

'You'd better be in tomorrow,' he says and hangs up.

Odious, weasel-faced toad, I think as I wander out into the corridor from the living room. Everyone else is asleep upstairs, my list of jobs before I can even contemplate sitting down are: waiting on the locksmith the he one recommended; calling work; and calling the children's schools.

I stop and stare when I step out into the corridor.

On the brown coir mat behind the door is a long, rectangular cream envelope addressed to:

Saffron Mackleroy

Wednesday, 24 April
(For today)

Don't call the police again, please.

Don't call the police again and I won't come into your house again. Is that a deal?

I hope you haven't done anything silly like tell them about me or show them the letters? I suspect if you had, they would have come for me by now. Although I'm not where they'd think to find me.

Don't call the police again. You really didn't have to do that. It's like I explained, I find it hard sometimes that I have nothing of his, that I missed out on so much by not being able to be a part of laying him to rest. I simply wanted to be in a place where he often was. Where he used to spend a lot of his time. He told me that he did most of the cooking. Did you do most of the eating, then? (Sorry, that was just our little joke we had.)

Don't be upset by this: but I can't imagine him with someone like you, sometimes. You don't seem his type.

Listen, I only wanted to be in his kitchen for a few seconds. Maybe touch a couple of the things he touched. It's not like I would have come upstairs and watched you while you slept. It's not like I would have done anything to you.

Really, don't call the police again. If they come
looking for me, they won't find me but I will know and I
will make sure you pay before I disappear for ever.

I'm not threatening you, far from it. I AM saying that
you can't be everywhere at once. Will it be you, Phoebe, Zane
or your lovely mother? She's at home all day, isn't she? I'd
hate for anything awful to happen to her.

Don't call the police again and we'll both be happy,
we'll both feel safe.

A

XXVI

They arrive at the same time but from different directions, probably for the same reason – to find out why my children weren't at school today.

With Imogen I can understand: she won't have been told by the school why Zane wasn't in, but Mr Bromsgrove, I'm sure they would have told. Maybe that's why he's here: he is concerned after hearing what happened in the baldest of terms – there was an attempted break-in and we were all up half the night – so had to check we were all still in one piece.

The other three slept until gone three-thirty and then were grumpy, hungry and subdued. I made them pizza and allowed them to eat in the living room with the television off as they all argued about what to watch. (Which defeated the point of eating in the living room but none of us were willing to brave the kitchen.) Now, they are all in their rooms, steeling themselves for the night ahead in case it happens again. I want to tell them that it won't happen again, that I'm not going to call the police, that I can't take that risk with any of them. It's wrong, of course, to rely upon the word of a killer, but for now, that's all I can do.

I watch Imogen and Lewis do the 'After you', 'No after you' dance at the gate, until Lewis says something that makes

Imogen lower her head and giggle in that way she does when she's flirting with someone. I watch them because I've been standing here all day, looking out the window, trying to work out where Audra is watching me from, how she can know so much about us. I'm sure she saw the locksmith/security man arrive and worked out by the amount of time they spent here that I'd changed the locks – minimum – and was having other bolts and locks installed, too. I'd love to have CCTV and burglar alarms fitted, to put bars on the windows and doors, but that would scare my family. It wouldn't make them feel safe, it would simply underline the fact we are vulnerable, that I believe it's going to happen again.

Imogen sashays up the steps, trying to impress Lewis with the sway of her body that she keeps trim by only eating a set number of calories a day and exercising, except when she's doing the latest diet and trying to convince me and anyone who'll listen it's the answer to all our problems. (I never engage in such conversations because that way madness lies.) Lewis, to his credit, doesn't watch her as she hopes he will, he turns his back and remains on the bottom step, until *Rat-a-tat-tat-tat-tat!* sounds at my door. Even if I hadn't seen her, I would know it was her from the knock – she always slips that extra tap in.

'Hello.' I turn on the smile, try not to let her know anything is wrong before she has got over the doorstep.

'Hi, Saffy!' she trills. 'Just thought I'd drop by and see if everything is all right since Zane wasn't at school today! And, look! I bumped into Mr Bromsgrove, Phoebe's teacher!'

They both enter the house and I usher them into the living

room; I'm not ready to share the kitchen right now. I've spent most of the day avoiding it unless necessary.

'It's nice of you both to come over,' I say. 'I mean, it's not as if there's been an invention where you can stay in your nice cosy house and still contact me or anything. That slacker Alexander Graham Bell needs to get a move on, we could really use something like that nowadays.' My sarcasm is unnecessary, but it niggles a little that neither of them thought that calling might be better.

'Ah, yes, should have called instead,' Lewis says. 'Sorry, I heard what happened and I wanted to check you were all OK. Stupid of me to not call.'

'Why? What's happened?' Imogen asks, overtly put out that she's the last in the loop.

'We're all fine. I want to reassure you of that. We're all fine. Someone tried to break in last night,' I say. 'We're all fine. The police came along and scared them away. We're all fine.' I repeat that because I know she's going to say:

'OH MY GOD! That's awful! I've always been so worried about you not having a man around the house and it's all come true.' Her body is trembling and anyone would think it was her house that had been broken into, her that'd spent the whole day having the locks changed and security 'upgraded' instead of her simply being a drama queen of the highest order.

'We're fine, Imogen,' I repeat. 'We're all fine. Tired, but fine.'

'*Sorry*,' Lewis mouths at me.

'I'd imagine so,' she says. 'Oh, Sweetheart, you must be so scared.'

'I'm not, actually. Just tired.'

'That'll be the shock talking,' she says to Lewis.

And there it is, that realisation that he is male. He is young. He isn't wearing a wedding ring. It dawns in her eyes first, then overtakes the smile on her face. She knows exactly what to do next. Exactly what I need.

'I actually came over to invite you to dinner Friday night, Saffy,' she says. She revolves slowly and dangerously towards Lewis. 'Why don't you come as well, Mr Bromsgrove? It'll be lovely to spend some adult time with Saffy and I can quiz you about the secondary schools in Brighton and Hove. If you don't mind, of course.'

'I haven't said I can make it, yet,' I mention as a by the way.

'Of course you can make it!' she says with a wave of her hand. 'What else would you be doing on a Friday night?'

'Staying home with my traumatised children.'

'You won't be out late. And besides, I think it'd do Phoebe some good for you to show her that you trust her to look after her little brother – especially after the trouble at the school the other day?' The last part of her sentence is directed at Lewis, to see if he'll tell her what she needs to know. She receives a blank expression from him. 'So, Mr Bromsgrove, will you come?'

'If Mrs Mackleroy can make it, then I'm sure I can.'

'Perfect! Eight-thirty at my house! Saffy has the address!'

'I haven't said I can make it,' I remind her as she pulls her small, pink leather handbag onto her shoulder.

'Of course you can make it.' She is excellent at dismissing me. *Excellent.* In two steps she is beside Lewis, within a second she has hooked her arm through his, scaring the life out of him. His alarmed eyes frantically seek out mine. *You should have called*, I want to say to him. 'Mr Bromsgrove, would you mind awfully walking me to my car? I'm a bit nervous now I know what's happened to Saffy.'

'Erm, yes, of course. I'm glad you're all OK, Mrs Mackleroy,' he says.

'Call her Saffy, everyone else does,' Imogen says.

Actually, almost no one does, I want to say, but don't bother.

What she is doing, by forcing him to walk her to her car, is to put me in a lose–lose situation. I can't persuade him right now to let me cancel dinner tomorrow night, so to do so I'll have to call him later. Which would be fine with her because we'd be talking on the phone in the later hours. And, by the time I ring him anyway, she will have given him the 'Saffy doesn't get out much, I think an adult meal with the four of us – my husband, Ray, will join us of course – will do her some good, don't you? After everything poor Saffy has been through, and after this latest trauma, don't you think she deserves some fun?' And she knows Lewis, by turning up tonight, isn't the sort of bastard who'd disagree with her. By the time I get Lewis on the phone, Imogen will have convinced him that allowing me to cancel Friday night's dinner would make him as heinous a person as the one who killed my husband.

I watch them leave the house, exit through the gate and walk away in the direction that Imogen came from.

Great. I'm going to dinner with Lewis Bromsgrove. That's going to go down so well with my daughter.

VII

Saffron.

I'm glad you didn't tell the police anything. I should
have known that you wouldn't since Phoebe didn't tell the
police what she knew last time. I had to be sure, though. I
couldn't take the risk that you'd talk this time.

I don't like giving you ultimatums, but you really left
me no choice.

Let's put all this behind us, OK? Let's try to move on.
You live in your world, I'll live in mine. I'd love for us to be
friends? We have so much in common, after all. Joel was
the one man we both truly loved. We're the same you and
me, we both loved him so much. That's why I'd love for us
to be friends. We can share our loss as well as our stories of
him.

Please don't be hurt by that. Yes, we were lovers. But,
I think deep down you knew that, didn't you? That's why
you had him ring me and say all those things. You could
see how important I was to him and you were trying to stop
it before it got out of hand.

It didn't work, but I understand why you would try.

I would do the same. I would kill anyone who got in between me and the man I love.

I mean that figuratively, of course. But you knew that, didn't you?

A

XXVII

Joel's Mum Calling . . .

flashes on my mobile as I walk into the house.

She must be desperate – she never calls my mobile. The house phone is her preferred method of communication because she hopes that one of the kids will pick it up and she can avoid speaking to me altogether.

That Day

After a few false starts, I'd managed to get Zane and Phoebe to sleep on my side of the big bed, after the pair of them had sobbed into the pillows as if the other wasn't there. I'd crept out of the room, shutting the door behind me. I had a desperate need to be outside, to have some air on my skin, to remind myself that I was still breathing. I didn't feel like I was, everything seemed to be going on around me and I was swept up with it, not influencing it. I wanted a sensory reminder that I continued to be a functioning being.

I descended the stairs and found Fynn sitting on the second step, his head cradled heavily in his hands, his shoulders violently shaking. He heard me on the step behind him and stood, swung towards me. His skin was blotchy, a roadmap of tears and pain, his solid body trembling where he stood. I crossed the distance between us and, on the step above him, threw myself around him.

He'd spent the hours since arriving doing things, talking to people, answering the phone, sending texts, coping with the things I couldn't do. And, finally, it was time for him.

He almost swamped me as he accepted my comfort, the juddering of his tears moving our bodies together. I couldn't speak, but he had understood I was there for him. I pressed a kiss onto the top of his head as I rubbed his back.

And she gasped. A slight, wispy noise that escaped from her unlipsticked mouth, but I heard it and looked over at her. She stood in the doorway of the living room, her coat still on so I guessed they hadn't long arrived. Fynn must have let them in and left them to it because while they intensely disliked me, they absolutely *hated* him.

I knew what it looked like to her, but then it would if you believed your daughter-in-law was trash and your son's best friend had ruined your boy's life.

Joel's mum had her husband to hold her, Fynn had no one else except me and the most important thing at that moment was being there when he needed me.

The day after *That Day*

She stood beside me in the kitchen. When there was an expanse of space, she placed herself beside me as I poured boiling water into two cups to make coffee for her and her husband. She had the milk in her hand.

'I didn't like what I saw last night,' she said quietly, as though anyone could hear us above the calamitous silence that shrouded the house. As though in all that had gone in the last twenty-four hours, this was somehow important.

It was all about appearances with her, *them*. They had come, not because they wanted to be with us, nor to hug their grandchildren, nor to be near where he was, but because it was expected. They had to be seen to be here. It was probably shock, too; an inability to quite believe what had happened so they focused that disbelief on what I was doing wrong.

'I know,' I said. 'And I'm sorry, Elizabeth.' That was the first time I'd used her name. If I had to call her anything it was Mrs Mackleroy, giving her the respect she commanded, trying to earn the approval I craved. It wasn't important any more. Now we were the same, we no longer slotted into the roles we'd had for all this time because the person we loved that had unintentionally put us into those niches was gone. Even though it was only hours later, we were suddenly redefined. That meant I could call her Elizabeth. 'I'm so sorry you lost your son. I don't think I could breathe if that happened to me.' I replaced the kettle onto its stand, moved the mugs of coffee towards her. 'There you go, your coffee ready for milk. I'll talk to you later.'

She was surprised. She'd thought I'd be the same as I'd always been, that I'd continue to turn myself inside out trying to earn her approval until the end of time. That they could silently remind me that they were hoping Joel would meet the woman who would turn his life around by taking him in hand, pushing him to fulfil his potential so he could become something.

I wanted to say to her, 'That Saffron doesn't live here any more' but I didn't because they'd find out soon enough.

Joel's Mum Calling . . .

my phone insists. I hit the call reject button. I'm too para-noid not to listen to the message, though, in case something has happened.

'Saffron, hello, it's me. We'd like to visit you all, if that's possible? Do give me a call back at your earliest convenience.'

That would be when Hell freezes over, I think at her. But I know it'll be sooner. It'll have to be.

Saffron.

Do you miss him? In those moments between breaths do you think you can't keep going because you miss him so much?

I've been thinking and thinking about this the past few days and I'm not sure you do miss him, actually.

I saw you in the street on Monday night with that guy. Sneaking out of the house, holding hands, hugging, arguing. All very passionate. All very inappropriate. It annoys me that you get to call yourself his widow and behave like that, while I get nothing. NOTHING.

Do you miss him? Ask yourself that, please. Do you really, really miss him like a woman who loves him should? Or do you miss him because the world tells you that you have to?

I think I know the answer.

They stone women like you in some countries, you know.

A

XXVIII

I'm about to eat a large slice of Resentment Pie.

This pie is thoughtfully constructed with its filling of large chunks of the last eighteen months. It is intricately seasoned with bitterness that Lewis exists, irritation towards Phoebe for bringing him so closely into my life, antipathy towards Imogen for trying to force us together, and a dash of umbrage towards Aunty Betty for – technically – being another adult with whom I can leave my children. The thick, creamy mash topping is of shame about Fynn. Sprinkled on like mixed herbs is resentment of Joel for putting me in this position in the first place: this isn't what I signed up for. 'Till death us do part' seems a pretty stupid promise in the light of what's happened. I could have stayed with him until the end of time, but I agreed death could come between us at some point, and I'm left to handle the fallout of that particular bargain.

It's a nice-looking pie, so many delicate, unique elements have gone into making it and I'm about to eat most of it. From the conversation I had with Phoebe earlier, it seems she's got her own pie to devour – although hers has one ingredient only: acrimony towards her mother.

'I really, *REALLY* hate that you're going out with Mr Bromsgrove,' she said to me earlier while I stirred chopped tomatoes into the softened onion, garlic and grated carrots on the stove to make a red sauce for meatballs.

'Why?' I asked.

'The fact you can't even see what's wrong with it says it all.'

'I'm not "going out" with him, Phoebe. He's not "going out" with me. We were both invited to dinner at Imogen's house and you know how she is – she wouldn't stop until we agreed.'

Phoebe's reply was a mouth grimace that conceded, at least, to Imogen's bossiness. 'Just cos someone wants something, doesn't mean you should give it to them,' said the pregnant girl who had unprotected sex because her boyfriend wanted her to.

My hand paused in shaking brown rice vinegar into the tomato mixture in favour of staring long and hard at her. You couldn't tell she was pregnant by looking at her. I suppose it was still so early that she probably hadn't had any symptoms such as morning sickness. When I got pregnant with Phoebe it took a while for morning sickness to start, with Zane it seemed to start the second the sperm fertilised the egg. 'What's your real problem, Phoebe? I mean, it's not as if Mr Bromsgrove and I aren't already linked by you and his son. I didn't march up to the school and say, "Oi, Bromsgrove, me and you, Friday night at my friend's house," did I? If you have a good reason for not wanting this to happen, I'd love to hear it.'

She was silent for a few minutes and I waited for her to speak. In that time she moistened her lips, examined me as if weighing up something. 'He's my teacher,' she then spat. 'You're my mother. It's just wrong.'

'OK.' I returned to the sauce, humiliation and disappointment pulsing through my head. I thought in that pause, from the look on her face, that she was going to let me into her life, tell me something, but no. Just my imagination.

'It is wrong, you know,' she continued, oblivious to how much those few minutes had hurt me.

'If you say so. I'm not going to argue.'

'But you're still going to go out with him, aren't you?'

'I'm not "going out with him", in the sense that you mean.'

'Whatever,' she mumbled and stormed off back to her room.

Lewis is uncomfortable when he picks me up. He has on a modern, dark grey suit and a white shirt, with the top two pearly buttons casually left open. I assume it is a casual thing, but he could well have sat in his car for an age opening and closing the top buttons, trying to decide which way would be suitable and wouldn't give me the wrong impression. The thought of that makes me smile. I haven't been through that ritual, obviously. After a day of meetings, sarky little digs from Kevin, the call from Joel's mum, the latest letter and cooking dinner, my effort has stretched to a quick underarm wash, and a change into a white T-shirt.

'Hi,' Lewis says, standing on the doorstep, tense and nervous, like a man about to go on a date. It isn't a date! Am I the only one who realises this? '*If it walks like a duck and talks like a duck, what do you think it is, Babes?*' Joel would have said.

'All right?' I say grimly and step out beside him. I shout, 'Bye' over my shoulder and then underline the fact we're not going in by shutting the door, which almost bumps him on his nose when it clicks into place.

'Oh, we're not going in then?' he asks.

'No, I think we should get going.'

Instead of moving, he stands, an impressive figure in his suit, switching his gaze between our black glossed wood door and me.

'Is something wrong?' I ask.

'I, erm, was hoping to see Phoebe,' he says.

A swift, chilling breeze of suspicion raises the hairs on the back of my neck, piquing the interest of the goosebumps on my arms and jangling my hackles. 'Why?' I ask.

'It's not obvious?' he asks.

I shake my head, sizing him up as the man who did this to my daughter because I do not believe it is down to Curtis. He seems too respectful, honest. Lewis stares back at me, openly sizing me up as a serious contender for The Worst Mother In The World award – again.

'She's my pupil, she's *pregnant*.' He whispers the last word possibly to stop the neighbours hearing, possibly so as not to enrage The Worst Mother In The World – me – with such loaded words. 'Since she hasn't been to school in three days, I would like to check she's OK.'

Of course he does, *of course* he does. What's wrong with me? The old me wouldn't even think such a thing was possible, the me before words like 'murder' and 'sexual contact with a child' became a part of my daily life wouldn't have even thought it possible.

'Remember how I said my daughter doesn't speak to me?' I say.

Lewis nods.

'Well, she's started speaking to me now. To tell me she hates that I'm going out with you even like this, as two people who've been invited to the same place at the same time by my bossy, pushy friend. You will not receive a positive welcome if you walk through that door.' *You might even get a taste of what it's like to be me sometimes.*

'Right,' he says. 'Well . . . I can't say I'm surprised. She must be going through so many conflicting emotions right now, her mother and her teacher going to the same place at the same time to not discuss her must be a huge thing.'

'Everything feels huge to her right now,' I say.

'Yeah, I'd imagine so.'

'I'll drive,' I offer.

'Are you sure about that?' he replies, following me down the concrete steps to the garden path and then to the front gate. 'I mean, if you drive, I might be able to drink and if I drink I may start to have ridiculous delusions that you and I are dating or something equally horrific.' With an 'I got the message' hitch of his eyebrow, he sidesteps me on the pavement and heads for his car.

'*If it walks like a duck and talks like a duck, what do you think it is, Babes?*'

'*A duck-billed platypus.*'

*

Technically, Imogen's house is within comfortable walking distance, but the plan had been to drive so Lewis and I didn't have too much time together alone. We'd get to Imogen's, we'd eat dinner, we'd go home. Not enough time for relaxing and chatting and 'getting to know each other' like you'd expect to on a date.

Bossy, pushy and big-hearted Imogen has obviously got other ideas into her head. She will have planned it all out: open the door looking radiant in a blue satin dress, complete with perfect hair and make-up; invite us in, herd us into the living room where Ray – who'd have been warned that any off-key remark would result in him sleeping on the sofa – will be waiting, before she sweeps off to serve us aperitifs and start the banter. The banter will carry us through drinks and then seamlessly through dinner, where she will be conducting the conversation like a maestro to bring out the best in Lewis and highlight all my good bits. After our laughter-soaked dinner, there'll be port on the sofas in the living room, then coffees before Lewis and I, laughing, exchanging longer and longer meaningful gazes, will share a taxi home. (One home, that is.)

The first spanner in the finely tuned mechanism of her plan is, of course, seeing the car keys in Lewis's hand, which means she can't ply both of us with as much booze as she'd like. The second spanner is seeing my black work skirt and white long-sleeved T-shirt under one of Joel's black and red hoodies. The third spanner is my lack of make-up. *Saffy is not playing,* she realises as she grins at us. *Saffy is not going to sleep with this man, no matter what I do next.*

'Hello!' She beams a little wider. 'Welcome to our humble

abode.' Understanding her as I do, her previous thought has been followed up by: *Saffy doesn't know what's best for her. She needs a man. And here he is. I'm going to make this happen.*

'You have a lovely house,' Lewis says. 'Thank you very much for inviting me.'

He sounds like someone who has been brought up properly, who would teach his child manners. That's part of the reason I don't believe it's Curtis: there's something about Lewis that makes me believe he *has* drummed into his son the importance of contraception and respect for girls.

'Great to see you,' I say, receiving her hug and planting a kiss on each cheek in return.

The smell of food coming from the kitchen reminds me that I've been so tense and resentful of being forced to spend time with someone I don't want to be attracted to, I've been so worried about what Phoebe will do, I've been so distracted by the increasing menace in the letters, that I've forgotten I have to eat in front of other people.

I am 10
'Finish what's on your plate, Saffron.'

'I'm full.'

'How can you be full? You haven't eaten everything.'

'I have.'

'Don't answer me back. Finish what's on your plate.'

'But . . .'

'You're too skinny because you don't eat. Finish what's on your plate.'

'But I'm full.'

'You children. You have no idea what it takes to put food on the table. If you did, you wouldn't sit there and tell me you're full and let good food go to waste. Throwing away food is a sin.'

It's not how Fynn said. I'm not bulimic. I'm not anorexic. I'm not a mixture of both. I know I don't have the healthiest relationship with food, but that's hardly unique.

Yes, if I have to go to a big event I immediately think that I have to lose a little weight to make sure I look acceptable. OK, if I'll be expected to eat with other people I'll try to avoid eating for a few days beforehand so I've got a buffer zone to stop me being heavier after the event, I'll just get back to where I was before. Admittedly, when I weigh myself in the morning, if the number is the same as the day before, I'm disappointed, if it's less, I'm relieved – not pleased, relieved. If it's more . . . If it's more, then it confirms what I know about myself, what I've always known by myself.

I am 12
'While I'm away, try to eat more fruit and less bread.'
'OK.'
'You need to lose weight.'
'OK.'
'Your hair is a mess, too. You look like a tramp.'
'Oh.'
'You're not like your sister, you aren't pretty. You are clever, but that doesn't mean you should look like a tramp. You need to lose weight and look after your hair. It's not hard.'

'OK.'

'If you eat more fruit your skin will look better as well. All those spots will go away.'

'OK.'

'You won't always be studying. One day, when you have become a doctor, you can take the time off to get married and have children. But that doesn't mean you have to look like you do until then. How you look is important if you want to go to a good university. No one will take you in if you look like a tramp.'

'Oh. OK.'

'Remember, Saffron, when I come back in three weeks, I want to see you have lost weight. Less bread and more fruit.'

'OK.'

'Good girl.'

I know that weighing myself every morning is setting myself up for a day of disappointment, uncertainty or failure; that my life is dictated by the scales. But I can't stop. Well, I can, I really can. And I do. I can go for days without getting on them, without needing to know, but then I'll get curious, I'll need to confirm that I'm all right. That I haven't become out of control, that my weight isn't rocketing or sneakily creeping upwards.

I am 14

'Look at her, who'd want to go near that?'

'She's my friend. You have to be nice to her.'

'What, like she's nice to all those pies?'

'She can't help that. It's only puppy fat. Last year she was really skinny for a few months but it came back. My mum says it's puppy fat. She'll be really thin and gorgeous again one day, you'll see.'

'That ain't puppy fat, that's a whole kennel of the stuff.'

'That's really nasty.'

'It's only nasty if it ain't true. My older brother said with a name like Saffron you expect her to be all shapely and exotic, not like that.'

'There's nothing wrong with her.'

'It ain't fair. Why haven't you got any other good-looking, normal friends? None of my mates would touch her with a barge pole so we can't hang around with them.'

'If you want to keep hanging around with me, you'd better start being nicer to her.'

'Yeah, all right, calm down. I suppose she has got big knockers. Shame about the rest of her.'

'What have I just said?'

'All right, all right, all right. I'll be nice to her.'

'Good, cos she's really nice.'

'Yeah, all right.'

'I do wish she hadn't put on the weight again, though. It's really embarrassing sometimes when she's trying on a size fourteen and the button won't close. She gets really upset about it and I want to say to her it's not my fault you're so fat again, is it . . . Don't laugh. It's not funny.'

'Oi, shhhh, I think I just saw her over there.'

'What? Where? No. It can't be her. She'd never come out on her own. Where?'

'There. Oh . . . The person's gone. I could have sworn it was her.'

'God, I hope it wasn't her. The film's about to start anyway. But *don't ever tell her I said all that. She's a really nice person. She can't help it if she's a bit on the big side.'*

It's not like I have a huge problem. Or even a problem. I'll be good for days and days. I'll be on the salads, I'll be on the juice, I'll be drinking lots of water. I'll even be able to cook and bake for the children but then, I'll find myself alone. I will look around and see all I have is what is inside me. All I can feel is what lives at my very centre. And it will start to unravel itself, it will start to reveal itself to me and the pain will be too much. Too much for me to handle, it will grow and expand as it uncurls itself and I know that soon, it will overwhelm me. I won't be able to function because what is inside – all the voices, all the reminders of the ways in which I am not good enough – will drown me.

I am 16

'My goodness, you're a big girl, aren't you? I'm not sure I've got any uniforms that big. I might have to order some in. What size are your normal clothes?'

'Fourteen-to-sixteen on top, twelve-to-fourteen on the bottom.'

'I don't know where you've been shopping, but I'd say you're more like eighteen-to-twenty, love. I'll have to see what I've got in.'

'This one fits.'

'I can't believe it! You know, it's your boobs, love. They make you look huge. I never thought in a million years you'd fit into a sixteen. Goes to show you can't tell, doesn't it?'

At the same time as I am being submerged by the voices of not being good enough, that packet of crisps will start to seem like the answer to my problems. It'll be the only way to deal with what hurts inside, my only chance to silence the agony at the centre of my being, where all the bad things live, where all the distant voices talk the loudest. And then I can't stop. When it's stuffed away, when it doesn't touch the sides going down, when a little bit of the edge of how I feel inside is shaved away because one of the voices is silenced, I'll want more. I'll want more of the peace; to have the agony blunted. I'll need more. I'll take whatever I can, eat whatever I can lay my hands on. In front of the fridge with the door open, in front of the pantry with the door swung wide as I search for anything delectable, palatable, even vaguely edible. I will stuff it down until the noise, the torment, the words are silenced.

I am 19

'I want to be good enough. I don't understand why I'm not good enough.'

'You are good enough.'

'I tried really hard, I did really well in all my subjects and I got into this university that so many other people didn't. And I'm still not good enough. I'm just not enough. I'm not pretty enough. I don't fit in.'

'You do. People really like you.'

'But they don't, not really. Everyone in halls has paired off into mates and they often don't remember I'm around to ask if I want to go to the bar or to a nightclub. No one in my classes seems to want to hang out with me away from the lectures. I'm just a nobody that no one ever notices. It's cos I'm not pretty, I'm not beautiful, I'm not special. No one wants to hang out with the fat one with bad skin and bad hair, and nothing to talk about. I'm always going to be the fat, clever one, aren't I?'

'None of this is true, you know, Saffron. You are nice, you are special, there are loads of people out there who think you're beautiful. Look at yourself in this mirror, really look, and you'll see that you are so pretty, and all the nice things about you shine through.'

'I am looking at myself in this mirror and I can't do that any more. I can't look at me like this any more. I'm not going to listen to you, any more, either. You don't tell me the truth. You only see what you want to see. You don't see the real me. I have to be better. I have to look better and be better than this.'

'It won't change anything.'

'It will. People will like me, they'll notice me, they'll want to be my friend. I'm going to be better than this. I'm going to be perfect and then everything will be better. Life will be better.'

'It's not that simple, Saffron, it really isn't.'

'When I was ill with pneumonia last year and I lost all that weight, everyone noticed me. They all kept talking to me and commenting on how much weight I'd lost. Everyone was impressed. And when I started to put it back on again, everyone stopped noticing me.'

'That's cos everyone noticed you weren't around and missed you.'

'If they missed me, they'd invite me to meet up in the holidays, they'd want to hang out with me. No one does.'

'Give people a chance.'

'I'm not going to listen to you any more. I told you. You can speak

to me all you want, but I'm going to ignore you. Because I know once
I'm thin again, everything is going to get better. It really will.'

Afterwards is the terror. The fear of what I've done, the horror
of how out of control I was – the unthinking, machine-like
way I have torn through my carefully ordered kitchen and
filled myself to this uncomfortable point with hideous,
high-fat, high-calorie food. And the terrors of that, of those
out-of-control moments, replace the silence inside. They
become louder, more physical, sitting there, festering away,
and I know I can't keep it inside. I can't live with all of that
inside me, I need to escape, to remove it as soon as possible.
After that comes relief, comes the emptiness, when there is
nothing inside to hurt me, nothing inside to weigh me down,
nothing to make me feel as worthless as I know I am.

I am 25

'What were you doing in the toilet just now, Ffrony?'

  'Erm, what do you think?'

  'I know what you were doing.'

  'So why ask?'

  'I want you to promise me you won't do it again.'

  'You want me to promise that I won't go for a wee again? Sorry,
but it's a biological imperative.'

  'I want you to promise you won't make yourself sick again.'

  'What are you talking about?'

  'I heard you. I've heard you before. And it all makes sense to me
now. I was so confused why you wouldn't have any dates in the

267

beginning that involved food. I didn't understand why whenever I invited you over for dinner you'd always end up seducing me instead of letting me cook for you. Why you always disappear at the end of meals if I manage to convince you to go to a restaurant. I want you to promise me.'

'I don't—'

'Don't lie to me. I don't like liars. Please promise me you won't make yourself sick again and that you'll stop starving yourself. Look, we'll get you whatever type of help you need. Whatever it costs. I've got money saved up, I don't care what it costs, I'll pay whatever it takes to help you. But please, don't do that to yourself again. Promise me you won't do it again.'

'Oh, Joel, I can't promise you and not lie to you. It's not that simple. I wish it was, but it's not that simple. But I'll try, OK? I'll do my very best and you won't have to worry about me ever again.'

I didn't do it for years and years. I don't even do it all the time now. Only sometimes. That doesn't make it what Fynn said. It's an outlet, not a way of life. It doesn't mean I need a label on me like he said. Like anyone else would if they knew the truth. I'm not that person. I simply need release sometimes.

I am 26

'Baby, I'm really scared. I'm terrified about whether I can do this. I want you so much and I'm scared what I might do. But then, I know I couldn't ever hurt you. So I'm going to eat every meal I have to, I'm going to keep every calorie I need in because I know I need to nourish you. I'm going to do this. For you, for me. I'm still scared,

but I'm going to do it anyway. And you, you concentrate on getting bigger and getting born. I'm going to do this. We're going to do this. OK? We're a team.'

After *that day*, I've needed that release a bit more. I've needed that control over who I am and the world that is my body. I had it for a while with Fynn, but that was becoming too complicated, so I stopped. And I went back to what I knew. But that doesn't mean anything. And it doesn't make me what Fynn said.

'You're very quiet this evening, Saffy,' Ray, Imogen's second husband, says. I glance up from my glass of wine and our gazes collide.

He's right, I've barely said a word since we were led into the large, pristine living room for drinks. I'm worried now. It's not so bad in a restaurant, where you can pick at different things, where you can find the food poor and inedible, where no one really notices if you don't 'fill your boots' as Joel used to say when I first met him. And, if it's one of those restaurants where the food is great, where they cook things just right, and the cutlery and crockery are clean, and you've been good for days so you can visit, they also have toilets. You can go and take care of yourself without anyone you're with ever having to know.

In someone's house, it's rude not to eat, it's noticed if you disappear to the toilet for long periods of time. It's not easy to control yourself, to purge yourself of the unknown fats, and carbohydrates, and additives and calories that have gone into that meal. In someone's house you are completely, frighteningly, out of control.

'Sorry,' I say. 'I've got a few things on my mind.'

Lewis bristles beside me, not much, only enough for me to notice. He thinks it's him, that I'm still hung up on the fact I'm out with him.

'Oh, I'm sorry,' Ray says. 'Anything we can help with?' His arm is casually slung over the back of the sofa he sits on and every now and again he reaches down to affectionately caress Imogen's bare shoulder.

A lump surfaces in my throat, a little kick is delivered to the centre of my chest. I remember what it felt like to be like that with someone. To touch each other, just because. I glance away from them, seek my fortune in my glass of rosé. 'No, you can't help, not unless you know anyone who'll take in a sixty-something-old woman who'll be trying to escape at every turn and who is a menace to any men over the age of . . . I was going to say fifty-five, but to be honest, anyone over forty-five is fair game as far as she's concerned.'

'Jo— I mean, your aunt is living with you now?' Imogen says, a note of disapproval in her tone. She's always advising me to not make rash decisions; to remember that I am bereaved and that will colour, shape and influence any choices I make. I haven't run this past her, haven't talked it through and looked at it from every angle with her, and she is not impressed.

'Yes, Aunty Betty has moved in. It's not as bad as I'm making out, she's actually quite fun and the chil—' It seems wrong to call Phoebe that. She'll always be my child, but when she is sitting a couple of miles away trying to make adult decisions with a child's brain, it seems wrong to call her a child. 'Phoebe and Zane love having her around. She dotes on them. She dotes on me in her own way, I just worry.'

'That's a big decision,' Imogen says gently, sounding more patronising than concerned – for the first time I can remember, since *that day*, it's a sharp nail down my blackboard of irritation.

'What are we having for dinner?' Lewis cuts in, helpfully. As a widower he's probably had this, he'll have experienced people telling him how he should be careful, what he should be feeling, when he should be moving on because he is bereaved. He's probably been patronised within an inch of his life. 'It smells divine.'

'Oh yes! I almost forgot about that!' Imogen is on her feet. 'Go on through to the dining room, dinner will be served shortly.'

She's used butter, I can smell it, I can see the way it's beginning to congeal, a slightly solidified second skin, on top of the whole baby carrots and roasted new potatoes. Even olive oil wouldn't have been as bad. It's bad in terms of fat content and calories, but it's not high in saturated fat. She's used all-butter shortcrust pastry for the top of the chicken pie, but it's shop-bought pastry, so I can't know what's in it. Some brands have more fat than others, some brands add preservatives if it's not been frozen. She's probably used cream in her white sauce, too. Probably non-organic chicken because she's only fanatical about organic produce when it comes to her children.

'This is lovely,' Lewis says. Even though I don't know him that well, I know he's lying. It might look nice, it might smell nice but I can guarantee it does not taste nice – because Imogen, for all her attributes, has no love or respect for food. She throws things together and arranges them nicely on beautiful plates and hopes for the best. She told me that herself. Usually, she buys it all ready-made, heats it up and serves it. Tonight, she must really be trying to matchmake between Lewis and me if she's tried to cook.

Imogen beams at him. 'Thank you.'

'Lewis, I'm impressed with anyone who can teach teenagers in this day and age,' Ray says. They're a good-looking couple, Imogen and Ray. He's only slightly taller than her, slender because he likes to take care of himself with three visits to the gym a week. He has flawless skin, strong features, perfect teeth (of course, being a dentist). Unfortunately, which is why I avoid lingering in their house as much as possible, he's more than partial to the odd diatribe. In the same way most people ask if you've watched anything good on telly recently to fill a gap, he'll start a rant about undesirables in society and won't stop until his audience walk away or agree with him.

Lewis doesn't know this. He thinks Ray's comment about teenagers is innocuous and so replies: 'A lot of people say and think that, but they're not so bad. In fact, one of the most rewarding things about doing my job is when you connect with a student and you know they're on their way to doing something with their lives. It doesn't happen with every student and, granted, some of them can be trying, but it's like any job – you take the rough with the smooth.'

'You sound so passionate,' Imogen swoons. 'I would have given anything to have had a teacher like you when I was at school.'

'You probably did have one,' he says, 'but it's an unfortunate fact that if you weren't trouble, those teachers probably didn't need to focus on you. We tend to notice and try to correct the squeaky wheel.'

I cut into my chicken pie and the white filling oozes out onto my plate, stretching itself as it heads towards the potatoes, turning my stomach as it moves. She didn't follow the recipe, there are no herbs, no black pepper, but there'll be a tonne of salt. Slowly, precisely, I swirl the tip of my fork through the sauce, moving it towards a cube of chicken. The fork goes into the chicken after I press hard on the handle and I know it's over-cooked and tough – she cut the pieces too small and cooked it for too long. I have to eat this. It'll upset her if I don't.

She's watching me. Maybe she's spoken to Fynn – she's been known to call him if she's worried about me. Maybe he's told her what he thinks. I'm not sure he'd do that, though. He's too good a friend. Smothering my gag reflex with my respect and love for Imogen, I raise the fork and slip the chicken, swimming in white sauce, into my mouth. The cloying globules of fat coat my tongue, the sharp excess of salt claws at my tastebuds. Too much salt, not enough herbs, the wrong type of cream. I hate myself for knowing this stuff. I hate myself for not being able to enjoy food at times like this; that I immediately seek out a problem so I don't have to eat it, so I don't have to be seen to stuff myself in front of other people.

'Please don't do that again. Promise me you won't do that again,' Joel says in my head. *'Look, we'll get you whatever type of help you need. Whatever it costs . . . But please, don't do that to yourself again.'*

'A good friend – a true friend – would have confronted you by now about your eating disorder,' Fynn says.

Nonchalantly to the outside world, but determined to prove to myself, to Joel and to Fynn that I have no real, discernible problem, just a bit of a quirk, I force more chicken pie into my mouth, taking in the crumbly, fat-based crust this time. I slice the butter-coated carrots in half and then put them in my mouth. Chew, chew. I force myself to chew, ignoring the saline flooding my mouth, the bile that stirs itself in my stomach, and swallow. The new potatoes go the same way. Chewed, chewed, swallowed, stuffed down. I can do this. I can do this. I don't have a problem with food, I don't need confronting, I don't require help. I do not have an eating disorder.

'See, that's where my problem is,' Ray is saying while I am eating, ingesting food like a normal person. 'I pay my taxes, I send my child to school like the law tells me I should and I don't get first class service. But some little scrote who lives on a council estate, whose mum got knocked up as a teen to get a free flat, hasn't got a dad on the scene and wouldn't know the meaning of the word work if it bit him, gets loads of attention. How is that fair?'

'Let's change the subject,' I say, lowering my cutlery. I stare at my plate, the horror of what I have done slinking outwards

through me from my stomach. *I need to have not done this thing.*
I move my line of sight up to Ray as he sits on his indignant, know-it-all perch. 'I don't like you describing other human beings in such a way, Ray, I'm sorry, it's not on. You have no idea about other people's lives, you might think you do, but until you've lived it and lived it for years under different conditions, you have no real idea. There are some people like that and there are lots of people who aren't. I don't like you describing people so nastily. So please, let's change the subject and not fall out over this.'

'Yes, I agree,' Lewis says, obviously relieved that I've said something before he's had to. 'Let's change the subject.'

'Yes, *Ray*, let's change the subject,' Imogen adds through gritted teeth. He is going to be in so much trouble later tonight.

I glance down at my plate. I am in so much trouble right now. I stand, placing my napkin over my half-eaten meal. 'If you'll excuse me,' I say. 'I just need to nip to the bathroom.'

I am 29

'I thought you'd stopped doing this, Ffrony. You said you didn't need any help and you promised me you would stop.'

'I didn't promise. I said I'd try.'

'Why can't you just eat and stop this?'

'I don't know.'

'This is killing me, Ffrony. It's killing me that I can't help you, that I can't get you to stop this. Don't I make you happy enough? Is it me preventing you from being happy enough to stop this? It'll destroy me to split up, but we can do that if it means you'll be able to stop this.'

'No, no, no. That's not what I want. I don't want to split up. Never. I am so happy with you and Phoebe, I don't know why I can't stop, I just can't.'

'If it's because you want to become thin, believe me, you're thin enough. You're perfect. I don't love you for what size you are. I don't care what size you are or what you weigh.'

'I know. But everyone out there does.'

'No they don't. And if they do, so what? Why does it matter what people out there think?'

'It doesn't. But, if I lose a little bit more weight I know that no one will ever be able to say anything about the way I look. They won't be able to think I'm a fat cow. They won't be able to see there's anything wrong with me. I only need to lose a little bit more.'

'You don't need to lose any more weight. You've never needed to lose weight.'

'You didn't know me when I was younger. That's why I've kept all the photos away from you. I was huge.'

'Even if you were huge, so what? What's wrong with being large?'

'What's wrong with being large? Are you mad? There's everything wrong with it. People look down on you, they think you're lazy and greedy and unattractive. You can't fit into clothes and everyone's always got some statistic about how you're going to die young because you're so greedy and lazy.'

'Thin people die, too. Everyone dies, no matter what their size. And I've read just a small amount about what you do and the permanent damage it causes: crumbling teeth, swollen salivary ducts, osteoporosis, irregular heartbe—'

'Everything is so much easier and better if you're thin. Life is easier and people treat you better. If you're large you're worthless.'

'And do you feel any less worthless now you've lost all that weight?'

'No.'

I manage to keep my pace normal, I do not tear up the stairs like I want to. I climb each one as though I do not have a volcano desperate to erupt inside me. I walk along the corridor towards the bathroom.

Exiting the toilet, the sound of a cistern refilling itself behind him, is Damien, Imogen's eldest son from her first marriage. He is tall, athletic without being too broad, and wears his hair long and floppy, so – I'd imagine – he can spend a lot of time sweeping it back off his face or hiding behind it.

He freezes, then falters in his step when he sees me coming towards him. The colour quickly drains away from his face as he tries to decide what to do with his expression: smile, grimace or do what he is currently doing – look terrified. A lot of people look like that – scared of me because they don't know what to say. They aren't sure what will make me cry or will make me scream at them, so they tap dance their way through conversations, the discomfiture of not understanding a bereaved person rolling off them in waves.

I have seen him many times since *that day*, though. He came to the funeral, he sometimes drops Zane off with Imogen. Last summer he finished and graduated from Lincoln University so moved back here. Around the time Phoebe began to spend hours on her phone, in fact.

'Hi, Damien,' I say.

'Erm . . . Hi . . . Mrs Mackleroy,' he says.

Maybe I am reading too much into this. Maybe he was always like this, maybe like everyone else he's always felt uncomfortable. How would I have noticed since it's only in the past few months I've started to notice much of anything?

'How's the job-hunting going?' I ask.

'Erm . . .' He steps around me, heading for his bedroom. 'Fine.'

'Not found anything yet?'

'Erm . . . No.'

'So that means you're around during the day a lot,' I say. 'Doesn't that get boring?'

'Erm . . . No. Erm . . . I hang out.'

'Who with?'

'Erm . . . friends.'

'Girlfriend, by any chance?'

More colour bleaches out of his skin.

'Erm . . . sort of.'

'What do you mea—'

'Erm . . . got to go. Sorry. Bye.' He moves so fast, dashes so quickly out of my sight to the staircase to the loft I can't say anything else to keep him talking.

If he's the one, God help him.

I shut the bathroom door, then quietly prepare myself to do what I came up here for. I can't take too long, I can't make anyone else suspicious about me and what I do.

XXIX

'I won't walk you to the door,' Lewis says as he pulls up outside my house. He's kept the engine running. 'You know, just in case.'

I want to kiss him. I would so love to kiss him and see what happened next, I feel incredibly still inside right now, so serene that I could take that step. I can't, of course, because my mouth was full of sick. I rinsed it out with water, but I'm sure if anyone came too close they'd be assaulted with the putrid stench of who I really am.

'It's nothing personal,' I say to him. 'It really isn't. I actually . . . I actually quite like you.'

The lines of his face, tense with being so restrained and neutral, relax as he allows himself a little smile. 'That's not the impression I get.'

'You're a widower, you must understand how hard it is when you meet someone and it opens up all these possibilities but to even contemplate the possibilities you have to let go a little of the person you lost. The thought of letting even a little of Joel go . . . It's impossible to my mind. What was your wife's name?'

'Hallie,' he says, his demeanour sombre and reserved.

'You did tell me, but when did she . . . ?'

'Four years ago.'

'Was she ill before she died?'

He nods contemplatively. 'Yeah, she was.'

'Have you been out with people, dating and stuff like that?'

'I have.'

'When did you feel all right about seeing other women and not extremely guilty at the very idea of being attracted to other people?'

'I'll let you know when it happens.'

'Well, if it's like that for you, can you understand where I'm coming from?'

His black-brown eyes run carefully over my features until they settle on my lips. 'Can I kiss you?' he asks.

A wave of embarrassment and humiliation crashes over me. 'I'd love it if you did, but I, erm, the food tonight didn't really agree with me and when I went to the loo earlier, I kind of . . . Kissing would not be a pleasant experience.'

'OK,' he says. Amusement dances around his lips. He doesn't believe me.

'It's true.' I have simply left out the part where I did it because I'd been forced to eat to prove I don't have an eating disorder.

'I see,' he replies, the mirth has moved to his eyes and is now a huge smile. At least he thinks it's funny, not hurtful, that I might lie about throwing up to avoid kissing him.

'And anyway,' I say after a glance up at my house, 'if I'm not mistaken, my daughter is in my bedroom, sitting at the window watching to see if we are just two people who went to the same place at the same time or if we're dating. The last thing either Phoebe or I need right now is another thing to fall out over.' *Plus she is out there somewhere, watching. Noting this down to write into a letter.*

With remarkable restraint, Mr Bromsgrove doesn't look around. 'Well, yes, there is that. Next time?'

'Next time,' I agree. I say it but it doesn't mean anything. It doesn't mean I have to do anything. 'Maybe.'

He creases up with another amused smile.

At least he thinks it's funny.

XXX

My early start, the chance to get the shopping out of the way before the others wake up this Saturday morning, has been thwarted.

From my place on the pavement, my reusable bags tucked under one arm, my handbag slung across my body, I stand and I stare at my car. All four of the tyres have been let down – the little rubber covers have been left neatly beside each tyre. I'm not sure if it's before or after the air was let out that the large slash mark has been made at the centre of each tyre. The cuts are long and wide, made with an obvious stab, a twist then a drag downwards. It looks like they've been made with a hunting knife to get through the thick rubber.

Under the left windscreen wiper, the one nearest the pavement, placed to be the first thing you spot after the tyres, is a folded-over rectangle of paper. No envelope for this, her anger was too urgent, too immense for her to bother with such formalities.

Whore

I thought no one, not even Phoebe, could resent me more than I did for wanting to spend time with Lewis Bromsgrove, but I was wrong. This person does. This person has shown me, with four re-enactments of what the kitchen knife did to Joel's abdomen, how furious she is with me.

Is there something wrong with me? Should I be reacting differently to this? Should I be on the phone to the police already, begging them for help? Or should I be refolding the paper, slipping it into my bag and working out how much it's likely to cost to get all the tyres changed today because I need the car?

I am in this halfway house between fear and anger. I am teetering between these emotions and not sure which one will help me to get through this without anyone else getting hurt.

Back in the house, I check the clock – 7:49 – before heading for the kitchen and my laptop, ready to search for someone who will fix my car. No doubt they'll have questions, no doubt I'll play dumb and pretend I'm going to call the police. The house phone bursts into the silence of a still-asleep household and I dive for it, forgetting it might be Joel's mum.

'Did you snog him?' Imogen. My heart sinks.

'Morning, Imogen,' I say.

The brightness of her smile is too much even down the phone.

'Did you?' she replies, unable to hide or contain her absolute glee. 'He's a bit yummy, did you do us all a favour and snog the face off him?'

'No, I didn't.'

'Oh,' she says. 'I thought I felt a vibe between you!'

'You probably did,' I admit reluctantly. I wander into the living room.

'Oh my God, but that's brilliant!' she squeals. I hear her settle her cup of tea – white, two sugars – on the table so she can clap her hands. 'I mean, it's obviously so difficult to think about all that stuff after what you've been through, but this is great. Really. It's not too soon at all, so don't you even think that! I can totally see you two together!'

'It's not that simple.' I think I need to tell her. I need to see if she has any clue about Damien and Phoebe. If she has, then the news of the pregnancy would give me a reaction that would tell me I was on the right track with thinking it might be Damien. It's not my secret to share, but I also need someone to talk to who isn't a man I've slept with, a man who I'm attracted to, or an older woman who is hiding something even though she is living in my house.

If Damien is the father though . . . It could complicate things. If Phoebe hasn't told him the truth – which I don't think she has – then that would mean putting her at risk of unreasonable pressures and demands.

'Oh? Why not?'

'I can't tell you,' I say to her. I rub my eyes. 'I wish I could, but it's not my news to tell and I can't talk about it. My head is well and truly wrecked.'

My poor blue car seems so defeated, looking at it from the living room window. So damaged and hurt. Why did she do that? What was she thinking? Or wasn't she thinking? Is it easier to stick a knife in and twist it as a solution to your problems if you've done it before and were never punished for it?

It's not that much easier for me to wake up every morning and know I face another day without Joel, but maybe that's because it was forced upon me. Maybe if I'd actively decided to be without Joel I wouldn't mind doing it again and again and again. Maybe it's the same for her. Maybe by the second tyre it was as easy as breathing.

'Oh, Sweetheart,' Imogen coos on the phone, her voice a welcome balm, 'maybe it's good that you and Lewis are getting closer. Phoebe might have a thing or two to say about it but you can't live your life according to the whims of a hormonal teenager. It'd be so good for Zane, too. He needs a father figure. He's got Fynn, I know, but it's not the same. When you are in a relationship with someone it'll make everything so much better.'

I spin away from staring at my car and return to the conversation in full. 'Better?' I query.

'You've done an amazing job with those children since . . . but I really think that you need to move on and being part of a couple will help them to feel more secure.'

'I don't believe I'm hearing this,' I say. 'Are you basically saying my being a lone parent is destabilising for my children, more than, say, their father being killed?'

'Please don't take it the wrong way. It's just that children need two parents, they need a mother *and* a father. It's not your fault that you're a single mum. I mean, look at last week and you being called up to the school about Phoebe. She used to be such a sweet girl, wouldn't say boo to a goose, but now she's getting in trouble. The way she spoke to me the other day when I was just asking how she—' She stops talking and the sound of her mouth dropping open fills the line. 'Oh my God, she's not pregnant is she? Is that why Lewis is taking an interest in her?' My heart stops in my chest. 'Or is it drugs? Underage drinking?'

'Nice to know what you think of me and my family, Imogen.' Maybe Aunty Betty had a point after all.

'Sweetheart, no. I didn't mean it like that. It's just . . . If you do get together with Lewis, properly, a man with a decent job and who obviously has a positive influence on wayward kids, it'll do wonders for all of you.'

'How's Damien getting on?' I ask to change the subject, to follow up what I was thinking about last night not long before my car tyres were brutalised.

'Damien? He's fine.'

'Has he managed to get a job yet or is he still under your feet all day?'

'It's so hard out there for graduates,' she says. 'I've applied for a few jobs for him and I'm sure he'll get something soon.'

'I expect he spends a lot of time with his girlfriend when he's not applying for jobs? I saw him upstairs last night and he got all embarrassed when I mentioned it. Bless him, he looked so cute. Like he was a teenager all over again.'

'You know that boy, always has an army of girls after him. I remember Phoebe had a crush on him once upon a time.'

'Yes, I think she did,' I say. I needed her to confirm that I am remembering it right. That it may well be him that is involved in this, not Curtis.

'We should all get together soon, you can invite Lewis.'

'I may just do that,' I say. *It'd be great to spend some time with Damien, it really would.*

As I ring off the phone, all the things I need to think about crowd in on me. If I knew what Phoebe wanted to do, I could talk to her about talking to the police. Until she decides, I can't put anything else on her. I have to put up with the stalking, with the judgement from Imogen, with the hurt I've caused Fynn, with the feeling I'm betraying Joel by even thinking about Lewis.

Until Phoebe knows what she's doing, nothing else can happen. I am stuck as I am, out of control in my own life, waiting on someone else.

XXXI

'What do you think I should do, Aunty Betty?' Phoebe asks.

They obviously do not know I am in here. Why would I be? Why would anyone be in the small toilet beside the kitchen unless they'd recently stuffed themselves with as much food as they could, pushing it in by the handful, filling themselves as much as they could, forcing down every single feeling they had, hiding away every unpleasant thought with every swallow, and then had purged until their throat was raw, their eyes were running and they were shaking with the pain in their chest from heaving? Why would anyone have collapsed onto the floor and stayed there, unable to move from the exhaustion and horror and disgust at what they'd done? Trembling because their heart felt like it might give up at any second.

As silently as I could, I shifted my still-quivering body until my back was resting against the white door.

'No one can tell you that, Child,' Aunty Betty replies. I wonder what they're doing up at this time. I thought it was just me who couldn't sleep. 'You are a child, but in this situation you need to make big woman decisions.'

'Mum always tells me what to do, I thought she'd tell me what to do now.'

'Your mum can't do that about this. It's your life and your body, your mum can't make those choices for you.'

'But I don't know which choice is the best one.'

'No choice is easy,' Aunty Betty says. 'There are three main choices, yes?'

'Yes.'

'Keep the baby, have the baby adopted, abortion.'

'Yes.'

'Which one is the one that you instinctively think might be right for you when I say it like that?'

Phoebe says nothing for a while. 'I don't know. Every time I think about one, another one seems better.'

'Child, you are fourteen. No choice is better than the other at your age. Every option will weigh heavy on your mind and heart. The only thing we can do in this sort of situation is choose whatever it is we think would be easiest to live with.'

'I don't know what that is and I don't know what to do,' Phoebe says. My instinct is to run out to her, throw my arms around her, tell her that it'll be all right, we'll work out the best thing to do together.

'I will tell you the secret that all of us grown-ups have, Sweetness – we don't know what to do. We never know what to do. We pretend we do until something works.'

'My dad always knew what to do,' she says.

'If you believe that, truly believe that, you're the biggest fool I've ever met.' Aunty Betty smirks, I imagine she shakes her head. 'Your dad always knew what to do. Ha ha! I've never heard such nonsense in my life. No one always knows what to do. No one.' I can imagine her shaking her head some more.

'Apart from me. I always know what to do. All the time.'

I hear the scrape of wood on tile. 'Are you going to help me upstairs?' Aunty Betty asks.

Phoebe also scrapes her chair as she pushes it back. How many times do I have to ask them not to do that? 'Lots,' younger Phoebe would have said in reply to that question. 'Lots and lots and lots of times.'

'Child, you don't know how lucky you are,' Aunty Betty says as they make their way to the door. 'I know girls whose parents threw them out the second they found out they were expecting. Knowing your mother, I bet she hasn't even shouted at you. You are lucky, lucky, lucky.'

'But she hasn't—' Their voices disappear into the house, away from where I can hear what they are saying, cutting me off from knowing what it is I haven't done that has left my daughter hating me so.

After some time has passed, I pull myself up, the trembling recedes as I become upright and is taken over by a wooziness from all the blood rushing away from my head.

Upstairs, I ignore the multicoloured 'Keep Out' stickers that are plastered all over the door to Zane's room and carefully open it. Cautiously, I cross the room to his bed. My little boy, who told me on the day of the funeral that he knew he was now the man of the house, is splayed out in bed. His arms spread wide, the bottom of his blue pyjama top pushed halfway up his torso, his summer duvet spilling onto the carpet like water over the edge of a waterfall.

He looks like his father. He has his cheeks, his long eyelashes, the shape of his plump lips. It's good to see him sleeping like that, open, free. After Joel ... *Afterwards*, he would sleep curled up, a tight, closed-off little ball, desperate to keep the world out while he slept; terrified that the dangers of the world would somehow find their way into his life all over again. I'm glad after the attempted break-in and my tyres being slashed he's OK enough to be this free in his sleep.

I wanted to see him. To look in on him and wonder how I'm going to let him down, too.

VIII

XXXII

What I'd love to do right now is go for a walk on the beach.

I'd love to switch off my computer, push out my chair, gather up my coat, my bag, my laptop, my piles of papers, and walk straight out of here, wave to security, walk down the road, turn at the corner, navigate through the throngs of people and make my way down and down and down the hill, always with the wet, bluey horizon in sight, until I was there. I'd cross the road, find a way down onto the front and at the bottom of the steps I would stop and struggle my feet out of my shoes. And then ... My whole body would thrill with the sensation of cool smoothness on the soles of my feet; would contract with slight shock then would relax with plea-sure. I would make my way to the water's edge, each step a new shock-and-relax routine with the different textures and temperatures of the pebbles, until I could stand on the dark, damp sandy part of the beach and wait for the sea to come gushing towards me to claim my feet and ankles as its own. That's the whole point of living by the sea: you can drop by any time to let it tease and play with your feet and ankles, your shins and thighs, your bum and waist, your chest and neck, your entire head.

Like a lot of things since *that day*, going to the beach is not an option for me any more.

6 months after *That Day* (April, 2012)

The soles of my feet, a covering of rough, uncared-for skin, began to disappear into the wet, sandy part of the beach, and little ripples of seawater rushed in periodically to cover the tops of my feet in cold, foamy puddles. If I stood here long enough, the proportions would change, the sea would continue to come in and out, staying in a little longer each time until it gradually filled up this part of the beach; covering it and revealing it, covering it and revealing it, until it stopped revealing it and I was completely covered.

If I stood here long enough, I could disappear just like Joel had. I wondered again, as I did each time I did this, which one would be more painful – the way he went or the way I would. I took a step forwards, then another, then another, vanishing away the tops of my feet, then my ankles, then my shins. I had my laptop bag, stuffed not only with a computer, but also with a report I had to write, pages of other documents to read, other things to edit. The bag, barely shut with all the work I had to do that night. Slung across my body was my handbag, another full item, stuffed and heavy with the essential detritus of my everyday life. On the pebbles behind me were my shoes. *All she left behind were her shoes*, they'd say. *Everything else she took with her.*

I didn't want to wait for the sea to claim me, to replace the air around me with water, I wanted to be proactive, to walk forwards, to keep moving forwards until I began to float. I wouldn't float, though, because I was heavy, weighted down by my new, complicated life. I wouldn't swim either, wouldn't be able to move my arms and fight to stay alive because even if I let go of the things I carried, I could barely swim. And I wouldn't bother trying. I would let the sea do what it wanted.

My feet surged forwards again. Ready to do it, willing to walk into the sea and disappear.

Phoebe's face, a small, gaunt, innocent oval, shimmered into view. Zane's face, smaller, rounder, just as innocent, appeared beside his sister's. Joel's face materialised, too.

As if. As if I could do this to them.

Find something else, I told myself in an uncharacteristic moment of gentleness. I was so used to hearing my thoughts berating me, scorning me, reminding me I wasn't good enough, telling me off – I was taken aback by the kindness of that thought. It was almost as if I was talking to someone else. *Don't come to the beach any more, don't do this any more. Find something else to do. Don't do this to yourself any more.*

The inner voice, this almost loving version of who I was to myself, was right. I wouldn't leave my children, but the urge itself was destructive, it was stripping off little pieces of my soul, wearing it away like the sea wore away the rough edges of pebbles and soon, I'd probably lose the will to live. I'd want to die but I wouldn't be suicidal, I wanted to be with Joel but not enough to do anything about it. If I didn't find something else, I'd become someone counting down the days until I was allowed to leave, missing the point of having the gift of life. That was no way to be in this world.

My foot slipped a little on the saturated sand as I took a

step backwards, and my arms flew upwards to protect the laptop from the sea if I fell, but I righted myself. Carefully, I turned on my heels, enjoying the sensation of them sinking into the sand, having fragments of shell dig into my feet, and began my way up the beach. I had to find another way to cope, another way to connect with the world.

Two days later I kissed Fynn.

Sometimes I wish I could go away and be with Joel, even for a little while, and not have to deal with all of the stuff here. It was being unable to go to the beach that forced me to try to look for him in other places. Finishing Joel's cookbook seemed the only way to connect to him, to find that perfect blend of flavours that would remind me of what he was like, what being with him was all about. I haven't even had a chance to think up something new, try out something new since I was called to the school sixteen days ago. My search for him has been stalled by the realities of everyday life, by the fact his killer is stalking me.

Imogen is standing outside my building. She's looking at the front of it as if she's about to enter, or maybe she's waiting for someone. When she tucks her bag determinedly onto her shoulder I realise she's been waiting for me.

'I'm sorry,' she says before I've worked out what to do with my face or whether to say 'hello' or 'hi' or 'are you waiting for me?'

'Sometimes I'm a big-mouthed, over-opinionated cow,' she

continues. 'I'm so sorry. I shouldn't have said all those things. It's no wonder you don't tell me things when I don't engage my brain before I run my mouth off.' Rather dramatically, I decide, her hazel-green eyes fill with tears. 'I think you do an amazing job with those children and I can't believe I implied that you didn't. I think you're an amazing parent and I know you're going to be an amazing grandmother.'

'Pardon?' I reply.

Again with the drama, she looks around, takes a step closer to me and lowers her voice. 'Damien told me about Phoebe being . . .' her tone drops to barely a whisper, '*pregnant.*'

'Damien told you? *Damien* told you? Why would *Damien* tell you that?'

'Please don't be angry,' she prefaces her reply. The children do that when they know I'm going to hear something that will mean a nuclear response can be the only option. 'After Saturday, I asked him to call her because they used to be quite close. I said to him that it'd be nice for him to find out how she's getting on and, if in the course of the conversation he happens to ask her how she feels about the possibility of you dating her teacher, then that'd be great. I'm sorry, I know I shouldn't have got involved, but I was so interferingly desperate for you to meet someone nice. I can see how lonely you get sometimes and Lewis seems so perfect.'

'During the course of this one conversation Phoebe just came out and said she was pregnant?' Given it took me a trip to the school and someone else saying the words to find out, given that she burst into tears when she thought I'd told Aunty Betty, given that I've been too frightened of the trauma it'd cause her if she knew I'd told Fynn, given that she barely speaks to me *at all*, she's managed to tell a relative stranger this news? As well as giving him and Imogen the implication that she's decided she's going ahead with the pregnancy. 'Why would she do that?'

'They are close.'

Or he is the father.

'That whole conversation we had the other day, I understand so much more now. I feel horrible about it. I shouldn't have said those things, I don't even believe them. I suppose I wanted you to see that a lot of your loneliness could go away if you took a chance on Lewis. I shouldn't have questioned your parenting. I'd have taken anyone's head off who did that to me.'

'Thanks, Imogen, for the apology. But right now, I need to go and have a few words with my daughter.'

I don't even wait for a reply before I step around her and hurry up the road towards the car park.

I've been *so stupid*. Giving her space, allowing her time to think about what she wants rather than imposing my will upon her or forcing her to talk to me. All along she's been plotting and planning, scheming behind my back, just like before. She has no respect for me. She knows that I am so scared of losing her love, she's probably unconsciously aware that I don't want her to feel about me the way I feel about my mother, that I'll almost literally let her get away with murder.

XXXIII

'Phone!' I say to Phoebe when I enter the house.

I don't bother to take my coat off, I hurl my laptop and bag onto the sofa and stand in front of my daughter with my hand outstretched.

Zane stops staring at the television screen and turns to me. Horrified, I'd imagine, at the fury broiling in my voice. I never speak like that, even before I started trying to be more like Joel, to keep him alive for them by trying to respond to them like he did, I never showed this much anger.

Aunty Betty, resplendent in her bobbed burgundy wig and matching lipstick, lowers her e-cigarette and does big eyes at me too. Phoebe looks up at me from the screen in her hand, trying to gauge how to react to my demand.

'*PHONE!*' I roar.

She meekly places it in my hand, not even bothering to try the battery trick.

'Get upstairs. We need to have a proper talk.'

Her widened, melted-wood eyes fly first to Zane, then to Aunty Betty, wondering if either of them is going to help her by stepping in. Neither of them is, of course. Zane has on a violent movie, Aunty Betty has an e-cigarette in her hand – they've both got problems of their own.

'DID YOU NOT HEAR ME?' I scream at her and she is out of her seat and taking the stairs two at a time. I revolve slowly to the other two piss-takers in the house.

'You.' I point at Zane. 'No more TV for two weeks. I've told you I don't want you watching anything over a twelve registration, but you can't listen to that, so no more TV for two weeks. And that includes no playing any games on it.' I spin on the spot. 'And as for you . . .' I march over to Aunty Betty. 'I've told you about this. There's no smoking in this house.' I go to snatch the cigarette off her and she refuses to relinquish it, struggling with me, clinging onto her black and chrome holder like life-support. Her sixty-six-year-old hands, although bony and wrinkled, like darkened, aged parchment, are strong and won't easily give up. I eventually wrench it free from her grasp. She gives me Phoebe-big eyes, unable to believe I've done that.

'Child, you can't expect me to go outside every time I need a little top-up. And it's cold out there. You really expect a woman my age to go out into the cold?'

'You really, really want to be able to smoke inside?' I ask.

'Yes, Child, yes.'

'Well then you shouldn't have got thrown out of the one place where you could do whatever you wanted, whenever you wanted, should you?'

She sits back, looking me up and down as if she is wounded by my words. Wounded, I doubt. Surprised, absolutely.

'Zane,' I say, normalising my tone.

'Yes, Mum?' he says, now on his feet.

'Please go and get ready, you and your Aunty Betty are going to get some chips for dinner tonight.'

'Yes, Mum,' he says and pegs it out of the room.

'You got a problem with that?' I say to Aunty Betty.

'No, no,' she says quickly. 'I'll pay for dinner,' she adds.

'I suspect I'll pay at some point in some way, but thanks for the offer anyway.'

Phoebe thinks hiding under her covers will save her. That I will see she has tried to shut out the world by curling up under her seaside-scene duvet and will respect the gesture; I'll leave her alone.

She's ignored my knock on the door, as I expected she would, and so I entered anyway. At the windows, on five individual threads hang the leftover crystal butterflies she strung together for the kitchen. They catch the light as they gently twirl, throwing small, glancing patches of colour on the walls and making the whole room look as if it is dancing. I don't often come in here. I've tried to respect her privacy, trusted her not to have crusty, moulding plates and cups, to sort out her own laundry, to keep things tidy for herself not because I want her to. I do often sit outside her room, waiting for her to fall asleep and whispering 'I love you' into the wooden door, hoping it'll transfer into the air inside the room and will diffuse into her mind as she sleeps.

I never had any privacy, I was never allowed any secrets, nothing I did went without scrutiny and I never wanted that for Phoebe. I wanted more openness, a closeness between us that I never had with my mother.

'You can cut that out, too,' I say to Phoebe as I sit on her office chair and swivel it towards the bed. 'There's no hiding from this right now, Phoebe, so I'd appreciate it if you would sit up and talk to me.'

The drive home had heated up my blood until it was boiling over when I stormed through the door. I kept seeing Joel's face, so still and peaceful, threaded with the agony of his last moments too; I kept experiencing the moment when I lost feeling in my fingers and that bowl of blackberries fell from my hands; I kept remembering seeing reporters outside the coroner's court, waiting for me as I went to the first day of the inquest and I had to tell the taxi driver to drive on because I couldn't cope (I knew Fynn and Joel's parents would be waiting for me but I couldn't do it). I kept thinking what a mug I'd been to give her so much space, when time was ticking away and the threat from my stalker, Joel's killer, seemed to be intensifying. I haven't heard from *her* in two days. It scares me, unnerves me that she is out there, and I can't go to the police because I'm trying to spare Phoebe. And Phoebe has been making decisions without bothering to tell me.

'*Phoebe,*' I threaten. Slowly her hands move under the cover to the top edge and she pulls the duvet down so I can see the chestnut-brown glow of her fourteen-year-old skin, the beautiful apples of her cheeks, the mini-me version of her small button nose, the set of her dark brown lips, the perfectly straight lines of her hair gathered into two pigtails.

'So, you told Damien you were pregnant?' I ask.

Her eyes, which had been defiantly glaring up at the glowing star-covered ceiling, widen in alarm.

'Is he the father?' I ask.

'No!' she says with disgust. 'You know Curtis is.' *Lie*. But I don't call her on it.

'Who else have you told?'

'No one.' *Lie*.

'So why did you tell him?'

'He asked because you'd already told Imogen.' *Lie*.

'I didn't tell Imogen. I wanted to because God knows I need someone to talk to when my head is so wrecked, but I didn't.'

'You told Uncle Fynn, though.' *Deflection*.

'Yes, yes I did. I was in shock and I told him.'

'See?' she says.

'See what? See that my daughter won't talk to me? That when she does talk to me she lies to me? That I'm once again terrified of what's going to happen next? Yes, I do see all that.'

She bunches her lips together and narrows her eyes as though trying to read something written about her on the ceiling above.

'Why did you tell Damien you were pregnant?'

'Because . . . I wanted to know what it felt like to say it out loud again. It doesn't seem real sometimes and I wanted to know what it sounded like.' *Truth. At last some truth.*

'Have you decided at all what you think you might want to do? Because it sounded from what Damien told his mother that you'd decided to go ahead with the pregnancy.'

'I never said that! I told him I was pregnant. And he said, "Oh, wow, I bet your mum's really pissed" and that was it.' *More truth.*

'What can I do to help?' I ask her. 'Is there anything I can do to help you come to a decision?'

'No!' she snarls. *Contempt. Because I've stopped shouting at her, because I've stopped being scary and unapproachable, she's back to contempt.*

'Fine. OK,' I say. It hurts at my core that she thinks of me like this, that I'm not good enough for her to want to talk to any more. That she can sit in the kitchen and tell her great aunt something but not me. I will not cry in here with her about this. 'Well, you know where I am if you want to talk.'

She snorts her derision.

'But Phoebe, we're going to have to go back to the doctor's soon. I know it freaks you out, but you need to decide if you're going to start on the folic acid and we'll need an early scan to check everything's OK, or if you're going to have to make another type of appointment. Whichever choice you make, just remember I'll support it a hundred per cent.'

Her eyes angle themselves to the left of the ceiling as she attempts to block out the annoying sound that is her mother.

'Here's your phone,' I say as I stand, and leave it on her desk. 'Oh, and by the way, I'm going down to call Mr Bromsgrove to let him know you're going back to school tomorrow. You and Zane are both going back tomorrow.'

'But—' she says.

'You're going to school tomorrow and we're going back to me taking you for breakfast club and picking you up after homework club.'

'But—'

'Yes?'

'Nothing. Fine.'

*

Lewis is silent for a while when I tell him that Phoebe is coming back to school in the morning. Then says: 'If you think it's best.'

'I think it's best she doesn't sit around doing nothing,' I reply.

'Has she decided what she—?'

'Not that she's telling me. She also says she hasn't told anyone else about it. What about Curtis, has he?'

'Not that I know of.'

'I'm not fooling myself that it's going to stay a secret for much longer, especially if she starts having symptoms soon, but I think it's best to be keeping up with school as much as possible.' I sound like a proper parent, there. Firm and decisive, not scared and confused.

'I agree,' he says. 'Erm, hang on.' I sense movement and I realise Lewis is moving, probably taking his phone elsewhere to get some privacy.

I walk the distance to the small shelf in the corridor, and hook the phone between my chin and shoulder so that I can leaf through the most recent post to have been delivered. Another unstamped cream envelope sits among the bills and fliers and circulars that have been pushed through our door. Another connection from the woman that ruined my life.

'Hi, sorry about that,' Lewis says, giving me a start. I hadn't realised how hard I'd been concentrating on the expensive envelope in my hands. I release my phone from its position on my shoulder, hold it to my ear in one hand, the letter in the other.

'Hi,' I reply.

307

'I . . . erm . . . Can I see you?' he says. 'Just you.'

My response is to exhale at length.

'I don't do this very often, Saffron. It's unfortunate the circumstances we've met under, but I'd still like to see you.'

I should say no. Instead I say, 'How did your wife die?'

If someone said that to me after I'd asked them out, I would hang up. Honestly, it's such an unnecessary intrusion. There's no reason for me to ask that except to maybe prod him where his question has prodded me, to get him to consider it's not as simple as saying yes or no.

Lewis is silent for several minutes, they tick by loudly as I wait for a reply or for Zane and Aunty Betty to return from the shop with our fish and chips dinner.

'I should go,' I say. He doesn't want to answer and he shouldn't have to.

'No, no, don't go. She died of cirrhosis of the liver. Alcohol related. Very difficult all round.'

'I'm sorry to hear that.'

'Is it guilt that's stopping you from saying yes?'

'Maybe.'

'I mean guilt about how he died? Do you feel responsible?'

It's obvious I'll feel guilty about the possibility of dating someone after Joel, but less obvious that I will feel guilty about how he died, too. And I do. It's a type of guilt that stirs the constant vat of sickness at the bottom of my stomach; the mixture of bile and desolation that never goes away, no matter how many times I throw up. I don't say that to anyone because they will tell me it's not my fault, that I shouldn't blame myself, that it was his killer who was responsible, not me. They'll say all those things and they'll have no idea what they're talking about.

'Do you?' I reply.

'Yes. I wish she'd loved me enough to give up drinking before it got to that point. I wish I'd managed to make her see what she was doing to Curtis when she was still drinking when she was ill. I wish that I'd been strong enough to take Curtis and leave so he didn't have to be exposed to the end of her life being like that. I feel very guilty.'

'OK, yes. We can meet up at some point, soon.'

'Is tonight too soon?'

'Yes,' I laugh, 'that's far too soon.'

'Well, let's not leave it too long, OK?'

'OK. Bye, Lewis.'

'Bye.'

I slide my finger under the flap of the envelope, bracing myself for what it's going to say. Her missives don't frighten me, they are better than trying to break into the house or costing me nearly two thousand pounds in new tyres and call-out expenses, and nonsensical explanations to my family.

All there is in the envelope is a photograph.

That Day
My fingers are numb, my body is numb, my entire being is suddenly without air. There are a dozen little splattering thuds of black-berries falling onto the ground, there's a crash of a white ceramic bowl hitting a white ceramic tile.

*

The photo lies on the maple-coloured floorboards of our hallway. It's been taken by a mobile phone so the quality isn't brilliant: the image is fuzzy, slightly blurred, but it's clear enough to show me what I need to see.

Phoebe and Joel, standing talking in the outside car park at the very top of Churchill Square shopping centre on the day he died.

XXXIV

That Day

'I'll see you later, Babes, I'd better get going. If I drop the car off early enough I should be able to get it back early.'

'OK,' I called from the bedroom. 'Are you sure you don't want to tell me what this extra special pressie you're going to buy me is?'

'Yes, I'm sure.'

The front door clicked shut and, wearing my dressing gown, I threw myself onto the bed. Joel had done the school run for a change and I could avoid getting dressed until the mood took me. For the first time in ages we both had the day off, so I could do as I pleased. What I pleased was to do nothing.

Seconds later, the front door opened and shut again, and I heard Joel take the stairs two at a time, not bothering to kick off his shoes.

'What did you forget this time?' I said, a laugh at his forgetfulness at the back of my throat.

'To kiss you goodbye.' He pressed his cold lips against my neck and sent that familiar, delicious shudder through me. 'See you later, Babes.'

'See you later.'

*

Phoebe and Joel stand close together, only visible from the waist up. He has his hands up, his fingers spread apart as he talks to her. Probably telling her off, reminding her that she'd promised not to do that again after the last time, but unable to do so without the look of absolute adulation he had for both his children on his face. They drove him mad but he couldn't do proper angry when it came to them. He'd try, but it'd end with him wanting to make it all better, smooth things over because he'd know whoever it was didn't mean it. He was rubbish at discipline so had to leave it to me.

Phoebe is in her grey school uniform, she has bunches that I put in that day because at that time I still did her hair for her: she sat on the floor between my legs while I manipulated her beautiful locks into hairbands or plaits or twists. In the picture she's doing big 'sorry' eyes at Joel, knowing he'll be OK with her, he'll sort it out with the school, will write a note saying he forgot he had to take her out for an appointment; knowing he'll tell me and stop me from screaming at her.

I drop to my knees, pick up the photo. Joel. This is how he was that last day. He was meant to come back to me. He had errands to run, his car to pick up, a present he wanted to buy for me. He was meant to come back and we'd cuddle up in the living room and watch something on television while talking. Or maybe do bubbles in the garden without the disapproving gaze of our children. He was meant to come back to me.

'*See you later, Babes.*'

'*See you later.*'

I saw him later: still, immobile, forever gone from me. But he couldn't see me. And he'd never see me again.

This murderer has a photograph of him from *that day*.

The letters, the break-in attempt, the tyres . . . all of them pale into insignificance against this. She has something of him that I'll never have and she is using it to needle me.

If I saw this woman right now, I think I could probably kill her.

XXXV

I'm searching for the perfect punnet of blueberries.

I spent a lot of time in bed last night going through my notebook and writing things down, making notes of recipe ideas, foods I could combine, to find that perfect blend.

My scrawlings – manic and wild, many, many crossed-out words, many underlined, lots of bad doodles – were my way of suppressing the photo in my head. I had to stop myself from seeing that picture. I'd hidden it less than two feet away from me, but it still felt as if it was in my hand. I could still see the captured lines of my husband's face in his final few hours. I was still experiencing Phoebe's mollified smile, a smile I haven't seen since before *that day*. Every time the image became clearer in my head, the faster, harder, I would write.

What I came up with was something with blueberries. They're about to come into season, so the ones on sale will be imported meaning they're either firm and tangy or soft and oozing with subtle sweetness – either way, the right ingredients can wash it away or enhance it. That something else will be soft apricots.

I was convinced by the time I fell asleep, anxious because I'd managed to resist silencing what was macerating me inside in the usual, familiar way, that this flavour combination would be it. It would be the flavour that I could put in my mouth and would remind me of what life tasted like before I lost Joel.

After dropping Phoebe at school – with firm instructions that if she wants to keep her phone, computer and ability to live in our house not under lock and key she's to wait for me to pick her up tonight – I've done a bit of a haphazard shop. I went for the jars first – small, squat jars each with a bright orange rubber airtight ring and wire-hinged lid – that I will have to sterilise either on the stove or in the dishwasher. Then I had to hunt around to find some fair-trade vanilla pods, and then I went for sugar. I'm going to make blueberry and apricot jam without pectin so it was a toss-up between sugar and honey but the sugar won. I picked up butter on the way back to the fruit and veg aisles (virtually at the entrance to the store, where I probably should have started), searching for the blueberries. I've got lemons, and the apricots, which are soft and furry-skinned but not enough to set my teeth on edge like peaches do. I've seen some blueberries but they're not organic. The ones I need for my jam have to be organic. They just have to be.

'I thought it was you!' Imogen says behind me. 'I kept looking over and thinking it must be you! But then it couldn't because you should be at work! But it is! It is you!'

Imogen often speaks in exclamation marks. In short, should-be-screamed sentences. It's actually quite irritating. Or is it that since the announcement of Phoebe's pregnancy, I've stopped being the numb woman who dropped the blackberries and I can feel again? The mute button has been lifted and I am experiencing life again. And life is painful. Since the photo last night, when I've had to make a gargantuan effort to be normal for the children, the world also seems to be loud and full of exclaiming people like the woman behind me.

'Imogen! Hi!' I say as I revolve to face her. I am doing it too, I am sending shards of pain into my ears, scraping agony across my skin.

'So! What are you doing here during the day?'

'Working from home, apparently!' I continue in my masochistic falsetto and hold aloft my wire basket. (Frankly, Kevin can swivel. I almost told him that, but instead said I'd get more done at home and if he wanted this urgent report – that his assistant director of operations should have done but didn't because it was beyond his capabilities – it was best I wasn't in the office.) 'Cooking from home would be more accurate, though! I need to do something calming before I knuckle down to work!'

Imogen nods sagely. 'I know what you mean! I'd imagine the hormone levels in your house are pretty high at the moment!'

Did I always have so much Imogen in my life? I wonder idly. She was at my house, then dinner, then the phone call, then showing up at my work and now this. I've had contact with her at least five times these past seven days. In the last eighteen months it hasn't been a problem, she's been such a help, but at what price? Since Saturday, I've been asking myself if I actually like her that much.

'I can't believe you're going to be a grandmother!' she says suddenly, excitement infused in every word.

Do I like you at all, let alone 'that much'? It's nothing personal to her, I am questioning everything.

'I only have to pick up a few bits,' she says to my 'not engaging' silence, 'do you fancy accompanying me and then we can go for a coffee or something?'

'I can't, I really do need to get some work done.'

'OK, spoilsport, walk around with me then. It won't take long.'

'Fine,' I say.

Apples
Milk
Eggs
50-50 bread
Cucumber
Butter
Sausages

Imogen's handwriting is completely different to the one of the letter writer. Hers is over-the-top curly, her 'e's look like they are trying to have a nice little rest, her 'l's look like they are stretching out their tips to the letters above, the bellies of the 'b's are filled with an additional ink swirl.

'I think you'll make a fantastic grandmother!' she says, chancing her arm again. 'You'll be young enough to enjoy your grandchild! That's such a bonus!'

I want her to stop acting as if there is only one choice in this. She did it outside my work yesterday and now twice in less than ten minutes. I want her to stop it. 'Phoebe hasn't decided what she's going to do yet,' I say, simply. My voice is now kinder on my ears, the falseness has been replaced by a monotone.

Imogen, my friend from the school gates, who was friendlier than the other mothers right from the off, stops in the middle of the meat aisle, in front of the rows of chicken, and regards me at length. Her perfectly shaped eyebrows are knitted together like the seam of a cardigan, her lips are pursed like a closed-up zip but open to ask: 'What do you mean?' before instantly zipping themselves up again.

'I mean . . . I *mean* my daughter is fourteen years old and nothing has been decided yet.'

She parts her tightened mouth to speak again: 'What is there to decide?'

When I don't say anything, she speaks again: 'Are you really going to make her do *that*?'

I don't like you, I decide. *Even though you were there and you helped to keep me going when the world fell apart, I don't like you. I'm not sure I'm allowed to think like that, that I'm allowed to 'not like' anyone who has helped me after I was bereaved, but I can't help this. I simply don't like you.*

Aunty Betty was right, Imogen is an emotional vampire.

'I'm not going to make her do anything,' I say. When you stand in front of the fridges for a while you realise how loud they are as they pump out cold air.

'She'll regret it for the rest of her life,' Imogen says, her voice pitched somewhere between hysterical and foreboding, as if she has unique insight into how my daughter will feel for however long she lives.

'How do you know that then?' I ask.

Ignoring my question, she says, 'It's bad enough she didn't keep her legs shut, but doing *that*? She'll never feel the same about herself. She can't right a wrong by doing more wrong. And what if she can't have another baby because of scarring? I can't believe you'd do this to your daughter.'

'What about the alternative?' I reply. I can feel the thrum of the fridges in my veins, they move through me in calming waves. 'What if my fourteen-year-old daughter has a baby? How will I pay for it? Because, let's be honest, I *will* be paying for it. How will I be able to work and take care of a baby because Phoebe will legally have to go back to school? I'll either have to find childcare or give up my job. How will we survive financially? Even with the mortgage paid off by Joel's life insurance, it is still a struggle to make ends meet. So, what am I supposed to do? Try to get benefits? Even if we managed to get any, your husband made it perfectly clear what he – and I suspect you – think of people who live on benefits. That's how people all over the place will look at us. Then there's Zane, why does his life have to be turned upside-down because of someone else's choices? And what about me? I only wanted two children, I've done the newborn and baby and toddler and young child years, I don't need or want them again. Is that all unimportant because I'm supposed to subscribe to some principle that *you* have?'

Imogen's mouth remains creased in on itself, a severe line of scrunched-up disapproval.

'But as I said, *nothing* has been settled upon. If Phoebe decides she wants to continue with the pregnancy, I will do my damnedest to support her and to find a way to make it work. But only if that's what she decides. And before you say anything, no, I haven't said all that to her about how it will devastate our lives if she goes ahead with the pregnancy because I want her to make up her own mind and make her own choice.'

'*That* shouldn't even be an option, though, can't you see that, Saffron? It's just wrong.'

I am getting nowhere here. Nowhere. And why am I even having this argument? What is it to her, anyway? 'You really believe that abortion is wrong, Imogen?' I say.

'Yes, yes I do,' she says.

'Well don't have one then,' I reply.

I drop my wire basket with my ingredients, and leave her standing in the cold food aisle. Reasoning with her is like trying to empty the sea with a teaspoon: frustrating, impossible and ultimately pointless.

Every step should rip at my already ravaged heart, because I thought I loved Imogen. I thought we were good friends and even if we disagreed, we cared enough about each other to take a step back, to let the other make their own mistakes and catch them if they fell.

Obviously, I've been blinkered, ignorant, *numbed* to the reality of this friendship so I feel nothing at all. In the reawakening process, it's one of the first things to go.

XXXVI

6 months before *That Day* (April, 2011)

'Did you know she'd been bunking off school?' Joel was enraged. Pacing the bedroom, trying and failing to keep his voice down.

'Yes, Joel, I did. In fact, I went out with her a few times myself.'

'This isn't funny,' he snapped.

'Oh, OK. "Not funny when I'm being sarcastic." I shall note that down on my CV.'

'*Ffrony . . .*'

'I'm not the one who bunked off school so I don't see why I should be getting into trouble. But if you insist on acting as if I am, I will continue to be unfunnily sarcastic. So, can you calm down . . . and *sit* down so we can talk about this properly?'

'Her and a couple of other girls have been bunking off and getting the train up to Worthing. Anything could have happened and we'd have never known what she was doing there.'

My head nodded as though that hadn't occurred to me, that I hadn't already played through several scenarios that would have ended badly. 'The problem is, Joel, me and you were two of those children who wouldn't even think to bunk off. We don't know her mindset.'

'I'll give her mindset,' he said.

'Yeah, right. You think it was just your bad luck that the school called you? Your twelve-year-old daughter knows what we all know – she has you wrapped around her little finger. A quick flash of the big eyes and a downturned mouth and "Oh, Daddy, I'm sorry" and you'll be helping her plan the next excursion.'

'I'm not that bad.'

'You are.'

'All right, I am. What do we do?'

'We hit her where it hurts. No phone and the pleasure of us accompanying her to and from school every morning for an unspecified amount of time.'

'Can I at least shout at her?' he said.

'You can try. But when you start crying instead of her because of the look on her face, don't come running to me.'

'I really am pathetic, aren't I?'

'Only when it comes to your children, Sweetheart. Which is why you've got me. I have no worries about shouting at her for things like this.'

'I'll be there when you do it, to show I back you up. I'll ask for the phone, too.'

'Fantastic. Once we're finished with her, she'll never even think about bunking off school again.'

XXXVII

The photo is still there.

I shut and lock the bedroom door, drop to my knees and feel for it, inside a clear plastic A4 wallet taped to the underside of my bedside table. My whole body relaxes and then tenses when my fingers brush over the cool plastic, feeling the outline of the shape and bulk of the envelopes.

Rap-rap-rap! at the door makes me jump. I snatch my fingers away and stumble back from my hiding place.

'Yes?' I call.

'Saff-aron,' Aunty Betty says. 'Can I talk to you?'

She is holding onto the wall when I step out of my bedroom. Today she has on a blonde chin-length wig and big pearl earrings. She is wearing her long, black silk kimono and her pink slippers with feathery balls at the front. No make-up, but she doesn't need it because she has an enduring beauty that is underpinned and fuelled, I think, by her 'I can do whatever I want' attitude to life.

'Of course,' I say to her. 'Let's talk in your room.' It'll give her a chance to stay upstairs after our chat. Aunty Betty sometimes walks as if she is being carried by angels and makes no sound, and then at other times, like today, she is slow, stiff, agonised. I've never asked her what is wrong, if it's the previously broken hip playing up or something else, because I suspect she'd curse me out for trying to turn her into someone she's not – i.e. an older person who talks about their ailments. I haven't even thought about registering her with a doctor. I need to add that to the list.

'It's nothing urgent,' she says. She uses the flat of her hand against the wall leading up to the loft to move her body, hefting herself from step to step. Maybe I should have put Zane up here. I didn't even think about that. The old Saffron, the one I was before I was the woman who dropped the blackberries, would have. She would have given Zane or Phoebe the upstairs room even though it runs the whole length of the house and has its own walk-in wardrobe in the eaves and shower-room with loo. The old Saffron would have booked Aunty Betty in to a doctor and dentist, she would have made sure Aunty Betty had access to everything she needed.

She drops heavily onto the bed, kicks off her slippers and rubs the hip she broke. 'If you were male, ten years younger and not related to me, I'd have you stripped to the waist and rubbing my feet by now,' she says and adds a dignified cackle.

'I really don't need to hear things like that,' I say.

In two weeks she has made this room her own: every flat raised surface is covered in photo frames – snapshots of the people she's loved, the places she's visited, the 'other celebrities' she's allowed to be photographed with her. The bed has been adorned with her shiny, chocolate-brown diamante-studded quilt. She has a chocolate-brown, ruched, heart-shaped rug on either side of the bed. In the belly of and around the fireplace she has piled up some of her books, probably her most precious ones. She has hundreds of them in storage. This is what her bedroom looked like in her old mansion flat, this is what her bedroom looked like in each of her 'apartments' in the various complexes she'd moved into. In the bathroom I know she has lined up all her wigs on black, faceless mannequin heads.

'My brother called me earlier,' she says, quickly, decisively like delivering unsettling news should be delivered. 'He wanted to know if I'd spoken to you because he said Elizabeth's been calling you for a while.'

'Yeah, she has.'

'Didn't want to speak to her?'

'Not especially.'

'They want to come and visit.'

'I know.'

'I told them the guest room is occupied by me – he was a bit surprised by that – so they've agreed to either come for the day or find a hotel.'

'Right. Did they say when?'

'This weekend, I think, because of the bank holiday. But you'll have to call them to check.'

'Yes, I suppose I will.'

'Do you want me to go and live with them?' she asks as quickly and decisively as she told me Joel's dad had called.

'What?' I reply. 'No! Why would you even think that? Have I made you feel unwanted or unwelcome? Because I'm sorry if I have.'

'No, no, Child, it's not that, there's so much going on here right now. You don't need me and my stuff cluttering up your life.'

'You're a part of what's going on, Aunty Betty. For better or worse, unfortunately for you. And do you know why we went through the deep, *deep* agony of having the attic converted? Joel always planned to have you living with us. Before you went into your different "villages" he knew you'd need to live with other people at some point. And then when you did move into your "homes" he knew you'd be chucked out of one place too many eventually and he wanted you to live here when you were. I thought I was the control freak, but turns out it was my husband. I wish you'd given me more notice, like, but that doesn't change the fact that this is your home now.'

Aunty Betty smiles her trademark grin of mischievousness. 'You're a good girl, Saff-aron. I like you.'

'Even though I won't let you smoke in the house.'

'Even then.'

'I should get on with work,' I say, despite it being the last thing I want to do right now. My mind keeps going to Phoebe, the brave look on her face as she marched in through the school gates, waving away any suggestion I come with her to see the headmaster and Mr Bromsgrove. My head goes to Zane, who is slipping back to being quieter than normal these days. Since Joel he has been quiet anyway, his exuberant nature whisked away almost overnight. He talks to Aunty Betty and for a while he was almost himself again, but now he's struggling. I've even rescinded the ban on telly because he seems so damaged, insular. My thoughts go to Fynn and how much I hurt him. My guilt goes to Lewis, who is at school unaware that I've decided I can't see him – not right now. My heart goes to the photo and letters downstairs and it begins to race, stirring the sickness within faster and faster.

'No one tells you, do they, that the biggest loss when someone you love dies is the loss of who you are,' Aunty Betty says.

I lower myself onto my seat and refocus myself on Aunty Betty.

'You get to my stage of life and you lose so many people. I remember when the first man I had sex . . . Now take that look off your face, Saff-aron. I had sex, get over it. Where was I? I remember when the first man I was intimate with died. He was the first person I was close to who passed. He wasn't that nice in the end, and it wasn't some big love, but when he was gone, I cried. I sat in my house and cried because he was the first. He was the first of the people my age to go, and I knew I was going to be losing people, they were all going to leave me until it was my turn. And there was nothing I could do about it.

'I was crying for myself because of all the loss to come, or so I thought. In time I came to see that I was crying, also, because the Betty I was when he was alive was gone. He was a part of me whether I liked it or not and he was suddenly gone. Who I was, how my role in the world was defined by him, was over. The closer you are to someone, the bigger that loss of part of who you are is, I think.'

For the first time, ever, I see Aunty Betty beneath the mask. She is incredibly human, suddenly, her face streaked with pain, her eyes, that unusual liquid-mahogany brown colour that Joel, Phoebe and Zane shared, are swimming in tears. I've never seen her cry. I don't think she's seen me cry, either. Despite everything, we have not cried together. Even without the tears, I've known how sad she was. Sad she is.

'I would have moved the moon for Joel,' she says while blinking away her tears. 'I'm lucky, I think, because I still have you, I still have the children, you're all a little part of him and you sort of play the same role in my life. I am still Aunty Betty. It's not the same, though, I'll never be the woman who did all those things his parents never knew about. You know, I bought him his first packet of condoms.

'Oh take that look off your face! I didn't want to be Great Aunty Betty before my time and my boy was so handsome. Lots of girls were after him. That's why I knew you were special when he brought you to meet me. You were the only one he willingly brought – with everyone else I had to engineer meetings.'

'Why doesn't that surprise me?'

'Do you feel angry sometimes that you're not the woman you were with him any more?' she asks. 'That sounds off-key, but you understand me, don't you?'

I nod. 'I don't feel angry sometimes, no,' I reply. 'To be honest, to be more honest than I've been for a long time, when I'm not numb and unable to feel anything, all I feel is angry. Really angry. With the world, with myself, with Joel. Everything. I can't talk about it, of course, because you're not supposed to feel that, are you? Especially if you're a woman because being angry will make you seem cold and unlikeable. I'm supposed to be all whimsical and fragile, and searching for someone to help heal my heart and really, all I want to do is scream at whoever's in charge for letting this happen. Or smash things to get all this rage out.

'I can't, but that's what's there all the time. I thought by now it'd be over with because that's what I was kind of promised by all these things that I read on bereavement. They said I'd feel angry and then I'd move on to something else, another "stage" like depression or acceptance or something else. *Anything* else. I think even despair would do. Unfortunately, it's still this deep, relentless anger.' I think sometimes that I live in my sleepwalking state because I do not want to deal with the anger that brews inside. I don't want to be the woman who gets angry. I don't want to be unfeminine, unpretty because I feel such a non-feminine emotion. I'm expected to be depressed, or quiet, or a sobbing wreck; it's easier to be the woman who wistfully stares into space while taking a demotion, while being patronised by teachers and friends, while being terrorised by a killer than to be the woman who feels so much rage at the injustice of everything. To be the person who fucked her husband's best friend because she needed sex and she needed physical release and she needed to feel what another person's skin felt like. I am the Angry Widow, but I can't be that on the outside because that's not what the world expects to see. Tears, yes; sticking up two fingers at everything because the world screwed me over, no.

'And then, of course, there's all that guilt,' Aunty Betty says.

Is it that obvious? I wonder. I must be wearing the guilt like a cloak for Aunty Betty to mention it after Lewis did yesterday, too. Or is it simply Aunty Betty guessing at what I might be feeling? 'What about the guilt?'

'Don't you feel more of that than anger?'

'Maybe. Maybe not. I don't know.' All I know is that I have a knot inside, twisted, convoluted, complicated, that I can't untie. Every chance I get, every time I think I've got a reason to smile, a reason to relax and simply be me, another strand will be added to the knot – woven through and tugged tight, cementing itself over the original knot.

Aunty Betty closes her eyes, then immediately forces them open.

'Time for me to get to work, I think.'

'Thank you for the talk,' she says.

'You, too.'

'Joel wouldn't mind if you found someone else,' Aunty Betty adds. 'As long as he was good to you and the children, Joel wouldn't mind if you found someone else, even for a little while.'

'You're probably right. But I'd mind. Quite a lot, actually.'

I'd love for us to be friends? Joel's killer wrote. For some reason that upsets me. I suspect she means it. I suspect she really believes anyone could be friendly with someone who killed the person they love. And that upsets me in ways I'm still not able to articulate.

XXXVIII

'How was school?'

One-shoulder shrug.

'Did you see any of your friends?'

Two-shouldered shrug.

'Did you see Curtis?'

'Yep.'

'Did you talk to him?'

'Yep.'

'About the pregnancy?'

'No.'

'Are you going to talk to me in proper sentences any time soon?'

Two-shouldered shrug.

Maybe sending her to school was a bad idea, it seems to have set her communication abilities back a few rungs on the evolutionary ladder.

'Considering how much you said you liked him, and how you ended up in this situation in the first place, I've got to wonder why you aren't talking to him more about the pregnancy and what you plan to do next.'

'You're going to tell me what to do, so what's the point of talking to him about it?'

'I'm really not, Phoebe,' I say. I hope she doesn't notice how my hands clench at the steering wheel, and how I delay changing gear a second too long because I fear I'll wrench the gearstick out of its socket if I touch it. Few people can frustrate me like her, I've realised. Few people know, with only a few words, how to get me going. 'If you want advice, if you want to sound me out about anything, or if you want me to find people for you to talk to, then I will, but I am not going to tell you what to do. I thought I made it clear that while I will support whatever you choose to do, this is your decision.'

I don't even need to see her thin, oval face to know she's cut her eyes at me, then rolled them.

'What did you and Curtis talk about then?'

'He told me that you and his dad were talking for hours on the phone last night and that you were going out with each other again and you were planning when you could hook up. That's what we were talking about.'

'I'm really surprised you can love a boy who lies so much. And so badly, too. First it was about not getting pregnant the first time you do it, now it's about hooking up with his dad after spending hours on the phone. What's he going to make up next? That the Loch Ness Monster lives in his attic?'

'No, that'd be our attic,' she mumbles.

I stop myself from smirking. 'Aunty Betty is a lovely woman, never let her hear you say that.'

'She'd laugh louder than all of us,' she retorts. 'And be gutted she didn't think of it herself.'

True. 'Don't change the subject. How do you feel about your boyfriend lying all the time? Because I'm not planning when I can "hook up" with his father and since you're pregnant . . .'

'He didn't lie to me actually, I misunderstood. He meant it was unlikely you'd get pregnant the first time, but if you've used tampons and stuff it can stop—'

'What, stop the woo-woo magic from working? My goodness, I think it's time I had a proper chat with this boy because he has got some really strange ideas about reproduction. Or maybe I'll just get his dad to explain it to him again. For some reason Mr Bromsgrove told me that he'd had the "always use a condom" chat with his son several times. Maybe he's lying, too? Maybe I should sit them both down and call them out. See what happens.' Theatrically, I look at the car clock. 'I reckon they should be home soon. Mr Bromsgrove gave me his address, maybe we can drop round now.' With as much theatre as the clock-checking, I peer into my rear-view mirror and hit my left indicator to pull into the next left. 'I'll turn the car around, and go back to his house and we can all sit down and get—'

'No, Mum, don't,' she says, alarm in her voice, in the way her whole body has tensed. 'He didn't say that exactly, I'm probably remembering it wrong.'

'Right.' I turn off my indicator and carry on past the road, ignoring the angry beep from the car behind me.

'You're not going to tell him or his dad off, are you?' she says after we've driven in silence for a minute or two.

'Not right now, no, but I might do.'

'If you do, I'll never speak to you again,' she states with the certainty of a teen.

No real change there, then, I'm tempted to say. 'If that's what you feel you have to do then I can't stop you, just like you can't stop me talking to Mr Bromsgrove and his son if I feel they are both lying to my daughter and thereby lying to me.'

'They're not lying,' she eventually says. 'It was a misunderstanding.' Every time she lies to me/defends the lies of the father to me, I know Curtis isn't the father. These are the manipulations of an older, more experienced man. Damien, possibly, but I suspect someone older who is used to subtly manoeuvring people to get what they want.

Outside our house, I turn off the engine and place my hand on Phoebe's arm to stop her leaving the car. 'Your dad's parents are coming to visit sometime this weekend,' I say to her as a warning.

Engraved into her eyes is a haunted, hunted look that has been there, prominent and evident, since Joel died. I should have known something was going on, that she was falling in love, because for those weeks before all this came crashing down around us, that expression had been erased. Replaced by a sun of joy that radiated throughout her body. She was happy, fizzing with excitement. I noticed but I said nothing because I thought she was starting to move on, that she was the first of us to reach that state of 'acceptance' I'd read so much about. I'd been pleased that for someone the pain was easing, and I'd been jealous that for someone the pain was easing.

'Great, I suppose you're going to tell them, too?' she says.

'No, it's your news, you tell them if you want and I won't tell them if you'd rather they didn't know.'

'Thanks,' she mumbles.

'The other thing is, Phoebe, I don't want to put any pressure on you, that's the absolute last thing I want to do, but you're going to have to make a decision quite soon. Whichever it is, the sooner we know the easier it'll be. You can change your mind, of course, but I want you to remember that, like the doctor said, every option has its time limits. And we need to make another appointment soon.'

'But no pressure, eh, Mum?' she snarks, pops open the door and gets out. She shuts the door normally, when I'd expected a slam. That simply goes to underline another thing I've been taught recently: I really don't know my daughter. At all.

Saffron.

How did you like the photo? Did it make you smile to remember how beautiful he was?

I am so angry with you.

I'm sorry about your car, but I couldn't believe my eyes when I saw you off out again with another man. If this was what you were like, and you must have been because no one gets over the love of their life so quickly, then why did you try so hard to keep him? Why did you make him say all those things to me?

Is it because you knew you weren't good enough for him so you let other men use you however they want?

The more I see of your life, the more I know it should have been you.

It was never meant to be him, but if it had to have been anyone, it should have been you. You were always there with us, uninvited and unwelcome.

We were fighting over the knife. It wasn't him I was going to use it on but myself. I wanted him to see that if I was hurt, I would bleed. And what he was saying, how he was repeating all those things that you'd made him say on the phone, was hurting me, so it was making me bleed.

Do you deserve to live, do you think?

When he's not here, do you deserve to carry on breathing like nothing has happened? Like you didn't cause all of this by not letting him go?

You're going to find what goes around, comes around. It's a really hard lesson to learn.

A

XXXIX

13 years before *That Day* (September, 1998)

'I think that went as well as can be expected, don't you?'

Joel sat in the driver's seat of his car, his eyes wide and unfocused, his breathing fast and shallow as though he had just sprinted in the Olympic Men's 100m final. He couldn't answer me straight away.

I was probably the calmer of the two of us, and I feared my fiercely hammering heart was going to crack the wall of my chest any second now and leap free.

'I suppose,' Joel said.

'I mean, if you look beyond the absolute horror and disgust on both their faces, and your mum taking you about three feet away to ask you in the loudest stage whisper I've ever heard if you were sure you were the father . . .'

'And me screaming my head off at her that if she repeated that I'd never speak to her again . . .'

'Yes, and of course your dad getting up to defend your mum by saying it was fair comment because no one really knew much about me and it was possible I'd tried to trap you . . .'

'And me screaming at him that the pair of them were seconds away from me walking out and never seeing them again.'

'Oh, yes, there was that, but if you look beyond all that, I think it went as well as can be expected. Your mum did hug me, after they both calmed down.'

'And Dad did shake my hand.'

'See? And they both managed to say they were looking forward to being grandparents, it was simply a shock because we aren't married yet. I mean, as I say, we've got off quite lightly.'

The nausea in my stomach rose and fell, rose and fell, as though my organs were surfing during a thunderstorm in the middle of the North Sea.

'We did,' Joel conceded. I'd never seen him like that; it was like the rage he'd been repressing about how his parents treated me had spewed out of him in one huge go. It felt like the walls of their house were shaking when he shouted. I never thought I'd see him yell at his parents.

'Right, so how long do you think it'll take us to get to my parents' house from here?' I said to him.

Appalled, Joel turned his head to me. 'What are you talking about?'

'I am not going through another day of this, mate. The build-up beforehand, the drive there, the telling them . . . I can't do it again. We go to my parents' place now and we tell 'em and then we go home, get into bed and never get out again. Cos your parents are amateurs compared to mine in this sort of situation. In my twenties, not married, other half not a doctor, lawyer or the prime minister – you haven't seen real dysfunctional parenting in action until you've told a Nzemi you're going to be a knocked-up, unmarried mother. It's no coincidence that my sister lives so far away – she moved to Japan because it was less guilt-inducing than going no-contact.'

'Eurggghhh,' Joel groaned. 'All right, give me a minute to get myself together. Don't think I can drive yet. Don't think I can breathe properly, actually.' After a couple of thumps to his chest to get his lungs working, he turned to me with an indulgent smile. 'We're a right pair, aren't we?'

'Hmmm.'

'The tragic thing is that I always thought I got on with my parents until the Cambridge thing. I've been one disappointment after another. Even then they've always been all right, manageable. I actually thought they'd be happy about this, though.'

'They will be. In their own way. Just like my parents will be. And once there's an actual baby, they'll want to get involved. They may not be happy about who the mother is, but they'll be happy about the baby.'

Joel's large fingers were reaching for the ignition but did not connect. Instead he threaded them through my fingers. 'I meant it, you know, Ffrony? If my parents ever made me choose between you and them, you'd win without me even thinking about it.'

'I know,' I said. 'I absolutely know that. Same with you about pretty much everyone.'

'Let's never be like them, Ffrony. Either of them. I know it's an awful thing to think let alone say, but I never want to put our kids through this. We've got to do our best to let them make their own mistakes and help to pick up the pieces afterwards.'

'I'll remind you of this conversation when you're punishing this one for something in the future.'

'Do. You have to promise me that you will. I never want to forget how awful this feels and I never want to inflict that on our children.'

'It's a deal. Right then, are we off to our next appointment?'

'Yes. Once more unto the breach, dear friends.'

'Once more.'

XL

Zane is the first to appear after he and the other two sloped off after breakfast to prepare for today's visitation. My little boy, although he hates me calling him that, is wearing beige chinos and a dark denim shirt with the top button done up. He's had another shower, and has been rather restrained with the body spray to give him his dues. He throws himself onto the sofa and picks up his DS, which he'd left on the floor on the other side of the armrest. He's so handsome. A better-looking version of Joel, if that's possible, with his pouty lips, rounded cheeks, and huge eyes. Last week I clipped his hair to a grade two all over and it'd made Aunty Betty gasp while her line of sight flew wildly between Zane and me. I saw her inhale a few times, deeply, slowly, trying to catch her breath, trying to remind herself that he wasn't Joel at ten, he was an entirely different person.

Phoebe is next, it's a shock to see her in normal clothes – in other words not in her school uniform and not in her pyjamas because since I've been collecting her and taking her to school, she rarely wears anything else, even at weekends. I haven't challenged her because, frankly, there are better things to fall out with her about at this stage. She has on a short-sleeved summer dress covered in dozens and

342

dozens of tiny blue and pink flowers, and she has styled her hair into two babyish pigtails – instead of her grown-up afro puffs – each one plaited to the bottom and secured into place with ribbons. No earrings, no ring on every finger, she's even found ankle socks with a flowery ruffle to complete the look. She throws herself onto the other sofa in the living room and flicks on the television, puts the remote on the seat beside her before immersing herself in the world on her phone.

The final person who is apparently going to brunch with the Queen or some other such dignitary is Aunty Betty, The Wimp as I rename her. The children I can understand because I spent years dressing them smartly to look the part for a visit to both sets of grandparents, but Aunty Betty? The rebel? The OAP who got slung out of a home for shagging in public? She has dressed the part of a Great Aunt in Residence with a navy blue cashmere twinset, a navy blue knee-length skirt, thick American tan tights and her grey, suede sheepskin-lined slippers. By the outline of her breasts, I'm guessing she's got out one of those old-fashioned bras that hoists and shapes your chest into two comical rocket shapes. She's even worn her black wig – chin-length, layered and styled on big rollers – which looks most how I'd always imagined her real hair did. I expected better of her, I really did.

'What time did they say they'd be here?' Aunty Betty asks, causing us all to glance at her and then to look again in sheer disbelief. Alarmed, more than a little unnerved, both Zane and Phoebe immediately frown at me. *What's wrong with her?* they're asking.

The same as is wrong with you, I silently reply. 'They didn't say a specific time, around ten-thirty to eleven,' I say to Aunty Betty.

'Didn't say a specific time? Is Norman sick, do you think? That's not at all like him. Or her.'

'I'm sure they're both fine,' I reassure. 'You look nice,' I add to Aunty Betty diplomatically.

All of them – including the lady herself – glare at me like I am mad. 'Fine,' I state to their collective incredulity. 'You look like a different person, is that what you want to hear?'

'It's closer to the truth,' she says. Her hand, the one that fought me for her cigarette holder, reaches up and adjusts her wig, then tugs at the back of her bra to force it into place. She must be really uncomfortable because I've never seen her do something like that – far too classless. The only time I've ever seen her with such a demure, monotone outfit was for the 'official' bit of Joel's funeral. When it came to the wake she reappeared in a crimson trouser outfit that had earned a smile from me and instant disapproval from her brother and sister-in-law. Maybe she's trying to make up for that outfit with this one.

There was a time, of course, when I would have been the same, the knowledge of their visit would have sent me to the scales, to working out how many calories I could get away with eating without alerting Joel to the fact I was restricting, to spend half the morning trying on different outfits to see which one would say, 'Not trash' or at least, 'Not fat trash'. Since *that day*, things like that aren't important any more.

*

They arrive in their old Ford Fiesta and have smiles on their faces as they walk through the door, hug the children and sit down and accept tea with the triple chocolate (white, dark and milk) banana muffins I made earlier.

I notice almost straight away the assessment of my wrong-doings has begun: the lingering gaze on Zane's hair tells me it's the wrong type of haircut for them; the uncertain stare at Phoebe's upper arms reveals to me that there is too much flesh on display there, and the look at Aunty Betty tells me that it's business as usual, despite her outfit. Once upon a time, my anxiety would have me babbling, constantly on my feet, hissing to Phoebe to put a cardigan on, willing Zane's hair to grow, wondering how I could make Aunty Betty accept-able. Once upon a time, *that* once upon a time I had a husband who knew how to help me reframe my anxiety.

'These fairy cakes are lovely, Saffron,' Joel's mum says. It might have been me being so traumatised by Phoebe's preg-nancy, the letters, the fight with Fynn, and the photo, but even to my Mackleroy-criticism-trained ear, she sounds like she means it.

'Thank you,' I reply, waiting for the slight, the backhanded part of the compliment that comes with almost everything she says to me.

'Did you come up with the recipe yourself?' she asks.

Why would she think that? I look at the children – which one of them has told her what I've been doing? Phoebe is smiling banally, probably counting down the seconds until she can escape back to her phone and her room, while simultaneously wondering if someone's going to tell on her to people she's actually scared of. It's Zane.

'Erm, yes,' I say. 'I've been experimenting with different ingredients with varying degrees of success.' *I've been looking for the perfect blend of flavours, the one that used to be Joel*, I want to tell her. *And when I find it, everything will be all right. He'll come back to me, to us. I won't be selfish, you know, I'll share him with you, it's only fair since you brought him up.* 'How did you know?'

'Zane told me,' she says. Before I can silently ask my son what possessed him to tell her this, she smiles at me. In response, I stare at her, transfixed. It's such a beautiful smile, one that our wedding photographer captured as she adjusted Joel's buttonhole minutes before the ceremony, one that she often gave to her son when she thought no one was looking. Her face, so set with the lines that sorrow has scored upon it, is suddenly alive with this smile – her eyes gentle and open, her lips slightly parted to show some of her teeth. The beam rips my breath away, and I have to look down because tears are spiking behind my eyes.

I didn't realise, not until this second, that I've longed for even the briefest glimpse of niceness from her.

'You'll have to give me the recipe,' she says.

'Right, yes. OK.' I cannot lift my gaze for fear of her smiling at me again and making me cry.

'Phoebe,' Joel's dad says, making all of us jump. 'How's school?'

'It's good, Grandpa,' she says. Sweetness and light. She can definitely turn it on for the people she's actually afraid of.

346

'Have you decided where you want to go to university yet?' he asks. Even if I wasn't on the verge of sobbing, I couldn't look up now. He asked her this the last time he saw her, well over six months ago, and she'd given him the stock answer of having to see which university had the best reputation for the course she wanted to do. What would she say now? *Actually, Grandpa, I'm pregnant so I may be delaying uni for a while, if not for ever because I'm going to be having a baby. Yes, that's right, I'm no better than my piece of trash mother.*

'Erm, no, not yet.'

'Well, don't leave it too long,' he says, good-naturedly. 'It does a person good to have a clear path in life. Even if it does take some pleasant detours along the way . . . Don't you think, Saffron?'

Me? He was talking to me? In that tone? As if anything I thought meant anything to him and them and the world? 'Erm, yes, I suppose so,' I say without facing him, either. If I look at him and he's smiling, I will have a breakdown. There are things that can send a person over the edge, and after eighteen months of nothingness, of business as usual with a side order of 'what if he hadn't met you, would this have happened to him?', sudden pleasantness is not something I can assimilate or process at all.

Aunty Betty has been strangely quiet, too. The tension we always seem to have in the air is coming from us, I realise, each of us waiting for our turn in front of the firing squad. Something is not right, here. I knew this before with Phoebe in the lead-up to finding out she was pregnant but I ignored it. I glossed over it because in the midst of everything, in the process of 'moving on' like a good bereaved person is meant to, I was jealous she was happier, I was grateful that she seemed to have moved on when I couldn't even contemplate it.

Something is wrong now, the world is off-kilter.

Before I know it, before I can tell myself I am being ridiculous and paranoid, I am on my feet. 'Zane, Sweetheart, can you come and help me with something upstairs, please?' I ask him.

He glances down at where he's left his DS, looks at each of his grandparents, then warily he rises. I'm right. It's a wrench in my already mangled stomach, but I'm right.

In his bedroom, I shut the door. His room is neat, tidy, everything slotted away in its rightful place even though I only do a minimal clean, vacuum and take the laundry down. He keeps it tidy himself, returns toys to their shelves, pulls his duvet over in the mornings, folds his pyjamas and leaves them neatly on his pillow – his dad's influence, in the main, but his own conscientiousness spurring on the rest.

I smile at him as we sit on his bed together. 'I'm sorry,' I say. 'I haven't paid you enough attention and I'm sorry.' I slip my arm around his shoulders, pull him towards me and gently kiss the top of his head. There's a stopper in my throat, preventing me from speaking properly, and there's a knife in the centre of my heart, stopping me from doing what I have to do. Is this how it felt for Joel? Knowing you're bleeding to death, knowing what is coming is inevitable but being powerless to stop it? Knowing that at this point, there is nothing you can do.

'It's all a bit much at the moment, isn't it?' I say to him. 'With Phoebe, with Aunty Betty, the drama last week, my car, me running around trying to fix things – it's too much, isn't it?'

'Yeah,' he says and I'm grateful at least, he can admit that. He's not going to pretend any longer.

I inhale, gathering strength from the ability to pull air into my body. 'Do you want to go and stay with Granny and Grandpa for a while?' I ask him. I do not breathe, do not move, do not even think as I wait for his answer.

It takes him all the time in the world to screw up his courage and tell me he doesn't want to be here any more. He doesn't want to be with me any more. 'Yeah,' he whispers.

Is this how Joel felt, when the knife was first inserted into his being? Like nothing could ever hurt this much?

'OK, Baby, OK.' On Tuesday I'll need to call St Caroline's, but they have been so considerate, offering support and staggered school days, I'm sure they'll understand now. I have to pack him enough stuff for his time away. I'll have to give Joel's parents some money. I'll have to find a way to file this away in my mind and my heart, to remind myself for every second of every day until he comes home that this is for the best, so I don't spend the next few days breaking down if I see a young boy in the street.

'Sorry, Mum,' he says quietly.

I tug him as near to me as possible, surround him with all the love I have for him, press my lips against his forehead again. 'You have nothing to be sorry for. It's me that's sorry that I didn't notice earlier that you need a time out. If staying with your grandparents is what you want for now, then that's fine.'

'Can I come home whenever I want?'

'Yes, of course. This isn't for ever, you're coming home really soon. Any time you want. Even if it's the middle of the night, call me and I'll come and get you.'

'For honestly, real?' He hasn't said that since he was six. His dad, on the other hand, said it right up until he died.

'Absolutely. Any time you need me, even if you just want to talk to me, just call me.' I drop another kiss onto his head. 'In fact, it's a condition of you going that you call me at least once a day. And, at least once every few days, you must call in the middle of the night for a chat and to complain about something. OK? Deal?'

I raise my hand and he averts his mortified face when he realises I was going for a high-five. Suitably shamed, I lower my hand and hug him instead.

'Right, I'd better get on with packing some stuff for you,' I say briskly, to cover the sound of the earthquake happening in my heart. 'Can you go down and get Granny to come up for a minute so I can talk things through with her?'

'Is this for honestly, real OK, Mum?' Zane asks.

'Yes, it's for honestly OK. It'll do you good to have some time with them, but I'm telling you this like I'm going to tell Granny, you're coming back really soon, OK? This isn't for ever. It's a bit of a holiday while things calm down. OK? Go on now, get Granny and I'll get packing.'

*

'Zane isn't your second chance,' I say to her when she has crossed the threshold and shut the door.

'I know that, Saffron,' she says, still with the pleasant tone that revealed she had been speaking to my son and they were buttering me up to convince me they could take care of him in my place.

I am arranging his clothes in neat piles on his bed. I'm packing fourteen of everything, so he can stay for up to two weeks without needing stuff washed. Under his clothes, hidden from view, I have put his memory box of Joel. I gave them both the A4-size boxes with individual photos of them with their dad, and the same group photo of them at the beach hut. I also put in a notebook, a pen and a note saying how much he loved them. It was the best I could do and I'd told them to fill it with whatever they wanted and I would never look in there. They could show me things, but it was their space to fill however they chose. Zane would need it if he was away from home, and he could maybe add stuff from his grandparents' place.

'Well, I don't think you do, actually,' I say. 'He may look like Joel did before he met me, when Joel was all yours, but Zane isn't Joel. Zane is his own person. And he's *not your son*.'

Her hand, placed tenderly on my shoulder, causes me to jump. 'I know that, Saffron,' she repeats, kindly.

'And this isn't for ever. I've told Zane that, and I'm telling you, this is only for a short while and then he's coming back home. Because *this* is his home.'

'I know.'

I can't start crying in front of her. It's always felt wrong to do so. No matter how she's treated me over the years, no matter how she treats me now, she has lost her only child. I don't know how I'd cope with that. It'd be churlish to cry in front of her, knowing that I could, theoretically, find another husband but she'll never find another son.

'I've told him, too, that he has to call me at least once a day. The day that passes without me speaking to him is the day I come and get him, is that clear?'

She nods.

'Good,' I say, aware that she still has her hand on my shoulder, probably the first time she has touched me so gently. 'And don't say anything bad about me to him. He *will* tell me, he *will* hate you for it and I *will* come and get him.'

'We wouldn't do that,' she protests, but at least she has the grace to not sound hurt or incredulous that I would suggest such a thing.

'Yes you would. So just . . . just cut out the snide remarks. If you've got *another* issue with me then take it up with me and leave Zane out of it.'

'Fine. Yes.'

I have her on the ropes, she'd agree to anything right now. *Admit you've been an unfair bitch to me all these years*, I should say. *Admit that I was actually good enough for your son.*

'We're going to look after him,' she says and I snap back to the stark reality where my son is leaving. 'That's not to say you're incapable of that. He just wants to be somewhere else right now.'

'I know,' I say. 'I know.'

There's only one reason I can pack his clothes, I can hug him goodbye, and I can watch him drive away in the old Ford Fiesta. I need to know he and Phoebe are safe, I can't do that if he's here right now. If he's in London, then he's safe. I don't think *she* would dare leave me alone for long enough to follow them up to London. If he's here, there's always the danger that she will use him to get at me.

IX

IX

Saffron.

I'd like to apologise. I haven't been fair to you.

As I explained before, I get so het up because my life was upended, too, when he died. I had to leave it all behind to go live abroad. I tried to get away from here because I couldn't live with the pain of what had happened.

He talked to me. That might seem insignificant, or even pathetic, but very few people talk nowadays. They text, they email, they connect on 'social media' but they don't talk. They don't listen. He talked, he listened and he waited patiently to hear what you had to say. It's an amazing way to make a person feel special. You don't concentrate on what you're going to say after what they say, you listen and hear and digest what they've told you then you talk and contribute what you have to say.

He did that. He listened, he heard, he seemed to understand. It was odd to hear him talked about in the papers and on the news and that's why I had to get away. I was gone for a whole year and when I came home, I tried to get my life back on track. There was a vacuum, though, where my heart should be. I think that was because the

357

person who listened, who heard, who tried to understand, was missing.

I lived for Wednesday evenings. Even when we didn't work together any more I still liked being around him. He was the shining one in the class, so much talent and everyone loved him. Being around him was magical.

Of course he loved you. Of course you loved him. I loved him, too. We're the same you and me. We loved him. We're lucky like that.

I'm sorry for the things I've said, the things I've done. I hope you can forgive me. I think it's time I backed off a little.

Take care of yourself, Saffron. Take care of your beautiful children. I'm going to go back to my proper life now and put this all behind me.

Good luck with the rest of your life.

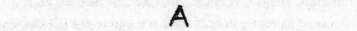

A

XLI

Lewis Bromsgrove is hugging my daughter.

I have no idea why he has his arms around her, but I assume they didn't want to be seen, which is why they are out here, on a small, out-of-the-way road at the back of the school. Getting sent by Kevin on a wild goose chase to drum up business from an uninterested company near Shoreham seafront is the best thing to have happened to me today. Without knowing why, my instincts told me to take this shortcut from Old Shoreham Road to Dyke Road back into town and there they are.

Neither of them notices me, of course, they are both too engrossed in each other. My whole being seems to leave my body as I drive on, not wanting to arouse suspicion by stopping, no matter how much I want to leap out of the car and rip them apart. I park up, a little way down on the opposite side of the road, behind a red, new-style Beetle so I can see them both.

I'm as confident as I can be they haven't noticed me as my trembling hand unclips my seatbelt and I turn to watch them out of the rear windscreen.

They've stepped apart now, but they're still standing close together, Phoebe's hunched shoulders and bowed head broadcasting that she is upset. Mr Bromsgrove, as he is to me anywhere near these grounds, is listening to what she is saying. I can't hear them, of course, but what she says is enough to cause him to put an arm around her shoulders, still listening and then, it happens again: he puts both arms around her and pulls her towards him, hugs her.

Teachers, as far as I know, aren't allowed to touch pupils in this way. If at all. Certainly not twice in less than a minute.

Mr Bromsgrove is hugging my daughter.

It's not Damien. It's him. It was him all along. That's why he has been trying to charm me, it is not me, it is my daughter he wants. He has kept me distracted with attempts to 'hook up', as Phoebe would say, so he could work his magic on her. I was stupid enough to believe it. I actually thought someone other than Joel liked me, found me attractive without knowing me first. When I was allowed to go to school discos, I was always the one stood on the side for the final slow dance, no one even glancing in my direction. By the time I went clubbing in my university days, I had mastered the art of dancing alone, enjoying it, revelling in it while all my friends were snogging or leaving with the men they met. I wasn't fat in those days, not like in school, but I wasn't the kind of thin that made me visible or appealing to anyone who hadn't entered the last chance saloon, either. No one spent the night trying to woo me into bed, they only saw me at one-thirty in the morning, when it looked like they would be leaving alone – and realised I was better than nothing.

Lewis Bromsgrove must have seen that in me, he must have known that I was the type of adult who grew from that kind of child. He must have guessed that I would fall for flattery and I wouldn't notice he was carrying on with my daughter. Filling her head with lies, allowing his son to take the blame for the things he had done.

They break apart, him obviously realising someone could see them. He steps back, puts a hand on each of her shoulders and lowers his head to talk to her. Phoebe's head is still trained downwards, but I can see her nodding, agreeing with whatever it is he is telling her. Probably some variation on, *We'll be together soon, Baby, I promise.*

Suddenly, surprisingly, he steps back even further, shoves his hands in his pockets and seems to be awkward. Even from this distance, I can tell that Phoebe isn't looking at him with longing, the way I expected her to look at the man she said she felt so close to that she wanted to sleep with him. She looks at him like she would a teacher, a father, really. Is that how he managed to seduce her? Confuse her, appeal to the part of her life that she misses?

Zane became quiet, Phoebe became a guilt-riddled version of herself. She carried on as normal, but blamed and still blames herself. Maybe she's been desperately searching for someone to be that father figure in her life, someone who can partially fill the gap left by Joel. I've been searching for him through cooking, Phoebe has maybe been searching for it through this man.

Phoebe continues to speak and Mr Bromsgrove shakes his head slowly, then suddenly opens his hands in hopelessness. Maybe she wants to come clean and he's telling her the world wouldn't understand – that once they've decided what to do about the pregnancy, once she's sixteen, they can go public.

I need to know what they're saying.

She won't tell me anything, he certainly won't. I can't allow this, though. Whatever 'it' is. There is something 'off' in the way they relate to each other; I'm not sure if it's because they have to pretend all the time in public, or if there is nothing there to see. I have watched them together, like I watch all people, I suppose, and there doesn't seem to be that latent intimacy people who are connected unconsciously show to the world; no awkwardness, no secret looks or forced indifference. There is something, though. For him to twice have so openly hugged her, for her to have accepted the hug so easily, there is something. Maybe my skills aren't as honed as I thought, maybe I have missed all of this and Lewis Bromsgrove has been grooming her and is now in the process of grooming me to miss what he is doing with his pupil, with a child – with my child.

She returns to school first, and Mr Bromsgrove stands in the street, hands in pockets, staring at the ground looking bewildered until enough time has elapsed before he goes back towards the main road and the main entrance to the school, too. I wait for them to leave before I can. I need to work out how to find out the truth about this.

'How was school?' I ask my daughter when she climbs into the front seat of my car.

Shrug.

'Anything interesting happen today?' I probe. *Did you hug one of your teachers who you may or may not be sleeping with?*

'No,' she replies. She turns her head and most of her body away from me, like she did the day I found out she was pregnant, to gaze out of the window, watching the world surrounding her school disappear behind us as I take us home. Even though I am driving and have my eyes on the road, I can sense Phoebe's thousand-yard stare. She has the pregnancy on her mind, no doubt, but is it because she was hugging the father today, or is it something else? What else it could be I have no idea, but I would bet Mr Bromsgrove would know.

'Phoebe,' I say after clearing my throat, after I try to dislodge the blockage of fear around my voice box. She doesn't stop staring out of the window, bobbing around lost and forlorn, like an untethered boat on the sea. 'Phoebe, you can talk to me about anything and I will listen. If you want me to listen to your thoughts on what to do about the pregnancy, I'm more than willing to do that. If you want to talk through your feelings for the father, we can do that, too. Anything, any time, talk to me and I'll listen.'

'You can't.'

'Yes, I can.'

'You can't, Mum, because you won't get it. Mums don't get it.'

She thinks that my life began with Joel, that nothing of me existed before him. My first time I was seventeen, so older than her, but I thought I was in love, too. Actually, I pretended I thought I was in love so that I could do it without too much guilt. I remember going back to his small, dingy flat in Central London after we'd finished our shift working at a department store. I'd fancied him for weeks and I convinced myself it was all right to let him undress me and to watch him roll on a condom and to kiss him back because it was love. What stuck with me most of all was the pretending. It wasn't awful, being physically, completely entered for the first time, but I pretended to him and to me that I felt something. That it was amazing, that I had experienced something other than the nothingness I did feel when he was moving on top of me and that I'd *die* if I didn't do it again with him soon. Pretending is something I did very well.

I pretended quite a few times with him until he decided the new girl in haberdashery was a better fit than me. I cried because I thought I was expected to, but the fact was, I didn't mind not having to do it again. What got to me was the humiliation of seeing him and the haberdashery girl together, public and loved-up, when he'd been adamant and determined that we keep our 'thing' a secret. Their constant canoodling sent me back where I had been: desperate to cope, to fit in, to look better, to be validated in a way I hadn't been for ages.

'Try me,' I say to my daughter. 'You may find that I do "get it".'

'No thanks,' she replies dismissively.

Bleep-bleep-bleep, intones her phone in her grey and turquoise, branded St Allison school rucksack.

'Phone,' I tell her, surprised it's not already in her hand.

'Yeah, I know.'

'Sounds like a text message.'

364

'Yeah, I know.'

'Are you going to read it?'

'I don't have to read every message the second it comes in,' she says, with her gaze fixed in that thousand-yard stare out of the window.

Since when? I think at her. 'How's Alzira, these days? I haven't heard you talk about her in a while.'

Phoebe snorts. 'Alzira's family moved back to Portugal.'

'When? You didn't mention it.'

'You didn't ask.'

'Oh, I suppose I didn't.' I leave it thirty seconds. 'So, Phoebe, any of your friends move to a foreign country today?'

'Ha-ha, very funny.'

'Which girls do you hang around with nowadays? Do you want to invite any of them round?'

She snorts again, an unpleasant sound loaded with the precise amount of scorn to show that I am irrelevant. 'So you can make weird comments and cook some of your strange food? No thanks.'

'Well, it's nice to know what you objectively think of me at least.' My ego smarts with the efficient way she has slapped me down.

'See?' she says.

'I suppose I do make what others might think of as weird comments. But, much as it might pain you, this is who I am so you're pretty much stuck with me.'

'Doesn't mean I have to expose anyone else to it, though.'

She is being uncharacteristically mean, unusually nasty. I know she hates me, won't speak to me most of the time, but this is low, uncalled for, and more than a little vicious. 'Is something bothering you?' I ask.

She waits a beat, a long enough moment to be filled in my mind with: *Yeah, you* then she says, 'No.' Her shrug that follows is a full stop to any more conversation; it tells me that I can talk if I want, but she's not going to dignify me with any kind of response – not even a shrug.

This has something to do with Lewis Bromsgrove and what I saw today, I know it does.

Friday, 10 May
(For Saturday, 11th)

Saffron.

I'm really disappointed. I thought after my last letter you might attempt to meet me halfway, at least.

Prove that you believe me when I say I'm sorry by at least leaving your blinds open or something.

It was never meant to be like this.

Please trust me. Please show you trust me by opening your blinds again.

A

XLII

'Thanks for dropping by,' Kevin calls as I rush to pack up my belongings.

I'm already pushing it – at five-thirty-five, I'll be lucky to get there just after six, let alone for six when homework club ends.

I'm sure Phoebe was meeting whoever the father is in the hours between finishing school and coming home, and I need to be there to see if I can spot anyone hanging around. I've spent most of the weekend, with the blinds still closed, tossing and turning between whether Lewis could be guilty or not, and I kept thinking 'not' but then the fact they were sharing something secret would make me cycle right back to 'guilty' again. With so much on my mind, I don't need this from Kevin.

I pause in stuffing my laptop into its black neoprene carrier. My boss stands in the doorway to his glass box, his weasely face contorted into a nasty sneer. I think of Joel, how he'd deal with this: he'd quietly work to prove Kevin wrong, would go over and above on every single occasion so that Kevin had nothing to say. This strategy had worked for the last few months but when my life started to fall apart again, and I wasn't there to immediately do his bidding, Kevin had started this up again. Joel's way only worked as long as I was doing exactly what Kevin wanted whenever he demanded it. I am being stalked by the person who killed my husband, why does that not scare me more than Kevin? Why am I putting up with this when someone could be planning how to end my life?

'My stated hours are nine to five-fifteen,' I say. 'It's home time. In fact, it was home time twenty minutes ago.'

Kevin surveys the large open-plan office, split up into desk banks of four, each person with a divider on either side of them so they can't easily chat to the person next to them, even though the desks face inwards. There are ten people in here still working, about thirty-five others have gone already, departed as soon as the clock hit five. It's only me who Kevin has made a comment to today.

'Yes, for some it is, I suppose,' he says, pleasantly with a smile. He knows full well that I often finish my work at home, that despite my demotion I mostly do the job I did before even though his good buddy Edgar has the title and salary for it. 'Like I say, thanks for dropping by today. Hope we see you again tomorrow if your family doesn't develop another drama overnight.'

I remember vividly, painfully, the unadulterated humiliation of walking away from my other desk, the one beside Kevin's glass office. It would have been bad enough to pack my belongings into a box and move to the other side of the room, but to have Kevin and my replacement, Edgar, stood over me was something unusually punishing. I've never fully recovered from the calculated cruelty of that. They even followed me to my new desk, near the exit and as far away as possible from the wall of large floor-to-ceiling windows. They wanted to underline to me and everyone else in the room that sitting outside the office of the Director of Operations was for the second in command and I now belonged where the new people sat. I was nothing any more – I hadn't been demoted, they wanted to show, I had been degraded, too.

I clatter my laptop back onto my desk and lean forwards to my computer, catching the satisfied smile that slimes across Kevin's face – he thinks I'm about to start work again because I've been suitably shamed. I've never been able to work out quite what my crime was against him, given that my work was always done and on time. Even when my life imploded my work was done. I sometimes wonder if it's because he's scared of death. That he thinks he has to distance himself and prove I'm a lesser being which is why Death chose to visit itself upon my life. And if he proves he is better than me then Death will leave him alone. Most of the time I accept it's probably because he's a weaselly-faced bastard.

Once he sees I am still at my desk, he retreats into his office. I observe him from under my eyelashes until he throws his wiry frame into his chair, picks up the phone and spins towards the window behind him, resting his ankles up on the wide, low window sill as he stares out over Brighton.

My fingers move over the keyboard to finish backing up my files to the black data key I'd inserted earlier, then I shut down my computer. I pick up my mobile and dart out of the office, down the navy blue-carpeted corridor, up the stairs and onto the top floor, the executive floor.

As I open the door onto that floor, a flush of embarrassment creeps through me – I once thought my career would bring me here. I thought I'd one day be in one of the five offices up here after all the hard work I'd done.

Apparently, the Universe and Kevin had other plans for me.

I walk into Gideon, President and CEO's outer office, which has dark wood panels on the walls, dark wood furniture and always inspires a reverential hush upon entering. His assistant, a new one since the last time I was up here, sits behind her expansive dark wood desk. She's on the phone and is about to say, 'Hang on' to the person on the phone to talk to me but she doesn't get a chance because I don't stop to speak to her, I carry on going. I don't want her to put me off by 'pencilling' me in to see Gideon at some other point. I don't want to give her a chance to get Gideon to speak to Kevin. I want to find out what's going on from someone I can trust to only focus on making as much money as possible for the business.

The new assistant is on her feet, her face an 'O' of horror that I am going straight in – it's not the done thing. He could be in the middle of a high-level meeting, but I don't care. In fact, it will show him how serious I am that I thought to interrupt rather than wait my turn. My knuckles tap briefly before I open the door and step in. I don't care any more, I really don't. I've given so much to this company and I'm still getting snide comments. I don't care who they think they are, but I'm going to show them who I am.

The swirl of my indignation and outrage is halted in its tracks by a pair of tight white underpants covered in red lipstick marks. They're at the top of tanned, hairy, flabby legs.

At the bottom of the legs are black socks. Above the underpants is an open white shirt revealing a slightly paunched, tanned stomach, and a pair of man's hands planted proudly on each hip, emphasising what is going on below the waist. What is going on below the waist, unfortunately for me, is an expectant bulge, straining against the tight material of the pants.

I rear up, horrified, and Gideon does the same. My body, thankfully not as frozen with alarm as my mind, steps back, swinging the door shut with me.

Brain bleach. I need brain bleach. I remember Phoebe said something about it the other day when Aunty Betty mentioned she'd snogged one of the members of a band Phoebe liked. I need some, desperately.

The new personal assistant is in the petrified position she'd adopted when I opened the door: phone in one hand, her other hand outstretched as it tried to stop me, her visage caught in its 'O' of fright.

I've met Gideon's wife a few times. She's a lovely woman who sent a personally written card after what happened to Joel. Poor woman. I wonder if she suspects? I doubt it. Gideon and his assistant could lock the door and do all sorts and he'd still be home for their children's bedtimes. And his betrayed wife would think he didn't have time or opportunity to have an affair.

Behind the door there are sounds of him scrabbling around. I should leave, walk away and pretend this never happened. I can't, though. Actually, I won't. No matter who he is fucking, I need this man to be honest with me.

I knock again and wait for a response this time before I enter.

'Saffron,' Gideon says. He is behind his desk, fully dressed and buttoned up, he even has a blue brocade tie around his neck. 'Shut the door, come in, sit down. Please.' As he speaks, his eyes are trained on the padded, black leather ink blotter on the desk in front of him.

I do as I'm told.

'How, erm, how can I help you?'

He is, thankfully, opting for the 'it never happened' way forward. My mind tries to summon up the frothing mass of indignation and righteous fury that had driven me up here, but it does not come – the white pants image has dampened all that.

'Do you have a problem with my work?' I ask.

He faces me full-on – my question has sliced away the embarrassment. He's always been about the business, the results, the making of money. He doesn't much care about anything else. 'Of course not, why would you ask?'

'If I may speak frankly, I am sick of the comments about the hours I work in the office. I work at home and even if I didn't, it's not mandatory for me to give my whole life over to this job.'

'No one has said you have to,' he replies.

'Yes, you have. Every day that I walk in this building and sit at my desk with my demotion hanging over my head, still doing Edgar's job but with no money or recognition for it tells me I have to. Comments about the time I'm leaving tell me I have to. Snide remarks about events beyond my control meaning I have to take the day off say I have to. The fact I'm sitting here having this conversation at all tells me I have to.'

'It's not that bad,' he says.

'I think I'm going to resign,' I say, my mouth running away with me. I need to be at home more, I need to supervise Phoebe better, and if I'm home it'll be better for when Zane comes back – he'll know I'll have more time for him.

'Resign?' Gideon leans forwards over his desk.

'Yes, resign.' This is absolutely the right thing to do. I can be there, too, during the day, when the letters arrive. I can see her face, I can maybe catch her at it and . . . I don't know. It might not make her stop, but for once in all of this I'll be in control.

'Can you afford to do that?'

'No, but that doesn't mean I should stay here and get treated like something Kevin stepped in.'

'If you think you're being bullied—'

'It's not bullying, it's unrelenting disrespect. It's the constantly being made to feel small and useless when I actually do a good job, and the— Actually, I suppose it is bullying now I've said that out loud. I don't want to deal with it any more, Gideon. Life is too short.' That's the first time I've said that since Joel died. I used to say it all the time when he was alive, probably even to him. I would utter those words when I was telling myself to do something that I knew technically I shouldn't do. Or if I wanted to appear cool and enlightened like all the other would-be hedonists I met. I never let those words slip from my lips because I meant them – back then, as far as I was concerned, I was always going to live for ever.

374

I said it because I could, because I'd never experienced the brevity of life. When it was proved to me in the most hideous way possible, I realised that I didn't believe life was too short. I simply believed that the succinctness of life would never have anything to do with me.

'How about a leave of absence?' he suggests.

'And come back to this, in fact, probably come back to worse because I won't have been here and there'll be a whole store of comments? No, thank you, it's a very kind offer, but I think I'll pass.'

He is silent, obviously thinking something over. 'Don't leave, Saffron. It doesn't sit easy with me that you felt you had to take a demotion when you had recently lost your husband.'

'I didn't feel I had to take a demotion, I suggested it so I still had a job at a time when my whole world was imploding.'

'Please. Please consider a leave of absence of a month and while you're off, think through your options properly. You don't have to come back, just consider your options.'

Ah, right. I see. 'I'm not going to go blabbing my mouth off the second I leave here,' I state. 'I don't care what you do. You don't have to keep me here so you can keep an eye on me.' *Although I'm not going to lie for you: if anyone asks, I'm not going to plead ignorance.*

A red that is dark and potent, the colour of the jumper I wore the day I dropped the blackberries, bleeds into Gideon's cheeks. 'That's not what this is about,' he replies. 'I would like you to consider taking a leave of absence, and thinking through your options. I think you're a good worker. I will do my best to speak to the people who run your department about their general attitude towards all staff. I have heard rumblings, but it's difficult to do something if no one will speak out first. This is the first time someone has officially told me about what is going on, therefore, now that I am aware of there being a problem, I have a duty of care to my employees to investigate it. I will sit down with the head of HR and we will look through the issues, see what people have said in their exit interviews and then work out how to tackle the problem.

'I am asking you, *begging* you, if need be, to give me time to address this problem. If you still feel after your leave of absence that you would like to resign, I will not argue with you. I will accept it with regret and we shall all move on. What do you say?' Once again, he considers every word so he does not commit himself to something he cannot see through.

'Fine,' I say.

His relief is evident. It's not me, I'm sure, employees are lining up to get work, it must be the company's reputation – maybe the people who have left recently and there have been a few, aren't keeping quiet about how they're treated. A business that works to help other companies successfully brand and market themselves survives on its reputation as well as its work. 'I'll have HR go over the contract with you and you can start as soon as possible.'

'Thank you.'

'Oh, Saffron?' he calls as I'm about to leave.

'Yes?' I brace myself to be admonished for walking in without knocking earlier, to be asked to pretend I had seen nothing.

'I'm assuming if we need any back-up in the next month or so you won't mind helping out?' I like Gideon, really I do. Although I like him a whole lot less now that I know he's a cheating scumbag, but if I didn't know that, I'd like him because he's very straightforward. He's all about the business, all about the making money and all about trying to get me to work for free as well, it seems.

'We'll see, shall we?' I say.

His shamefaced personal assistant is glaring a hole into her computer screen when I exit his office, silently agreeing that I saw nothing.

XLIII

It's like a scar, a jagged-edged, shiny, bright scar that runs the length of the driver's side of my car. Made by *her*, probably with a screwdriver, sometime between the hours of nine-thirty and five-fifty-five.

She's slipped in here and done this. She's placed it below the handle so I can't miss it. So she can make her point. She's following me to work – to make sure I don't decide to drop into a police station at any point, I'm sure. Well, at least that's one bonus – if she's here, watching me, she won't be in London with Zane, she won't be in Queen's Park with Aunty Betty, and she won't be in Hove with Phoebe. She'll be wherever I am. There's an odd, unsettling comfort in that. It removes a layer of rawness to the vat of sickness at the pit of my stomach.

I am not going to freak out. If she's watching, then what she wants is for me to break down or to start screaming (what I'd like to do) because what she is desperate for is a reaction. A way to know she's got to me, especially because I've refused to open the blinds.

I cast a cursory glance around the car park, searching briefly in the gloom for any additional shadows beside the squat pillars; for someone lurking behind the other parked cars; for anyone breathing in the quiet of the underground level of this car park. I'm trying to sense someone, anyone, *anything*. I should be able to, especially now that I can experience the world in full, but there's nothing there. It's almost as if a ghost is doing this. Someone who leaves no trace of themselves is stalking me without actually being real.

There's traffic, which I think is odd for a Monday evening.

Cars stretch bumper to bumper along Dyke Road: the red lights, like a line of glassy, blinking eyes, are extinguished as the cars move and then lit up again as the cars have to stop. I've been calling Phoebe with the hands-free and there's no answer. I don't have the number for the teacher who is covering library duty.

I could call Mr Bromsgrove, but I'm loath to give him more reason to talk to my daughter than necessary. She'll be fine. She'll wait outside for me and it'll be fine. The panic that is fuelling the frenzied stirring of nausea in my stomach is only from general anxiety about being imprisoned here in traffic. It's not the worry that *she* might not have stayed to see my reaction to scarring my car, that she might have gone after Phoebe now. It's not fear that Phoebe will see her and will freak out that this person is around again.

I hit the call button on my steering wheel and my daughter's phone clicks straight to answer machine. There's nothing unusual about that. She's probably run out of battery since she's never off the damn thing – apart from the past couple of days when she doesn't seem to want to pick it up at all.

The car in front of me is a huge people carrier type affair

that holds one driver and three passengers. Joel had been angling for us to get a campervan not long before *that day*. He'd been willing to sell his BMW because we'd only be allowed two residential parking permits. I'd had to remind him several times that I wasn't the camping sort. 'I'll take the kids on my own, then,' he'd say happily. I wonder if the four people, two adults at the front, two child seats just seen over the top of the back seats, are a family in the traditional sense? Two children, two parents? I wonder if they go camping? I wonder, if Joel was alive, if we'd have gone camping?

There's a surge forwards as we come up to new traffic lights where Dyke Road becomes Old Shoreham Road. I pull my car onto it and the knot of anxiety loosens in my chest, it won't be long before I'm there. Probably around six-fifteen. Late, but not too late. She'll be fine. She'll be there. She knows not to go off with anyone else.

I pull up outside the school and park on the double yellows, not caring that I might get a ticket – the parking inspectors being that conscientious until eight o'clock. As I exit the car, the way the school is in darkness, with no sign of Phoebe outside, whisks up that terror inside to a new level. It's like those times you're looking for something you've forgotten. You look and you look but even as you're turning everything upside-down, and opening every drawer and cupboard you *know* deep in your soul that it's gone. I used to do that in the early days with Joel. I would walk around the kitchen looking for something, looking for him, even though deep down inside I knew he was gone.

Deep down inside, I know Phoebe is not here. I know she's gone.

But I will not panic. I will not go to the extreme place right away. I won't connect Joel's killer to this, this is simply me being late when I shouldn't have been. There is nothing more sinister going on here.

I dial her number on my mobile.

'*This is me. Leave me a message. Or don't. It's really up to you,*' her recorded voice cheerily tells me after a click without a ring. I forget sometimes that Phoebe can sound happy, that she has the capacity to be and sound joyful, young, delighted with everything.

'Pheebs, it's me. I'm waiting outside. I'm really, really sorry I'm late. See you in a minute or two.'

My body starts to tingle, the sickness twirling inside. Phoebe is gone. I know she is.

No she isn't, the sensible, sane part of me replies. *You're overreacting.*

I would be overreacting if Joel hadn't been murdered, if I wasn't getting those letters, if we weren't being stalked.

From the darkness of the school, two figures approach: one is tall, the other a little shorter. As they draw nearer, the smaller one two paces behind the taller one, I realise it's Mr Bromsgrove and Curtis. He has a box filled with books in his arms, as well as his laptop case over his left shoulder, his school bag slung over the wrist of his right arm. Curtis is walking with his school bag over his shoulder while fixated on his phone.

He's good-looking, is Lewis Bromsgrove. It's not only the

way his large, dark deep eyes stare at you, it's not simply the way a smile is never far away from his full, oh-kiss-me-now lips, it's not just that he has irresistible features. It's also the way he stands, the way he exudes a quiet, gentle confidence, the way he looks in clothes. He is the entire package. It's hard to believe he could be involved with Phoebe in ways he shouldn't be, but it's not an impossibility.

'Mrs Mackleroy,' he says, overtly pleased to see me. 'Hello. What brings you here?'

Curtis looks up at hearing my name, then immediately dips his head, abandoning his phone in favour of his feet.

'I'm picking up Phoebe,' I say.

'Phoebe? She went hours ago. I was on library duty and she told me someone was picking her up.'

Curtis, who carries on inspecting his feet as if he has only recently discovered them, develops a renewed and vigorous interest in them.

'I am meant to be picking her up. She knows she only leaves school with me.'

I don't need to see to know that Curtis's face is twisted with anxiety, a partner in whatever Phoebe is embroiled in now.

'Do you know something about this, Curtis?' I ask him. 'Do you have any idea why she would lie to your dad?'

He shakes his head without raising it.

I return my attention to his father with my eyebrows raised. 'Curtis?' he says in a modulation that suggests he's not going to be impressed if his son is lying to him.

'She didn't really tell me anything. Just that someone was

giving her a lift home and I should cover for her,' he mumbles.

'She didn't say who?' Mr Bromsgrove asks before I can.

Curtis shakes his head. 'Honest,' he adds.

I am not going to panic, I am not going to panic. Nothing has happened to her. Nothing is going to happen to her.

I am not going to panic, but Mr Bromsgrove is: his face tightens with apprehension, the same worry unpeeling in his eyes. He knows something I don't know, no one worries like this over a teenager sneaking off. He balances the cardboard box in one arm, roots in his pocket until he produces his car keys. 'Go wait in the car for me,' he tells his son in an agitated tone.

Once his son is shut away, he turns back to me.

'Why were you hugging my daughter?' I ask.

Thrown, he frowns as he replies. 'What?'

'I happened to drive past the school last Thursday and I saw you hugging her, why?'

The lines on his forehead deepen. 'Are you thinking . . . Because if you are, we can go straight to the police to sort this out. I'm not even going to entertain any idea that I might have been inappropriate with her.'

'Don't overreact,' I say. I will go to the police about this. If he is a manipulative bastard, he'll think that I won't, he'll believe him saying that will make me back off. It won't. 'I am simply asking why you were hugging my daughter. It's a fair question.'

'I was hugging her because she was upset.'

'Why?'

'I . . . I can't tell you. I said to her I wouldn't tell you.'

'Really? You promised my pregnant, fourteen-year-old daughter that you would keep things that have upset her from me? *Really?*' My voice is barely restrained. '*REALLY?* Tell me why I shouldn't punch you out right here and now?' *Apart from the fact I'm not violent.*

'Phoebe needs someone she can trust.'

'No, Phoebe needs someone who will keep her safe before having someone she trusts. If she's not safe, no amount of people who she trusts will matter. What was she upset about?'

Has she told him? About us keeping vital information from the police?

'At the end of last week, we don't know how, it became public knowledge that she's pregnant. She's been getting messages online about it ever since. Some of them are hideous, and she doesn't want me to tell the school officially, nor for me to tell you. I told her that if it hadn't died down by tomorrow morning, I'd have a duty to tell the school and you.'

'You kept this from me?'

'I was trying to do my best for Phoebe.'

'Well, you haven't. What do these messages say?'

'I can't . . . I can't repeat them. You have to see them yourself. She's deleted a few, but on some sites she can't so they're still there.'

'Sites? More than one?'

'Yes.' Jostling the box, he goes into his pocket again and pulls out his mobile. He attempts to unlock the screen with one hand, changes his mind and drops the box onto the ground. 'I've seen online bullying, but this is the nasty end I haven't really experienced until now.'

I was panicked before, now I am sliding into pure terror, even before he hands me the phone.

'Phoebe,' I say, 'I need to know where you are. I need to know you're safe. Please, call me. Or text me. Just let me know you're safe. Please, Sweetheart.' I need to calm down. In this state, the key won't find its place in the ignition slot, my body won't placate itself enough for me to check a mirror or to put the car into gear. Eventually, I find the ignition, insert the key.

I pause, pick up my phone, thrown onto the passenger seat, hit redial. 'Phoebe. It's me again. If you don't want to talk to me, that's all right. Call Curtis, Mr Bromsgrove, Aunty Betty or your uncle Fynn. Even Zane. Anyone. Just let them know you're OK. That you're safe.' *Safe*.

I need this to turn out the right way. I need to not be that woman with the bowl of blackberries ever again.

Before I drive away, I make another call.

He used to say your name, not like the expensive, fragrant spice but like it was something sour, bitter and poisonous. A bit like you, really.

XLIV

Knock-knock!

Phoebe has a key and I doubt she'd knock, but I run to the front door and snatch it open anyway because you never know.

Fynn.

'*I know you don't want to speak to me right now,*' began the message I left earlier, '*but Phoebe has gone missing. I need your help. A couple of other people are out looking for her, and Aunty Betty is here in case she comes home, but I need someone else out looking for her before I call the police. I hope you don't ignore this.*'

My disappointment is so evident that it's him and not Phoebe, I have to explain: 'I thought you were her.'

'When did you last see her?' he asks. He is not looking at me: he stares at the wall beside the kitchen door at the end of the corridor, way beyond my shoulder. Way out of reach of eye contact with me.

'I dropped her off at school this morning. She's been staying a bit later so I can pick her up after school. I got there a bit late and the teacher who covers library duty said she hadn't come in. Mr Bromsgrove, you know, her form tutor, said she'd told him she was getting picked up instead of waiting for me and left at three-thirty.'

'Did you have a row or something?'

'No, but a few days ago people found out at school she's pregnant. And she's been getting nasty messages online and probably texts ever since. She never told me. I was trying to give her space. I didn't want to pressure her until she'd made a decision, so I've not checked her Facebook, Twitter or anything like that. I'm so stupid. She's out there, alone and scared and probably has all those things running through her head – I saw what they'd written – because I was too stupid to just clamp down on her. I'm so scared for her.'

He inhales deeply. 'Who's out looking and where have you looked?' he says evenly. He is scared, like me. He too is back at *that day* and he is telling himself that it will turn out fine.

'Is it her?' Aunty Betty calls from the living room.

'No. It's Fynn,' I call back. I return to speaking to Fynn: 'Mr B—'

'Does he know where she is?' Aunty Betty interrupts.

'No! He's come to help look for her! ... As I was saying, Mr B—'

'Tell him hello from me!' she interrupts again. 'And thank you!'

'For the love of ... Yes! I'll do that!'

Before I attempt to speak again, I wait a second, then another, to give Aunty Betty a chance to interrupt.

'Lewis is out looking for her with his son. And I've driven around a bit, visited a few places in Brighton where she likes to go, but I came back to check on Aunty Betty. I'm about to go out again.'

'Where do you want me to cover?'

'I'm not sure. Mr Bromsgrove is doing out towards the marina and Saltdean. I think I'll try up Preston Park way next.'

'I'll do Hove,' Fynn says.

'I'm really panicking. I know this isn't your problem, but . . . What if something happens to her? What if someone's taken her?'

'Who would take her?'

'I don't know. Who would kill Joel?'

The same thought strikes us at the same time: Joel.

'Have you . . . ?' he asks.

'No. It never even crossed my mind. I'm *so stupid*. Why wouldn't I think of trying there? I've got to go there.'

'I'll drive you.'

'It's fine. I'll go by myself.'

'You're shaking, you look as if you're about to fall over – you're in no fit state to drive. I'll take you.'

'How've you been?' I ask him.

We have driven for five minutes but it has felt like five excruciating hours have crawled past without either of us speaking. I was leaving it to him, taking my cues from him and his cue has been silence.

Silence that has its hands around my throat and is suffocating me to the point where I may start to hyperventilate in order to breathe properly.

'Fine,' he replies. Succinct, formal. 'You?'

'Fine,' I reply. This is the man who held me for hours after Joel died, who slept on my sofa so he could take care of me when my night terrors started, who I love with all my heart. He will not talk to me. He has nothing to say to me. From anyone else – apart from the kids – I could probably stand it. From him, it is like a drip-dripping torture at the centre of my forehead that is burrowing into my skull.

'It doesn't have to be like this, Fynn,' I tell him. 'If we could just talk properly.'

'Is Zane at Imogen's house?' His formality remains secured over his words, and keeps the gap between us prised open. 'Do we need to pick him up on the way back?'

'No, he's . . . he's in London, staying with Joel's parents for a while.'

The expression that passes over Fynn's face is one I understand, I'd have made it too, if I hadn't been desperate, if Zane hadn't been quietly falling apart. On the phone I can hear his happiness, his relief. He's probably not worried any more about being in the house. He misses us, but he can't be with us. If things were normal with Fynn I could explain and he'd understand that. In this moment, I can't explain anything. He has nothing to say to me, and he is not getting involved.

The entrance to the cemetery is a red-brick Gothic structure with five peaked arches, the largest at its centre. The outer two arches have fixed iron railings, the inner two arches are the foot entrances with iron gates, and the large centre arch has double gates for cars to drive in. On the other side of the locked gates, only a few feet away, is the admin office, another red-brick structure that looks like a shrunken Gothic mansion, where there are lights on. A huge, thick-trunked tree stands outside each foot gate, immobile and threatening like nature's own bodyguards for the residents inside.

As we pull up to where the double gates are locked and chained, I see her, sitting with her back against the left-hand gate, her knees pulled up to her chest, her arms wrapped around her legs, her head resting on her knees. Every part of my inner being is simultaneously turned upside-down and inside out. I barely wait for the car to come to a standstill before I rip off my seatbelt and bolt out of the door.

I throw myself to my knees and gather her in my arms. She's breathing, she doesn't look hurt, I can still touch her. She's not gone, she's not 'evidence of a crime', she's still here with me where she should be. 'Are you all right?' I whisper into her hair. 'I thought something had happened to you. I couldn't stand it if something happened to you. You're my world, Phoebe. You and Zane are my world. Are you all right?' I hold her as near as I can. She's cold and shivering slightly.

'I wanted to talk to Dad,' she mumbles, her forehead against her knees. 'But it was closed.'

When she was four, after a bright February morning in the garden, Phoebe was running to the house to fetch her new ball, when she tripped on an uneven flagstone. I watched it happen in horror as she fell forwards, hitting her chin and hands at the same time, the rough uneven surface of the patio stones scraping the skin off her chin and the palms of her hands. Joel, who was nearer to her, leapt out of his seat and ran to her, ready to scoop her up into his arms. 'No,' she wailed at him, while I, eight months pregnant, was strug-

391

gling to become upright. 'No, Dad, I want Mum. I want Mum. I want Mum.'

'I'm sorry he's not here, Pheebs,' I say. 'I'm so sorry.'

'Do you think he'd be ashamed of me?' she asks.

'Of course not! Why would he be ashamed of you? Your dad . . . he thought the Sun and Moon rose and set with you and Zane. Of course he wouldn't be ashamed of you. Why would you even think such a thing?'

A shrug.

Shrugs always have their root in something to do with the man who got her pregnant. 'Is this something to do with the person who got you pregnant?' I ask.

'No!' she exclaims. She lifts her head to make sure I know the truth. 'It's just, Imogen texted me and said she wanted to talk so she'd meet me after school. We got in her car and we went to a café and she said all these things. And she said I'd already let Dad down by getting pregnant so young that if I killed this . . . you know, she said Dad would be ashamed of me. I don't want Dad to be ashamed of me.' She sniffs, her nose runs from being out here for hours in the cold. 'She was so sure that I thought she must be right.

'I didn't know what to do. I'm so confused. So then, I thought if I did something like walk in front of a bus then I wouldn't be pregnant any more and the problem would go away and Dad wouldn't be ashamed. That's why I came to talk to him. I wanted to say sorry for letting him down. And I wanted to ask him what it was like to be dead. And if he'd be waiting for me if that's what happened to me.'

I have to remind myself not to breathe too quickly. Slow

breaths soothe away the sickness enough to help me to find the right words.

'It's not true,' I state. 'You haven't let him down. Don't listen to Imogen. I knew your dad for so much longer than her. I loved him, I had children with him, I ate with him, I rowed with him, I even got to smell his farts and wash his dirty socks. I knew him. I knew him so well and I know, without a doubt, that you haven't let him down and he wouldn't be ashamed of you.'

Her young eyes search my face as her mouth crumples into a line of uncertainty: she's not sure if she should believe me. She's wondering if I'm saying what I'm saying because I want to help her or if her father would never be ashamed of her.

'I did some pretty stupid things when I got together with your father,' I say.

'Drugs?' she asks, aghast. More, I think, that I'd be the one doing them rather than the fact it was drug-taking per se.

'No,' I say. 'I've never taken drugs – and you shouldn't either. No, it was stupid though, and potentially dangerous.' Fynn is watching us, and I flash back to what he said to me in the street and how I turned on him. 'Well, your dad found out about it. And he confronted me and he told me that he loved me, and he wanted me to get help. At no point – *no point at all* – did he say or act like he was ashamed of me. He could have been, but he wasn't. When you love someone it takes a lot to make you ashamed of them. He loved you so much. You should have seen the pride on his face when you were born. He called everyone he knew, even people who he hadn't spoken to in years, to tell them. Obviously that went down well with the woman he was on holiday with when he met me. She was overjoyed to get *that* phone call, as you can imagine. What I'm saying, Phoebe, is you'd have to do more than make a mistake for him to be ashamed of you.

'He would have been upset that you're in this situation and that you have such a hard decision to make, but he wouldn't be let down by whatever choice you make if it's the right one for you.'

She says nothing, but I think she believes me, the words have soothed part of her because she remembers what her dad was like, who her dad was.

'Come on, let's get you home, Aunty Betty was so worried. We all were.'

'Were you an alkie, Mum?' she asks as we get to our feet.

'No. I'm not going to tell you what it was so you can stop asking.'

'Do you think I'm a slut?' she asks.

'No,' I reply. 'I don't think anyone is a "slut". It's horrible to call someone that. The things that were written about you were so horrible and not in any way true.'

Something shifts between us, something as ethereal as air, but as tangible as our bodies, and this newly formed connection between us is cracked, the fractures evident in multiple places.

'You read my Facebook? Even though you promised you wouldn't, you read it. I should have known I couldn't trust you.'

'Phoebe, you can trust me. I didn't promise not to read your Facebook or Twitter or anything else, I said I wouldn't look unless I had reason to. And I did have reason to, I needed to see what was written so I could work out how to help you. Mr Broms—'

'He probably agrees with them, too, doesn't he?'

'No, he doesn't.'

'Why not? Everyone else does. They all think I'm a slut and a whore and really stupid for getting pregnant and that I should do anything to get rid of it. Why not you and him?'

'Only stupid, thick, disturbed people who hide behind a computer to say those things think that. All the people who know and love you don't think like that, either.'

'Imogen does.'

'That's different.'

'How is it different? She said what they all said but used nicer words. It all means the same thing. Even you were angry when you found out.'

'I'm allowed to be angry, Phoebe,' I reply. Memories of what I thought and felt at that moment aren't easy to access, they slip away from me like running water through my fingers. 'I don't actually think I was angry,' I tell Phoebe. 'I was shocked and then I was disappointed because it looked like my beautiful, bright daughter who was going to university and then would go on to change the world had suddenly had her life shunted down a completely different track. I'm allowed to feel that and to forget for a minute that having a child doesn't mean you can't do those things, or having an abortion means you'll be scarred for life, or that having a baby adopted means you won't see them at some point in the future. I'm allowed to forget all that for a little while and to react not perfectly to one of the most shocking pieces of news I've ever had because I'm only human.'

'But I'm not, am I, *Mum*?' she retaliates. 'I'm not human. I have to be perfect all the time, I have to do everything right all the time otherwise it's the end of the world.'

She's not talking about the pregnancy, she's talking about the day Joel died. What she did on the day that picture secreted away in my bedroom was taken. 'No one expects you to be perfect, Phoebe. I've never expected that of you.'

'Yeah, right. I made one mistake one time and you act as if it's a reason to go through my things.'

'I don't go through your things, Phoebe. I only looked because I was worried about you. And the agreement when you signed up for those things and when you were given your phone back was that I would look whenever I felt it necessary.'

'Yeah, like I could ever trust you to stick to that.'

'You, trust me?' I reply. 'What about me trusting you? How about every time I trust you, you pull some kind of stunt to obliterate that trust? Even tonight. You were told not to leave school without me so you go off with someone else. Before you start talking about trusting me, think about if I can trust you.'

Fynn, who must have heard the tail end of the conversation because we are right by his car, opens his door and gets out because things are getting out of hand.

'I think we should all calm down,' he intercedes. 'I'll drive you back and you can sit down at the table at home and talk this out.'

'No. Thank you but no,' I say before Phoebe can utter a protest about being in the car with me. 'Fynn, can you drive Phoebe home? I'll call a cab.'

Phoebe's protest, which had grown rapidly on her face, withers where it began, replaced by a new crop: disbelief at what I am doing.

'Don't be ridiculous,' Fynn says.

'I'm not being ridiculous,' I reply. 'I think Phoebe needs to spend time with her uncle Fynn and I need to either walk home or get a taxi. I'm not getting into that car so you can ignore me.' I'm talking to both of them – I'm not giving either of them the chance to blank me.

My daughter is genuinely surprised, and a tiny shard of admiration lurks in there, too. I love her, I am so relieved she is all right, but I can't be around her at the moment. Same with Fynn.

'I love you, Phoebe,' I say to her. I want to fold my arms around her as I say that. I want to envelop her and let her know that, like before, I will do everything I can to protect her. She won't let me, though. The wall around her is definite, she has a boundary that she doesn't want to be breached right now and I need to respect that.

She says nothing and gets into the car.

'I'll make sure she goes into the house,' Fynn says.

I nod at him. '*I love you*,' I mouth to him when he turns away to climb into the car. '*You're my best friend and I love you.*'

I can't watch them drive away, instead I drop to the ground, lower my head and give myself up to the agony that is expanding inside.

9 weeks after *That Day* (December, 2011)

'I didn't go to school that morning,' Phoebe said to me, pausing between each word. 'I bunked off to meet Molly in town because she was suspended. One of Dad's friends saw me and called him. Dad came to get me before I found Molly. And his friend gave him a lift. His friend waited for him in Churchill Square car park until he found me, then they gave me a lift back to school and Dad came in and gave them a note saying I'd had a dentist appointment. He said he didn't like lies and this was the last time he'd ever do that and that he was going to tell you later and I'd be in big trouble. But he didn't want me to get in trouble with the school if I promised to never do it again.'

'I don't understand.'

'Your mixing bowl, Mum. Dad bought it that day. It was on the back seat of her car and I sat next to it.'

'Her?'

'Yes. She was from his cooking class. He said he was going to explain everything to you, so I shouldn't.'

'I don't understand why you've waited this long to tell me, though.'

'Your mixing bowl. It was in her car. And then it was in the boot of Dad's car.'

I suddenly realised what she was saying: his car had been in the garage that morning for a service and it was still in the garage after he was killed. The garage was miles away, and they remembered him arriving too early to collect it. They remembered him saying he had to leave the bowl in the boot because he had to go and find his lost phone. But they didn't remember how he arrived or how he left, they only remembered that he didn't come back like he said he would.

He'd obviously been dropped off by his 'friend'. He'd probably been taken to collect his phone by his 'friend'. But the police never did find out where his 'lost' phone had been because it must have been off when it wasn't with him, and from tracking its signal, the last time it was turned on was on Montefiore Road, where he died. And since it was beside him, wiped clean it seemed of fingerprints apart from his blood-smudged ones, it'd come to nothing; another unanswered clue in the mystery of why he died.

The police checked his phone records and everyone on the list who had called him that day – including me – had an alibi. No one except our family had seen him that day, apparently. Except now I knew that at least two people weren't where they said they were: Phoebe, and his 'friend'. Audra.

It was her. She had done it. She had lied to the police about why she spoke to him for those brief minutes in the morning, and then lied again about her whereabouts – if they had checked her alibi, they'd find out it was false. And she knew that Phoebe had lied to them, too. That Phoebe hadn't told the police about her because they never questioned her again.

'Are you going to tell the police?' Phoebe asked.

'I think I have to.'

'But I'll get in trouble because I didn't tell the truth first of all.'

'You won't get in trouble, you did nothing wrong.'

'But what if they think I did it?'

'They won't think that, Phoebe.'

'Please don't, Mum.'

'But, Phoebe—'

'Please don't, Mum. Please. Please. Please. Please. Please. Please. I'm scared. I'm really scared.'

'Phoebe, we can't—'

'Please, Mum. I'm really sorry, but please, don't.'

'Shhh, shhhhh. It'll be OK, I'll make it all OK.'

Phoebe was terrified, she was already traumatised and being eaten up by the guilt of what she'd done, with thinking she had caused this to happen to her dad – she didn't need to speak to the police on top of it. I was going to tell them anyway, I had to. But then the FLO started asking about prostitutes, hinting that Joel might have had a secret life. And I knew they would destroy an already fragile Phoebe. Their questioning – brutal, crude and immensely unsympathetic – would be too much for her at that time. So I made the decision, one that I knew Joel would have approved of, to protect our daughter at all costs.

While I wait for the taxi, I stand at the gates of the cemetery, too exhausted, too drained to be scared or spooked out. What is there to be spooked about, anyway, when Joel is in there? He'd wanted to be cremated, to have his ashes scattered in the sea outside our beach hut. But we were robbed of that, too. As a homicide victim whose killing hadn't been solved, we weren't able to do that. That was one of the conditions of being allowed the body back within four months of his death

– we agreed they could exhume it whenever they wanted to carry out more tests. We had to agree to let him rest in peace in a way deemed acceptable by someone else.

He's a little further in, up the winding, uphill path. A bit of a walk, then around the bend and towards the pond. Near a tree, not far from the water, the best I could do because I couldn't scatter his ashes.

I don't come here often enough.

It's too much. Whenever I come here, I'm overwhelmed. Unlike the usual potholes in time I live with, thoughts of him crowd into my head, my body, my heart in an immediate rush. I am filled with him in a sudden, gluttonous binge of remembering. I can't separate them, experience or even contemplate enjoying them. It is a homogeneous mass that takes over. I usually stand at the graveside, unable to do anything but allow the binge to take over.

And when I leave, the memories are ripped away; abruptly and viciously snatched from me so I go home empty. Not the emptiness I feel after a purge, not the emptiness I felt after the sex I had with Fynn, it is a total, petrifying barrenness of a hole at my core that nothing can fill because what has been gouged out can never be replaced.

Coming here is too much for me, so I avoid it as much as I can.

XLV

Usually, I reach for the brass, lion-shaped knocker because I can modulate the level of sound I create inside the house and not disturb anyone, but right now, I do not care who is unsettled by my visit: I press the doorbell hard and create a loud ring that trills through the house.

Imogen's concerned face, a blonde-topped oval, peers around the door. 'Saffy?' she says, surprised. 'Is everything OK?'

'Erm . . . not really, can we talk inside for a few minutes?'

'Yes, sure,' she says. It doesn't occur to her that I know what she did to my daughter. If it does dawn on her, she's being very blasé about what my reaction would be. But Imogen doesn't know me. I am the person she wants to see, the widow she talks over and dismisses so I will do what she thinks is best. Maybe she's so deluded about who I am that she thinks I've come to apologise for walking away from her in the supermarket the other day.

'Come into the kitchen! I was making up Ernest's sandwiches for the morning! Everyone else is upstairs in various rooms, on various electronic devices!' she chatters. I haven't noticed before how much she chatters, as if silence is too much for her to tolerate, so she always has to be filling it with words and exclamatory sentences. She gesticulates in an exaggerated manner, her body swaying in time with the movement of her hands.

Bright light assaults me when I enter the kitchen from the darkness of the corridor, momentarily stopping me before I follow her into the room with its maple-wood units, black granite worktops, a large rectangular table at the centre where they eat breakfast. Many times I have picked up Zane after a sleepover and he's been sitting in this room, perfectly slotted into the Norbet family, welcomed into the fold like one of their own. That's what is the biggest betrayal in what she has done. She knows my family: she's not one of those faceless people on the internet who can say whatever they want from the brave and ignorant distance that being behind a computer gives them; she's not one of those people who stands up and makes impassioned speeches about something without knowing the individual stories. She knows my daughter. She knows what my daughter has been through and she is capable of *using* my child's trauma to try to control her.

'What was it I could do for you?' Imogen asks. She has returned to her place at the worktop area nearest the sink. The detritus of making ham sandwiches is on the wooden chopping board in front of her: the cellophane-covered organic ham packet is peeled back, two slices of it resting on one medium-cut slice of the organic 50-50 bread. The top part of the sandwich sits beside it, ready to be lowered into place. The organic pre-washed lettuce waits in an unopened bag, while the small plum tomatoes are on the chopping board, sliced and ready to be dropped onto the ham. It's this that launches me off into the deep end, like a champion diver leaping from the highest perch. Before I came here I could probably have talked calmly and rationally to her, I could have had a row with her about what she did, but seeing this normality, that she has simply gone back to life as though she did nothing different today is too much. My life will probably never be normal again, and that is not fine, but it is something I am coming to terms with – Imogen has no such worries. She can hurt people and because she believes she is right, she can come home, eat dinner with her boys and then make sandwiches.

How blithely she has all but destroyed my daughter triggers something inside and my eyes start to search a little manically for something in her kitchen. I know where it is in mine, but in the familiar strangeness of hers, it's a full minute before my gaze finally settles on the sleek, black land-line handset, resting in its discreet silver cradle. My fingers close around the handset, causing a bleep as I lift it clear then toss it underarm to Imogen. Baffled, she dips her body slightly to catch it in the crook of her arms.

'Call the police,' I tell her calmly.

She does not speak, she does not do as I have asked, instead, her slender body draws back, and she frowns a little at me. Slowly her lips bunch together in confusion.

'I mean it. Call the police and tell them that there's a woman about to smash up your house.'

She smirks, a bewildered response to what I've said.

'I *fucking mean it*.' I force the words through my gritted teeth. Rarely do I swear, rarely do I react like this to anything.

My anger is usually internal. Even when it should be directed outwards at specific people, it's usually fired at me, it dwells inside, eating at me, gnawing at me until I have to silence it in the only way I know how. 'You don't come into my house, my family, and start smashing things up without thinking I'm going to do the same to you.'

'I haven't smashed anything up,' she says, disgusted as well as perplexed.

'It didn't occur to you that the little chat you had with my daughter might wreck her head, smash up her mind?' I say loudly. 'Maybe make her suicidal?'

Imogen darts to shut the kitchen door to prevent her family from hearing what she's done today in between breakfast and dinner.

'She was so distressed after talking to you that she was thinking of walking in front of a bus to solve the problem.'

'What? No, not because of anything I said to her.'

'My child was thinking about killing herself so she wouldn't continue to let her dad down and she wouldn't make him even more ashamed of her.'

'She took it the wrong way, she obviously didn't understand what I meant.'

It's Imogen who doesn't understand, who thinks that she can sidle out of this with a mealy mouthed explanation that blames her victim. She can get away with a lot, but this trying to blame a child for her adult actions unleashes a tornado of rage inside me. 'CALL THE FUCKING POLICE!' I scream. 'CALL THEM NOW!'

Imogen begins to shake as the realisation of what she did,

what she almost pushed someone to do, sinks in. She flattens herself against the door, her hand over her mouth. 'Is she all right?' she asks through her fingers. 'Tell me she didn't hurt herself, please.'

I take a step backwards, those questions, the worry behind them, are a cure for my hurricane of rage. Another step back and I am in front of a chair. It makes sense to sit down, to calm myself. 'She hasn't hurt herself, but that's no thanks to you.'

'Oh, God, I didn't mean . . .' Imogen says. She drags her feet heavily and crosses the room to drop into the wooden chair at the diagonal opposite end of the table to me. The blinds are drawn and the shiny red cherries on a white background add a forced cheeriness to the room. That's what's so odd about Imogen, this house and everything she does – it is forced, as if nothing comes naturally, it's all about appearances and that appearance has to be happy, bright, positive. *All the time*.

I inhale deeply and exhale at length. My head is buzzing with what has happened in the last few hours; buzzing constantly with what has happened in the last few days, weeks, months, years. My brain cannot relax – ever. 'What were you thinking?' I say to her. She's a nebulous outline, slumped in a chair on the very periphery of my line of sight. If I look at her, if I see her properly, I'll probably imagine her mouth moving as it torments Phoebe and I will lose it again.

'Saffron,' she says heavily, patronisingly, obviously unaware how close she is to unleashing my rage again, 'I wish you would understand – what she was going to do was wrong. Someone had to explain that to her. *I* had to explain that to her because no one else would. I didn't think it would upset her so much and for that I'm sorry, but I needed her to think about it. *Really* think about it. She has no idea how it'll scar her for life.'

'Scarred or not, at least she'd still be alive. And how many times do I have to tell you: nothing's been decided. Even if it had, it's got *nothing* to do with you.'

She witnessed how every day after Joel's death we couldn't think straight, couldn't eat, could barely sleep. She saw how broken Phoebe was and is. She has seen Zane's personality being stripped away, hidden behind layers of fear and silence and uncertainty. She's seen this, she's been there, and she can still do this to Phoebe.

'It has got something to do with me. Abortion is wrong. It shouldn't even be an option. She will never be the same again afterwards. Your little girl will be gone for ever and I want to save her – and you – from that.'

'You don't know how she'll be after an abortion or how she'll be if she has a baby. None of us knows.'

'Yes, I do!' she insists.

'How do you know? Do you have some kind of crystal ball that tells you everything everyone's going to feel after every little thing they do?'

'No!' she snaps.

'Then spare me. If you don't have incontrovertible fore-sight, then stop it.'

'I know because I had one. All right? I had one and there's not a day goes by when I don't feel *horrible* about it.'

I scrutinise the cherries on the blinds again, then I move on to the brightly coloured mugs hanging from the metal hooks screwed into the underside of the wall cupboards beside the kettle, then I take in the multicoloured chopping boards lined up against the counter to the right. To avoid facing her, and this confession I'm sure she never intended to make, I scan the room, ingesting the imposed joviality that seems to drip from every visible element of their lives. *You really believe that abortion is wrong, Imogen? . . . Well don't have one then*, I hear myself say. I had no idea.

'I fell pregnant very quickly after Damien,' Imogen is saying. 'I couldn't believe it, I was breastfeeding and I thought we'd been careful, but six months after Damien I was pregnant again. My husband, my first husband, he made all the right noises in the beginning, said he was pleased but I could tell he wasn't. I knew he was worried about how we'd cope moneywise because it would mean I couldn't go back to work for a bit longer than we planned.

'I didn't care about all that, but the more we talked about it, the more I could see he was right. We really couldn't cope with another . . . I didn't want to do it, but it was the only way to keep my husband. If I didn't I knew he'd leave me and I couldn't handle being a single mother. Children need two parents. Damien deserved the best and I couldn't give him that if it was just me.'

She pauses to draw breath and I still can't bring myself to look at her, instead I continue to examine the cherries on the blinds.

'So I went through with it, and I . . . I cried for a week afterwards. I was so broken by it. I felt like I'd let Damien down. Nothing ever felt right after that and I never forgave my husband for making me do it.' She sniffs, and I sense her wiping her nose, trying to mop up her tears with her fingertips. 'The worst part is he left me anyway. Had a grubby little affair with some young tart who threw herself at him, and then left. I should never have done it for him.' More sniffing, more tear-wiping. 'You see? I *do* know what I'm talking about, I *do* have some idea of what it'll do to her.'

'No, you don't,' I reply quietly. I feel awful for her, but what she has done to Phoebe is still bubbling away in my chest. 'I am so *so* sorry for what you went through, Imogen. It sounds horrific, but all you know is how *you* were affected by it. Just because you felt like that doesn't mean everyone else will.'

'How can they not?' she says. Her tears have evaporated and she is back in the position of 'right about everything'.

'Oh come on, Imogen, everyone's different, how they react to things is different. You *know* that. You are *not* Phoebe. You can't know what she'll feel whether she goes ahead with the pregnancy or not.'

'I think I—'

'If you were fourteen when you had your abortion, that might take you a step closer to understanding her,' I interrupt. 'If your father was killed when you were twelve and they still hadn't caught the killer, then that might take you a step closer. If you had a mother who has been on the edge of a nervous breakdown since your father died, that might take you closer. If some bastard lying to you to get into your knickers resulted in a pregnancy you never wanted, that might take you fractionally nearer. But you are and were none of those things so you have no idea how she'll react. None of us have any idea about anything that hasn't happened, not even Phoebe, so *please*, let's drop this.'

'Saffron—'

'Unless you are about to say, "Saffron, I'm really sorry for being so unutterably vile to your daughter, I'm going to apologise unreservedly to her and tell her I was wrong" then please do not finish that sentence.'

'I hope someone can talk some sense into you before you let—'

The rage boils my veins, blisters my muscles and scorches my chest as it erupts through my mouth: 'STAY AWAY FROM MY DAUGHTER! STAY AWAY FROM ME! NEXT TIME, I WILL NOT GIVE YOU THE OPTION OF CALLING THE POLICE FIRST!' My bellow is a sound I've never made before. It doesn't matter who hears me, it's not important who is frightened by my words, all that matters is that Imogen understands. I don't care what she believes, I don't care if she expects the whole world to do as she says and not as she does, I simply need her to believe that if I ever again have to listen to my daughter talk about killing herself, permanently removing herself from me because of something Imogen has said, it will be the end of Imogen. 'DO I MAKE MYSELF CLEAR?'

Although most of Imogen's body is rigid, her large, hazel-green eyes are fixed on me as she nods.

These are the things I know about her: Imogen wears make-up every day, she has her hair professionally washed and styled every week, she started to go to church to get her son into St

410

Caroline's because of its outstanding Ofsted report and her house being technically out of the catchment area; she runs her home with military precision.

These are the things she doesn't know about me: I have done some unthinkable things to protect my daughter; I'd do virtually anything to protect my daughter and my son; if it came to a choice between hurting Imogen and allowing my children to be damaged, there'd be no choice at all.

'I was about to come out and look for you. I was worried.' He doesn't want to be around me any longer, he doesn't want to speak to me, but Fynn has waited here for hours for me to come home. My heart aches at the thought of that, at the thought of him.

'Thank you,' I say. 'For the lift to get Phoebe, for bringing her home, and for staying here to wait for me. And for being worried.'

He won't look at me, he stares straight ahead as I speak.

The walk home hasn't cleared my head, it has simply made it swim, made me feel as if I am on a piece of driftwood in the ocean, bumped around, taken here and there on the will of the tide, the whim of someone else. I need to cook something. Or eat something. I need something that is going to make all of this *everythingness* go away. A talk to my best friend might do it.

'Fynn—'

His navy blue eyes look sharply at me, then. Cold, unflinching; warning me not to do it, not to go *there*. It was done with and we all had to get on with it.

'Nothing. I'll see you.'

'Take care of yourself,' he replies, his line of sight back on the windscreen. He pulls away from the kerb without looking in my direction again.

Entering my house seems too much effort right now. I sit on the fourth stone step, my bag on my lap, the cold of the night air seeping into my skin. I know she's probably out here, watching me from wherever she is. But if I go inside I will not be able to stop myself from bingeing. I will need to stuff away all these feelings, all this hurt, and I don't want to. I need to, but I don't want to. I can't fight it for much longer, but being out here will delay it a while.

I hear the car before I see it. It has a familiar growl, it is a striking British racing green colour, it has a driver with navy blue eyes who looks in my direction and meets my gaze. He throws a regretful but affectionate half-smile at me before accelerating away.

Come back, I think at him. *I want to do it again.*

X

Saffron.

I think it might be a good thing that Joel didn't get to live to see this happen. His precious, adored daughter is as big a slut as her mother? It would break his heart.

I didn't even know she was pregnant. I wanted you to see how badly you were letting her down, how you weren't protecting her from all the bad people out there. Do you know how easy it is to befriend her friends online? Too easy. They don't even bother to check who a person is before they become 'friends'. I know Phoebe kept rejecting my requests, but her friends accepted me. And I just made up the rumour and put it out there. And suddenly it's true. She's a slut, just like her mother.

She doesn't know when to keep her legs shut.

As I said, maybe it's a good thing he isn't here to see this. It would break his heart.

Some lessons need to be taught the hard way. I'm sorry, Saffron, but you've just learnt one. I think you may have to learn a few more.

A

XLVI

In my fantasy I am not here. I am at the beach.

In my fantasy, the beach isn't the place where I go to explore thoughts of ending the pain. In my fantasy I am sitting at the beach hut, with the doors propped inwards. We have put up the rickety camping table, its Formica top cracked and peeling away from its metal surround. We have canvas deckchairs – four in total, but we have room for five people because one of the deckchairs is a doubler. In my perfect life, I am curled up on my husband's lap as he reclines in the double deckchair, his long legs support my body and I am substantial and real, but not grotesque and huge as I often feel. He has his arm slung around me, the other playing with my hair. My eldest child, a girl, has her legs curled underneath herself and she is alternating between texting and reading a book. My youngest child, a boy, is sitting on the hot, uneven tarmac in front of his deckchair, sorting through his heaped pile of stones and shells, industriously categorising them.

In my mind, I am landed here, on my beach, with the sea rushing in and out to say hello like an excited, noisy child who can't quite believe how many people have turned up for a visit. There are people wandering past on their way to somewhere else, but we are cocooned inside our little world, the pieces of our lives slotted together, so from up close, from far away we are the same: a complete picture. We are a family.

In my real life I am here. My grey-white dressing gown puddles at my feet when I discard it to step into the shower. Instead of my usual rush to move straight into the shower, avoiding the faint reflection of my shape in the limescale-splattered glass of the shower cubicle and the full-length mirror behind the door, I stop. Air goes in and out of my lungs, forced to expand and contract my chest, giving me courage. I have not done this for a long time. I have weighed myself every day but this I avoid. I have repeatedly binged and purged but I have side-stepped this. I constantly take handfuls of the excess parts of me, feeling their disgusting mass ooze between my fingers, but I have shunned this.

I am naked, and I turn first to the ghostly reflection in the shower cubicle's glass. It has a build up of white flecks of limescale because it was Joel who used to do the bathrooms. I haven't kept up with that job as regularly as he did.

A very faint version of me is there in the glass, and the outline is not what I expect. From the numbers on the scales, from the amount that goes in and comes out, from the touch of myself sometimes, this should not be my outline. My outline should be bigger, much, much bigger.

'I thought you'd stopped doing this, Ffrony. You said you didn't need any help and you promised me you would stop.'

'You are thin.'

I hear those words all the time, they are with me constantly, in there in the never-ending swirl of thoughts, feelings and memories I constantly hear in my head.

My body revolves until, slowly, bit by bit, who I am when everything is stripped away is revealed to me in the mirror.

In my fantasy life this is not who I am. I am perfect, and whole, and relaxed. It doesn't matter what my body looks like, it doesn't matter what the number on the scale says, I am complete. This outer part of me doesn't matter, all that matters is what's inside me. I will be loved no matter what, I will be held and cherished and wanted. In my perfect life I can let go of the digital numbers that go up and down, I can release the need to stuff things down and away, only to do *whatever it takes* to feel empty again. In my mind, my clear mind, I know that food is not love, it is not reward, it is not punishment, it is not perfection, it is not control, it is not unmanageable, it is not hate, it is not a sin, it is not one of the many things I use to torture myself with every day. Food is fuel.

In my dream existence I know that thinness is not perfection. Thinness is not happiness. It is not the answer to all my problems, it is not the place I need to be so my life can begin. Wanting to be thin is another way of being elsewhere while life goes on around me. It is no different from being fat. Large. Big. Obese. Thinness is not going to change my life because I am thin and I am not happy. I am in control of my food and my body and I am not happy.

In my ideal life I do not look in the mirror and see what I do now. I don't see that I am thin and know that I am not happy. I don't see that I am in control of my body, I control every element of it, and I am not happy. In my ideal existence, I don't look at myself in the mirror and I don't see the only thing Joel and I ever really argued about, I don't see that Fynn was right.

In my blissful world, I don't remember the voice inside I chose to ignore when I was nineteen so I could restart on this journey to thinness and I don't see clearly and painfully why I split myself in two so I can make it through the day.

I often cry in the shower. With my hair pushed under an elasticated clear shower cap, I stand facing the large metal head and I let the water drum onto my face, I let its rhythm resonate over my sensitised skin and I cry. I allow my body to shake, I wrap my arms around myself and I sob, I breathe in and out rapidly, like the short bursts of a machine gun. I can do that in here with the sound of running water as cover so no one can hear me. I am never alone enough to properly cry, to completely let go and wail. So I do it here, as alone as I can get.

When I am exhausted, tired of crying, agreed that this is enough for today, I right myself. I force myself to stand upright, I release my body from my own tight grasp and I open my eyes ready to focus and face reality.

It takes longer today, to right myself, to drag myself out of the fantasy life where I long to dwell and into this life. In this life I have devastated my body, I have constantly painful teeth that are so damaged they have often crumbled from eating cereal; I haven't taken care of my family and they are fragmented, frightened, fragile; I have lost my best friend. I have messed up on every level. It takes longer but with determination, I prise my eyes apart, reaching to the side for the sliver of unperfumed soap that should be sufficient to wash my body. As my eyes, probably a vivid crimson and thick with the heaviness of attempting to weep my heart out, open they take their time to focus.

Once the world around me is in view again, I see him. He has a perfect, cylindrical but tapered body; neat, evenly spaced black and yellow stripes; four clear, fragile wings; a long, protruding line at his bottom.

9 years before *That Day* (May, 2002)

'You do the spiders and slugs, Babes, I'll do the wasps.'

'We hardly ever get wasps.'

'That doesn't mean we don't need a dedicated wasp ridder.'

'How come I get two and you get one?'

'Wasps are more dangerous, Ffrony.'

He would find this hilarious, he really would. The slugs have had their way with my plants, I see evidence of spiders and their webs all over the place and now this. I can't remember the last time we had a wasp in the house.

'You absolute bastard,' I say to the grin Joel's no doubt wearing wherever he is. 'You'd do anything to get out of dealing with things like this, wouldn't you?'

I stare at the wasp, wobbling its way up the condensation-soaked shower pole, as if attempting to climb to the top of Mount Everest.

This is Joel all over. He was expert at reminding me that you need to put your problems into perspective. Right now, my biggest problem isn't all the things I've been crying about, it's getting out of the shower without being stung.

'*Let's see how you get out of this one then, eh, Ffrony.*'

XLVII

With my notebook splayed open, a pen nestled like a blue, crystal-encased caterpillar in the valley in the middle of the pages, I sit at the kitchen table.

In my notebook I have written:

Food is not love.

and

Love is love.

and

Food is food.

and

Nothing can taste like love.

and

Everything tastes amazing when you love what you are eating.

and

Love what you eat.

and

Eat what loves your body.

I mean it all. I know it all on an intellectual level, I know what I need to do, I know how I need to see myself move towards a cure for what I have, but it is living it that will make a difference.

If I let go of what I have now, I will be back there in no time. I will be back to being the little girl told to stop eating bread and eat more fruit by her well-meaning mother, I'll be the best friend who's ever so nice and would suit my name if I lost weight, I'll be the worker who needs special clothes because I am huge, I'll be the woman at college no one notices because I am large. I'll be fat and ugly and unsuccessful. I'll also be the woman that Joel fell in love with. And I'll be the woman who dropped the blackberries, the woman who hadn't prepared for every eventuality so losing her husband nearly destroyed her.

I know what I have to do intellectually; emotionally I'm too damn scared right now. But if I write things down, I can come back, I can see what I believe. And maybe it will click in my mind and my heart and I will be able to do it. If I write things down I'll remind myself that I can't think clearly when I binge and purge, and right now I need to think clearly.

Now, I have little pieces of Joel in front of me. These scrawlings of his bring me closer to him, remind me he was more than his death, he was alive, too. He was so much, and he was this – a collection of recipes, each containing the foods he loved.

I adore his funny, sloping writing, the way he crossed his 't', the way he curled his 's', the longer slope of 'J' because, I guess, it was the most important letter to him. He has notes on scraps of paper, a few filed away in a notebook, some on different-shaped and rainbow-coloured stickies. Some of the sheets are crumpled and creased, others are bisected in two directions from the way he folded them up.

I've been looking for a blend of flavours that, when I slip them between my lips, will bring back everything good about my life with him. I'll close my eyes and the taste will take over my senses, and I'll be transported back to another place when I was with him. I'll be that person who can look in the mirror and not worry about who I'll see looking back at me. I'll be the woman who can experience a bad feeling and not be terrified it's going to consume me. I'll be the person who can cope with things. I can deal with wasps in the shower. I can deal with the person who is going to try to kill me.

If I find the perfect mix of flavours, I'll be with him again. He'll come back to me. I'll find that love that made me feel normal and safe.

Joel liked to follow traditional recipes as much as possible and would add one little Joel twist. Unlike me. I keep trying out different things, mixing ingredients up, replacing one or two elements to see what they taste like together. If they'll be him. And us. And the life we had before *that day*.

I have a whole month to indulge myself in this if I so wish. I can pretend that everything else is OK with the world and I can immerse myself in cooking and baking and making and creating. Or I can face up to what is going on and deal with it head-on.

'What are you doing still in your dressing gown?' my daughter says to me, causing my heart to lurch. Instinctively, I cover the papers with my hands to hide them. Then I remember that it's Phoebe. It's not someone who's going to mock what I'm doing.

'I'm off work for a month,' I say. I release the papers and notebooks then start to gather them up, to put them in some sort of order.

'Why?' she asks.

After the venom of last night, the way she spoke to me, the hatred behind her words, I'm surprised she hasn't packed her bag and left.

'It's a long story,' I say. I'm amazed, too, I can still speak to her after last night, to be honest. What she said, it cut at me in ways I'd forgotten I could hurt. My daughter stands in her grey and turquoise uniform, her bag over her shoulder, ready to go to back to school. Ready to face all the words that have been fired at her. I don't talk to her enough. I don't let her know what I'm thinking so why would she let me know what she's thinking? 'But the short version of why I'm not at work is that I've been really unhappy there so I decided to go see the big boss, the President. And *boy* did I get more than I bargained for there.' I shudder. 'Anyway, he told me to take a month off to consider my options so here I am, considering my options.'

'After breakfast are you going to take me to school?' she asks, uninterested in my story.

'No. I don't think you should go to school today. Or even for a while. I'm going to talk to Mr Newton about it on the phone, but I think you should stay home.'

'I want to go to school. '

'You're being bullied, Phoebe, pretty hideously from what I saw.'

'You can't run away from bullies. You've got to stand up to them.'

'Yes, you're right,' I say to her. 'But you know what? Sometimes it's best to take a rest, to step out before you go back into the fight. And it's even better to fight when someone has your back.'

'Do you even know how you sound when you say things like that?'

'Phoebe, I know it goes against everything you believe in, but I'd be really grateful if you could do me one favour.'

'What?'

'Don't go to school for a few days. Give things a chance to simmer down, let the school deal with the main culprits if they can find them, then go back if you really, *really* want to.' Before then, though, I will have found her a new school. Even if it means going back to work for Kevin to magic up money from somewhere to send her to a private school, she is not going to go back to St Allison.

It won't have occurred to Phoebe, but whatever she does from now on, how the people at school react to that, react to her, will shape how she feels about herself for so many years to come.

Something like this follows you everywhere. It seems to go

away, to be buried and forgotten, then when you have dared to forget, it comes for you. Sneaking out of the mouth of someone who didn't even know you at the time, written in white on a black chalkboard for everyone to see, repeated by a headteacher for your parents to hear. You never get over this type of thing, you can only pretend it never happened, stuff it down as soon as it rears up in your head. You can only do the best you can to live with it as a smudge on your psyche.

Part of who I am comes from this sort of thing. An element of who I am is from seeing the words on a blackboard about something I shouldn't have let a boy do to me – something I never thought he'd tell anyone after he persuaded me to let him touch me. For only a second, but once it was done, it never went away.

I never thought my daughter would be there, too. This is so public, so exposed, this is scored permanently onto the fabric of time that is the internet. It won't only follow Phoebe around, it'll be there in the histories of the people who said it. They'll always be known – even the anonymous ones – as architects of someone else's despair and anguish.

'Why were you unhappy at work?' She drops her bag, lowers herself onto a chair and her gaze begins to wander inquisitively over the papers on the table in front of me as if she hasn't seen them before.

'It's really been one person making my life a misery. Making snide little comments, questioning the time I get in, the time I leave, what I do, whether I go for lunch.'

'What, kind of like what you do to me?' She almost explodes with laughter. I wish she could see herself, the way her face has opened up and how she is radiating pure joy. This is what she was like before her father died.

'Yes, I suppose if I was you that's what I would think,' I reply, desperate to hear her laugh again. 'But it's my job as a parent to do those things.'

Her naturally slender body leans forwards as if she would love to pick up the pieces of paper and have a closer look. Only Joel and I have touched them. Whenever I get them out, I try to feel him in the pages, imagining where his fingers would have touched, where he would have planted his hand to begin writing. But if she did touch them, it wouldn't be the end of the world.

J's House Ratatouille catches my eye. I often look at it because it seems so complicated, that it would take courage, true fortitude to attempt it.

'How would you like to be my sous chef while I make J's House Ratatouille?' I ask her.

'Mum, we're not in some teen show where you give me a cute little assignment and we bond and become besties.'

'That's me told then, isn't it?' Smarting, I examine the recipe again:

Aubergines
Courgettes
Peppers
Tomatoes
Onions
Basil
Herbs de Provence
Olive oil

It's not *that* big a list, reading the instructions, it's not *that* complicated, it has simply seemed that way. I've built it up to be something it's not in my head. I'm not going to be scared by this. I can do this. I'll be chopping till the end of time, but I can do this.

'Well, I'm going to get changed, then I'm going to the shops and I'm going to buy all the ingredients to make this. It was amazing when your dad made it. I've never been brave enough to try it. I'm going to do it.' I stand, feeling that familiar, almost comforting feeling of light-headedness because I haven't had breakfast. I will. I will eat.

I honestly will. I'll go and get this stuff first, then I'll sit down and have breakfast. I will try to focus on what I've written in my notebook. I will remember I need a clear head.

'Why don't you ask Curtis if he can bring your homework round after school?' I suggest to Phoebe. It kills me that he hasn't been treated the same way she has, that he hasn't had messages calling him a slut and saying he should have kept it in his trousers, or any of the other hideous things that have been fired at Phoebe. Even if he is the father, he'll escape from this fairly unscathed.

She shrugs. 'I'll leave school for now,' she says.

'Great. If you don't mind, could you make Aunty Betty some breakfast when you make yours?'

'Yeah, fine.'

'Thank you. I'll see you later then.'

I take a chance and circle her with my arms.

I sense her rolling her eyes, I feel her sigh in exasperation, but she doesn't pull away or push me off, she doesn't reject my love. She accepts the hug, accepts me. It's working, I'm managing to chip, chip, chip away at her.

I'm finally getting through.

XLVIII

The large wooden rectangular chopping board, its surface marked with thousands of cuts, has been laid on the largest unbroken run of worktop in our kitchen. There are four different-sized pans on the different-sized rings of our six-ring stove top. The large stainless steel colander and the smaller colander, which used to be the steaming basket part of an old metal steamer, are waiting beside the sink to be filled and used.

Phoebe rises from her seat as I enter the kitchen. I notice with a hitch in my heart and a jerk in my throat, that over her red jeans and white T-shirt, she's tied on Joel's black Run DMC apron we bought him four years ago. It hasn't moved from its metal hook behind the kitchen door since he died. Joel would sing, '*J-J-J-J's House!*' every time he reached for it to let us know he was about to start cooking.

The plug of memories that often blocks my throat forms, and I pause in the doorway. I mustn't mess this up by smiling or crying or doing anything that will have her ripping off the apron and marching upstairs.

Determined to not ruin this, I bustle like a busy matron on a hospital ward into the kitchen and place the heavy and bulky bags onto the floor.

I daren't ask her to help me empty the bags in case that sets her off, so I start to unload them myself. I'm halted briefly, my heart hitching itself to the plug in my throat, when I notice she has draped my white apron over the back of the chair I usually sit on at the table.

Phoebe reaches into the other bag, pulls out the shiny, black-purple aubergines, weighing them in her hand. Out come the speckle-skinned dark green courgettes, the large, brown papery onion, the bulbous, shiny red tomatoes, the mug-shaped red, green and yellow bell peppers, and the pot of herbs de Provence. I have olive oil, I have basil leaves from the plant on the kitchen window sill.

'Aunty Betty was asleep,' Phoebe says, unnerved, I think, that I haven't spoken. 'She didn't stir when I went in, so I left the tray on the side.'

'She didn't stir?' I ask, concerned.

'She was snoring her head off but didn't wake up,' Phoebe clarifies.

'Ahh, right.'

More things come out of the bags: fresh chicken pieces, rustic bread flour to use in the bread machine, which I have barely looked at in over eighteen months. We used to wake up to the smell of baking bread, having programmed the machine the night before, and it'd be a special treat every morning to have fresh bread for breakfast but, like a lot of things, that ended over eighteen months ago.

'Do you want to start on washing the vegetables while I put the bread on?' I say to Phoebe. The words melt delicately and delectably on my tongue; they drizzle stars of happiness into my ears – I am spending time with my daughter because she wants to. I am cooking with my beloved little girl and I haven't forced her to be here.

'OK,' she says, without a dismissive shrug, without an irritated eye roll, without an exasperated sigh. It's almost too delicious to believe.

'How do you want me to chop the peppers?' Phoebe asks.

'Into large chunks.' I resist the urge to go and show her. 'I find it's easiest if I lay the top down on the chopping board, slice it in half downwards. Take out all the seeds and stalk, then slice the halves into quarters lengthways and then cut them up into three? But that's how I do it. You may find it easier to do it another way.'

'I'll do it your way,' she says.

I am making chunky rounds of the aubergine. Once they are all on the chopping board like large, green-tinged white counters for a game, I start to halve them, to make them big enough to not disintegrate while cooking, but small enough to be bite-sized. The secret, apparently, to not creating a tasteless pot of gloopy stew when making ratatouille is to cook the ingredients separately first, then to combine them all towards the end of cooking. Joel loved aubergine. I could live without it, personally, but he would eat it every day if he could.

'This reminds me of when you were a baby,' I say. 'When you were about six months old and I had to start weaning you onto solid food, I used to drive your dad mad with the time I spent cooking. I'd be obsessed with trying to make the healthiest foods for you, I didn't want to feed you any of the shop-bought stuff so the moment you were asleep I'd be in the kitchen, steaming sweet potatoes and carrots and broccoli. No, no, not broccoli after the first time because it stank! Then I'd be mashing it through a sieve and putting it into little pots and ice cube trays and freezing them.

'Sometimes I'd spend whole Sundays doing that so you'd have fresh, homemade food to eat all the time. Most of the time you'd just spit it out – probably because it all tasted the same after it'd been defrosted and heated up – and fixate on what your dad and I were eating. Always making a grab for it. After all the stuff I read and cooking I did, I'd catch your dad giving you sneaky bites of his baby corn or garlic bread or something. I remember one time, when you were about one, he gave you a couple of chippy shop chips.

'I got *so* mad because I'd spent so much time on getting the nutrients right in your meals and he did that. But he was like, "Seriously, Ffrony, it's a couple of chips. All food is all right in moderation." He was right, but still . . . By the time Zane was born pretty much everything was labelled organic and I'd lost the will to purée anything ever again so I let your dad do what he wanted. Poor kid. Speaking as one of them, most second-born children get a rough deal.'

The only sound that comes from Phoebe's direction is the phumping of the knife as it comes through the peppers and hits the wooden chopping board, scoring more cuts onto its surface. I stop my chopping and close my eyes in regret as I realise what I've done. It wasn't intentional, but the effect is the same.

'What's it like,' she says, quietly, 'having a baby?'

'Do you mean the actual physical having it, or all the stuff that comes afterwards?'

'Both, I suppose.'

'It's different every time. Well, it was for me, anyway. Having you and having Zane were very different experiences although I was terrified both times because I didn't know what to expect. That's only part of having a baby, though. It takes a while to get your head around, but you're not only having a baby, you're starting the life of another person. By that I mean they don't stay babies for long, you turn around and they're one, five, seven, ten, fourteen. They've got their own little personalities and it's amazing. And it's hard and it's relentless, and I've never experienced love like it.' And sometimes I wish I had my other life back, I wish I weren't tied down and responsible for someone else's existence. I could never say that to Phoebe, pregnant or not, because that would hurt her in ways she doesn't need to be damaged – she could never understand what I meant until she was there herself. 'And it's pretty damn scary because, if you're like me, you're always conscious of the ways you're going to screw up, you're always scared of hurting your child, and then you go and mess up in ways you hadn't even thought of. I suppose what I'm saying is that when you think about having a baby, you need to remember that you're giving birth to a whole new life – *your* whole new life, not just the child's.'

'Have you ever had an . . . you know? Have you ever done it?' she asks.

'No,' I reply.

'Would you tell me if you had?'

'Normally, no I wouldn't because there are some things you don't need to know about your parents, but in this instance, because of your circumstances, yes I would. I think it'd be important for you to know that I'd done it and survived. I do know a couple of people who might talk to you about it if you want?' I glance sideways at her.

She shakes her head and reaches for the green pepper, concentrates on dismantling it for our dish.

'What would you do if you were me?' she asks.

That is the question she asks, but I know the question she really wants me to answer. I stare at the greeny-white sides of the aubergine slices I am halving. I struggle to find the right words, the perfect blend of words that will tell her what she needs to hear. I know how Joel would say it, but I have to say it. She has to hear it from me, in my way, otherwise she will not believe me. 'Phoebe,' I say as gently as I can, 'I wish with all my heart I could tell you what to do. As your mother, I want to make everything as easy as possible for you, and especially after everything that happened with your dad . . . but I can't.'

'You tell me what to do all the time.'

'This is different. This, this is such an important decision, and I wish wish *wish* that you weren't in this situation and that you weren't having to make such an adult decision when you can't legally do most of the stuff an adult can. I will help you make the decision, I will answer your questions, I will write lists with you for and against each option, I will listen to everything you have to say, and I'd like to sit down with you before you make the final decision and go through them in case there's something you haven't thought of, but I can't –

won't – tell you what to do. The final decision has to come from you. It's your choice. You are not me, and what you choose has to be the option *you* think you will find it easiest to live with. If I don't let you do this, I will be ruining your life. There are no simple answers, only what you think will be easiest to build your life around. And whatever choice you make, I will support you one hundred per cent, but it has to come from you and what you think will be easiest to live with.'

'That's what Aunty Betty said.'

'She's a wise woman, then.'

We say nothing, the rapport of our knives chopping sounds out of time, like two hearts close together but beating to their own rhythms.

'Mum,' she says suddenly, sounding like my lost little girl. 'I'm scared. I'm really, really scared.'

It takes two strides to reach her, it takes a second or two to remove the knife from her hand and place it carefully beside the jumble of peppers. It takes two seconds more to put my arms around her and pull her towards me. And it takes no time at all for the misery, suspicion, anger, hatred, despair, pain, guilt and unrelenting loss that has kept us apart since *that day* to dissolve away.

Her sobs are loud, uncontrolled, rising; each one ploughs a new groove of grief into my heart. I place my hand on the back of her head, another in the middle of her back, holding her as close to me as I can.

All the desperate, jagged moments in the fragmented shell of our lives come together and I have her back. I have my daughter back. She has her mother back.

XLIX

8 months before *That Day* (February, 2011)

'Are you listening to my heart beating, Babes?'

His hand strokes lightly through the curls of my black hair.

I nuzzle my head as near as I can to his chest, the material of his T-shirt caressing my cheek. 'Yes. I like to make sure you're still ticking properly.'

'And am I?'

'Yep, working perfectly.'

'Great. Can you sit up now, then? I can't keep the TV this loud without the sound distorting.'

'Sorry, mate, it stays that loud as long as I need to listen to your heartbeat *and* hear the film.'

'How long will that be?'

'For as long as it takes.'

L

We've come to the beach.

After her tears had subsided, we needed to get out of the house. We needed space, the expanse and freshness of being outside to talk without the fear of Aunty Betty, who seems to walk on air sometimes, appearing unexpectedly. She can't hear this conversation, no one can.

I've set aside my guilt and self-disgust and opened up the beach hut. Fynn has taken care of it. It's been repainted, sealed, aired; loved and cared for in the time he 'owned' it. I can tell, though, that he hasn't used it. He hasn't sat here and enjoyed the view, or watched people go by or – as Joel often did – used it to get chatting to people. When Phoebe was in school and Joel would take Zane out so I could work even though I was technically on maternity leave, he found that the combination of a beach hut and a baby were the strongest people magnet there was – especially for mothers with young children. He'd come home with several numbers and offers of play dates. (*Play dates for who, exactly? Our son is seven months old,*' I'd say to his grin.) I could tell that Fynn simply looked after it for us.

Between us, we wrestle the double deckchair out of the hut and set it up to face towards Worthing. From here we can see Worthing pier. I pull my jacket around myself and sit on the deckchair first, Phoebe drops herself on top of me, and turns her body into mine like she used to when she was much younger.

It's a cool, blustery day; the temperature lowered by the strength of the wind that whips foamy peaks into the surface of the sea. The blustery breeze and cold have seen off all but the most dedicated joggers and dog walkers. Almost all the beach huts I can see from here towards Brighton and towards Worthing are locked up tight – no other owners are insane enough to venture down here. Except for one beach hut, far down in the distance, which has someone working on it, his tools laid out on the promenade, a workbench all set up with power tools, a portable generator by its side. I cuddle Phoebe close to me, sharing my body heat with her, revelling in the ability to do this with her, and watch the man, in his forties, portly and with a ponytail, work. His fingers must be numb in this wind.

'Why don't you talk about Dad?' Phoebe asks me.

'I do,' I reply.

'You don't. Earlier, when you were going on about feeding me is the first time in ages and ages you talked about him without me saying anything first. I always say stuff about him and what he'd do because you don't talk about him.'

'I didn't realise.'

'Is it because of what I did?'

'What did you do?'

'Is it because . . . because you're angry about what I did that day and so you're angry with Dad, too, because he didn't call and tell you, like, right away?'

'No.' I tug her as near to me as possible. 'No, it's nothing like that at all. It's because . . .' It's because I avoid fresh pain, I avoid digging up old pain, I avoid current pain, I avoid all pain at all costs even though it seems to hunt me down, seek me out and rub my heart in it. Pain wants nothing more than to snuggle up to me and make me its new home. I avoid pain so it does its best to live itself through me. 'I don't know how to talk about him without breaking down. Even now. I think about him all the time, please believe me. Almost everything I do or say has a thought of him in there somewhere, but it has to stay there as a thought so I can function.

'Not many people want to deal with a woman who bursts into tears nearly two years after her husband has died because they've mentioned they were thinking of going to Lisbon on holiday and that's where she met him. The only way I can function in normal society is to not talk about him much.'

'Is it all right if I do? And Zane?'

'Of course.' I kiss her head, enjoy that unique smell of her. 'Of course you can. I'm sorry you didn't feel as if you could. You two can talk about him as much as you like. Do you talk about him with each other?'

'Yeah. We write in those books you gave us and put stuff in the memory boxes. But you knew him the longest, so there's stuff I want to ask you. And Zane does.'

'Like what?'

She thinks for a moment, then: shrug. 'Dunno. Just stuff.'

'When you remember what this "stuff" is, feel free to ask.'

'Are you going to get married again?'

'No. Next question.'

'Are you going to marry Mr Bromsgrove?'

'No.'

'You do *like him* like him, though, don't you?'

A few hours ago I convinced myself that I needed to be more honest and open with Phoebe. I'd forgotten *that* needs to be filtered through the sieve of 'Things you don't need to know about your parents'. 'He seems like a very nice, decent person.'

'He's still my teacher, though, so I don't think you should go there.'

'Duly noted.'

'I always thought I would marry Uncle Fynn,' she says, dreamily.

An icicle of shock slips unpleasantly down my spine. When she was five Phoebe would regularly ask me who she was going to marry. She would relentlessly question me about who it would be, running through the names of all the male non-relatives she knew – even a couple of our elderly neighbours – asking if he was the one. I don't remember her ever including Fynn in her list, not once.

'Fynn?' I say, as unsuspiciously as possible while every single hackle is raised. 'Why Fynn?'

'Don't you think he's well hench?' she asks, obviously forgetting who she's talking to and about.

'Hench?'

'You know, *hench*.'

'He's old enough and close enough to be your father,' I say. Shrug. 'Still hench.'

If it was him, she wouldn't be talking so openly about him

and his looks, would she? She would keep it quiet, as she has been from before all this came out. She wouldn't say all that, knowing it could make me guess about them. It sounds to me that I am trying to convince myself that it couldn't be him. But it couldn't. He is not that man.

Her phone beeps in her pocket and after hesitating for a few moments she takes it out. All social media has been deleted from her phone, but there were still texts. Messages from people who must have been her friends to get her number. Phoebe braces herself before looking at the screen.

UNCLE F

She heaves a sigh of relief and repockets the phone. It's a coincidence, of course. He said he couldn't be around me, not that he couldn't be around the kids. I'm sure he's texted Zane, now that he knows he's not here. And he wouldn't be who he is if he didn't contact Phoebe today after the drama of last night.

Another icicle slides down my spine. *It can't be him.* He's not that person. Phoebe is like a daughter to him, she'll be like a sister to any children he goes on to have, he wouldn't do that to her.

'Phoebe,' I say, seriously. I need to step away from those thoughts as they will not only drive me crazy, they will distract me from what I need to do. I brought us here with a specific purpose, I needed to be away from the house and from the potential of being overheard for a reason. I have been looking around while talking to Phoebe and I can't see anyone here that seems to be lurking, I can't see anyone who is near enough to eavesdrop. The man who is working on the beach hut is too far away, too engrossed in his task to pay us any mind.

'Yes?' she replies cautiously.

'I have to tell the police what we know.' Quick, clean, precise.

Until this moment, when she grows still and fearful against me, I haven't noted how free, mobile and unburdened she has been since she cried. She is now like a lump of rock in my arms. 'Why?' she eventually mumbles.

'It's not the best timing with everything else that's going on, but it needs to be done. We can't live with this indefinitely.' Now I know how far *she* will go to hurt me – spreading rumours about Phoebe being worse than anything she can write or any violence she can visit upon my car – I have to end this. To do that, I have to take away the power she has by confessing all our secrets. 'Also, Phoebe, people like Zane, your grandparents, Aunty Betty and Uncle Fynn, they deserve to know who did this and to have the person who did it brought to justice. This limbo they're living in is horrible. We – *I* – have to put an end to that.'

She remains silent, stays still.

'You're not a young girl any more, you're much stronger, and I know the timing could be better, but the police won't tear you to pieces, I'll be with you every step of the way to protect you and to stop them if they upset you. But, we need to tell them so they can catch her.'

'What if they don't? What if they can't prove it? If they

444

arrest her and let her go, she might get really angry and she'll know it was me, so she might come after me.'

'You told me earlier that you have to stand up to bullies, and you're right. And, you'll hate me saying this, but I really have got your back. We have to do everything we can.'

'It was her who tried to break into our house, isn't it?' Phoebe says.

'Why do you say that?' I ask, horrified that in the midst of the pregnancy and all the troubles surrounding it, she has made the connection.

Shrug. 'I just think it was. I'm right, aren't I?'

'Yes, you are.'

'And she let down your tyres, didn't she?'

'How do you know all this?'

Another one-shouldered shrug. 'You let Zane go away. You hate Granny and Grandpa but you let him go stay with them. You wouldn't ever let either of us go away unless you were really scared.'

'I don't hate your grandparents,' I offer lamely. 'We simply don't get on. Why didn't you say anything if that's what you thought?'

'Cos this is all my fault. Everything that happened is because of me.'

'No, it's not. The only person at fault here is the person who did this to your dad.' And me.

'Zane and Granny and Grandpa and everyone are going to hate me, aren't they?' she sobs.

'They won't. Because they'll know it's not your fault. You didn't do this and they'll understand why you were too scared to tell anyone. I promise you, no one is going to blame you.'

'I'm scared, Mum,' she sobs.

'I know, Sweetheart,' I say. I hug her close, kiss her head. 'I know you are. And so am I.'

Saffron.

How about we make a deal? You open the blinds and
I'll find a less harsh lesson to teach you next?

I only want you to open the blinds because I want you
to show you can trust me again. You can trust me.

What I've done in the past is just frustration, me
lashing out because I feel so powerless about what
happened to him. Do you understand?

I think we can help each other. This deal would be a
good way to start, don't you think?

I never wanted it to be like this. I hope you realise
that.

A

LI

'Saff-aron, what are you doing?'

My heart goes through the roof, as she's done it again – managed to come all the way through the house from the attic without making a sound.

'Do you know what time it is?' she says. She hasn't noticed, clearly, that her appearance has caused me to lean on the worktop, clutching at my chest.

'About two o'clock?' I gasp.

'Yes, why are you up?'

Because I don't sleep any more.

'And why are you cooking?'

Because if I don't cook, I'll binge on all the food in the house and then I'll purge it. Then, because I am so anxious, I'll probably drive out to the twenty-four-hour supermarket at the marina to not only buy more food to replace what I binged on, but to get more stuff to binge on and then purge. If I cook, I can concentrate on something else, I can concentrate on the measuring, the weighing, the mixing, the method. I can wash up and clean up afterwards, I can possibly sit myself down when it is cooked and maybe even eat it. Maybe taste it in the eating process. See if it is that perfect blend of flavours that will bring Joel back to me.

'I'm thinking,' I say to Aunty Betty. 'Cooking helps me to

448

think. I have a lot of thinking to do.' If I'm bingeing and purging, I can't think. And I need to think. I have to work out how to screw up my courage to talk to the police. I have to put aside all the worry I have about them. And I have to be careful, the killer, the letter writer, can't know. She's been clear about that, if I go to the police, she'll know and she'll disappear, but not before she's hurt one of us. I could probably stand to be hurt if Zane and Phoebe still had their dad, I couldn't stand for any of the others to be hurt. I can't sacrifice one of them to get justice.

'What are you making?'

'Galette des rois. It's a pastry dish that Nathalie, a French friend, taught to me many years ago. It's ground almonds, eggs, sugar, rum and pastry. I'm experimenting, adding fruit to the mix. Trying different shapes with the pastry.'

She moves to the large pantry cupboard at the end of the kitchen and opens it, peers in. Her entire arm disappears into the opening as she reaches for the very back of the top shelf. Without her heels, she has to push up slightly onto her toes to reach past the tins and packets of pasta, lentils and rice, until she gets what she wants. Her arm reappears, clutching onto the dark glass bottle of Late Bottle Vintage port. She's been drinking it – only the good quality stuff – since the holiday where Joel and I met and he brought her back two bottles from Portugal. Ah, yes, now it's all clear: she's trained herself to walk silently because she sneaks down here in the middle of the night for a tipple. The simple option, of course, would be to have a bottle in her room, but when has Aunty Betty ever done anything the simple way?

She settles herself at the table with her bottle of port and a squat, ribbed glass that she always seeks out to the exclusion of all the other glasses in the cupboard (including the actual port glasses).

'What is it that you're thinking about?' Aunty Betty asks.

'Stuff.'

'Like?' she replies, accompanied by the subtle 'pop' of the cork coming out of the bottle.

'Like . . . stuff.'

'Like you "hooking up" with young Fynn?' she asks.

My head whips round. 'Pardon me?'

She delivers that Aunty Betty Grin at me above the three-quarter-filled glass and throws in a hitch of her eyebrow for good measure. 'I've seen the *tings* between you two.'

'Really? And I've seen you try to bluff stuff out of people. Even if there's *nothing* to bluff.'

'Hmmm,' she replies. She imbibes a delicate sip of her drink. Eventually she concedes, 'It was worth a try.'

'It surely was. And please, don't use "hooking up" ever again. It's bad enough when Phoebe uses it.'

'I can promise you nothing.' She takes a deep sip of her port. 'What are you thinking about?'

'Phoebe. Zane. You. Joel.' I say his name because I need to. I need to do it more so that Phoebe and Zane will know it's all right to talk about him in front of me. That I haven't forgotten him.

'Why aren't you thinking about you, too?'

'What's to think about me?'

'How many times have I told you, Saff-aron, if you don't

look after yourself, you won't be able to look after anyone else?'

'Erm, you've never told me that.'

'Oh. Well, I meant to. Especially since I've been here.'

Slowly, I stir the ground almonds into the melted butter in the stainless steel pan on the stove and it becomes a mass of beige, freckled ripples with the action of the wooden spoon. I turn off the heat and continue to stir until the butter absorbs the ground almonds. In goes the sugar, then the beaten eggs. The spoon coaxes them together before the rum and vanilla join them. It's hypnotic, stultifying almost, doing this. I know there's an answer, if I switch off by doing this, I know the answer will present itself to me. I will find my own least worst solution like Phoebe has to find hers.

'Joel constantly told me how blessed he felt to have you,' Aunty Betty says, and I nearly jump out of my skin again.

She wants to talk and I am not going to get anywhere with broken shards of conversation puncturing my thinking, so I abandon my pastry filling and go to the table. She has placed a glass on the table for me. She refills hers, then moves onto mine. 'Enough,' I say after she has glugged in about a third of a glass.

She raises a perfectly arched eyebrow at me.

'All right, a little more, then.' Black-red and giving off heady scents of red grapes, the liquid sounds thick, promises to be satisfying as it pools in the glass.

Aunty Betty is in her chocolate-brown silk dressing gown and her real hair is hidden under the purple silk sleep scarf on her head. She looks smaller, older, without one of her wigs framing her face.

Nearly three weeks ago, Aunty Betty sat at this table with Phoebe and my daughter told her what I wasn't giving her. Nearly three weeks ago, I had a binge so hideous my throat and chest hurt with the lumps of food I barely chewed before I forced them down, and then the purge ripped new havoc through me. The relief afterwards didn't even feel better, the emptiness and stillness not as fulfilling because my entire torso, jaw and throat throbbed with agony. My face was wet with pain, and with anger at myself for being weak enough to go back to that. And then I was listening to Aunty Betty and Phoebe talk and a new sorrow began as I heard I had let her down. I want to ask Aunty Betty what it was that Phoebe felt I wasn't giving her. What she thought I could do.

I open my mouth. Close it again.

'Come on, speak your speak,' Aunty Betty says, even though she isn't looking at me. Her eyes, the same liquid-brown mahogany as Joel's, meet mine. 'Ask me whatever it is you've been aching to ask me since I moved in here.'

'When did Joel find out you're his birth mother?'

Her smile is shackled like barbed wire onto her lips as she glugs more port into her glass, filling it to the brim so she has to lower her head and sip it while the glass is still on the table. When she raises her head to look at me, the barbed-wire smile is back, her eyes are like laser beams.

'I don't know,' she eventually says. 'He never asked me about it, and like I agreed with his parents, I wouldn't say anything unless he asked. How did you find out?'

'I saw his birth certificate after . . . after he died. It obviously has mother's maiden name down as Elizabeth Mackleroy. I didn't even twig until it said under father: "unknown". Then I realised his mother obviously wasn't born a Mackleroy.'

'Look at you, Columbo.' She laughs like punctured old-fashioned bellows being pumped – a small, breathless in-and-out sound with a wheeze that trails in its wake.

'You never talked about it with him?' I ask.

'Some things are not meant to be talked about.'

'I've always wondered why his parents treat you with such disdain but never seem to want to cut you out.'

'They couldn't have children, and when I "got myself in trouble" they were more than willing to help me out. You wouldn't think I was mid-twenties, the way they carried on – you'd think I was like Phoebe.'

'That doesn't sound very fair,' I offer diplomatically.

'They can't help it,' Aunty Betty says. 'A lifetime of disapproval of me wasn't going to vanish overnight. When it was clear I wasn't going to disappear and leave them to it, they had to do the best they could while still looking in my big fat face. Elizabeth doesn't like being reminded that I wasn't a good girl, I didn't keep my legs shut waiting for the man who would marry me and I still got "rewarded" with a baby while for her, who did everything right, everything by the book right down to going to church every week, it never happened. She wanted me to leave. I couldn't do that.'

'You were all right with being so close to him?'

'Of course! I am a natural born aunt. Saff-aron, I could not do what you do. I could not be a mother.'

453

'Yes, you could.'

'Look at you. You worry about everyone else first all the time. Me, no way. I am the most selfish person on God's green Earth. You would do anything for your children, probably without a second thought. Me, I think about how something is going to impact upon *me* – no one else – just me, before I say yes or no. I loved Joel like no one else on this Earth could but that wasn't enough for me to bring him up. I believe, truly believe, that every child born must be wanted more than anything, and I gave him to the mother who would do anything for him without a second thought. They *wanted* him, I would have just had him.'

'You're a strange one, Aunty Betty. Always going on about only caring about yourself first, but that's not true. You got yourself thrown out of the complex on purpose to come and be here with us. To help take care of the children.'

'I did not—'

'Yes you did. I can understand it, of course, who wouldn't want to live with a stroppy teenager, a computer-obsessed boy, and a neurotic widow? People are queuing up to live with us.'

Her hand curls around mine. 'Oh, Saff-aron. Remember who you are. You're the woman who stood up to the Mack-leroys. I never thought it was possible, but you stayed when others ran away. You made my beautiful Joel so happy, you have brought up two children for the last eighteen months all on your own. And all with your secret.'

'What secret?' I ask. I can tell by the glint in her eyes and the set of her features she is not bluffing.

'I come down here almost every night, that's why I don't

454

get up early in the morning. I know, Saff-aron. I know what you do to handle the pain.'

I unravel my hand from hers, lay it in my lap next to my other hand. Shame and humiliation fire up in my cheeks and I have to fix my gaze on my scarred hands, to stop myself from shouting at her, from reacting to her like I reacted to Fynn.

'I don't know what you're talking about.' The port I sipped suddenly tastes like cheap malt vinegar, sour and disgusting, in my mouth.

'Please, don't be upset. I understand how much pain there is when you lose someone, how out of control you feel and how it changes who you are. I understand why you do what you do.' I can tell she wants to reach out to me again. 'I'm sorry. Truly, I'm sorry. For your loss, and for what I have just said.'

'It's fine.'

'Can I say something to you?'

'Sure.'

'Please believe in yourself, Saffron.' I look up at her because, for the first time ever, she's said my name properly. 'What I was trying to say before I upset you is that you have all these things going on, and you are coping brilliantly. Please believe that. That is all. You can do this. You can do more than cope, you can do more than get through the day, you can thrive. Please believe that.'

'Thanks,' I mumble.

'You will believe me one day,' she says. Suddenly she waves her hand as if to dismiss me. 'Now go, go, finish your cooking, your thinking, whatever it is you are doing. I want to finish my port in peace.'

I stand and return to my place in front of the metal saucepan Joel used to make his cement-like porridge in, and where I've laid out the pastry sheets to warm up to room temperature. The white-bristled, rubber-wood pastry brush waits to be dipped into the bowl of water to seal the pastry edges, and then into the beaten egg to sweep over the top. I don't know what I'm doing. These all look like alien items to me and I'm supposed to do stuff with them – I know what that stuff is, but I have no clue how to do it.

'I loved him, the man who gave me Joel, very much,' she says. 'He was a part of me, and when I lost him, like you, I found a way to hide from the world. I found a way to live in the world again, too. I hope you will as well.'

My mind won't take me back to where the baking was my cipher for thinking, and what I was doing made sense. I am in trouble. I need help. But I can't explain that to her. I can't tell her what I did nineteen months ago to protect my daughter.

I can't explain to her that what I used to do was from when I was desperate. I was desperate when it first started as a thirteen-year-old who no one paid attention to unless it was bad and no one approved of no matter how much she tried. I stopped for years, I lived with being large for years. And then I was desperate again at college when I needed friends. I needed to not be the fat clever girl all the time. And then I fought with myself for years, I got myself onto an even keel. I was balancing myself and Joel would kiss my palm and say how proud of me he was. Then *that day* happened. I made it to six months but I was desperate a year ago. I had to get back into control, numb the pain in another way because sex with

456

Fynn had been a bad idea. But now, I am not that kind of desperate. I am in a place where I need to be clear-minded and rational. I need to solve this problem and save my family, so no matter how much I want to stuff down these raw layers of pastry, or spoon the uncooked filling into my mouth, I won't. Because I don't do that any more.

When I turn around to tell her this, to say that I had my reasons and I don't do that any more, she's gone. Whisked away and upstairs, as though taken by the silence of angels.

Saffron.

Fine. Have it your way. But remember, whatever happens next, you could have avoided it by simply opening your blinds.

A

LII

flashes up on my phone. I want to talk to him but at the same time I don't. His presence in the world is complicating enough without the additional conflict I feel about him keeping secrets with Phoebe from me. It niggles at me. What else isn't he telling me? What else would he be willing to keep from me?

In the midst of trying to work out how to bring an end to the stalking before *she* can further hurt Phoebe, maybe turn her attention to Zane, I don't want to work out how I feel about Lewis as well. It is a complicated strand in the knot that is already inside.

He's called every day for the week and left long messages. He's said to me that the school has found some of the culprits of the bullying, and have suspended them with a promise to put it on their permanent files. He's told me that Curtis has been in touch with Phoebe and he's pleased that she and I are finally talking. He's explained that he's sorry for not letting me know earlier what was going on. He says the right things and I know he means them, and if I wasn't paranoid about Joel's killer and worried about everything else, I could maybe talk to him. But the truth is, I can't. I can't. I can't. I can't.

My finger hits the call reject button. I'm about to give myself up to the guilt of that when I hear something in the corridor. I wander out and stop halfway along between the kitchen and the living room door.

'And where do you think you're off to?' I ask Aunty Betty who is clearly readying herself to all but sneak out of the house. I've asked her to let me know if she's going out so I can come with her, but this request has fallen on deaf ears, obviously.

She is wearing her normal-looking black wig and has carefully applied foundation, powder, eyeliner (with a little flick at the ends of her eyes) and mascara. Her lips have a gloss but no colour. She has on her beautiful black wool coat with the wide, stylish lapels, and she's carrying a cute little square patent black bag with a gold clasp.

'Just down to the post office,' she says. Aunty Betty always sounds like she has something to hide.

'What for?' I ask.

She stops examining herself in the full-length mirror beside the coat rack and slowly rotates to look at me. 'What do you think I'm going to the post office for? To post a letter.'

'Just a letter?'

'Yes.'

'I have stamps. Large letter ones and normal ones, first class and second class of both. They're in the box on the mantelpiece. Which do you need?'

'It's OK, child. I need the walk.'

'Really?'

'Yes, of course. I need a walk, that's all.'

'I may have been one of the worst mothers to a teenager ever, but even I know when a person is sneaking out to see some guy. Who is he?'

My sixty-six-year-old teenager cuts her eyes before she rolls them at me.

'Have you ever seen that work when Phoebe does it?' I ask.

'You can't tell me what to do, you're not my mother.'

'I literally have heard it all now,' I reply. 'OK. Wait there, I'm going to get my bag and my socks and I'm going to come with you.'

'But—'

'Either I come with you or I give you one of my stamps. Which is it?'

'You can come with me,' she mumbles.

'Great. I'll get my stuff.'

'Buurrrnnnned,' she mumbles miserably as I take the stairs two at a time.

We walk down to the bottom of our road and then cross onto the side of the road where Queen's Park begins. Every step I take I am aware that *she* is watching, *she* is examining what I do to make a comment on it. That's why I've asked Aunty Betty to let me come with her whenever she goes out. She has no idea the danger she – and all of us – are in. Phoebe is upstairs and knows not to open the door to *anyone*.

'This is all your fault,' Aunty Betty admonishes as our pace of walking slows with our approach to the Rislingwood Road Post Office because it is near the top of a steep hill. 'You keep

461

getting letters – sometimes every day – and it made me want to write to young Zane.'

'You've been writing to him every day?'

'Yes, and sending him five pounds. You don't mind, do you?'

I shake my head. 'Not at all. Phoebe will when she finds out, though.'

'Yes, you're right there. Who are your letters from? A secret admirer?'

'Something like that,' I say.

We swing the door open and there's a queue right up to the door, and we have to squeeze ourselves in behind them as if we're joining the world's slowest conga line. There are two men behind the counter, one of them looks up over his half-moon glasses, his tanned skin setting off the white of his thick locks and he brightens up like sunrise on a summer morning when he sees Aunty Betty.

Oh, well, I think and shimmy forwards with the slight surge of our conga line, *at least someone's happy*.

LIII

My life seems to be draining away too quickly. Like I am in an hourglass and my life force, the time I have to find a solution, is running out for me. Time is running out for me, but all I can do is wait.

Wait for Phoebe to make a decision. Wait for another letter. Wait for my heart to move on to another stage of grief so I can feel something different inside. Wait for the time when my son can safely come home. Wait for something huge to happen to bring things to a head.

I have to go to the police. I know this. I fear what it's going to do, what it will unleash in *her*.

None of this would be happening if it wasn't for her. And for me, of course, because I was the one who got him those cooking lessons, I am the one who set him on that path. It's my fault that he died in the way he did, it's down to me that he isn't here any more.

This morning I heard Phoebe bolt to the toilet, and I think she's started to have more pregnancy symptoms, namely in the form of morning sickness.

I watch my eldest's slender form wander up towards the back of the health food shop. She moves slowly, rolling her right shoulder back as if it is aching. I remember the backache that came with both my pregnancies: twinges and tugs like over-stretched elastic bands between the muscles. General pangs and spasms appeared overnight, too, accompanied by a strange, almost metallic taste in my mouth no amount of water could clear, and my skin seemed to cycle from clear to spotty to clear within hours. We'd been trying for a baby, but it wasn't until my body started to change in ways I hadn't counted on that the terror descended for real. It wasn't simply about putting on weight, how I looked was different, how I thought seemed different. Nothing could prepare me for that first pregnancy. I'd wanted Phoebe to make her decision before this stage, if I was honest. If she was going to carry on with it, then she'd be able to embrace it, if she wasn't, then physically it might not be so arduous before it was ended.

I catch up with Phoebe. 'I need to ask you something and I need you to give me an honest answer,' I say to her.

'Oh, God, what?' she asks. Her eyes, dulled by the aches of her body and probably from throwing up, avoid me. Instead, she leans heavily on the trolley.

'I need you to tell me who the father is.'

'I've told you.'

'It's not Curtis.'

'It is!' she insists loudly, then lowers her voice. 'It *is*.'

'I've seen you and Curtis together, he is not the person you were talking about five weeks ago. He's a lovely lad, and I don't for one second believe he lied to you about not getting pregnant first time. He's not that sort of boy. You love him like a friend, yes, I can see that, but he doesn't make your heart race and he doesn't make you so desperate to be with him that you'll convince yourself you really believe any cock and bull story you're fed about contraception. Tell me who he really is.'

She wriggles her body as if trying to free her back and rolls her shoulder in a circle while she stares down at the items in the trolley.

'I thought we'd got to a really good place, you and me,' I say. I'm not usually into emotional blackmail, but needs must. 'I thought we'd got to the stage where we could trust each other with almost anything. I'd really like you to tell me who it is. I'll try not to get angry.'

'I can't tell you,' she says quietly. 'He'd get in so much trouble.'

'With who?'

Shrug. 'Everyone.'

I step forwards, place my hand on her bare forearm. Her skin is clammy and cold under my fingers. I take her face and tip it to face me, her eyes are unfocused and bloodshot. A line of sweat is collecting across her forehead, and she reaches down to rub her stomach. 'Are you in pain?' I ask her.

Shrug.

'How long have you felt like this?'

Shrug.

'Why didn't you tell me you were feeling ill?'

Shrug.

'We need to get you to a doctor,' I say, reaching for the bags in the trolley. In between my stretch for the bags and saying the word doctor, Phoebe's eyes roll back in her head and she crumples to the ground.

LIV

I want to cry.

The ache in my throat, the caught air in my chest, the wet smarting behind my eyes are all parts of it, are all parts of the anatomy of tears I want to shed.

I can't let myself do it, though. Right now, crying feels like the weak option. Normally I wouldn't think that, but in this moment, any tears will admit that everything is still falling apart when it was meant to be getting better.

I want to feel better. I need to feel better. I need to feel full, crammed with so much stuff there is no space for anything else; not even the smallest cavity for this dread and anguish. I want to purge, too. I want all of this stuff that's inside, the worry, the uncertainty, the guilt, to be excavated so I am empty; so I am nothing.

Is this what happens when you ask to feel something else? Do you need to be specific and say exactly what you want to replace the anger with because you'll get what you're given? What I've been given to replace the anger is terror, torment and even more guilt.

I'm sitting in an easy chair in a hospital room in the children's hospital of the Royal Sussex County Hospital, The Alex, as they call it. Phoebe has had surgery to remove an ectopic pregnancy as well as the resulting ruptured Fallopian tube and I am waiting for her to wake up. I am waiting for her to wake up before I call Aunty Betty and Zane, before I have to introduce new worry into their lives.

This little room, only a bit bigger than my bedroom at home, is surprisingly full with machines: electronic panels on the walls, a mechanical arm with a small television screen that hangs over the bed like a dentist's close-work light, and two portable units she's hooked to that bleep intermittently and have colourful displays of her heartbeat and blood oxygen levels. Despite those bleeps and flashes, everything feels still in here. Tranquil, almost. Phoebe seems peaceful as she sleeps, her face in profile against her puffy pillow.

I've noticed the furtive looks amongst the staff when they hear or read her date of birth and find out she was pregnant: they wonder if I'm up to the job of being her parent; they silently ask how I let this happen in the first place; and quietly question how I allowed this to continue without her having a proper appointment with a midwife or GP. Their scorn and disdain aren't necessary – no one can hate me more than I hate myself. I hate myself for not noticing, for not hurrying her up so she could have gone for a proper consultation with a medical person no matter what her final choice was going to be. I hate myself for not predicting this was going to happen.

My gaze wanders over the lines of her young face, her hair pulled back into the low ponytail she's taken to wearing since not being at school. She seems so untroubled in this moment. Even when I look in on her most nights she doesn't look completely relaxed – there's always that shade of loss we often take with us into the dreamworld. Now that powerful drugs have knocked her out, she can sleep, she can finally let go.

I've been holding her little black and silver box of secrets in my hand since they took her down to surgery. Before I had to call the ambulance, it felt like I was getting through and that she was about to tell me who was really responsible for this. She confirmed there was another man involved and he was still on the scene, probably still manipulating her. All she had to do was give me his name.

All I have to do is unlock this phone and I'll have all the information I require.

I'm desperate to find out the truth, to arm myself with the information that I thought she was about to give me. The second I look, though, I will have crossed a line. I will have actively invaded her privacy and that goes against everything I believe in. My parents had no sense of boundaries, I was never allowed privacy because I wasn't an autonomous being as far as they were concerned so they had a right to know everything, all the time. Even when my mother came to stay in my flat in the years before I moved in with Joel she would open my post, sometimes go through my belongings because I was still her child in her mind and I required no privacy. I've tried too hard to go the other way, and it's ended up here – with Phoebe hospitalised because I allowed her too many secrets that I convinced myself was privacy. There's a fine line between privacy and secrecy – Phoebe has crossed the line. I have to cross it too as her parent, but it stirs up all sorts of uncomfortable feelings inside.

I feel like I am reverting to type, I'm being my mother.

Phoebe knows I check the history on her computer, the rules being if it looks like anything has been deleted or that she's been using private browsing, she loses her computer indefinitely. I can check her phone whenever I want, too, and if it looks like anything has been deleted or the calls and texts don't match up to the bills then she loses her phone. I have never checked her phone. I check the computer because, I convinced myself, all the danger was on that nebulous thing called 'the internet'. It wasn't other people she knows and cares for in real life. It wasn't the real-life friends she hung out with on social media. It was chatrooms and perverts and porn – strangers, not the people who had her phone number, who were friends in the physical world. When you hung out on social media with the people you hung out with in the real world, your mother could relax. She'd tell herself not to fret that you're bunking off school, that you're somewhere you shouldn't be which leads to your father being there too, and meeting up with the person who was going to take him away for ever.

It was all of it, of course. I should have been involved, should have known what she got up to via her phone – I should have checked.

The main reason I didn't check her phone was because I wanted to believe she'd earned back the trust she'd lost because Joel would have wanted me to try to trust her again, he would have convinced me that she'd made a mistake and was genuinely, heartbrokenly sorry and wouldn't do anything like this again.

Over and over goes the phone in my hand. Over and over, spin, spin, spin.

I'm scared to check in case it is Fynn. Or it is Lewis. Or it is any man I know. If he's familiar to me, I'm worried I'll lose the plot and go after him and all the anger I feel at the loss of Joel, the devastation of my life, the powerlessness created by the letter writer will be unleashed upon this man. He'd deserve it, but Phoebe and Zane don't. They don't deserve to lose another parent, probably to prison this time. The rational me understands and believes that, but the me who would want to hurt the man who has done this to my daughter might not be as reasonable.

If I don't check, though, I can't go to the police about the stalker because having that sitting there, a ticking bomb for any reporter to unearth and detonate at some later date, is too big a risk to take with Phoebe.

Through the strip of window embedded in the wall opposite where I sit, I spy the panorama of Brighton: the buildings slotted together like irregular, multicoloured building blocks, and the mysterious misty seascape beyond the buildings. From this angle I can't see the beach, from this height I can't see the people. They're both there, they both exist even though I am looking right at them and I can't see them. The answer to what I do next is probably the same: staring me right in the face and I can't see for looking.

What would Joel do? I ask myself.

What would Joel do? I ask the Universe, God, Whoever is out there. *What would Joel do?* I ask Joel.

The answer diffuses through me – my skin, my lungs, my

heart – like an expensive, delicate perfume until it arrives in my mind.

I am not Joel.

It doesn't matter what Joel would do because I am not him. I am me. And I need to do what I would do.

Slowly I type the password, the key to the secrecy box, into the waiting space. I almost hear the latches being drawn back, the handle being turned and the door being thrown open to Phoebe's secret life.

It takes seconds to find him. It takes minutes to work out who he is. It takes twenty minutes to read through their message chain. And it takes a microsecond to know that, like the Mount Vesuvius eruption that levelled the ancient cities of Pompeii and Herculaneum, my explosion is going to level everyone and everything in his immediate vicinity.

My hand shakes as I place the phone on her bedside table. It's set back onto the last message to Curtis it was on so she won't know what I read, what I discovered until I confront the bastard and I tell her that I looked.

'Mum?' she croaks. She tries to move but doesn't manage anything beyond a slight shift of her torso – her body probably feels like it is weighted down by boulders, her throat will be arid and tight. She doesn't open her eyes, probably too much effort at the moment. I clasp my hand around hers.

'I'm here, lovely girl, I'm here.' I smile at my daughter who can't see me but can hear me.

Not being able to touch Joel at the morgue was something that underlined my loss in so many ways in the following days and weeks and months. Since I first clung onto his hand on the flight to Lisbon, I loved to touch him, I loved to be touched by him. Being restrained, ordered not to connect with him physically, added a cruel dimension to losing him. The policeman's grip on my forearm, a stern restraint from interfering with 'evidence', underlined how totally he had been snatched from me – reminded me that my connection to him in the physical world was gone. I promised myself then I would touch the people I loved as much as possible in case I was ever denied that again.

I lean over the bed, stroke my daughter's face and press my lips to her cool cheek. She usually protests at my touches, doesn't understand that I need to do this in case I'm not allowed to do it again. Right now, her entire being seems to relax when I make contact with her.

'I'm right here, beautiful girl. I'm right here.'

LV

'You need to stay here until I come back,' I tell Aunty Betty.

She hasn't had time to change from today's visit to the post office, which she's done alone. For the past three days I've accompanied her there, which is why Phoebe and I were up and out early, so I could be back in time to take her, but she's sneaked off to do it alone. I don't have time or the spare amount of annoyance to bring it up with her now. I do, though, need her to understand how important it is that Phoebe isn't left alone. I don't want her waking up alone, to be confused why I'm not there.

'I don't understand where you're going,' Aunty Betty replies.

'I have something urgent I need to do. It can't wait. But I want you to promise me that you won't leave her. Play the old woman card and I'm sure one of the nurses will get you anything you need. The loo's right there. Don't talk to anyone who isn't a doctor or a nurse and who can't prove they should be in here. If they can't prove they should be in here, kick up the biggest fuss you can.'

'Child, you want me to check if someone can prove they should be in here?'

'Yes.'

'Why would some—' Aunty Betty stops talking and her usually animated face draws still, wary. She's a smart woman, she understands what I mean. 'The letters?'

I nod.

'You're going to sort that out now?'

'No, this is something else entirely.'

She jerks her head questioningly towards a fast-asleep Phoebe.

I nod, gravely.

'I won't leave her side.'

'Don't tell her where I've gone, I'll do that myself later. If she wakes up and asks for me, call me. If you can't get hold of me, call either Brighton or Hove police station because that's where it's likely I'll be.'

For a moment, when our eyes meet, I have a flash of Joel staring at me, and the way her mouth is set reminds me of how his mouth would contort itself right before he would ask me not to do something.

'You do what you've got to do,' Aunty Betty says.

If she'd asked me not to do it, I would have thought twice. I would have tried to find another way. But I have to do this. He deserves to experience this now, while I am this angry. If I've had time to calm down, to be reasonable, to decide to talk it out, I'll let him get away with it. And he'll do it again. He's probably done it before.

'Thanks,' I state.

A kiss and a hug for Phoebe. I turn from her, a mountain in my throat from how fragile she is, how close I came to losing her. I bend to hug Aunty Betty, the moment awkward and unnatural. I keep doing it though, despite her whole body stiffening in my arms, I'm going to keep my promise to myself – I'm going to touch the people I love before it's too late.

From my house I retrieve the items that I need right now.

I stuff them into my black soft-leather bag, grateful once again that I'm not one of those people who can carry her life around in a bag no bigger than a cigarette packet. Before I leave, I'm seized with a sudden need to run from room to room, to check that there's nothing else I need. I pause in the living room, stare at the picture of Joel with the children on the mantelpiece.

I'm sure he'd tell me not to do this. I'm sure he'd tell me to find another way. It would work if he was here, he'd do it his way and the consequences wouldn't be as extreme. In my chest my heart is beating in staccato again, my breath is shallow and ragged.

Maybe I shouldn't do this.

Trust me . . . other adults don't want you falling in love . . . so they won't tell you the truth . . . you can't get up duffed your first time . . . so don't worry about the pill . . . and don't ask your mum . . . she won't under-stand . . . she'll tell you anything to stop you . . . no one cares for you like I do

The words of his texts replay themselves in my mind and the rage descends all over again. He doesn't get away with this, this man who has groomed my daughter, he doesn't walk away from this unscathed.

I'm probably a bit too shaky to drive, but I do it anyway because I need to do this now. Waiting on more taxis, trying to avoid making chit-chat with the driver will only delay this and will only make me doubt myself again. I need to do this while the Sun is still up, while it's early enough in the day for me to possibly get away with it, while the blood is still bubbling and fizzing in my veins.

He does a half-day today. Gives him time at home for other pursuits, so I'm as sure as I can be that he'll be there when my finger presses hard against the doorbell.

My heart sounds in my ears, drowning out the gushing of my adrenalin-laden blood. Inside my head is a loud place right now.

He answers the door and his first instinct is to grin. To flash his flawless smile, and to open his perfect mouth and say, 'Saffron! This is an unexpected pleasure.'

I can see why she likes him. If you are fourteen, I'd imagine you'd form an attachment to someone who treats you like an adult, who plies you regularly and consistently with confidence boosters and compliments the way a party rapist would ply you with booze. I can see why you'd think that this was what you wanted when you feel responsible for your father's death, your mother is distracted by grief, your brother is too little to understand and you think you know and trust this man. He is an attractive man if you are fourteen and scared and looking for love and understanding wherever you can get it.

'My daughter is in a hospital bed right now, because of you.'

'Phoebe?' he asks, confused. 'Is she all right?'

'No, but she will be. Because I'm going to do whatever it takes to make sure she is. And if that means going to the police about you sending her sexually explicit material and seducing her, then that's what I'll do.'

'Wait, I never—'

'Don't even bother lying about it. I saw the text messages.'

'No, no, it wasn't like that. It was a silly thing. I saw her on her way home one night after school so I gave her a lift. It was all perfectly innocent.'

'"I get hard just thinking about your lips." That's innocent, is it?'

'Saffy, out of context, that can be taken—'

'She's fourteen!'

'She doesn't act fourteen,' he says. 'Girls mature much faster and they know what they want—'

'*Fourteen!* Even if she was sixteen you'd be a pervert but *fourteen*?'

'No, Saffy, it's not like that. It was only a bit of fun,' he protests.

'Fun? Really?'

I reach into my bag. My fingers close around the handle of what I retrieved from my kitchen and pull it free from my bag. 'I'll show you fun,' I say, brandishing my blue and white iron, the white and grey striped cable wrapped around its base. It's heavy and solid – exactly what I need for this.

477

'Darling, what's taking so long?' Imogen appears behind her husband in the gash of the open doorway. 'Oh, it's you,' she says coldly. 'What do you want? And what are you doing with an iron?'

'I'm showing your pervert husband what fun is,' I say. Along their posh, well-to-do road in this posh, well-to-do area of Brighton, the cars seem to have all come from the same template of car ownership: a colour palette of navy blue, silver or black; a sleek design, a sunroof, an expensive manufacturer badge at the front, matching extravagant model type on the back. Ray's car stands out though – sleek, pricey and lavish like the others, but it is an eyesore metallic bronze that makes it easily identifiable to the woman with the iron.

I pause for a moment beside his pride and joy, to ensure he is watching, and he can accurately predict what is about to happen.

'No!' he shouts.

His car's blemish-free bonnet shudders violently as I bring the iron down upon it with my full weight behind it. A jagged-edged dent appears beneath and around the iron.

'Are you having fun yet?' I shout at him.

I bring the iron down again, another shudder quakes through the car and another part of the bonnet crumples in like screwed-up paper.

'Stop this, Saffron! Stop this right now!' Imogen screams. Her hands are on her face, her eyes are wide with horror. How she looks is how I've felt almost every day since *that day* – paralysed by the horror of what is happening right before my eyes.

Around me, people spill out of their front doors to see

478

what is going on in their usually quiet and placid street; others pull back curtains or hold apart blinds.

'I'm calling the police!' Imogen shrieks and disappears into the belly of her house.

Ray is incapacitated. Not only by shock, but also by circumstance – he needs to come up with a plausible explanation for this. He needs to formulate different stories with different wording that will work on Imogen *and* his neighbours.

I slam down the iron again. 'How about this? Is this fun?' This dent caves in the front left side of the car. Another slam, another devastating dent. 'FUN?'

I wriggle the iron at Ray, a man as white and immobile as a statue. 'This is brilliant fun, isn't it?' After two heavy, determined blows, the driver's-side window gives a sickening crunch before the glass buckles and smashes into beads that scatter mostly over the front seat.

With one last blow to the bonnet, which is now like a crater-filled planet, I leave the iron embedded there.

Heaving air into my lungs, I stand and regard Ray. He is tall, he is well-built, he is handsome. He is a disgusting specimen of a man.

Between gulps of oxygen I say, 'You stay away from my daughter,' loud enough for our audience to hear, and noisy enough to drown out the sound of my heart thundering in my head. 'You stay away from other little girls, too. Because I don't care how many perverts make statements in the papers, or how many crappy TV dramas pretend it's all right, or how many paedophile apologists tell you the teenager wanted it, grown men going with children is NEVER all right. And if I see you near my daughter again in her lifetime, I *WILL* come after you again.'

Ray has not moved. Even though I can hear the sirens in the distance, and I see Imogen in the doorway behind him, he does not move. He is stuck. Everyone around us has heard what I've said, including his stricken-looking wife. His lies will have to be epic to get out of this.

You should have thought of that before you started sexting my daughter, I want to say. *You should have considered the consequences before you started to browbeat her into an abortion by telling her 'I can't love you in this state, you need to sort it'. You should have cut off all communication when she stopped responding to your texts instead of stepping up the mixture of sex talk, love talk, and 'get it sorted' talk to try to get her to re-engage.*

'I think we understand each other now,' I say to him.

Imogen is frozen, petrified, in her doorway with her thin hands still on her face. The look of horror is gone, replaced by a mask of shock and despair. *I know how you feel*, I want to say. But of course I don't. People said versions of that to me after Joel died and I wanted them to stop it. They didn't know. No one knew. How could they when they didn't know him like I did and they weren't me? I don't know exactly how Imogen is feeling now, but I can suspect. I can imagine what it feels like when the world around you starts to collapse but you're expected to keep on standing through it all. I would never say that to her, though. I would never presume to tell her that I know how she feels when I can only really guess.

My gaze shifts to the pavement beneath my feet. I've done what I needed to do, I've delivered my message visually as well as verbally, and I don't want to keep looking at Imogen's face.

Two police cars draw up and I do not move. There's no point. I wasn't sure one of them would do this, but they have, so I am not going to compound my troubles by resisting arrest. I simply stand where I am, waiting for them to come for me, to ask me my name, to tell me my rights; I am waiting for them to put handcuffs on my wrists, to bundle me into the police car and take me away from here.

Waiting. I always seem to be waiting.

LVI

My cell is quite cosy, all things considered.

I sit with the thin, PVC-coated mattress beneath me providing no kind of padding between my bottom and the hard metal of the bed. The rough-surfaced breeze blocks of the wall are painted an odd off-white that I suppose is meant to make the room appear larger than it is. High up on the wall there is a window with frosted, thickened (I assume) glass. At the foot of the bed there is a metal toilet and a metal, wall-hung sink. It smells in here, of course: a mixture of sharp, chemical-heavy disinfectant, stagnant water in the toilet, as well as the sweat of whoever has recently languished in here. Maybe it's deeper than that, maybe that stench comes from the crimes of those who've been in here; maybe it rolls off them and seeps into the walls, lurking there like a communicable disease, waiting for another criminal to add to it, building incrementally into a smelly putrid disease that crawls nefariously up the nose of the next occupant. Maybe everyone adds to the smell so no two arrestees smell the same thing or leave with the same crime infection inside them.

I dismiss, then wrestle away those mad thoughts because, I remind myself, *this cell is cosy*.

It is *not* small, confined and claustrophobic. It is not

making me want to scream and claw my way out through the metal door, or to climb the walls to the window to smash a chunk of air into here.

They've taken my trainers as well as my bag and coat and belt and socks. My shoes, I assume, will be standing outside, facing my cell door, like all the other shoes I saw lined up outside the cells when I was brought here.

My heart jerks to attention and my whole body jumps as the door is unlocked and swings open. It's the he one who was once my Family Liaison Officer. He pauses in the doorway. I vividly see what I am about to do: leap up, knock him aside and make a run for it. I'd have to stop to scoop up my trainers and I'd get nowhere without my bag, and would I even remember the way out of here? It's a ludicrous idea but haven't most of my actions been unhinged of late?

The he one sighs, deeply, the sigh of a confused, frustrated, concerned friend and arranges his face to reflect his sigh before he comes to sit as far away as he can on the narrow, short bed. At least he's left the door open. At least he's given me the option of doing a runner.

'I didn't think I'd be seeing you again so soon, Mrs Mackleroy.'

'I wanted to see if you'd get my name right twice in a row. And, hurrah! You did. Well done.'

The he one doesn't find this funny but he is mildly amused. 'What's going on, Mrs Mackleroy? I couldn't believe my eyes when I saw your name on the detention sheet. Criminal damage?'

He is genuinely concerned for me. I'm almost over-

483

whelmed by the wave of affection I feel for him suddenly. He's so young and he seems to have changed so much in such a short amount of time. 'What's your name?' I ask him.

He blinks at me. 'You don't know my name?'

I shake my head.

'I never told you or you forgot?'

'You never told me. When you came to my house that very first time neither of you told me your names. You told me probably the worst news I've ever had and you were nameless people to me. And then, after that, you never said what your name was. All the other people who came introduced themselves but you never did.'

'I must have done.' He is wild-eyed as he searches through his memory, examining that time; he wants to pinpoint a moment when he would have told me what he was called. *I was in her house every day*, he's thinking, *I must have told her my name.* 'I must have done,' he repeats, unable to locate that moment in time when he allowed me to know who he was.

I shake my head.

His eyes slip shut in regret. 'I look back sometimes at your case and regret so much,' he says, more to himself than to me. 'I've learnt so much since then.'

'But not how to tell me your name, clearly,' I joke.

'Trainee Detective Clive Malone.'

'Pleased to meet you, Clive Malone.'

'Mrs Mackleroy, you're in a police cell, I don't think you have much to be pleased about.'

'No, you're right. My daughter's in hospital and it'd be great to get back to her.'

484

'You're going to be here for a while, I'm afraid. There's nothing I can do to make this go away.'

'I don't want you to. I needed to show that man, the man whose car I attacked, that he had to stay away from my daughter.'

'There are better ways of doing that,' he replies.

'Yes, there are. I wanted to be arrested. I've been such a bad mother, I've been absent, I haven't been paying attention and I didn't even notice how awful things were getting. I wanted to be locked up for a bit as punishment. Scaring the living daylights out of the bastard who's been abusing my daughter was a bonus. I'm not going to prison, though, am I?'

'No. If you're willing to accept a caution, I'll see if I can get your interview moved up and get you out of here as soon as possible.'

'Thank you, Clive Malone.'

'It's the least I can do, given everything.'

'Don't suppose you can leave the door open?' I ask him as he prepares to leave.

'Afraid not. But I'll see if you can be moved to an interview room.'

'Thank you,' I say.

Clive Malone smiles at me before he disappears. I pull my knees up to my chest and lower my head onto them. I deserve to be here. I really do. Not only for smashing Ray Norbet's car, but for all of this.

I'm going to turn this around, though. I am going to make everything OK again. I have to.

*

485

Aunty Betty and Phoebe are both asleep when I get back to the hospital.

Aunty Betty has worked her magic and someone has found her a full-recline chair and she's made herself comfortable under a couple of white waffle blankets. In the darkness of the room I drop into the easy chair I occupied earlier, the beeps punctuate the silence, the flashes push pinholes in the darkness.

I want to take a shower, I want to wash off the crimes I sat amongst in the prison cell. I want to cleanse myself so that I can start again all clean and new. That'd be good, wouldn't it? It'd be symbolic.

As quietly as I can, I shift the chair closer to Phoebe and reach out for her. I rest my forehead on our linked hands. Without her, without Zane, there is no point.

I close my eyes and sleep. Everything's going to be better in the morning.

Saffron.

We're so alike, you and I.

When you were attacking that bastard's car, you felt the rage like I did, didn't you? I saw it in your face, it was a power rush like no other. It's like you become another person.

I heard what you said, too. I'm glad you told him. He's disgusting. I'm sorry I thought Phoebe had been sleeping around. It's awful what he did to her.

Someone told me that you accepted a caution, which is why the police let you out so soon? Why did you do that? If I was you, I would have explained what he did and they would have realised that you were completely justified.

I think they'd understand why I had to do it, too. I didn't plan to, but when it happened I felt like you did – I was almost blind with rage at what he was saying to me. They were words you'd put in his mouth, but he didn't have to say them, did he? I'd arranged it so we were alone. There was no one around who would know and there was no one who could tell you. And he kept saying those things.

It didn't have to be that way. I was so . . . enraged. But you understand now, don't you? You see why what happened to him, happened. I didn't murder him, I didn't plan it, but the rage took over.

It's not that far a leap from a car to a person, if you think about it.

I think we should meet, and talk it all through. I think we could be friends, I really do.

LVII

I read the letter, delivered with flowers to Phoebe, while I sit on the closed toilet lid of the shower room that's attached to Phoebe's room.

This woman is everywhere that I am. She follows me, she doesn't seem to sleep, she doesn't seem to miss a thing. She's getting braver, too. It doesn't seem to matter to her whether or not I spot her, if she was there yesterday, close enough to hear what I said to Ray, near enough to see my face. I have no doubt in my mind now that she's coming for me. I have to be ready and waiting. I return the letter to its envelope, then fold it in half, cutting her words in two. I fold it again, cutting them again. Then they are shoved into the back pocket of my jeans. They'll have to stay there until I can add them to the others.

I wash my hands, cleansing her from me, then return to Phoebe's room. Aunty Betty has charmed her way into a shower and a proper lie down in one of the nurses' rooms. I went back to the house and collected changes of clothes for both of us early this morning – having to take a taxi there and back because my car is still at Imogen's house, probably with several parking tickets covering the windscreen and the serious danger of being towed.

Phoebe has had breakfast, she's had her consultant visits and now she is sitting up wearing her white gown, her cannula still taped like a white whistle to the back of her left hand, and her name written on a white band around her right wrist. She is obsessively flicking through the limited channel range on the small TV hanging above the bed as she has been all morning.

My daughter looks about six, right now, her face waiting for the wonders of the world to be visited upon her. I drop heavily into the seat beside her bed and she gives me a sideways glance. 'I know that look,' she mumbles before she switches the television off. I move it out of the way so I can see her properly.

'So, Curtis really would have been the father,' I state.

She attempts a shrug but can't because the nerve connection between her shoulder and the operation site/the ectopic pregnancy mean shrugs and turning too quickly are agony. 'I told you.'

'Yes, you did. But you didn't act like he was because of Ray.'

Her dark eyes, surrounded by red veins widen in trepidation. 'You know about that?'

'Yes. I went through your phone. And before you start to freak out, I should have done that a long time ago. I have no insight into your life, Phoebe, and that's wrong. It's my job to protect you from the bad things in the world and I did a terrible job of that partly because I didn't want to be like my own mother. I went too far the other way. That ends, now. I'm going to check your phone and your computer regularly and anything amiss then you lose privileges, OK?'

She wants to shrug, I can see it in her face. 'It's not fair.'

'Yes it is. You are young. I know you feel like a grown-up, and that you want to do whatever you want, but you can't just yet. You can have some freedom and independence, but not totally. And things like phones and the internet, you can have but only if I'm able to check regularly what you're up to and to make sure you're not getting into things you can't handle. I'd love for you to talk to me about your life, too. I'd like you to tell me what's going on with you and ask my opinion and for advice but I can't force that. All I can do is to promise that I will try to balance being your mum who makes the rules with being someone you can talk to. Does that sound fair?'

'Suppose.'

I rest my head back on the seat and stare up at the ceiling. I must stay awake, I must not slip off into a deep, deep sleep that lasts for a thousand years.

'Aren't you going to tell me off about Ray?' she asks cautiously.

'Not right now. I haven't the energy.'

'Are . . . are you going to tell him you know? And Imogen?'

'I've told them. And they know not to come near any of us again.'

Her eyes triple in size along with her gasp. 'What did you say? What did they say? Are they angry with me? Is Imogen going to tell me off again?'

'They weren't happy, but like I said, they know not to come near any of us.' I'm going to think about moving Zane's school so he can be away from Ernest. It's not his fault, but the less contact Zane can have with that man, the better.

I rub my fingers across my eyes, they feel like burning coals in the ice-cold furnace of pain that used to be my head.

'Mum?' Phoebe asks.

I lower my head to look at her.

'He was nice to me. Remember you asked me if he was nice to me? He was. Curtis, I mean. He wanted to use a condom and I kept saying we didn't have to because of what Ray had told me.

'Curtis is, like, my bestie even though he's a boy and I told him that I didn't want Ray to think I was a stupid little girl. I wanted Ray to like me so much. And Curtis said he wasn't into hooking up and that he liked me so he wasn't sure if it was a good idea if we did it. I was so gutted because I thought, if I wanted to do it with Ray he'd be put off if I wasn't, like, experienced. And then, Curtis, like, changed his mind out of the blue and he said he wanted to. And we did it at his house after school when his dad was still at work.'

I'm in the perfect state to hear this, to ease myself into a relationship with my daughter where she is open with me, because I'm too exhausted and drained to run around with my hands over my ears, screaming at her to shut up talking to me about sex.

'He was really nice to me. He kept asking if I was sure and if I was all right. And he said if I wanted to stop at any time we could and we didn't have to do it at all. I felt really safe.' *I'm sure that's why he changed his mind*, I think. *He knows my daughter, he knew she'd find someone else and he wanted her to be safe the first time, to be treated well.* 'It was nice, too. I kind of, you know, like, enjoyed it.'

'I'm glad.' Joel was the first person I had that with. I'd had sex so many times and it'd been great, enjoyable, orgasmic most of the time, but the first time I had emotionally safe sex, where I wasn't worried about hiding what I felt, was with the man I married. *That's what it was like with your dad*, I almost say, but catch myself – there really are some things you don't need to know about your parents.

'I wanted to tell you cos I didn't want you to hate him or nothing like that. He didn't do anything wrong and he was nice to me.'

'I don't hate him. Have you told him what's happened?'

'Yeah, and Uncle Fynn. They're both coming in later. Is that OK?'

'Yes, tell anyone you like. Apart from your grandparents. Either set. I don't need the hassle right now. We'll tell them another time or never, I haven't decided yet.'

Phoebe's face falls. 'Oh.'

'Oh, Pheebs! You could at least have warned me. When did you tell them? I need to get my story straight for when they show up.'

'Buuurrrnnneed!' Phoebe chuckles. She holds onto her stomach so she doesn't damage herself in the process. 'Not even I'm that stupid, Mum.'

Her face, lit up with laughter, is one of the most beautiful things I've seen in my life. It almost makes up for the letter burning a festering hole in my pocket and the clock ticking over my head that's counting down the time to when I have to confront my husband's killer.

LVIII

I'm walking the corridors waiting for Fynn to finish his visit with Phoebe.

If I keep walking, I won't fall asleep. Both Phoebe and I have dozed on and off this afternoon, but nothing deep enough to make me feel refreshed instead of tired and grubby. Aunty Betty has found a whole new life in the hospital and keeps dropping in to let me know she's OK, then she's off. I'm not sure how she's managed to gain access to so many other wards when everything has a security lock on each entrance and exit, but I don't question it. She's like a giant toddler: playing happily and nicely somewhere I can mostly see her so I let her get on with it.

I stop beside the door to Phoebe's room and lean back against the wall. It's cool and solid against my back, much like a bed. My eyelids come together and I drift. Float away from all of this. Allow myself the freedom to let go of consciousness and succumb to the beauty of—

'You look exhausted.'

My senses snap to attention and I struggle upright. 'It's always good to get updates from the talking mirror,' I state.

After a smile of recognition, he becomes serious. 'You should have called me, Saff,' he states.

My tired heart is aching. It is aching at the centre of my chest and I want to tell him that. I want to talk to him, for him to be my best friend again. For us to get back what we had. 'Should I?'

'Yes, you know that.' He rests his gaze on the wall beside my head, down the corridor over my shoulder, to the ceiling above, but never on me. Anywhere but on me. He still can't stand to even look at me. I should take his hand and press it to my chest, ask him to feel this very real and very painful ache that echoes across my heart because of how we are with each other now.

'Can't we talk about this, Fynn? See if—'

'Come on, Saff, what's to talk about? My feelings haven't changed, have yours?'

'It's not that simple.'

'I'll take that as a . . .' Fynn's words trail away. His line of sight is fixed over my shoulder and then it isn't. Instead he is hanging his head, he is struggling to disguise a mixture of emotions on his face, the main one I can see is betrayal. My stomach, a vat of constantly churning nausea, starts to turn itself inside out: I know what he's seen, *who* he's seen. He thinks I called Lewis and not him, that when Phoebe could potentially have died, I didn't think to contact him but I instead phoned the new man in my life. 'No. I'll take that as a no. I'll see ya, Saff.'

'I'll see you, Fynn.'

I screw up my eyes and bite down hard on my lower lip so I don't have to watch him leave me again. It's been too many times already, my heart can't take much more of this.

'Trust our children to bring us together again,' Lewis Broms-grove says.

We are in the café on the ground floor of The Alex and the last time the kitchen door swung open, I'm sure I saw Aunty Betty back there in a pinny and hairnet. But I'm probably hallucinating. I *hope* I'm hallucinating.

I offer him a wan smile. Beside his large cappuccino, I have in front of me a large black coffee in a cardboard cup and a Danish pastry. I don't want the pastry. I can't remember the last time I ate, but I don't want the pastry. I often buy something like that as a cover, though, when I meet another person for coffee or tea. I'll start to eat it and will 'find' a hair or a patch of mould in it so I can't possibly devour it but I don't want to cause a fuss, so it sits there, uneaten. It's the perfect disguise because whoever I'm with thinks I eat, and I have the chance to test myself. To test my willpower and how strong I can be in resisting food.

Sometimes, I'm not that strong, so I'll strip what I have to pieces. I'll take the icing off a cupcake, the cream off a carrot cake, the filling out of a pastry – claiming they're too sweet – and eat the other stuff. The stuff with fewer 'empty' calories. And then, as soon as I can, I'll do whatever it takes to not keep those calories in. Right now, I don't want this pastry and I don't bother with my elaborate ruse. I ordered it because that's what I do when I have coffee with someone else.

We sit, the busy café carrying on around us, without speaking for long minutes.

'I'm sorry,' Lewis eventually says. 'I should have told you straight away.'

'I don't know if you should have, actually,' I admit. 'I've been thinking about it a lot and, as Joel would have pointed out, it was good that she had an adult she could and did turn to at such a desperate time. You did a good thing for a frightened young girl and that's honourable.'

'But?'

'I'm not Joel. I can't square it in my head that you would keep something so big from me. It took me a while but I finally twigged that it's only a problem because we're attracted to each other and there's all this potential between us.'

Lewis grimaces in agreement.

'If you were simply Phoebe's teacher, what you did would be fair enough and understandable. But, there's this thing between us – if anything happened, you'd potentially become a stepfather-type figure in Phoebe's life, and it would drive me insane with worry wondering what other secrets you had with Phoebe or Zane.'

Lewis removes his gold-rimmed glasses and clatters them on the table, almost like a prize-fighter throwing in the towel. He nods, resigned it seems to what I'm saying, what it means, and rubs tiredly at his eyes.

'Apart from with Curtis, I suspect you'll always be a teacher who wants to help children, first, which is commendable, but not great for someone like me who already has huge trust issues.'

Another nod. I wonder how much he can see without his glasses. I'm slightly delirious and have an urge to pick them up, put them on and parade around going, 'Hello, I'm Lewis Bromsgrove and I'm so delicious that Saffron wants to lick me.'

'Were you having some kind of weird fantasy moment then?' Lewis asks when I return my gaze to him. 'Your eyes went off to another land or something.'

'Yes,' I admit. 'I was wondering what you'd do if I put on your glasses and pretended to be you.'

He grins at me, so beatifically I have to glance away. He really is delectable.

'And this has got nothing to do with that guy, Fynn?' Lewis asks, serious again.

'Why would it have anything to do with him?'

'He's not exactly friendly towards me. I'm guessing I might have some competition there.'

'I'm not a prize to be won or lost,' I remind him. 'And Fynn or no Fynn, it doesn't change the fact I can't square in my head what you kept from me.'

'True. I suppose we can call this a classic case of failure to launch,' he states about the potential of us without bitterness.

'I guess so,' I say. 'But a lot of the fun in these things is the "will we, won't we?" part anyway. At least we got that.'

Lewis's laugh is deep and throaty, it reverberates happy sprinkles down my spine, and it makes a couple of people turn around with awed looks at how touching his laugh is. 'That really isn't the fun part,' he chortles. 'Not by a long shot.'

'You know what I mean.' I laugh, too. It's an experience being able to laugh. When was the last time I did that? I can't even remember.

'I'd like the chance to change your mind,' he says.

'Yeah, sure, why not?' I reply. As I said to Phoebe earlier, I don't have the energy to argue. 'But just so you know, I rarely change my mind.' He doesn't know there have been enough secrets in my family, I don't need to invite in the potential for any more.

'And just so you know,' he states with a smile, returning his glasses to his face, 'I like a challenge.'

LIX

'Mum! Mum! Wake up!'

My eyes fly open at the urgency of the voice and the weight on my body.

I do not know where I am for a moment, I've been here for three days, but still I wake up every time disorientated. I wince slightly, at the brightness of the world outside my eyelids – it's clearly not early morning or the middle of the night. My body feels heavy, weighted down and something is far too close to my face for me to focus on it. The object pulls back a bit so I can see what it is. What it is, is divine.

'Zane?' I whisper. I'm afraid to say it too loud in case I wake myself up from this dream. 'Zane?'

'Yep!' he says, happily. He bounces on me, twice, and the curves of his knees crush most of my internal organs. He's towering over me because he seems to have doubled in size since he left three weeks ago. 'I came back. Can't believe what Pheebs has done now!'

If he's here, then so are they and that means ... They stand on the other side of Phoebe's bed like twin peaks of disapproval. They're not sure who to aim their disapproval at – when one is glaring at me, the other looks at Phoebe, then they swap.

'Betty called us,' Joel's mum says. 'She thought we should know.'

'Oh, OK.' I can't believe Aunty Betty would stitch me up like this. This is the last time I take her in.

'I can't believe she got to ride in an ambulance,' Zane says. 'Flashing lights and everything, she said. Not fair.'

I cuddle Zane, draw him close to me to stop him causing me any more physical damage, and because my little boy is home. I'm going to bask in that for a moment. I'm not going to allow thoughts that having him here is another point of weakness, because I don't care right now. He's back, he's here and I can put my arms around him.

'You could have called us, Saffron,' Joel's dad says. 'We would have come sooner.'

The temperature hadn't dropped enough in hell for me to do that, I think.

'Please,' Joel's mum says suddenly. She is staring right at me, and there is a look I've never seen before on her face. On anyone else I would think it was humility, regret. 'Please,' she repeats. 'Can we start again? I know Joel isn't here to see this, but let's put the past behind us. Let's be kinder to each other. And move on with a new understanding.'

Bloody hell, what did Aunty Betty say? I wonder.

'Yes, of course,' I say. I take the opportunity to snuggle my face into my little boy's neck, to smell him and hold him. I'm so lucky that I'm allowed to do this, that it's my purpose in life to do this.

I could point out that none of it was me, it was all them. I could remind her that I'd turned myself inside out for years attempting to be good enough, and they wouldn't have it. I could say that I thought things would be different after Joel died and was gutted beyond reason when I realised things were going to carry on as before. I could say all that but I don't. None of it matters because they've brought my baby home. I can forgive them almost anything right now.

XI

LX

She's going to come for me today.

It's one of those things I have been waiting for and today is the day it will happen.

I feel it.

There've been no letters at the hospital for three days, I don't know of any new attacks on my car because it has been towed and I haven't the time to go get it. I do know that someone called the hospital and asked when Phoebe would be sent home. The nurse who answered said they couldn't give out that information but she did confirm that Phoebe was a patient. I knew it was her, checking to see if we were still there, finding out if I'd called the police and we were under police guard. Trying to work out how much longer I'll be alone in the house for stretches of the day so she can come kill me.

Every day for the past four days I have come home from the hospital at the same time to get more clothes, return dirty clothes and cook some food for me and Phoebe. Aunty Betty comes and goes as she pleases during the day – getting fed by various people – but she always stays with Phoebe when I'm not there.

I can feel *her* approach like the coming of a bleak winter.

The sensation hangs in the air, a chilling, threatening menace of things to come. She has always been coming for me, I realise. If I read the letters from the beginning, it's obvious that they were simply the precursor to today.

It's going to be today because Phoebe is meant to be leaving hospital tomorrow, so we'll all be here again, the house will be alive again and I won't be alone – properly alone – like this for a long time.

She's coming for me and I'm ready.

I stopped off on the way home to buy some blackberries. They are my flavour I love. I haven't had any since *that day*. I don't even look at them in shops, my eyes seem to develop a blind spot wherever they are. I skim over recipes with them in books and on the internet. I loved, all that time ago, the tanginess of blackberries. I adored the sensation of several little explosions on the tongue. *That day*, I was going to sit down with my bowl of blackberries and read a magazine with the radio in the background and wait for my husband to come home. Instead, *that day* I began my wait for today.

She's coming for me today and it's what I've been waiting for.

I'm in the kitchen, of course. That's where I'm going to wait for this to happen. I'm not going to eat the blackberries, I'm going to make my recipe for the book. I'm going to use it to create something I love.

I have laid out what I need and I examine each of them closely, running my fingers lightly over the surface of them to ensure I truly have everything:

Blackberries
White sugar
Lemon juice
Vanilla extract
Butter
Light brown sugar
Salt
Ground almonds
Plain flour

I have also taken out the beige ceramic mixing bowl that Joel bought me on the day he died from the cupboard under the sink. I put it there because I couldn't look at it. For some reason it became a symbol of what had gone wrong. It had been in her car and I wondered often if he hadn't bought it as a surprise for me, would he have come home instead of dropping it off in his car? Would he still be alive? I have washed it out, and it sits beside the ingredients. This will be a good thing, an *appropriate* thing to do while I wait.

The berries explode and disintegrate under pressure from the fork in my hand. They become mush against the white sides of the bowl and every few seconds I have to stop, to look at the stain on the tiles, to remind myself what I'm doing this for. For Phoebe. For Zane. For me. For Joel. Especially for Joel.

'J-J-J-J's House!' Joel echoes to me. *'J-J-J-J's House!'*

'Your husband has been involved in an incident,' the he one echoes.

'So, Unc, what you been up to?' Zane echoes, too.

'*Everyone hooks up,*' Phoebe echoes behind him.

'*I think it's great. The idea of finishing the cookbook and the talking,*' Lewis echoes.

'*It was only sex to you?*' Fynn echoes.

'*Please believe in yourself, Saffron,*' Aunty Betty echoes.

All the voices, all the things that have been said, the utterances of the people of my life are alive in here. They talk at once, they've all made their impression on the fabric of the heart of our home and now they fill the room, fill my head. I stop what I am doing and allow the strands of my life, the flavours of the different types of love I've experienced, to descend.

They are so loud, so clear, so present, I almost miss the first one: *Knock-knock.*

My heart is drumming out its usual rhythm, my chest creates its normal in and out. I should be scared, terrified, of who is on the other side of the door. But I'm not. This is inevitable, so I don't need to be frightened.

Knock-knock comes again. Louder this time.

My heart flits over a beat. Maybe I was wrong, maybe I am scared and I simply don't know it. Maybe I've been living in a state of fear for so long, ever since *that day*, that what I think is normal is what most people think of as being terribly afraid.

It takes me seconds to reach the door. My hand is shaking. I *am* scared.

'*If you don't hear from me in two hours, call the police and tell them to go to the house and call Fynn and ask him to come here to be*

508

with you,' I told Aunty Betty as I left her this morning. I have fifteen minutes left to call her, then she will do as I asked.

My trembling hand makes contact with the doorknob and I turn. I edge it open.

A boy not much older than Zane stands on my doorstep. His skin is alabaster white, his curly hair matches the colour of the freckles dotted across his nose. He has striking green eyes and he's dressed like he is on his way to hang out with his homies in da (posh boy) 'hood: branded hoodie, branded low-slung jeans and NYC baseball cap – all brand new, all ridiculously large on him.

'Yes?' I wait for her to leap out at me, to appear from beside him on the doorstep and to barge her way in, like a battering ram making light work of a barricaded door.

'This lady told me to give you this.' He holds up a cream envelope.

Saffron Mackleroy

is scrawled on the front.

'Which lady?' I ask and don't take the envelope.

'Dunno,' he replies with a shrug.

'If you don't know her, why did you take something from her?'

'Cos she gave me a fiver.'

'Don't you know you're not supposed to take stuff from strangers?' I say to him. I am stalling, of course. The longer I talk to him, the longer the time is until what is going to happen will happen.

'It was a fiver,' he says.

'Why do you have a cockney accent?' I ask him.

'Dunno.' Shrug. 'Do you want this or not?'

Not. I think. *Absolutely not.* My hand trembles as I relieve him of his envelope.

'Do yourself and whoever loves you a favour, don't talk to strangers any more,' I say.

'Yeah, all right,' he says. He thinks in this scenario that I'm the weirdo. Not the person who paid him to deliver a letter, not himself for doing it and not simply running off with the money. But me, the person who has been targeted.

The letter is heavy in my hands because it contains the weight of my rapidly growing fear; it contains the final message.

My fingers shake as I open it. I'm aware as I do that the house isn't empty any longer. I am no longer alone. I slip out the single sheet and drop the envelope where I stand to use two hands to unfold the message.

SURPRISE!!

is written large across the page. Large and, indeed, surprising.

I drop the cream sheet too, and walk towards the kitchen. I know what's going to happen once I'm there. The house no longer feels empty because someone is waiting in the kitchen for me.

I should turn around and run. I have children to think of. What would they do without me? But I keep walking because I have children to think of. If not me then it'll be them. And as Aunty Betty pointed out, I'd do anything for my children without a second thought.

I know her. She's one of those people you pass in the street, you stand behind in the queue for the pay machine in the car park, you clash trolleys with in the supermarket. She's one of those people who you sometimes throw a confused half-smile at in case you know her because you vaguely recognise her face but you're not sure where from.

She is every person you've ever not met properly. She's the person you could see every day for your whole life and never notice.

She is standing in front of my back door. The hood of her black top is pulled up but it doesn't quite obscure her face. In her right hand, held close beside her leg with the blade pointing down, is a black-handled chef's knife. The type that killed my husband.

'Don't run,' she says. Her voice is normal, ordinary, like she is. I expected maybe a witch's cackle, or a husky, villainous drawl. But she is ordinary.

And I smile. My smile may show on the outside, but it's there on the inside. What a ridiculous thing for her to say. Running is the last thing I'm going to do.

LXI

In the year I was forty-one, a woman broke into my house to murder me. She murdered my husband and then she decided to kill me. I let her in by leaving the back door unlocked while I went to the front door. I knew she wasn't the type to knock at the front door, but she was the type to sneak in and wait for me, to try to end me the way she ended my husband.

When she killed him, I think she thought she'd put a full stop onto his life and who he was. She hadn't, of course, and that's what drove her insane in the end. He was still alive, in his children, in his wife, in his family, in his friends. He did not end, did not cease to exist because of her, she'd wielded the ultimate power of killing someone and she thought it would make her the most important person in his world. That the world would focus on her when they thought of him, that he would not continue to exist for anyone unless they thought of her as well.

That didn't happen. His wife continued to go to work, his children continued to go to school, his aunt moved to be near his family, they didn't take part in the appeal, they didn't spend all their time at his grave. They carried on as he would have wanted them to, but without her at the centre of it. And that didn't work for her.

She'd spent a year in hiding, living in France, waiting for the knock on the door, for them to come for her. But no one did. The anniversary came and went and no one came for her. No one questioned her beyond asking why she'd called him that morning. 'About a recipe from cooking class,' she'd replied and no one said anything else.

His daughter didn't tell she'd seen my husband with her that day. And so she said nothing. She waited and waited and waited. And it never happened. So she moved back to England. Back to her house, back to the life she had before. She even got another job and everything went back to normal. But she wasn't normal, ordinary. She was *someone* now. She was the woman who had done that thing everyone had talked about for months in the papers. She had held someone's life in her hands, how could anything be the same again?

It only meant something to her, though. His wife slept with the blinds open like nothing bad had ever happened to her, that she didn't need to lock up tight at night. His wife went to the supermarket and didn't break down in the aisles at certain foods – not like she did when she ever saw an ingredient they'd used in class. The wife let her children come home from school by themselves as if they were safe. His wife even looked her right in the face on Brighton seafront and threw her that 'do I know you from somewhere' smile you gave to strangers you vaguely noticed. Nothing had changed for his wife, the woman who was meant to love him more than life itself. The Wife was the reason why this had happened in the first place and nothing had changed for her.

It had to.

The Wife had to know who she was. And then she had to be scared. And then she had to be removed. But only when The Wife knew that once she was gone, there was nothing she could do to protect her children. His end had been unplanned, quiet and horrifically sad. The Wife's had to be slow and as terror-filled as possible. This was all her fault, after all.

In the year I was forty-one, I had two children and a late husband, and a woman several years younger than me stood in my kitchen and tried to kill me.

The first words she said to me were: 'Don't run.'

And I smiled at her. I smiled at her because running was the last thing I was going to do.

LXII

'Don't run,' she says.

'Why would I run?' I reply. I sound brave, I seem courageous. I am also completely terrified. Completely. My heart cannot beat properly because of this fear. I'm not even shaking. My eyes want to focus on the blackberry stain but I can't stop looking at her, for even a second, because that's when she'll come at me. 'I don't even know who you are.'

'I have to kill you, you know that, right?'

'Erm, no, I don't know that, actually. Why would you do that? Who are you?'

'It should have been you. I should have killed you instead of him. If you were gone, I could have supported him through it and been there for him. He would have fallen in love with me. We would have been together properly, then.'

'I thought he already did love you. That's what you said in your letters. You were lovers.'

'He did love me.'

'He just had no clue that he loved you or that you were lovers, right?'

Her body jerks forwards, ready to cross the kitchen and use the knife on me, but she restrains herself, holds herself back because she has more to say.

Time is almost up, I think. *Aunty Betty will be calling Fynn and the police any second now.*

'This is all your fault. He would be alive if it wasn't for you.'

'That's what his parents think,' I say. 'They think if he hadn't met me he would have gone on to marry some nice woman who would have made him become a doctor or something and he'd still be alive. I feel sorry for you thinking like his parents.' I hear Phoebe say in my head, *'Do you even know what you sound like when you say things like that?'*

'You don't think I'm going to kill you.' She snarls a smile at me and I know she's going to do it. I've run out of time. This wait is over.

'You're not going to,' I say. 'I don't think you killed Joel, and I know you're not going to kill me.'

'How did I get his back door key, then?' My heart jerks to a standstill, my breath snags in my chest.

She takes a small but definite step forwards. 'How do I know the knife was twisted before it was dragged across his stomach?'

I clamp my painful teeth together as a barricade against her words, I don't want to hear this.

Another step. 'How do I know that he was left on Montefiore Road because there is no CCTV on it or any of the surrounding roads?'

'I don't want to hear this,' I state through my gritted teeth, my eyes aflame with dry, outraged tears.

Step. 'How do I know that he thought he'd lost his phone? But really, when he took his daughter into the school, he left it in my car. So I turned it off and kept it.'

516

'I don't want to hear this.'

Step. 'You don't want to hear that I wanted him to come to my house and I even drove us there? But he didn't want to come in, just wanted to pick up his car.'

'No. I don't want to hear it.' I *cannot* hear this.

Step. 'You don't want to hear that I dropped him off to pick up his car but I knew he'd work out where his phone was, so he'd come back to my house to get it?'

'I . . . I don't want to hear this. Please stop talking.'

Step. 'You don't want to hear that even though we were alone he still wouldn't admit there was something between us? He was still saying what you told him to say.'

Step. She is almost at the blackberry stain.

'Please. Just stop. I don't want to hear any more.'

Step. 'You don't want to hear any more? *You* don't? What about me? What about how much he hurt me by saying all those things to me because you told him to? We could have been so happy but he had to keep saying those things to me.'

Step. 'I wanted him to understand how much I hurt. How it felt to be humiliated once in public and then again in my own home. So I showed him. With this.' A brief wave of the knife.

Step. 'He understood all right.'

Step. And she is there on the stain; she is where it all started for me. 'It would have been fine, he'd be alive right now if it wasn't for *you*. He persuaded me, even when he was bleeding all over the place, to take him to the hospital, saying he wouldn't tell them what I did.'

Step. She is closer to me now. So very close. 'And in the car he tried to send you a message. That's why I stopped and dragged him out. Left him there with his mobile out of reach because he didn't deserve to live if all he'd want was you. What's so special about you?'

'I can't hear any more of this,' I tell her. It's enough. What she has told me is enough. Any more and she will not be able to go for me because I will go for her. I will kill her.

Step. Three more steps and she will be close enough to stab me – and I'll be close enough to put my hands around her neck. 'The last thing he did was to type a text to you saying "Love you xxxxx" that he never got to send because the thought of him doing that when I was the one trying to save his life was one insult too far.'

'You didn't have to do that to him.' The words tumble out through my clenched teeth. 'You didn't have to kill him.'

'No, I didn't. But I do have to kill you.'

Her hand gripping the knife comes up, her face twists with a type of rage I've never seen before and the back door explodes as it is kicked open. Suddenly, brutally, the world around us is alive with an unsynchronised chorus of voices shouting, ordering, screaming at the same time: 'STAY WHERE YOU ARE!' 'PUT THE KNIFE DOWN!' 'DROP YOUR WEAPON, NOW!'

All at once, Trainee Detective Clive Malone is in front of me, putting himself between me and the woman who is wide-eyed, shocked and furious at what is happening around her. He wants to be a barrier between us in case she decides to ignore all the warnings and lunges for me.

She won't, though. This has taken her too much by surprise. 'PUT THE KNIFE DOWN! NOW!' someone screams again, and her eyes scowl her hatred at me as she slowly raises her hands above her head like they do in the movies and then drops the black-handled chef's knife. It clatters as it hits the floor and creates a small nick, not far from the stain, on one of the tiles – another scar on the skin of my life. Another mark to remind me, this time, of where it ended, where this circle came around to meet and complete itself.

We stare at each other as they handcuff her.

'Did you really think I'd let you get away with what you did to Joel, to me, to Phoebe, to my family?' I say to her. 'Did you really think that I'd let you come into my house, my home, to destroy me and not fight back? You really are deluded, aren't you? Pathetic and deluded.'

She surges forward but is held back by the small male officer to her left and the tall female officer to her right. We continue to glare at each other as the officers inform her of her rights and take her away. Even as she is led out of the door she continues to twist her head to glower at me until her head will not go any further around to finish visually eviscerating me.

'You did so well,' Clive Malone says to me, now able to face me because I am safe from her. 'We've got a full confession which, as I said, means Phoebe probably won't have to testify. If we can get her to plead guilty, it's unlikely anyone will ever know about Phoebe seeing her that day. That must have been an awful experience for you to go through, but you got us exactly what we needed. You've done so well.'

4 days ago (May, 2013)

'Mrs Mackleroy, can you tell us for the tape in your own words what happened?' Clive Malone said. He sat beside another, older uniformed police officer who could not look more bored if he tried.

'Eighteen months ago my husband was murdered,' I began. 'Everyone thinks I've been coping so well. But they have no idea of the things I have done to keep myself going. And then six weeks ago my fourteen-year-old daughter asked her headmaster to tell me she was pregnant. A boy she knew confessed that he was the father, but I knew it had to be someone older, more worldly wise who had manipulated her to not use contraception. And that week, I got the first letter from my husband's killer. She's been writing to me for six weeks now. I know who she is because my daughter saw her with my husband on *that day*. The day my husband was killed.

'She's been watching me, I don't know how long for, but she tried to break into my house, she's vandalised my car more than once and started to spread rumours about my daughter.

'I found out today who the man who has been sexually grooming my daughter is and I knew what I had to do. I had to get myself legitimately and publicly arrested so that I could tell you this. That's why I smashed up his car and made some over-the-top speech – every word I believe, by the way – so I could get here. I couldn't tell you this in the cells because I don't know who could be listening. I don't know who she knows. I'm taking a risk even with telling you this, but I have no choice. I think she's going to try to kill me in the next few days because when I'm not at the hospital, I'll be alone in the house.

'I am begging you to do nothing to investigate her for the next few days. I am begging, begging, *begging* you to let me carry on as normal so she thinks I haven't said anything and she won't disappear and she won't try to hurt anyone else in my family. Maybe when I'm at the hospital you could get someone to watch my house to see if you can spot her going there to leave a letter and then you'll be able to arrest her.

'That, in my own words, is what happened. I wouldn't normally behave violently, but I don't want to die and leave my children and I do want her to leave me alone and to be put on trial for killing my husband.'

They were both silent after I finished speaking. That wasn't what they expected to hear and because of that, they had nothing to say. And neither did I. So the three of us sat in silence for a full five minutes before Clive Malone uttered, 'Oh.'

'He's not coming back, is he?' I say to Clive Malone. I knead the base of my thumbs into the inner corners of my eyes, the site of my pain, the place where I am about to cave in. 'All this time I've been trying to keep him alive, I've been clinging on to every little thing of his that I can because I convinced myself he was coming back. And he's not. He's not coming back.' My legs refuse to hold me upright now that I've been struck with this news, this reality. 'He's not coming back. I'm never going to see him again.'

No matter what I do, what I say, how I behave, I'm never going to see him again.

Clive Malone stands in front of me and acts as a shield to the police officers who are slowly leaving the room. The realisation continues to rise up from my cells, my bones, my blood where I've always known and accepted this and starts to diffuse into my muscles, into my organs, into my mind, into my memory.

I am never going to see him again because he is never coming back.

When I am alone except for Clive Malone, my human shield, I start to scream. Real screams, the kind I've never been able to do because I'm usually surrounded by colleagues, or children, or friends or the world.

I can do this now. I have to do this now.

I have to empty all of the silent screams out into the air, I have to make them real and loud because the love of my life is never coming back.

XII

WOMAN ARRESTED FOR MURDER OF BRIGHTON FATHER OF TWO

A woman has been arrested in connection with the 2011 fatal stabbing of Joel Mackleroy. The thirty-five-year-old woman from Ramonant Road in Hove was detained yesterday morning on suspicion of murdering the popular father of two from Brighton. A police spokesman confirmed that the woman will also be facing multiple other charges including harassment, criminal damage and attempted murder. 'We have in custody the person we believe to be responsible for this crime as well as several others. We will be able to reveal more as our investigation continues,' the spokesman added.

From the *Brighton & Hove Evening News*

LXIII

'Please don't do that again, Saff,' Fynn says to me at the front door. He has borrowed a friend's people carrier to drive us back from the hospital, one day later than intended because forensics were still working on our house the day we were meant to return and I needed to buy a new back door.

Fynn still won't look at me. He's been visiting Phoebe every day, he insisted on driving us all home, but I am a trigger for his pain and because of that, he won't look at me. He doesn't realise how awful it is when a person you love purposely refuses to see you, even if you're right there in front of them they pretend that the space you occupy is blank. Vacant. He doesn't realise that literally blanking me cuts me up inside as much as his refusal to be around me.

'Don't do what?' I ask.

'What you did with the police and didn't tell any of us. The woman killed Joel, she's incredibly dangerous. If she'd . . . Just don't, OK? I'll wring your neck if you put yourself at risk like that again. Is that clear?'

'Crystal. And, Fynn?'

'Yes?' he replies.

What I want to say is: *Did you know Joel isn't coming back?* 'Don't call me Saff any more,' I say.

His gaze focuses on me now, a mass of confusion beneath the ridges of his frown. 'Why not?'

'Only my friends call me Saff. You don't want to be my friend any more, so stop doing things only a friend would do.'

I watch Fynn swallow at a lump in his throat and he lifts his head slightly as examines me, scrutinising my face to see if I'm serious.

What I want to ask is: *When did you realise he wasn't coming back? Do you feel as hollowed out as I do now that you know it's for ever?* 'What's the matter?' I ask. 'Aren't I playing this role properly? Am I supposed to quietly accept you ending our friendship and put up with you blanking me?'

'It was you who—'

What I want to utter is: *Does this desolate feeling get any better? Because you said I'd learn to live around the pain and I am, but what about this desolate, hollowed out barrenness? Will that ever go?* 'It was me who wanted to talk but you refused,' I utter.

He lowers his tone: 'Talk about what? I'm *just* a friend to you. What we shared was *just* sex. What is there to talk about?'

What I want to beg is: *I just need to know this will get better and that everything is going to be all right again.* 'Please, you know it's not that simple,' I beg.

'There's nothing to talk about,' he tells me.

'There is.'

He shakes his head. I know why he won't talk. It's for the same reason that I won't verbalise all of those feelings: the thought of the pain the answers will bring is too much to withstand; and I'm not the only person who will go out of their way to avoid pain, Fynn does it too. 'I won't call you Saff again,' he states.

'Fine,' I reply. 'That's perfectly fine.'

I have to walk away before he steps out of the door and clicks it shut behind him. I can't watch him walk away again. He keeps doing it and it hurts a little more every time, especially now it is certain I can't rely on him any more to be the one to tell me it'll all be OK.

Phoebe is installed on the sofa under her seaside scene duvet, plump white pillows propped behind her and the silver remote control firmly in her hand. Zane, who has barely left her side since his return two days ago, sits with his back against the sofa by her head, so they're as close as possible. Aunty Betty is dozing in the armchair in the bay window. It's been a very tiring few days in the hospital, I don't think she knew she had it in her. She's now volunteered to become a hospital visitor and to find funding for and to run a mobile book-lending service. She's planning on starting it with the books she has in storage but it essentially means I'll be funding it and taking her to and from 'work', as she calls it.

For the first time since I've known her she has gone several days without wearing a wig. Even when she was in hospital with a broken hip, by the time visiting hours came around she had her wig in place and some basic make-up on. Now, her chin-length hair is combed out and frames her face like wispy grey-streaked black clouds. She looks like a different person, even though she still has her eye make-up and lipstick. She's stopped hiding behind her make-up, I've realised these past couple of days, now she wears it to enhance her features, not to disguise them. Aunty Betty is finally ready to face the world, it seems.

At this moment, her head is thrown back, her mouth is wide open, her teeth with their patchwork of grey-black fillings are exposed to the entire room. She doesn't quite fill the brown leather seat, not like Joel used to. That was 'his' chair and once upon a time I would have encouraged her to move by saying she would be more comfortable elsewhere. Now, I simply leave her. It doesn't matter if she sits there now, he's not coming back. He won't sit there again. He really is gone.

'Who wants a cup of tea/hot chocolate/coffee/apple juice – delete wet substance as appropriate?' I ask.

A resounding silence is my reply.

'Fine, I'll take care of myself,' I say.

'OK, Mum,' Phoebe says.

'It's going to be all right, you know, Mum?' Zane says suddenly and unexpectedly.

I frown at my son.

'It is, you know,' Phoebe adds with a nod.

'Right.' I glance at Aunty Betty, expecting her to add something equally poignant. She snorts a little snore at us.

The kids crack up and I find my own smile.

It's going to be all right, you know, Mum. I hear those words for the rest of the day. And when I climb into bed that night, I don't simply look over at Joel's side of the bed, I spread myself over it, I try to touch both sides of the bed by stretching my arms right across.

It's going to be all right, you know, Mum.

My fingers don't come anywhere near each side, but I keep at it, I pull myself apart as far as I will go because I am desperate to touch the sides. I am desperate to do the impossible. Because it seems impossible that it's going to be all right. That life will work when he's not coming back.

I finally give in, stop stretching myself, stop attempting the impossible and I am still.

I am still and listen to those words again:

It's going to be all right, you know, Mum.

'It is, Ffrony,' I fancy I can hear Joel say, '*I promise you, it's going to be all right.*'

LXIV

Fynn has no shirt on and is kissing a woman on his front doorstep.

I watch them from the end of the black and white tiled path that leads to the tiled steps up to his flat. He lives in one of the four apartments in a large house in Hove on one of the roads that goes down to the street that runs parallel to the seafront. There really is no need for him to be doing that out there when he has a doorstep inside.

She's really quite beautiful, this woman. As tall as him in her designer heels, extremely slender, a well-cut navy blue suit and swathes of long, shiny, ebony black hair that cascade right down to the middle of her back. She has one hand on his face, he has his hand nestled at the base of her spine as they snog like two people who've blatantly spent most of last night screwing. And probably this morning, too.

This, I do not need to see. Whether she's a new girlfriend or a one-night 'hook up' I do not need to be watching this. Apart from everything else, it's confirmation that in the four weeks since we last saw each other it hasn't bothered him that we're not friends any more. How things stand between us – with him regularly speaking to/texting the kids and often

Aunty Betty – is fine with him. He's simply getting on with his life without me in it.

The canoodling couple break apart and simultaneously grin at each other, a secret shared without words between them. They say their goodbyes and she smiles, flashing her light blue eyes at me, on her way past. She has on last night's clothes but she has fresh make-up, and she's showered, her vaguely woody, musky scent is one that Fynn often smells of. I smile back because it's the polite thing to do. I even manage a smile for the man at the top of the black and white steps.

He replies with an unfriendly tightening of his lips and a glare, but leaves the front door and the door to his flat open when he goes inside.

The flat is in partial darkness because the living room blinds are drawn and I'm guessing the ones in the bedroom are, too. All the other doors that lead off the corridor are closed, so the flat is subdued and almost sombre. Fynn moved here after he got divorced eight years ago. He was married for two years and neither of them could explain why they got married – they did it in Vegas – nor why they split up. I liked her, but she moved away after they broke up and didn't want to keep in touch. 'Need a fresh start away from everyone,' she texted. 'I know you'll understand.'

By the time I enter the flat, Fynn has, thankfully, pulled on a T-shirt and he walks from section to section of his bay window and jerks the strings to open the blinds. He also opens the sash windows as far as they will go with the window locks to let some air in. The whole flat needs proper airing because everything reeks of sex.

He moves around his living room, righting it after last night's activities: he picks up the wine glasses on the table in front of the television and carries them through to the kitchen. He returns for the shot glasses and the nearly empty bottle of whisky. While screwing up the empty crisp packets and snatching up the empty condom packet that was partially hidden under the coffee table, he finally speaks: 'What, have you come over to watch me tidy up, or to tell me what else I can't do because we're not friends?'

'Neither . . . I came here . . .' I hold out the white paper bag in my hand, in it is a muffin I made earlier with him in mind. All the flavours I know he loves. 'Look, see? I brought this muffin: white flour, white sugar, white chocolate, coconut – which is of course white – all in a white paper bag. I mean, yes, it's got blueberries and the coconut was slightly toasted, but in essence, baked goods crammed with stuff to be used as a white flag.' I wave the bag around. 'Ceasefire?'

He says nothing, glowers at me from his 'hunched over cleaning my coffee table' position, before he stands upright and pads into the kitchen. His bare feet make an almost comical slapping sound as they hit the tiles.

I follow him. I know he's hurt, but I am too. The world doesn't feel right without him *and* Joel, I can't believe he doesn't feel the same.

'Isn't it weird to you that we've not spoken in a month?' I ask.

He shrugs dismissively and fills a large tankard I know he and Joel brought home from Oktoberfest 1997 in Munich with water from the tap. Joel confessed it was one of the worst trips of his life because for the first time ever he had memory blackouts from the drinking and hated the thought of not remembering what he'd got up to.

'So, who was your friend?' I try again as a punt on something that might make him talk.

Fynn lowers the glass from his lips and aims his head dangerously at me. I think for a moment he's going to scream at me to get out of his house, to stay out of his life, and brace myself for it. 'Are you having a laugh?' he replies.

Maybe this wasn't such a good idea, after all. 'No,' I say. 'I'm asking because I am interested.' I inhale deeply, an attempt to take the edge off the panic that is amassing inside. I have a normal way of quelling the panic but I am trying not to do that any more. I don't want to be that person any more. It hasn't worked completely, but I am getting there. I am here to face the panic instead of continuing to run.

'Interested or jealous?' he challenges.

'Jealous. Of course I'm jealous,' I say. The panic rises. I lower my gaze to the muffin in my hand. I want it. I want to rip open the bag and cram it whole into my mouth to silence myself, to stop myself from doing this. I toss the bag onto his work surface and turn my back on it.

His surprise is evident, but he does not speak.

I have to redirect my eyes as I continue. 'You know I'm jealous. You know that I . . . Wanting you, sleeping with you, was never the problem, Fynn.'

'That's not what you said.'

'I know. I just . . . both of those conversations caught me off guard. I'm not very good at this. Speaking about what I feel is not easy for me. If it was, I doubt I'd have half my issues. Lord knows I've had a crash-course in it recently, but it's not second nature. I get scared. I panic. I want to do things perfectly and I become so incredibly frightened when it might not work out, and then my mind races ahead to every possible thing that could go wrong which leaves me completely frozen. Except these past few weeks every issue I've ever had seems to need to be dealt with. It's been . . . It's been so hard. And with you, I panicked because there were so many trigger points in those conversations.'

Deep, deep, deep breath in, long, long, long push out. 'I need you back in my life. I want you back.'

'You've got Lewis.'

'He's not you.'

'What are you saying, Saff, sorry, Saffron, because you're not making any sense?'

Although my hands are trembling, I take his glass from him, place it on the countertop beside the sink. 'Fynn . . .' The panic, it billows up inside, sheets and sheets of soft, feathery panic welling up to smother me from the inside out.

My quivering hands rest gently on his face. I want to see him when I say this. I want him to see me, to watch me speak so he understands.

'Fynn . . . I . . . I *love* you. So much. It makes my heart ache when I think about how much I love you. Not just as a friend. You'll never be "just" anything to me. Yes, it was sex, but I couldn't have had sex with just anyone.' I squeeze my eyes together, push and shove at the panic to get it out of me; to free it with every word I say. When I am brave again, I open my eyes. 'I do love you and if I was ever going to have any more children, of course I'd want you as the father. You're practically a father to Zane and Phoebe as it is. And, yes, I admit a part of me has been expecting us to get together and settle down, too.'

Silent and wary, he watches me speak.

'But, I can't be with you.' The panic continues to gush out of me. 'You're too much like him. You talk alike, you think alike, you find the same things funny. You react in the same way he would to things and you put yourself out so often for the people you love. You're amazing. And so was he. In so many of the same ways.

'If we got together, I would lose him all over again. I already lost him once. I was trying so hard to find him again with the cookbook, to bring him back almost. And it didn't work. And then all the stuff with Phoebe where I had to stop trying to do things his way and do it my way, I had to give up some more of him. I can't let any more of him go. Not for any reason.

'Being with you would blot him out. I wouldn't know where he ended and you began. It'd happen slowly, I probably wouldn't notice it at first, but then I'd try to remember something he said or did and it would be mixed up with you and soon there'd be nothing of him left. I can't let that happen.'

Fynn cups my face as though nurturing a flower in the cradle of his hands, and gently his thumbs stroke away some of the tears on my cheeks. His tears are briefly dammed by my fingers, before they continue their downward journey over and around my hands.

The panic, the terror, is not as loud now; it does not seem

536

as overwhelming and dangerous, that it will smother me in its thick, white folds now that I have been honest. 'Do you understand?' I ask.

He nods, forcing his pink lips together into an unhappy smile.

'And do you understand why I couldn't tell you this? It's a huge thing to admit to myself that it's not been two years yet and I've fallen in love with someone else, let alone admit it to you when I so want to be with you and I can't.'

Another unhappy nod.

'I'm sorr—'

'Shhhh,' he hushes, 'don't say sorry. Not about that. Be sorry about other things, but not that.'

He takes his hands away from my face as I drop mine from his, then presses the palms of his hands onto his eyes, before he rubs roughly at his cheeks to dry his face. He leaves a trail of red marks as he rubs. 'God! Why am I always crying with you? It does my reputation no good, you know. You're no good for me, woman.'

'You're not the first man to say that.'

Blotchy-faced, he steps forwards again and slips his arms around my waist. 'So, fancy a couple of hours in bed for old times' sake?' he jokes. I know he's joking, what he is doing. He is taking my hand and leading us back to surer ground, to where we were. He wants, like I do, for us to go back to who we were before my attempt to find another way to obliterate the pain led to me kissing him when I didn't want him to leave one night. Before he tried to do the same and we almost irreversibly damaged ourselves in the process. Fynn wants to find the spark of who we were amongst the wreckage of the last twenty months of our lives. We both know we were friends, first and foremost, and we both believe we can have that again.

I laugh, ruefully shake my head while I dab at my eyes and fix my expression to suit the change in conversation. 'Erm, correct me if I'm wrong, but isn't there another woman's DNA all over your bed right now? Probably all over this flat.'

'Details, Saff, details. Although you could have a point.'

He closes his eyes and pulls me close. His face against my neck, he murmurs into my skin: 'I love you. Always.' The words imprint themselves onto me like an invisible tattoo, to be carried with me for ever.

Before I can reply, he takes several steps away from me. 'I love you, too,' I whisper back. 'Always.'

He grins at me with all the warmth and affection I'd grown accustomed to with a genuine, easy Fynn smile.

'Will you be my friend again?' I ask.

'Of course.'

'Good. Thank you.' I pause, inhale as deeply as I can to expand my chest, to make room for as much courage as I can muster. 'I'm going to get help, too,' I say. If I utter it aloud I will do it. I *will* do it. 'For the . . . For my eating disorder. I'm going to get proper help and I'm going to get through it.'

He stares cautiously at me but doesn't speak. It's hardly surprising he is wary of talking about this again after I lost the plot last time. He's probably worried, too, that I'm saying those words because it's what he wants to hear and not because I'm actually going to do it. But I am.

'I really am going to get help this time.'

'Did Joel know?' he asks.

I nod. 'It's the only thing we ever really argued about.'

Fynn picks up the bag with the muffin. It is heart-shaped in case I needed to be a bit more obvious about my feelings. 'Let me try this,' he says. 'Which is your favourite flavour?'

He's testing me. 'I'm not sure,' I confess. 'I haven't tried it.'

Decisively, he breaks a piece off the muffin and I watch as small crumbs rain down into the bag. He puts it into his mouth and immediately chews. As if it is the most natural thing in the world to simply put food in your mouth and chew. His eyes close briefly before he opens them again. 'My God, the flavours in that!' he says. 'They're incredible.' He eats another piece, reacting in the same way. 'You have to try this, Saff.' He breaks off a third piece and he visibly inhales, steels himself before he holds it to my lips.

The panic billows up and I am suddenly drowning in the feathery, wispy fronds of my fears. I can't do it. I can't do it. I want to do it, I want to be able to do this, but I can't. 'I can't,' I say.

'Try,' he encourages. 'Just try.'

'I can't.'

'Try.'

I close my eyes, open my mouth and let him slip the food inside. Tears of terror escape from my closed eyes. I can't do it.

'Which is your favourite flavour?' Fynn asks.

I need to spit it out, to remove this poison from my mouth.

'*Try, Ffrony,*' I'm sure I can hear Joel say. '*I know you can do it, just try.*' This has been happening more since I screamed and cried in the kitchen, I can hear him, feel him, it's like he has come back to me. I'm no longer falling through potholes in time to be with him, I can sense what he would say. I can feel him when I need him to be there. '*Try, Ffrony.*'

I bite down, *chew*, and tastes explode quietly in my mouth: the creaminess of white chocolate, a tang of under-ripe blueberries, a subtle stroke of coconut. I haven't tasted food in so long: I stuff food down, I bring food up, but I rarely eat it, enjoy it, know when I have had enough. I often never start because the fear I won't be able to stop is too immense.

I haven't been present while I eat in so long. But it's incredible. Tasting food is amazing.

'Go on then, which is your favourite flavour?' Fynn asks again.

I shrug like Phoebe, frown like Zane. 'All of them, I think.'

November 2013

(It's been about 2 years, 1 month)

LXV

'I'm not sure what you'd like to know.

'Or if, where you are, you already know. The children, they're fine. I finally bit the bullet and got them proper, professional counselling. I should have done it a long time ago, but I've done it now so I'll try not to beat myself up too much about the delay. Phoebe is much better. She's sort of dating Curtis but they're mates first and foremost, allegedly. Watch this space for more teen angst, I suppose. I try not to freak out when she tells me stuff about them being unsure about restarting their physical relationship. It's not easy to hear, but at least she's talking to me. I found her a new school, which is a bit of a drive away, but she seems happy there and has made new friends. She talks to me sometimes about the pregnancy, it still plays on her mind, but at least she talks about it and what she thinks she would have done. I'm proud of her, you know, Joel. Really proud of how she's grown from this experience.

'Zane is still at St Caroline's, I didn't want to take him away from the place where he was so happy and secure. He is so much happier, I wish you could see him. He talks much more, laughs again, and he loves to spend weekends at your parents' house every few weeks. You couldn't get Phoebe there if you paid her, but that's her prerogative.

'Ernest and Zane are still friends. A few weeks back Ernest told Zane his dad doesn't live with them any more, so I'm guessing Imogen and Ray have finally split up. Knowing Imogen, and how much she hated the thought of being a single mother again, I think she probably did all she could to sweep it under the carpet to make it work. But it didn't. Imogen and I acknowledge each other in the playground but that's it. She has her problems like I have mine.

'Aunty Betty is still in the attic and her whole life is now centred around the hospital. I spend a lot of time taking her there and picking her up. When I can't, Fynn does. It's like we're divorced co-parents of a teenager. It's funny that the most selfish woman on God's green Earth, as she branded herself, has found her true calling helping others.

'Fynn is Fynn. You understand what that means. I'm sure he spends copious amounts of time talking to you, anyway, but we take care of each other, we're the best of friends again, which of course means he drives me insane, sometimes, but that's what friendship is, isn't it? I love him as much as you did. He's helped me put up a greenhouse where the vegetable patch used to be so no more slug orgies. And I'm getting the money together to pay him back for the beach hut.

'Lewis and I hang out as friends occasionally and it's nice. Going nowhere despite his best efforts, but that's all right because it's nice. He's nice.

'And me? I feel better now that *she*, Audra, has been sentenced. She pleaded guilty to manslaughter, as we hoped, but also pleaded guilty to attempted murder of me, which meant no trial, thank goodness. She's finally got a minimum twenty-five-year tariff. She's been warned that if she tries to contact me again the harassment charges will be reinstated so, hopefully, I don't have to have anything else to do with her. That has helped everyone so much, knowing where she is and that she's going to be there for a long time. The world seems a less uncertain, scary place.

'The job is going well, too, now that there is no Kevin and no Edgar. I'm still working on getting that image of Gideon out of my head. But, moving swiftly on, it helps that I'm back in my old role and there's a possibility of promotion one day.

'And . . . and . . . the big elephant in the graveyard. The other stuff. I'm doing OK with that. It's been six months since I first got help and three months since I last purged. Getting better doesn't seem to happen fast enough sometimes and I want to give up, go back to what I know but I remind myself that I can't. That way of living, coping, hiding was killing me. And I know I have to be kind and patient with myself. I have to believe and accept it'll take as long as it takes to get better.

'And you, my lovely, Joel, how are you? I hope you're surrounded by others, I hope you have the chance to be who you are wherever you are. I hope it's peaceful but you're able to be that bouncy energetic man you always were. And I hope you don't spend any time worrying about us. We're OK.

'I'm still pissed off at you. I'm still incredibly angry that you're not here and that I have to keep doing this life thing without you, but that's not all I feel any more. I feel other things, and some of them are fantastic and some are awful, but I'm feeling again and that's a good thing. A great thing.

'*The Flavours of Love* continues to be a work in progress,

545

like me, like most things in life, I guess. I'm learning what foods I like by cooking them and tasting them and I'm adding recipes all the time. It's going to have thousands of recipes, I think, when I finally put your ones and my ones together, but it'll be ours. Something for us to share even though we're apart.

'I have to go now. We're taking Aunty Betty's boyfriend from the post office out to dinner. I mean all of us – Aunty Betty, Fynn, Phoebe, Zane, Curtis and me. He doesn't know that yet, poor guy – he'll wonder what hit him.

'I miss you. I love you. For honestly, real. I'll see you soon.'

epilogue

I'm going home tomorrow.

I don't know if I want to return to that life I have over there. I don't know if I can do it. Maybe I should just stay here. I love Lisbon, I love the cobbled streets, the sandstone-coloured buildings that don't so much rise up from the ground, but feel like they are there to comfort you, cuddle you. Maybe I should stay and leave all the other stuff back at home. I'm normal here. Even on my own I don't feel so panicky and scared, I'm not on edge and terrified all the time.

I have no money left to stay, but if I go home, take that job in Brighton, carry on living in Worthing, I could maybe do it again. I could come back, maybe to see more of Portugal. Maybe travel is what I can do with my life. Maybe I can start saving really carefully again and then take the time to see the world. Maybe the panic will subside if I just let myself go and move around the world in small, manageable chunks.

The air is warm, fragrant, filled with the promise of a light rain. I come up the narrow, winding street from the Avenida da Liberdade and round the corner to my hotel. The man from the plane, the one who held my hand during the hideous turbulence, is sitting on the edge of the tiled evergreen-filled planter opposite the hotel's entrance. He stands as I approach the hotel. I've been seeing him and his girlfriend – a woman who is obviously a model – everywhere. It's like we're pre-following each other around.

He smiles as he comes towards me, and I smile back.

'Hi,' he says.

'Hi,' I say, confused.

'This is going to sound like a cheesy chat-up line, and if you get to know me like I hope you will, you'll get to know that I'm not like that, but there's something about you . . . I think you're part of my future. I know it sounds stupid and strange and I honestly don't believe in all that spooky stuff . . . But I think you're part of my future.'

I stare at him: he's tall and well-built, but not overtly so, and I know he's strong because of the way he held my hand on the plane. His cheekbones are smooth but slightly prominent, his eyes are dark and look how mahogany would if you could melt wood. And his mouth, plump and inviting, keeps moving to smile at me. There's something about him . . . there's something about him that tells me he could be right.

'It doesn't sound as weird as it should,' I say to him.

'You think so? For honestly, real?'

'Don't you have a girlfriend?'

'Um, no, not any more. I'm booked to go on a flight home tonight, three days early because she dumped me. All I do is stare at you, apparently. She said she had too much self-esteem to stick with a man who kept staring at a lass who didn't even know he existed. I tried to explain to her that it was because I saw my future with you and she didn't take it very well.'

'I can't imagine why.'

'Yeah, I have a bit of a problem with honesty.'

'It's a good problem to have.'

'Can I give you my number? Will you call me when we get home?'

'Yes.'

'For honestly, real?'

'Yes, erm, for honestly real. My name's Saffron.'

'Saffron. Sa*ffron*. Ffron. *Ffrony*. I like that. I *love* that.'

'No one's ever done that with my name before.'

'Cool, huh?'

'Yes, it's cool.'

'It's great to meet you, Saffron. I'm Joel.'

acknowledgements

(aka Dorothy gets gushy)

Thank you to you, the reader, for buying this book, for taking the time to read it and, if you're that way inclined, for letting me know what you think. I'm grateful, always, for your continued support.

Thank you, also, to:

My lovely family and my equally lovely in-laws for being the people I can count on. A special mention goes to the real life Aunty Betty for letting me use her name and some of her stories.

My fantastic friends. You're all so understanding and still speak to me even when I go to ground to finish my latest book.

The amazing Ant and James, always there with the best advice and chats. Love you guys.

The fabulous Quercus peeps for being so, well, fabulous.

To brilliant Jenny for the delicious cover & brilliant Emma for the fabulous PR – keep doing what you do so brilliantly.

To Divine Jo Dickinson (you should totally call yourself that) for everything, really. Thanks for continuing to push me, believe in me and for trusting me to deliver on time, sight unseen.

The experts who helped in so many ways: Nathalie Sansonetti for help with the recipes; Polly Hockaday for the help with bereavement research; the people at Victim Support, especially Mark Hazelby, for info on the homicide process; the people at B-eat for info on eating disorders; and the brave women who generously shared their stories in order to help put this book together.

And finally . . .

E, G & M I'm not sure there are enough thank yous in the world for me to express my gratitude to you all for your being my support system, but I'll keep trying. Big love to you.

About *The Flavours of Love*

With my ninth novel, *The Flavours of Love*, I found my life was opened up in many different ways. Apart from having to confront some issues that I've been avoiding for many, many years, I rediscovered my love for cooking.

In the book, Saffron Mackleroy decides to finish writing the cookbook that her husband, Joel, started before he was murdered. Joel wanted to write a cookbook filled with recipes that each contained at least one ingredient – one flavour – that he absolutely loved. Saffron, in her grief at losing Joel decides to experiment with different ingredients and flavours in an attempt to find a taste that would remind her of what life was like when Joel was alive.

When I was writing the book, I decided to do what Saffron was doing and experimented with flavours and ingredients – and the results were incredible. Sometimes incredibly bad, admittedly, but often the meal was unexpectedly delicious. Even now, more than six months after finishing the book, I still experiment – I have the confidence now to go 'off recipe', knowing that what I'm making may or may not work, but I've had fun trying.

If you feel you're not confident enough to go 'off recipe' straight away, maybe you could try one of the recipes in this book and add an additional spice, herb or ingredient that you love, and see what happens. If that turns out OK, try grabbing one of your cookbooks and doing the same. Keep trying until one day you can make up a recipe from scratch, knowing that it's filled with the flavours that you love.

© Dorothy Koomson 2014

Recipes

Basil & Rocket Pesto

Carrot, Butternut Squash,
Apple & Ginger Soup

Triple Chocolate & Banana Tray Bake

Ratatouille

The Flavours of Love Muffins

BASIL & ROCKET PESTO

After Saffron is called to her daughter's school,
she makes gnocchi to go with this pesto while she
and Phoebe, her daughter, are having an emotionally
charged conversation.

The stuff you'll need

50g pine nuts
25g Parmigiano-Reggiano cheese
1 small or half a clove of garlic
20g rocket
20g basil
Extra virgin olive oil

The amount
1 x 0.25 litre jar

The how to

1. Lightly toast the pine nuts in a dry pan for a few minutes.
Turn off the heat and allow to cool.

2. Into a small food processor bowl put the pine nuts with
the hunk of Parmigiano-Reggiano cheese, the peeled garlic
clove, and a couple of glugs of extra virgin olive oil to
moisten. Pulse for a few seconds until the nuts resemble
largish breadcrumbs.

3. Wash the rocket and basil and pat dry with kitchen towel or in a salad spinner.

4. Put the rocket into the food processor on top of the blended pine nuts mixture, then push in the basil if there's room. On the slowest speed on your food processor, mix for a few seconds until the leaves are all incorporated.

5. Use straight away or put into a cleaned, airtight jar. Cover with olive oil and store in the fridge for a couple of days.

6. Stir a couple of spoonfuls into freshly cooked gnocchi or pasta, according to taste. Sprinkle with freshly grated Parma Reggino and serve.

CARROT, BUTTERNUT SQUASH, APPLE & GINGER SOUP

While talking to Fynn, Joel's best friend, Saffron begins to make this soup for her family. She discovers she hasn't got any butternut squash, and makes it without it.

The stuff you'll need

Olive oil or butter
1 tbsp cumin
1 red onion, chopped
Salt and pepper
1 tsp turmeric
1 clove of garlic, crushed or finely minced
1cm piece of ginger, peeled and finely sliced
1kg carrots, chopped into slices*
1 small butternut squash, peeled and cut into small cubes
2 red apples (gala or English), chopped
1l stock (either fresh or from cubes)

The amount
Four large bowls

The how to

1. In a large pan heat the butter or olive oil then add the cumin and turmeric. Stir for a few seconds before adding the crushed/chopped garlic and chopped red onion. Stir for a few minutes until the onion is soft.

2. Add the sliced carrots, cubed butternut squash and chopped red apples. Stir as much as you can to coat the vegetables in oil and herbs. Add a little salt and black pepper.

Put on a lid and on a low heat, allow the vegetables to sweat for a few minutes.

3. Add the stock, take off the lid and bring to the boil. Once boiling, lower the heat and allow to simmer without the lid for about 20 minutes.

4. After 20 minutes, test one of the larger pieces of vegetable for softness. If still firm, allow to cook for a bit longer. If soft, turn off the heat and allow to cool slightly before blending very carefully with a handheld blender or transfer into a food processor and blend until smooth.

5. Ladle into bowls, and season with salt and black pepper.

Serve with crusty bread or a salad.

* I don't peel, only wash, if they're organic carrots

Adapted from a recipe by Nathalie Sansonetti
http://www.newleafnutrition.co.uk/

TRIPLE CHOCOLATE & BANANA TRAY BAKE

When Joel's parents, who Saffron has issues with, arrive for an unexpected visit, she serves them these in muffin form with tea.

The stuff you'll need

130g butter, softened, or olive oil
100g soft brown sugar
3 bananas
1 tsp vanilla extract
2 eggs, lightly beaten
1tsp bicarbonate of soda
1tsp baking powder
250g plain flour
60g dark chocolate chunks or chips
(or chocolate broken into chunks)
30g white chocolate chunks or chips
(or cooking chocolate broken into chunks)
30g milk chocolate chunks or chips
(or cooking chocolate broken into chunks)
45ml milk

The amount
About 16 small rectangles and six large muffins.

The how to

1. Preheat your oven to 160 degrees C (fan) and butter or line two 22 x 24 cm cake tins or one 22 x 24cm cake tin and put paper cases into a six-hole large muffin tin. (Don't forget to butter/line the sides of the tray)*

2. In a large bowl, cream together the butter and sugar. Mash the bananas (I only do this now because the bananas

go brown) and add them with the vanilla and eggs to the bowl.

3. Sieve the flour, baking powder and bicarbonate of soda together into the bowl. Once well mixed, add the chocolate chunks and milk, then stir.

4. Spoon the mixture out into the trays or tray and muffin tin to about three-quarters full.

5. Bake on the middle shelves of your oven for about 20 minutes (checking constantly to see if they're done – depending on your oven they may take longer to cook).

6. Remove when a skewer or knife inserted into the middle comes out clean.

7. Allow to cool slightly and slice up into rectangles while in the tin with a palette knife or normal dinner knife. Remove from the tin and serve.

8. You can store for up to two days in an airtight container.

RATATOUILLE

The making of this dish marks a turning point in the relationship between Phoebe and Saffron.

The stuff you'll need

350g courgettes
350g aubergines
350g peppers (any colours)
1 large onion finely sliced
6 tsps olive oil
750g fresh medium sized tomatoes quartered
1 bunch of fresh basil finely chopped
2 tbsps herbes de provence
Salt and pepper

The amount
Serves 4

The how to

1. Slice the peppers and sauté in 2tsps olive oil together with the finely sliced onion.

2. When the peppers are soft add the tomato quarters, 1tbsp herbes de Provence and add salt and pepper to taste.

3. Simmer your mixture for 45 minutes.

4. Cut the aubergines and courgettes in thick slices and cook them separately in 2 tsps of olive oil each and 1 tbsp herbes de Provence, until soft.

5. Add the soft aubergines and courgettes to the peppers and tomatoes and simmer for another 10 minutes.

6. Add the finely chopped basil, salt and pepper to taste. Serve with BBQs, meats, pasta, fish, or great as a filling in your fajitas or on top of a baked potato.

You can freeze extra portions for later use too.

Recipe by Nathalie Sansonetti at
http://www.newleafnutrition.co.uk

THE FLAVOURS OF LOVE MUFFINS

(Blueberry, Coconut and White Chocolate Chip Muffins)

These muffins are made at an important point in the book for Saffron. The flavours shouldn't technically work together, but they do.

The stuff you'll need

100g desiccated coconut
200g plain flour
1 tablespoon baking powder
0.5 teaspoon salt
250ml milk
60g butter
1 egg
150g fresh blueberries
80g caster sugar
70g white chocolate chips
1 tablespoon plain flour
(to coat blueberries)

The amount
12 large muffins/6 large muffins and 6 heart-shaped muffins

The how to

1. Preheat your oven to 200c/Fan 180 C /Gas mark 6.

2. Heat a dry frying pan (non-stick is best) and then toast the desiccated coconut until it is very slightly browned. Remove from the heat and set to one side.

3. Grease a 12-hole large muffin tin or line with paper muffin cases.

4. Weigh and sieve together into a large bowl the flour, baking powder, sugar and salt.

5. Stir in the cooled toasted coconut and then stir in the white chocolate chips.

6. In the frying pan you toasted the coconut – melt the butter. Remove from heat and set aside to cool slightly.

7. Beat the egg in a separate bowl then add the milk and melted butter and mix together.

8. Add to this mixture to the dry ingredients.

9. This will go against the grain, but mix lightly until combined.

10. Wash the blueberries and then pat dry with a clean paper towel. In a bowl, coat them with the 1 tablespoon of plain flour. Gently fold them into the batter – being careful not to over-mix.

11. Spoon the batter into the muffin cups/paper cases.

12. Bake for 12 to 17 minutes. When a wooden skewer inserted into the middle comes out clean, they're cooked.

13. Leave the muffins to cool for about 10 minutes before turning them out onto a wire tray or removing from the tray if using paper cases.

14. Store in an air-tight container for up to 2 days.

Hopefully you will have already read the book and you'll know all about Aunty Betty. This is a story about her . . .

Revenge Is Almost Sweet . . .

'What do you think you're doing?' His voice is loud and booming, filled with authority.

She knows instinctively there's a policeman standing behind her. If I stand still long enough, pretend I'm a statue, maybe he'll leave me alone, she thinks.

'Did you hear me? What do you think you're doing out here in the middle of the night?'

'Don't know?' she replies.

'Can you turn around and look at me, please?' the man with the big voice asks.

She sighs. There's no way out of this. As she rotates on the spot, she whips the object in her hand behind her back, out of sight.

There are two police officers. They seem extraordinarily tall, but maybe that's just the way the light from the street lamp catches their reflective jackets and their pale features.

'What was that you hid behind your back?' the one with the booming voice asks.

'Nothing,' she says, trying to sound brave.

'That is not, nothing,' he says, 'show me.'

Instead of doing as she's told, she drops it. The spray can clatters loudly onto the pavement and rolls a little distance away into the gutter.

Both of the tall men look at the can of green paint and then at her. 'How old are you?' the other one asks.

'Old enough,' she says.

'Do your family know you're out this late on your own?'

'They won't care. They let me do what I want.'

'We'll see about that, shall we?' PC Booming Voice says. 'What's your name and where do you live?'

'I don't remember,' she says, defiantly.

'OK,' the other one says. 'Let's see if there's anything with your details in this bag of yours.'

He indicates to the small pink rucksack sitting beside the pink and white trainers she's wearing. 'That's not mine,' she says hastily.

'And I suppose that can of spray paint you dropped wasn't yours, either?'

'No, I just found it.'

'Well you won't mind if I take a look in that rucksack and see who it belongs to,' the other one says.

'Course I don't,' she nonchalantly bluffs, hoping it'll stop him from doing what he is doing.

Her stomach is aflutter as the younger officer reaches for her backpack. He unzips it, opening the top wide so the street lamp can shine its orangey light in on the contents. She shouldn't have put that red spray can in there, should she? But red was Philip's favourite colour and before she'd even thought about what she was doing, she'd picked it up with the blue can.

Philip, her former boyfriend, was in that house behind her right now with the woman he'd dumped her for. Philip didn't even have the decency to tell her before he moved in with this bit on the side – she'd had to hear the others, who were supposedly her friends, gossiping about it. That was . . . intolerable. That was why she'd snuck out to do this. She was going to tag the front door to their nice new love nest with her initials. She wanted them to know they hadn't got away with it. She'd planned to be out and back before anyone knew she'd gone. Just her luck she got caught by the fuzz.

She watches the policeman search in her bag and before long he reaches further into its depths and then removes her travel pass. She tries desperately to hide the way her heart sinks.

'How extraordinary,' he says. 'This looks remarkably like you.' He shows the pass to the officer with the booming voice. 'What do you think?'

'Why, they could be twins.'

'I do actually have a twin,' she offers lamely.

'I'm sure you do, Elizabeth,' the man with the booming voice says. 'I think it's time we took you home.'

'No, you're all right. I'll just go back by myself. You don't want to be waking everyone up.'

'Oh, I think we do,' he replies. 'And I'd love to meet your twin.'

'She doesn't actually live with me.'

'Oh, that's a shame. Never mind, it'd be nice to meet the rest of your family all the same.'

'Now, you see, I don't actually live where it says I do on the pass. I moved so many times since—'

'Well, it'd be a good place to start, seeing as you don't remember where you live. Right this way.' He indicates grandly to the back door of the police car.

This isn't fair, Elizabeth thinks. Being brought home in the back of a police car again and she hasn't even been partying. Philip so isn't worth this.

Elizabeth doesn't say anything as they pull up outside the big building with gated entrance fifteen minutes later. She waits sulkily in the car for the policeman with the booming voice to open the door for her to get out. Framed in the door-way to the building is the woman that they'd radioed the station to wake up to greet them.

The tall woman waits for them wearing a pink, quilt-ed dressing gown, with rollers in her hair and her arms fold-ed angrily across her chest.

'This is the final straw Betty, it really is,' she says.

'Does this sort of thing happen a lot?' the policeman with the booming voice asks.

'More than it should with a sixty-two-year-old woman with a previously broken hip who lives on the first floor,' the woman replies.

Elizabeth rolls her eyes.

'Tomorrow morning, I am calling your family. They will have to find you a new retirement village to live in.'

'Whatever,' Elizabeth mutters. She relieves the policeman of her rucksack with a wink. 'Nice to meet you, Mr Policeman. Hope to get a ride from you again, sometime,' she says with a broad smile before disappearing through the retirement home's hallway.

A version of this story appeared in _S_ magazine in November 2013.

© Dorothy Koomson 2013

'I could kill them for what
they've done to me.'

FIRST CAME LOVE.
THEN CAME MURDER.

DOROTHY KOOMSON
THE ROSE PETAL BEACH

THE *SUNDAY TIMES* BESTSELLER